CORRIDORS
OF
POWER

CORRIDORS OF POWER

C. P. SNOW

NEW YORK

CHARLES SCRIBNER'S SONS

To Humphrey Hare

NOTE

By some fluke, the title of this novel seems to have passed into circulation during the time the book itself was being written. I have watched the phenomenon with mild consternation. The phrase was first used, so far as I know, in *Homecoming* (1956). Mr. Rayner Heppenstall noticed it, and adopted it as a title for an article about my work. If he had not done this, I doubt if I should have remembered the phrase myself; but when I saw it in Mr. Heppenstall's hands, so to speak, it seemed the appropriate name for this present novel, which was already in my mind. So I announced the title, and since have been stuck with it, while the phrase has kept swimming in print before my eyes about twice a week and four times on Sundays, and has, in fact, turned into a cliché. But I cannot help using it myself, without too much inconvenience. I console myself with the reflection that, if a man hasn't the right to his own cliché, who has?

I would like to make one other point. This novel is about "high" politics and, like all novels on the subject, carries an unresolvable complication. This one is set in the period 1955–8, and in the year 1957 the Prime Minister has to be introduced. Now there was a real Prime Minister at the time. His name was Harold Macmillan. The Prime Minister in this novel is quite unlike Mr. Harold Macmillan, as unlike as he could reasonably be. Short of introducing real personages as characters, there is no other way. None of my imaginary Ministers is connected with anyone in office during the Eden or Macmillan administrations, and I have deliberately used, as the major public issue in the novel, one which didn't come openly into politics at that time.

Since I have had to mention Mr. Harold Macmillan, I should like, out of gratitude, to mention something else. If it had not been for his intervention, in one of his less public phases, my books would not now be published under the Macmillan imprint in London.

During the writing of this book, I collected other debts of gratitude. Politicians on both sides of the House of Commons have given me their time and trouble: it would look too much like a roll-call to write down all the names. But I should not feel comfortable if I did not make two specific acknowledgments. One to Mr. Maurice Macmillan, with whom I discussed aspects of the book long before a word was written: and the other to Mr. Maurice Edelman, who—being both a novelist and a member of Parliament—welcomed me on to his own proper territory and has been more generous and helpful than I can describe.

C. P. S.

CONTENTS

CORRIDORS
OF
POWER

I
THE FIRST THING

CHAPTER I

A LONDON DINNER-
PARTY

I stopped the taxi at the corner of Lord North Street. My wife and I had the habit of being obsessively punctual, and that night we had, as usual, overdone it. There was a quarter of an hour to kill, so we dawdled down to the river. It was a pleasant evening, I said, conciliating the moment. The air was warm against the cheek, the trees in the Embankment garden stood bulky, leaves filling out, although it was only March, against the incandescent skyline. The light above Big Ben shone beneath the cloud-cap: the House was sitting.

We walked a few yards further, in the direction of Whitehall. Across Parliament Square, in the Treasury building, another light was shining. A room lit up on the third storey, someone working late.

There was nothing special about the evening, either for my wife or me. We had dined with the Quaifes several times before. Roger Quaife was a youngish Conservative member who was beginning to be talked about. I had met him through one of my official jobs, and thought him an interesting man. It was the kind of friendly acquaintanceship, no more than that, which we all picked up, officials, politicians of both parties: not meeting often, but enough to make us feel at home in what they sometimes called "this part of London."

Prompt to the last stroke of eight, we were back in Lord

3

North Street. A maid took us upstairs to the drawing-room, bright with chandeliers, drink-trays, the dinner-shirts of two men already standing there, the necklace of Caro Quaife glittering as she took our hands.

"I expect you know everyone, don't you?" she said. "Of course you do!"

She was tall and pretty, in her middle thirties, just beginning, though she was still elegant, to thicken a little through the waist. Her voice was warm, full, and often disconcertingly loud. She gave out a sense of natural and exuberant happiness —as though it were within the power of everyone round her to be as happy as she was.

Other people had followed us up. They all knew one another, establishing Caro's principle of mutual intimacy: Christian names flew about, so that, when the principle broke down, I didn't know whom I was being introduced to. There was, in fact, only one man whom Margaret and I had met as often as the Quaifes. That was Monty Cave, who, according to the political talent spotters, was another coming star. He had a plump face, lemur-like eyes, a quiet, subtle, modulated voice.

As for the others, there appeared to be three couples, all the men Tory back-benchers, none of them older than forty, with wives to match, young, strapping matrons such as one saw in the Kensington streets at four in the afternoon, collecting their children from fashionable pre-preparatory schools. There was also an elderly woman called Mrs. Henneker.

As we sat down and drank, Roger Quaife not yet present, they were all talking politics, but politics which any outsider —even one as near to it as I was—needed a glossary to follow. This was House of Commons gossip, as esoteric as theatre-gossip, as continuously enthralling to them as theatre-gossip was to actors. Who was in favour, who wasn't. Who was going to finish up the debate next week. How Archie pulled a fast one with that question.

There was going to be an election soon, we all knew: this was the spring of 1955. They were swapping promises to speak for one another: one was bragging how two senior Ministers were "in the bag" to speak for him. Roger was safe, someone said, he'd give a hand. What had the P.M. got in mind for Roger "when we come back?" Monty Cave asked Caro. She shook her head, but she was pleased, and I thought she was touching wood.

The other men spoke of Roger as though he were the only one of them whose success was coming soon, or as though he were different from themselves. The gossip went on. The euphoria grew. Then the maid came in and announced, "Lady Caroline, Dr. Rubin is here."

It was not that Roger Quaife had a title—but his wife was the daughter of an earl, one of a rich aristocratic family who in the 19th Century had been Whig grandees.

I looked round, as Caro stood up with cries of welcome. I was taken aback. Yes, it was the David Rubin I knew very well, the American physicist. He came in, very quiet and guarded, pearl cuff-links in his sleeves, his dinner jacket newer and more exquisite than any man's there. He was, so my scientific friends said, one of the most distinguished of scientists: but unlike the rest of them, he was also something of a dandy.

Caro Quaife took him to my wife's side. By this time the drawing-room was filling up, and Caro threw a cushion on the floor and sat by me. "You must be used to women sitting at your feet, mustn't you?" she said. She couldn't understand, she went on, why Roger, the old devil, was so late. She spoke of him with the cheerfulness, the lack of anxiety, of a happy marriage. When she spoke to me directly, it was in a manner at once high-spirited, deferential and aggressive, eager to be impressed, used to speaking out and not thinking twice.

"Hungry," said Mrs. Henneker, in a trumpeting tone.

She had a fleshy, bulbous nose and eyes which stared out, a fine bright blue, with a disconcerting fixity.

"Sorry. Have another drink," said Caro, without any sign of caring. In fact, it was not yet half-past eight, but it seemed late for a dinner-party in the 'fifties.

The conversation had switched. One of the members' wives had started talking about a friend of theirs who was having "woman trouble." Just for once, they had got away from the House of Commons. This friend was a banker: he had "got it badly": his wife was worried.

"What's the woman like?" Caro gave a loud, crowing chuckle.

I observed David Rubin's sad face show signs of animation. He preferred this topic to the previous one.

"Oh, madly glamorous."

"In that case," cried Caro, "I don't believe Elsa" (the wife) "has much to worry about. It isn't the glamorous ones you ought to watch out for when the old man's showing signs of absent-mindedness. It's that little quiet grey mouse in the corner, who nobody's ever noticed. If *she's* got her claws into him, then the best thing is to call it a day and wonder how you're going to explain it to the children."

The other wives were laughing with her. She was not a beauty, I thought, she was too hearty for that. Just then her eyes lit up, and she scrambled off her cushion.

"Here he is!" she said. "And about time too!"

As Roger walked through the room from an inner door, he looked clumsy, a little comic, quite unselfconscious. He was a big man, heavy and strong: but neither his face nor his body seemed all of a piece. His head was smallish, for a man of his bulk, and well-shaped, his eyes grey and bright, pulled down a little at the outer corners. His nose was flattened at the bridge, his lower lip receded. It was not a handsome face, but it was pleasant. His colleagues in the room, except for

Cave, were neat, organised, officer-like; by their side he was shambling and uncoordinated. When I first met him, he had brought back my impression of Pierre Bezukhov in *War and Peace*. Yet his manner, quite unlike Pierre's, was briskly competent.

"I'm so sorry," he said to his wife, "someone caught me on the 'phone—"

It was, it appeared, one of his constituents. He said it simply, as if it were a matter of tactics that she would understand.

He had considerable physical presence, though it was the opposite of an actor's presence. He shook hands with Rubin and me. All he did and said was easy and direct.

For a moment he and his fellow members had edged away, and on the periphery of the group Mrs. Henneker laid a substantial, ringed hand on my arm.

"Office," she said.

I found her conversation hard to cope with.

"What?" I replied.

"That young man is going to get office." By which she meant that he would be made a Minister if his party were returned again.

"Will he?" I said.

She asked, "Are you an idiot?"

She asked it with a dense, confident twinkle, as though I should love her for being rude.

"I shouldn't have thought so," I said.

"I meant it in the Greek sense, Sir Leonard," she said, and then from a heavy aside discovered from Caro that my name was Lewis Eliot. "Yes, I meant it in the Greek sense," she said, quite unabashed. "Not interested in politics, y'know."

She was so proud of her scrap of learning. I wondered how often she had trotted it out, knowing as much Greek as she did Eskimo. There was something childlike about her self-satisfaction. She was sure that she was a privileged soul. She was sure that no one could think otherwise.

"I am rather interested in politics," I said.

"I don't believe it," said Mrs. Henneker triumphantly.

I tried to hush her, for I wanted to listen to Roger. His tone was different from that of his friends. I could not place his accent. But it was nothing like that of Eton and the Brigade; any of the others would have known, and Mrs. Henneker might have said, that he did not come "out of the top drawer." In fact, his father had been a design engineer, solid provincial middle-class. He wasn't young, despite Mrs. Henneker's adjective. He was only five years younger than I was, which made him forty-five.

He had interested me from the beginning, though I couldn't have said why. Listening to him that evening, as we sat round the dinner-table downstairs, I was disappointed. Yes, his mind was crisper than the others', he was a good deal heavier-weight. But he too, just like the others, was talking about the chessboard of Parliament, the moves of their private game, as though nothing else existed under Heaven. I thought that, with David Rubin present, they were all being impolite. I became impatient. These people's politics were not my politics. They didn't know the world they were living in, much less the world that was going to come. I looked at Margaret, who had the eager, specially attentive look she always wore when she was bored, and wished that the evening were over.

All of a sudden, I wasn't impatient any longer. The women had just gone back upstairs, and we were standing in the candlelight. "Come and sit by me," Roger said to Rubin, and snapped his fingers, not obtrusively, as if giving himself a signal of some kind. He put me on his other side. As he was pouring brandy into Rubin's glass, he said, "I'm afraid we've been boring you stiff. You see, this election is rather on our minds." He looked up and broke into a wide, sarcastic grin. "But then, if you've been attending carefully, you may have gathered that."

For the first time that evening, David Rubin began to take a part. "Mr. Quaife, I'd like to ask you something," he said. "What, according to present thinking, is the result of this election going to be? Or is that asking you to stick your neck out?"

"It's fair enough," said Roger. "I'll give you the limits. On one side, the worst that can happen to us" (he meant the Conservative Party) "is a stalemate. It can't be worse than that. At the other end, if we're lucky we might have a minor landslide."

Rubin nodded. One of the members said: "I'm betting on a hundred majority."

"I'd judge a good deal less," said Roger.

He was speaking like a real professional, I thought. But it was just afterwards that my attention sharpened. My neighbour's cigar smoke was spiralling round the candle-flame: it might have been any well-to-do London party, the men alone for another quarter of an hour. Then Roger, relaxed and solid in his chair, turned half-right to David Rubin and said: "Now I'd like to ask you something, if I may."

"Surely," said Rubin.

"If there are things you mustn't say, then I hope you won't feel embarrassed. First, I'd like to ask you—how much does what we're doing about nuclear weapons make sense?"

Rubin's face was more sombre, worn and sensitive than those round him. He was no older than some of the other men; but among the fresh ruddy English skins his stood out dry, pallid, already lined, with great sepia pouches, like bruises, under his eyes. He seemed a finer-nerved, more delicate species of animal.

"I don't know that I'm following you," he said. "Do you mean what the U.K. is doing about your weapons? Or what we're doing? Or do you mean the whole world?"

"They all enter, don't they?" Everyone was looking at Roger as he asked the matter-of-fact question. "Anyway, would you start on the local position; that is, ours? We have a certain uncomfortable interest in it, you know. Would you tell us whether what this country's doing makes sense?"

Rubin did not, in any case, find it easy to be as direct as Roger. He was an adviser to his own government; further, and more inhibiting, he was hyper-cautious about giving pain. So he did a lot of fencing. Was Roger talking about the bombs themselves, or the methods of delivery? He invoked me, to help him out—as an official, I had heard these topics argued between the Americans and ourselves for years.

There were other considerations besides the scientific ones, besides military ones, said Rubin, back on his last line of defence, why the U.K. might want their own weapon.

"It's our job to worry about that, isn't it?" said Roger gently. "Tell us—look, you know this as well as anyone in the world—how significant, just in the crudest practical terms, are our weapons going to be?"

"Well, if you must have it," Rubin answered, shrugging his shoulders, "anything you can do doesn't count two per cent."

"I say, Professor Rubin," came a bass voice, "you're kicking us downstairs pretty fast, aren't you?"

Rubin said: "I wish I could tell you something different." His interlocutor was Mrs. Henneker's son-in-law, a man called Tom Wyndham. He confronted Rubin with a cheerful stare, full of the assurance of someone brought up in a ruling class, an assurance which did not exactly ignore changes in power, but shrugged them off. Rubin gave an apologetic smile. He was the most polite of men. He had been born in Brooklyn, his parents still spoke English as a foreign language. But he had his own kind of assurance: it did not surprise him to be told that he was the favourite for that year's Nobel physics prize.

"No," said Monty Cave, "Roger asked you to tell us." He gave a sharp grin. "He usually gets what he asks for."

Roger smiled, as though they were friends as well as allies. For five years, since they entered the House, they had been leading their group of back-benchers.

"Now, David, if I may call you so," he said, "do you mind if I go one step further. About the United States— does your policy about the weapons make sense?"

"I hope so."

"Doesn't it depend upon the assumption that you're going to have technical superiority forever? Don't some of our scientists think you're under-estimating the Russians? Is that so, Lewis?"

I was thinking to myself, Roger had been well briefed; for Francis Getliffe, Walter Luke and their colleagues had been pressing just that view.

"We don't know," said Rubin.

He was not at his most detached. And yet, I saw that he had respect for Roger as an intelligent man. He was a good judge of intelligence and, courteous though he was, respect did not come easily to him.

"Well, then," said Roger, "let us assume, as I should have thought for safety's sake we ought to, that the West— which means you—and the Soviet Union may get into a nuclear arms race on something like equal terms. Then how long have we got to do anything reasonable?"

"Not as long as I'd like."

"How many years?"

"Perhaps ten."

There was a pause. The others, who had been listening soberly, did not want to argue. Roger said: "Does that suggest an idea to anyone?"

He said it with a sarcastic twist, dismissively. He was pushing his chair back, signalling that we were going back to the drawing-room.

Just as he was holding open the door, bells began to ring in the passage, up the stairs, in the room we were leaving.

It was something like being on board ship, with bells ringing for lifeboat-drill. Immediately Roger, who a minute before had seemed dignified—more than that, formidable—took on a sheepish smile. "Division bell," he explained to David Rubin, still wearing the smile, ashamed, curiously boyish, and at the same time gratified, which comes on men when they are taking part in a collective private ritual. "We shan't be long!" The members ran out of the house, like schoolboys frightened of being late, while David and I went upstairs alone.

"They've gone off, have they? Time something broke you up." Caro greeted us robustly. "Whose reputations have you been doing in? Men ought to have—" With lively hands, she exemplified cat's whiskers sprouting.

I shook my head, and said that we had been talking about David Rubin's expert subject, and the future. Margaret looked at me. But the division bell had quite smashed the mood. I no longer felt any eschatological sense, or even any responsibility. Instead, in the bright drawing-room, all seemed serene, anti-climactic, and slightly comic.

They had just started on what was becoming more and more a sacramental subject in such a drawing-room—schools for the children, or, more exactly, how to get them in. One young wife, proud both of maternity and her educational acumen, with a son born three months before, announced that within an hour of his birth he had been "put down" not only for Eton, but for his first boarding-school—"And we'd have put him down for Balliol too," she went on, "only they won't let you do that, nowadays."

What had Caro arranged for her children? What was Margaret doing for ours? Across the room I watched David Rubin listening, with his beautiful, careful, considerate courtesy, to plans for buying places thirteen years ahead for children he had never seen, in a system which in his heart he thought fantastic. He just let it slip once that, though he was only forty-one, his eldest son was a sophomore at Harvard. Otherwise he listened, grave and attentive, and I felt a desire to give some instruction to Mrs. Henneker, who was sitting beside me. I told her that American manners were the best in the world.

"What's that?" she cried.

"Russian manners are very good," I added, as an after-thought. "Ours are some of the worst."

It was pleasing to have startled Mrs. Henneker. It was true, I said, getting immersed in comparative sociology, that English lower-class manners were rather good, appreciably better than American; but once you approached and passed the mid-point of society, theirs got steadily better and ours got steadily worse. American professional or upper-class manners were out of comparison better. I proceeded to speculate as to why this should be.

I had a feeling that Mrs. Henneker did not find this specu-lation profitable.

The men came pelting up the stairs, Matthew in the rear. The division was over, the majority up to par. From then on, the party did not get going again and it was not later than half-past eleven when Margaret and I took David Rubin away. The taxi throbbed along the Embankment towards Chelsea, where he was staying. He and Margaret were talking about the evening, but as I gazed out of the window I did not join in much. I let myself drift into a kind of daydream.

When we had said good-night to David, Margaret took my hand.

"What are you thinking about?" she said.

I couldn't tell her. I was just staring out at the comfortable, familiar town. The Chelsea back-streets, which I used to know, the lights of Fulham Road: Kensington squares: the stretch of Queen's Gate up towards the Park. All higgledy-piggledy, leafy, not pretty, nearer the ground than the other capital cities. I was not exactly remembering, although much had happened to me there; but I had a sense, not sharp, of joys hidden about the place, of love, of marriage, of miseries and elations, of coming out into the night air. The talk after dinner had not come back to my mind; it was one of many; we were used to them. And yet, I felt vulnerable, as if soft with tenderness towards the town itself, although in cold blood I should not have said that I liked it overmuch.

The dark road across the Park, the sheen of the Serpentine, the livid lamps of Bayswater Road—I was full of the kind of emotion which one cannot hide from oneself, and yet which is so unrespectable that one wants to deny it, as when a foreigner says a few words in praise of one's country, and, after a lifetime's training in detachment, one finds oneself on the edge of tears.

CHAPTER II

THE OLD HERO

The election went according to plan, or rather according to the plan of Roger's friends. Their party came back with a majority of sixty: as prophesied by Mrs. Henneker at that dinner-party in Lord North Street, Roger duly got office.

As soon as the appointment was announced, my civil service acquaintances started speculating. The rumour went round Whitehall that he was an ambitious man. It was not a malicious rumour; it was curiously impersonal, curiously certain, carried by people who had never met him, building up his official personality for good and all.

One summer afternoon, not long after the election, as I sat in his office with my chief, Sir Hector Rose—St. James's Park lay green beneath his windows and the sunlight edged across the desk—I was being politely cross-questioned. I had worked under him for sixteen years. We trusted each other as colleagues, and yet we were not much easier in each other's company than we had been at the beginning. No, I did not know Roger Quaife well, I said—which, at the time, was true. I had a feeling, without much to support it, that he wasn't a simple character.

Rose was not impressed by psychological guesses. He was occupied with something more businesslike. He assumed that Quaife was, as they said, ambitious. Rose did not find that a matter for condemnation. But this job which Quaife had taken had been the end of other ambitious men. That was a genuine point. If he had had any choice, there must be something wrong with his judgment.

"Which, of course, my dear Lewis," said Hector Rose, "suggests rather strongly that he wasn't given any choice. In which case, some of our masters may conceivably not wish him all the good in the world. Fortunately, it's not for us to enquire into these remarkable and no doubt well-intentioned calculations. He's said to be a good chap. Which will be at least a temporary relief, so far as this department is concerned."

The appointment had more than a conversational interest for Hector Rose. Since the war, what in our jargon we called "the co-ordination of defence" had been split up. The greater part had gone to a new Ministry. It was this Ministry of which Roger had just been appointed Parliamentary Secretary.* In the process, Rose had lost a slice of his responsibilities and powers. Very unfairly, I could not help admitting. When I first met him, he had been the youngest Permanent Secretary in the service. Now he was only three years from retirement, having been in the same rank, and at the same job, longer than any of his colleagues. They had given him the Grand Cross of the Bath, the sort of decoration he and his friends prized, but which no one else noticed. He still worked with the precision of a computer. Sometimes his politeness, so elaborate, which used to be as tireless as his competence, showed thin at the edges now. He continued to look strong, heavy-shouldered, thick; but his youthfulness,

---

* These official designations are confusing. A Parliamentary Secretary is a junior Minister; these appointments are political, selected by the Prime Minister from Parliament. Usually, though not always, a Parliamentary Secretaryship is the first office given to an aspiring politician. A Permanent Secretary is a civil servant who has attained the highest rank in the administrative class: such an official has as a rule entered the Civil Service in his early twenties and is not affected by changes of government.

which had lasted into middle-age, had vanished quite. His hair had whitened, there was a heavy line across his forehead. How deeply was he disappointed? To me, at least, he did not give so much as a hint. In his relations with the new super-department, of which he might reasonably have expected to be the permanent head, he did his duty, and a good deal more than his duty.

The new department was the civil servants' despair. It was true what Rose had said: it had become a good place to send an enemy to. Not that the civil servants had any quarrel with the Government about general policy. Rose and his colleagues were conservatives almost to a man, and they had been as pleased about the election results as the Quaifes' circle themselves.

The point was, the new department, like anything connected with modern war, spent money, but did not, in administrative terms, have anything to show for it. Rose and the other administrators had a feeling, the most disagreeable they could imagine, that things were slipping out of their control. No Minister had been any good. The present incumbent, Roger's boss, Lord Gilbey, was the worst of any. Civil servants were used to Ministers who had to be persuaded or bullied into decisions. But they were at a loss when they came against one who, with extreme cordiality, would neither make a decision nor leave it to them.

I had seen something of this imbroglio at first hand. At some points, the business of our department interweaved with theirs, and often Rose needed an emissary. It had to be an emissary of some authority, and he cast me for the job. There were bits of the work that, because I had been doing them so long, I knew better than anyone else. I also had a faint moral advantage. I had made it clear that I wanted to get out of Whitehall and, perversely, this increased my usefulness. Or if not my usefulness, at least the attention they paid to me, rather like the superstitious veneration with which healthy people listen to someone known to be not long for this earth.

Thus I was frequently in and out of their offices, which were only a few hundred yards away from ours, at the corner of the Park. Like everyone else, I had become attached to Lord Gilbey. I was no better than anyone else, and in some ways worse, at getting him to make up his mind. A few days after that talk with Rose, I was making another attempt, in conjunction with Gilbey's own Permanent Secretary, to do just that.

The Permanent Secretary was an old colleague of mine, Douglas Osbaldiston, who was being talked of now just as Rose had been, nearly twenty years before. He was the newest bright star, the man who, as they used to say about Rose, would be Head of the Civil Service before he finished.

On the surface, he was very different from Rose, simple, unpretentious, straightforward where Rose was oblique, humbly born while Rose was the son of an Archdeacon, and yet as cultivated as an old-fashioned civil servant, and exuding the old-fashioned amateur air. He was no more an amateur than Rose, and at least as clever. Once, when he had been working under Rose, I had thought he would not be tough enough for the top jobs. I could not have been more wrong.

He had studied Rose's career with forethought, and was determined not to duplicate it. He wanted to get out of his present job as soon as he had cleaned it up a little— "This is a hiding to nothing," he said simply—and back to the Treasury.

He was long, thin, fresh-faced, still with the relics of an undergraduate air. He was quick-witted, unpompous, the easiest man to do business with. He was also affectionate, and he and I had become friends as I could never have been with Hector Rose.

That morning, as we waited to go in to Gilbey, it did

not take us five minutes to settle our tactics. First—we were both over-simplifying—there was a putative missile on which millions had been spent, and which had to be stopped: we had to persuade "the Old Hero," as the civil servants called Lord Gilbey, to sign a Cabinet paper. Second, a new kind of delivery system for warheads was just being talked about. Osbaldiston, who trusted my nose for danger, agreed that, if we didn't "look at it" now, we should be under pressure. "If we can get the O.H.," said Osbaldiston, "to let the new boy take it over—" By the new boy he meant Roger Quaife.

I asked Osbaldiston what he thought of him. Osbaldiston said that he was shaping better than anyone they had had there; which, because with Gilbey in the Lords Quaife would have to handle the department's business in the Commons, was a consolation.

We set off down the corridor, empty except for a messenger, high and dark with the waste of space, the lavish clammi-ness, of the 19th Century Whitehall. Two doors along, a rubric stood out from the tenebrous gloom: Parliamentary Secre-tary, Mr. Roger Quaife. Osbaldiston jabbed his finger at it, harking back to our conversation about Roger, and re-marked: "One piece of luck, he doesn't get here too early in the morning."

At the end of the corridor, the windows of Lord Gilbey's room, like those of Hector Rose's at the other corner of the building, gave on to the Park. In the murky light, the white-panelled walls gleamed spectrally, and Lord Gilbey stood between his desk and the window, surveying with equable disapproval the slashing rain, the lowering clouds, the seeth-ing summer trees.

"It's a brute," he said, as though at last reaching a con-sidered judgment on the weather. "It's a brute."

His face was pleasant, small-featured, open with that partic-ular openness which doesn't tell one much. His figure was beautifully trim for a man in his sixties. He was affable and had no side. And yet our proposal, which had seemed modest enough in Osbaldiston's room, began to take on an aura of mysterious difficulty.

"Minister," said Osbaldiston, "I really think it's time we got a Cabinet decision on the A——." He gave the code-name of the missile.

"On the A——?" Gilbey repeated thoughtfully, in the manner of one hearing a new, original and probably unsound idea.

"We've got as much agreement as we shall ever get."

"We oughtn't to rush things, you know," Gilbey said reprovingly. "Do you think we ought to rush things?"

"We got to a conclusion on paper eighteen months ago."

"Paper, my dear chap? I'm a great believer in taking people with you, on this kind of thing."

"Minister," said Osbaldiston, "that is precisely what we've been trying to do."

"Do you think we ought to weary in well-doing? Do you really, Sir Douglas?"

The "Sir Douglas" was a sign of gentle reproof. Normally Gilbey would have called Osbaldiston by his Christian name alone. I caught a side-glance from my colleague, as from one who was being beaten over the head with very soft pillows. Once more he was discovering that the Old Hero was not only affable, but obstinate and vain. Osbaldiston knew only too well that, immediately he was away from the office, Gilbey was likely to be "got at" by business tycoons like Lord Lufkin, to whom the stopping of this project meant the loss of millions, or old service friends, who believed that any weapon was better than none.

That was true; the latter being an argument to Osbaldiston for not having a soldier in this job at all. It was not even that Gilbey had been a soldier so eminent that his juniors could not nobble him now. When they called him the Old

Hero, it was not a jibe; he had been an abnormally brave fighting officer in both wars, and had commanded a division in the second. That had been his ceiling. If he had been even reasonably capable, the military in the clubs used to say, he couldn't have helped but go right to the top, since it was hard for a man to be better connected. His peerage had come by birth, not as a military reward. So far as there were aristocrats in England, he was one.

"Minister," said Osbaldiston, "if you think it's wise to prove just how much agreement there is, we could easily run together an inter-departmental meeting, at your level. Or at mine. Or Ministers and officials together."

"Do you know," Gilbey said, "I'm not a great believer in meetings or committees. They don't seem to result in action, don't you know."

For once, Douglas Osbaldiston was at a loss. Then he said: "There's another method. You and the three service Ministers could go and talk it over with the Prime Minister. We could brief you very quickly." (And, I had no doubt Osbaldiston was thinking, we could also see to it that the Prime Minister was briefed.)

"No, I think that would be worrying him too much. These people have a lot on their plate, you know. No, I don't think I should like to do that."

Gilbey gave a sweet, kind, obscurely triumphant smile and said: "I tell you what I will do."

"Minister?"

"I'll have another good look at the papers! You let me have them over the weekend, there's a good chap. And you might let me have a précis on one sheet of paper."

Then he broke off, with an air of innocent satisfaction.

"What do you think of this suit I'm wearing?"

It was an extraordinary question. No one, whatever accusation he was bringing against me or Douglas Osbaldiston, could possibly think of us as dressy men: which, in a gentlemanly way, Lord Gilbey was. He sounded innocent, but, though he might not be capable of making decisions, he was entirely capable of pushing them out of sight.

It looked very nice, I said, with a total lack of interest.

"You'll never guess where I had it made."

No, we found that beyond us.

"As a matter of fact, I had it made at ————." Gilbey gave the name, not of a fashionable tailor, but of a large London departmental store. "It doesn't sound very smart, but it's *all right*."

Inconsiderately, we had to bring him back to the point. This was my turn. I didn't know whether any news had reached him, but there was a kite being flown for a new delivery system: from what we knew of Brodzinski, he wasn't going to stop flying that kite just through lack of encouragement. Wouldn't it be prudent—Rose and Osbaldiston both agreed with this—to deal with the problem before it got talked about, to bring in Getliffe, Luke and the Barford scientists straight away? It probably wasn't pressing enough for the Minister himself, I said, but it might save trouble if Quaife, say, could start some informal talks.

"I think that's a very good idea," said Osbaldiston, who did not miss a cue.

"Quaife? You mean my new Parliamentary Secretary?" Lord Gilbey replied, with a bright, open look. "He's going to be a great help to me. This job is altogether too much for one man, you've both seen enough of it to know that. Of course, my colleagues are politicians, so is Quaife, and I'm a simple soldier, and perhaps some of them would find the job easier than I do, don't you know. Quaife is going to be a great help. There's just one fly in the ointment about your suggestion, Lewis. Is it fair on the chap to ask him to take this on before he's got his nose inside the office? I'm a great believer in working a man in gently—"

Amiably, Lord Gilbey went in for some passive resistance.

He might find his job too much for one man, but nevertheless he liked it. He might be a simple soldier, but he had considerable talent for survival; quite as well as the next man, he could imagine the prospect of bright young men knocking at the door. On this point, however, we had a card to play. My department would be quite willing to take over these first discussions, I said. If Luke and the other scientists took the view we expected, then the business need never come into Gilbey's office at all.

Gilbey didn't like the idea of delegating a piece of work within his own department: but he liked the idea of the work totally escaping his department even less. Finally, in a sweet, good-natured fashion, he gave us a hedging consent. He said: "Yes, perhaps that's what we should do." Without a blink, Osbaldiston took a note and said that he would minute it to the Parliamentary Secretary.

"We mustn't overburden the poor chap," said Gilbey, still hankering after a retreat. But he knew when he was beaten, and in a crisp tone, suggesting an efficiency expert addressing the woolly-minded, he said:

"Well, that's as far as we can go. I call it a good morning's work."

As we knew, he had a Cabinet at twelve. One might have thought that he would have shied from the approach of Cabinet meetings, feeling them above his weight. Not a bit of it. He loved them. As he was preparing himself for the occasion, he took on a special look, a special manner. As a rule, leaving Osbaldiston or me, or the secretaries in the room outside, he would say: "So long," sounding, as he often did, as though transported back before the first war, when he was a smart young officer in the Household Cavalry. But, leaving to go to a Cabinet meeting, he would not have thought of saying, "So long." He inclined his head very gravely, without a word. He walked to the door, slow and erect, face solemn and pious, exactly as though he were going up the aisle in church.

CHAPTER III

A SPEECH IN
THE COMMONS

After we had by-passed Lord Gilbey, I began to see Roger at work. He was ready to listen to any of us. He did not show much of his own mind. There were things about him, one above all, which I needed to know: not just for curiosity's sake, though that was sharpening, but for the sake of my own actions.

In the middle of July, Roger was making his first ministerial speech. I did not need reminding, having drafted enough of them, how much speeches mattered—to parliamentary bosses, to any kind of tycoon. Draft after draft: the search for the supreme, the impossible, the more than Flaubertian perfection: the scrutiny for any phrase that said more than it ought to say, so that each speech at the end was bound, by the law of official inexplicitness, to be more porridge-like than when it started out in its first draft. I had always hated writing drafts for other people, and nowadays got out of it. To Hector Rose, to Douglas Osbaldiston, it was part of the job, which they took with their usual patience, their usual lack of egotism: when a minister crossed out their sharp, clear English and went in for literary composition of his own, they gave a wintry smile and let it stand.

Osbaldiston told me that, on the present occasion, Roger was doing most of his own writing. Further, it was Roger who was taking over the final draft of Gilbey's speech. They were each to make statements for the department on the same day, Gilbey in the Lords, Roger in the Commons.

When the day came, I went to listen to Roger. I met Osbaldiston in Palace Yard: half an hour before he had gone through the experience, in the line of duty, of hearing Lord Gilbey. "If anyone can make head or tail of that," he reported, with professional irritation, "he damned well ought to be an authority on *l'explication du texte.*"

As we were on our way to our customary listening-point, his phlegm, usually impregnable as that of any of his colleagues, was wearing thin.

In the central lobby, I smelled scent near by me, and, glancing round, saw Caro Quaife. Her eyes were full and bright: she did not pretend to hide her nervousness. "I'd better sit somewhere out of the way," she said. "Otherwise I'm going to fidget you."

I said that he would be all right. Instead of going to the civil servants' box, we walked up with her to the Strangers' Gallery. "This sort of speech is hell," said Caro. "I mean, when there's nothing to say."

I could not argue with that. She knew the position as well as I did, and the House of Commons much better.

We sat in the front row of the gallery, deserted except for a party of Indians. We looked down on the Chamber, half full of members, on the sea-green, comfortable benches, the green carpet, hazy in the submarine light filtering through from the summer evening.

"I've got the needle," said Caro. "This is a bit too raw."

Within two or three minutes of his getting to his feet, she must have been reassured. Down there, speaking from the despatch box, he looked a great hulk of a man. From a distance, his heavy shoulders seemed even more massive than they were. I had not heard him speak before, and I realised that he was effective quite out of the ordinary. Effective very

much in a style of our time, I was thinking. He didn't go in
for anything that used to be called oratory. Nearly everyone
in that chamber, and men like Osbaldiston and me, felt more
comfortable with him because he didn't. His manner was
conversational; he had a typescript in front of him, but he
did not glance at it. No metaphors, except in sarcasm. As
Caro had realised, he had "nothing to say"—but he didn't
make the mistake of pretending he had. There was no policy
settled: the decisions were complex: there weren't any easy
solutions. He sounded competent, master of the details of
the job. He also sounded quite uncomplacent, and, listening to him, I believed it was that tone which went straight
home.

So far as I could judge Commons receptions, his was a
warm one, not only on his own side. Certainly Caro was in
no doubt. Gazing down with an expression that was loving,
gratified and knowledgeable, she said, "Now I call *that* a bit
of all right."

On my other side, Osbaldiston, still preoccupied with professional values, was reflecting: "I must say, it does make us
look a bit more respectable, anyway."

In the lobby, where we went to meet him, he was being
congratulated. Members whom he scarcely knew, hounds of
success, were trying to catch his eye. Shining with sweat and
well-being, he nevertheless wanted our opinion too. "Satisfactory?" he asked Osbaldiston and me, with a vigilant look.
It was not until he had had enough praise that he switched
to another topic. Now he was ready to think about some of
the scientists' troubles, he said. He and Caro were going out
to dinner. Could we come round to Lord North Street after
eleven, and start straight away?

Later that night, I sat in the Quaifes' drawing-room, waiting for them. I was sitting there alone, since Osbaldiston,
who lived out in the suburbs, had left me to it. They were not
late home: they ran up the stairs brimming with excitement:

but it was a long time before Roger and I got down to business.

They were excited because they had been dining with the editor of the *Times,* and had been given a glimpse of next day's (Friday morning's) paper.

I was amused. This was real privilege, I said. In London at that time, one could not buy the earliest editions until the small hours. The other notices they would not see before the morning. Still, Roger was prepared to concede, the *Times* was the most important. They couldn't have done him better. His had been the statement they examined, while Lord Gilbey, his boss, received a few indifferent lines.

He saw me watching him. I asked, what did Gilbey's speech look like on paper? Roger shrugged his shoulders, said he had been too close to it. He didn't know how it would read in the House of Lords Hansard.

Caro, radiant, gave us more drinks and took a stiff one herself. She was as excited as he was, but much more confident. She could trust her judgment about success much more easily than he could. He was still thinking of next morning's papers. That evening in the House, he had sounded grown-up, unusually speculative, responsible. It was arguable, unless one believed that we were wholly at the mercy of blind and faceless fortune, that his decisions might turn out to be important. More than most men, that was the feeling he gave one. Yet, in the bright drawing-room in Lord North Street, all he was thinking of, without any deviation or let-up, was what the *Telegraph,* the *Guardian,* the popular press, would say next day. Caro sat stroking the side of her glass, proud, loving, full of certainties. She could have written the headlines herself.

Of the people I knew, I often thought, it was only the politicians and the artists who lived nakedly in public. The great administrative bosses, the Roses and Osbaldistons, scarcely ever heard a public word about themselves, certainly

not a hostile one. As for the industrial tycoons like Paul Lufkin, as soon as they got near the top, they would have felt
the virtues outraged if they had heard so much as a whisper
of personal criticism. Those lives were out of comparison
more shielded. It was the politicians and artists who had to
get used to being talked about in public, rather as though
they were patients in a hospital visited daily by troops of
medical students, who didn't hate them, but who saw no reason to lower their voices. Of course, the politicians and artists
had asked for it, or rather some part of their temperament
had. Yet, though they might have asked for it, they didn't like
it. Their skins did not thicken, even if they became world
figures. I was sure that Roger's never would.

I wished that I were as sure of what, in his job, he intended
to do. That night, at last, we were talking business. He was
as familiar with "the papers" (which meant a drawer-full of
files, memoranda marked "Top Secret," and even one or two
books) as I was. He had mastered both the proposals of the
Brodzinski group, and what Getliffe and the others argued in
reply. All Roger said was intelligent and precise—but he
would not give me an opinion of his own.

I did not get any further that night. We went on in the
same fashion, sniffing at each other like dogs, in the weeks
before the summer recess. He must have guessed where I
stood, I thought—even though guardedness was catching, and
soon one didn't put out one's feelers as far.

Intermittently, during the summer, on holiday with the
family, I wondered about him. It was possible that he was
testing me. It was possible that he had not yet made up his
mind.

As a rule I would have waited. This time I had to know. It
was often naïf to be too suspicious, much more naïf than to
believe too easily. It often led to crasser action. But there
were occasions—and this was one—where you needed to trust.

In September, arriving back in London, I thought it would

do no harm if I tried to spend an evening with him alone.
Then, my first morning in Whitehall, I felt the sensation of
having put one's shoulder hard against a door already on the
latch. A telephone call came through before I had glanced
at my in-tray. I heard a familiar, rich, off-beat voice. Roger
was asking me whether I had any time free in the next few
days, and whether we might spend a bachelor evening at his
club.

CHAPTER IV

SOMETHING IN
THE OPEN

At the Carlton, Roger and I had our dinner at a corner table. Although he waved now and then to passersby, he was concentrating on his meal. He was enjoying himself, we were sharing a bottle of wine and he ordered another. When I had been with him before, he had not cared what he ate or drank, or whether he did so at all. Now he was behaving like a gold-miner coming into town. It struck me that he had the irregular habits, the mixture of rapacity and self-denial, which I had seen before in people who set themselves big tasks.

Through the dinner, I was stone-walling. He wanted something out of me: I wanted to find out something about him. But I could afford to let it ride. So we talked about books, where he uttered strong opinions, and about common acquaintances, where he was more interested and would not utter any opinion whatever. Rose, Osbaldiston, Luke, Getliffe, a couple of top Ministers: we discussed them all. He produced detail after detail, but would not admit that he liked one more than another. I taunted him by saying that this neutrality didn't suit his style. He was putting on the neutrality of men of action who, except under extreme provocation, never admitted that one man was preferable to another.

Roger gave a boisterous laugh, a laugh so unrestrained that I saw other people glancing towards our table.

It was a point to me. Without any introduction, preparation or lead-in, Roger leaned across the table and suddenly said: "Lewis, I want your help."

I was taken by surprise, and went back to stone-walling again. I looked, not at him, but at the people round about us, at an old man with a crimson face who was chewing with exaggerated slowness, at a serious youth impressed by his first glimpse of a London club.

I said, "What for?"

"I thought you had just been blaming *me* for being neutral."

"What am I being neutral about?" I asked.

"I can play that game as long as you can. Is it going to get us anywhere?"

Roger had seized the initiative and held it. He was speaking easily, with inexplicable intimacy, with something like anger.

A few drops of wine had spilled upon the table. He flicked them together with his forefinger, then made a cross with them, as if to emphasize an end to something.

"You've got some insight, haven't you? You're supposed to be a man of good will, aren't you? I believe you want some of the things I do. The trouble with you, you like to sit above the battle. I don't know that I've got much use for that. You're prepared to get your hands a bit dirty, but not very dirty. I'm not sure that that's as creditable as you would like to think. I must say, I sometimes lose my respect for people who know as much as you do, and still don't come and fight it out."

He gave a comradely, savage grin, then broke out: "Anyway, just to begin with, don't you think you might treat me as a moral equal?"

This was my second surprise—so sharp, it seemed I hadn't heard right and simultaneously knew that I had. We looked at each other, and then away, as one does when words have burrowed to a new level, when they have started to mean something. There was a pause, but I was not premeditating. I said: "What do you want? What do you really want?"

Roger laughed, not loudly this time. "You must have learned a *little* from your observations, mustn't you?"

His body was heaved back in his chair, relaxed, but his eyes were bright, half with malice, half with empathy, making me take part.

"Of course," he said, "I want everything that politics can give me. Somehow you never seem to have wanted that. If you'd been slightly different, I've sometimes thought you could have done. But I don't think you were humble enough."

He went on: "Look, a politician lives in the present, you know. If he's got any sense, he can't think of leaving any memorial behind him. So you oughtn't to begrudge him the rewards he wants. One of them is—just possessing the power, that's the first thing. Being able to say yes or no. The power usually isn't very much, as power goes, but of course one wants it. And one waits a long time before one gets a smell of it. I was thinking about politics, I was working at politics, I was dreaming of a career nowhere else, from the time I was twenty. I was forty before I even got into the House. Do you wonder that some politicians are content when they manage to get a bit of power?"

He said: "I'm not, you know."

Once more angry, intimate and simple, he said he thought he could have done other things. He believed he could have had a success at the Bar, or made money in business. He said in passing that money didn't matter much, since Caro was so rich. He went on: "If I were content, it would all be nice and easy. I happen to be pretty comfortably placed. It isn't a matter of being liked. I doubt if they like me all that much. Being liked doesn't count so much in politics as outsiders

think. Being taken for granted, becoming part of the furniture, counts for a great deal more. I've only got to sit on my
backside, and I should become part of the furniture. If I
played the game according to the rules, nothing could stop me
getting a decent, safe Ministry in five years or so." He gave
a smile at once sarcastic, matey, calm. "The trouble is, that
isn't good enough."

He said, as though it were straightforward: "The first thing
is to get the power. The next—is to do something with it."

There was a silence. Then, heaving himself up, he suggested
that we might have a change of scene. We went into the drawing-room, where he ordered brandy. For a moment or so he
sat in silence, as though uncertain. Then he snapped his
fingers and looked at me, with a glimmer of amusement.
"Why do you imagine I'm in this present job at all? I suppose you thought I wasn't given any choice?"

I said that I had heard speculations.

"Oh no," he replied. "I asked for it."

He had been warned against it, he said, by all who believed in him: encouraged into it by some who didn't. It was
of course a risk, he added, that a politician at his stage ought
not to take. He looked at me, and said, without emphasis:

"I believe I can do something. I don't guarantee it, but
there is a chance. For a few years the situation is comparatively fluid. After that, I confess I don't see much hope."

It was quiet in the drawing-room, only four other people
there besides ourselves, and they were far away across the
room. It was, as usual, rather dark, or gave the impression of
darkness. There was no sense of time there, of the hurrying
clock, or the inevitability of morning.

For some time we went over arguments which we both
knew well. They were the arguments over which for months
we had been fencing, not declaring ourselves. Yet, as he had
known and I had suspected, we disagreed little. They were
the arguments which had been implicit in his interrogation

of David Rubin, that evening in the spring: when, so it seemed now, Roger was already preparing himself.

Neither of us needed to make a coherent case. Knowing the details of the debate so intimately, we used a kind of short-hand, which at that time would have been understood by a good many of our acquaintances, in particular by Getliffe and most of the scientists. To put it at its simplest, we believed that most people in power, certainly in our own country, certainly in the West, had misjudged the meaning of nuclear arms. Yet we had got onto an escalator, and it would take abnormal daring to get off. There were two points of action, Roger and I both knew. One was in our own, English, hands. It was not realistic for us to try indefinitely to possess our own weapons. Could we slide out and manage to prevent the spread? The second point, about which I myself felt much more strongly, was not in our control. We might have an influence. If the nuclear arms race between the United States and the Soviet Union went on too long— how long was too long? none of us could guess—then I could see only one end.

"It mustn't happen," said Roger. Neither of us smiled. It was an occasion when only a platitude gave one support. Roger went on speaking with energy, calculation and warmth. It had to be solved. There were enough forces to be used, by determined and skilful men. He sounded impersonal, im-mersed. He wasn't thinking about me; both his pyschological attention and his vanity had dropped away. He was utterly sure that he could be of some use.

After a time, when the concentration had slackened, I said: "All this is fine, but isn't it curious, coming from your side?"

He knew as well as I did that I was no conservative.

"It's got to come from my side. It's the only chance. Look, we both agree that we haven't much time. In our kind of society—and I mean America too—the only things that can

possibly get done are going to be done by people like
me. I don't care what you call me. Liberal conservative.
Bourgeois capitalist. We're the only people who can get a
political decision through. And the only decisions we can get
through will come from people like me.

"Remember," said Roger, "these are going to be real decisions. There won't be many of them, they're only too real.
People like you, sitting outside, can influence them a bit,
but you can't make them. Your scientists can't make them.
Civil servants can't make them. So far as that goes, as a
junior Minister, I can't make them. To make the real decisions, one's got to have the real power."

"Are you going to get it?" I asked.

"If I don't," said Roger, "this discussion has been remarkably academic."

In the last moment before we got ready to go, he was preoccupied, but not with decisions to come. He was thinking
how soon he could manage to sit in Gilbey's chair. He mentioned the name, but he was being careful not to involve
me. He was sensitive, perhaps in this case over-sensitive, to
what he could ask his supporters. It sometimes made him
seem, as now, more cagey, evasive, tricky than he was at heart.

He was, however, happy with the evening's talk. He fore-
saw that, when he had the power, he would be plunged
in a network of what we called "closed" politics, the politics
of the civil servants, the scientists, the industrialists, before
he got any scrap of his policy through. He thought I could
be useful to him there. After this evening, he believed that
he could rely on me.

When we had said good-night in St. James's Street, and
I made my way up that moderate incline (with a vestigial
memory of how, when I was younger and had spent nights at
Pratt's, it had sometimes seemed uncomfortably steep) I was
thinking that he did not find his own personality easy to
handle. It was not neat or sharp, any more than his face was.

Like a lot of subtle men, he must often have been too clever by half, and taken in no one but himself. Nevertheless, when he spoke about what he wanted to do, he had not been clever at all. He knew, and took it for granted that I knew, that in their deep concerns men aren't clever enough to dissimulate. Neither of us had been dissimulating that night.

CHAPTER V

THE SCIENTISTS

Within two days of that dinner at the Carlton, Roger asked me to make some arrangements. He wanted us to have lunch with Francis Getliffe and Walter Luke—"in a private room," he specified. After lunch, we would all pay a visit to Brodzinski. As I stood with Getliffe and Luke in the room at the Hyde Park Hotel, looking down at the Row and the bronzing trees, I was puzzled and the others more so. There was nothing specially mysterious about the private room, if we were to discuss secret projects: but Roger met them both regularly on one of the defence committees. Why should he make an occasion of it now? Neither of them had any inclination to spend time with Brodzinski, nor saw any value in it.

As we waited for Roger, Francis was vexed. He was getting more irritable, more occupied with punctilio, as he grew older. He and I had been friends since our early twenties. At this time he was fifty-two, and already an elder statesman of science. He had thought more effectively about military-scientific strategy than anyone we had, and it was his views which had influenced us most. But now he had to force himself to produce them. He had found a new field of research, and was working as obsessively as when he was a young man. It was a physical strain to be torn away from it, to be dragged up from Cambridge for that lunch. He stood by the window, his face sculptured, hidalgo-like, his fingers nervous, as he spun the stem of a glass.

By his side, Walter Luke looked seamed, confident, grizzled, low-slung, more prosaic. Yet the scientists said that he had been unlucky: he had a scientific imagination as powerful as Francis's, or more so: in a peaceful world, he might have done work of genius. As it was, he had been busy on what he called "hardware" since 1939: he was still not forty-four, but he had been head of the Atomic Energy establishment for years. He was not as vexed as Francis, but was swearing like the dockyard hand his father used to be.

When Roger arrived, he was friendly, businesslike, but did not exert his personal arts on either of them. As we ate, he was asking them questions about Brodzinski's project—as though refreshing his memory, or making certain they had not changed their minds, for in fact he had heard their opinions times before and knew them off by heart.

"I go on saying," said Walter Luke, "I believe technically it might be on. At least, there's a fifty-fifty chance it might be on. Brod's no fool, he's got a touch of the real stuff. And if we had these bloody things, we could call ourselves independent in nuclear weapons, which we're not now except for guff, and which we're probably never going to be. The whole point is, we keep coming back to it—what price are you willing to pay for that?"

"What price are you?"

"Not this."

Luke bristled with energy. From his manner, no one would have guessed that he hadn't enjoyed coming down on this side. He had a simple, integral patriotism. He had shared the scientists' moral concern, but if his country could have kept the highest military power, he would have made any sacrifice. His tough mind, though, told him it was impossible, and he put the regret behind him. "We just can't play in this league. If we spent everything we've got, that is, everything we now spend on defence, and I mean *everything*, we might bring this off—and what the bloody hell have we bought at the end of it? The priceless thought that we could take out Moscow and New York simultaneously. The only thing that scares me is that too many people never grow up."

Roger turned to Francis Getliffe.

"You know what I think, Parliamentary Secretary," said Francis with stiff courtesy. "This business of Brodzinski's is a nonsense. And so are the views of more important people."

Francis, who did not often go in for public controversy, had not long before screwed himself up to write a pamphlet. In it he had said that there was no military rationale behind the nuclear policy. This analysis had got him into trouble, mostly in America, but also in England. In some Right-thinking circles, it had seemed not only preposterous, but also heretical, and something like wicked.

As we drove through the autumnal streets to the Imperial College, I was still not sure why Roger was playing it this way. What was he aiming at? Was he reckoning that Brodzinski, that lover of English flummery, would be softened by the attentions, the paraphernalia?

If so, sitting in Brodzinski's room, gazing out at the lonely-looking Colcutt tower, the pale green dome making the aesthetic protest in the solitude of sky, I thought that Roger had reckoned wrong. It was true that Brodzinski loved English flummery, with a passion that made Roger's more conservative friends look like austere revolutionaries. He had been a refugee from Poland in the late 'thirties. During the war he had made a name, working in one of the Admiralty scientific departments. Afterwards he had spent some years at Barford, had quarrelled with Luke and others, and recently taken a professorship. It was true that he had immersed himself, with fanatical devotion, in what he thought of as English life. He knew all the English snobberies, and loved them so much that they seemed to him morally right. He had dedicated himself to the politics of the English ultra-right. He addressed Francis Getliffe and Walter Luke, with extreme relish, as Sir Francis, and Sir Walter. Despite all that, or perhaps because of it, he was unyielding about his idea, and instead of listening to Quaife's persuasions, he was determined to make Quaife listen to him.

He was a tallish man, very thick in the chest and thighs, and his muscles filled his clothes. His voice boomed against the walls of his office. He had beautiful pure transparent eyes, in a flat Slavic face; his fair hair, now mingled with grey, was the colour of dust. He was always on the look-out for enemies, and yet he was vulnerable to help, appealing for it, certain that anyone, not already an enemy, given intelligence and willingness, would be convinced that he was right.

He explained the project over again. "I must inform you, Parliamentary Secretary," (he was as familiar with English official etiquette as any of us) "that there is nothing techni-cally novel here! There is nothing that we do not know. Sir Walter will tell you that I am not overstating my case."

"With reservations," said Luke.

"With what reservations?" Brodzinski burst out, brilliant with suspicion. "What reservations, Sir Walter? Tell me that, now?"

"Come off it, Brod," Luke was beginning, ready to settle down to a good harsh scientific argument. But Roger would not let it start. He was treating Brodzinski with a mixture of deference and flattery—or perhaps not pure flattery, but an extreme empathy. Just as Brodzinski felt a brilliance of sus-picion when Walter Luke spoke, so with Roger he felt a brilliance of reassurance. Here was someone who knew what he had to fight against, who knew his urgencies.

"But, Parliamentary Secretary, when do we get something

done?" he cried. "Even if we start now, *tonight,* it will take us to 1962 or '63 before we have the weapons—"

"And they won't have any strategic meaning," said Francis Getliffe, irritated at the way the conversation was going.

"Sir Francis, Sir Francis, I believe there is meaning in having weapons in your hands, if the country is going to survive. I suppose you mean, I hope you mean, that America will have their own armaments, much greater than ours, and I hope they will. The more the better, and good luck to them. But I shall not sleep happy until we can stand beside them—"

"I mean something more serious—" Francis interrupted. But once more Roger stopped the argument.

Brodzinski burst out:

"Parliamentary Secretary, when can we get some action?"

After a pause, Roger replied, carefully, considerately:

"You know, I mustn't raise false hopes—"

Brodzinski raised his head. "I know what you're going to say. And I agree with it. You are going to say that this will cost a thousand million pounds. Some say we cannot afford to do it. *I* say, we cannot afford not to do it."

Roger smiled at him. "Yes, I was going to raise that point. But also I was going to say that there are many people to convince. I am only a junior Minister, Professor. Let me say something to you in confidence that I really oughtn't to. Within these four walls, I think it will be necessary to convince my own Minister. Without him behind it, no government could even begin to listen—"

Brodzinski was nodding. He did not need explanations about the English political machine. He was nodding, passionately thoughtful. As for Luke and Getliffe, they were looking stupefied. They knew, or thought they knew, what Roger wanted as a policy. They had just heard him, not exactly state the opposite, but leave Brodzinski thinking that he had.

Soon Roger was saying goodbye, inviting Brodzinski to
visit him in Whitehall, repeating that they would keep in
touch. Brodzinski clung to his hand, looking at him with
beautiful candid eyes, the colour of sea-water. Brodzinski's
goodbyes to Walter and Francis were cold, and when they
were back in the car they themselves spoke coldly to Roger.
They were, in their different fashions, straightforward and
honourable men, and they were shocked.

Roger, apparently at ease, invited them to tea before the
car had moved a hundred yards. Utterly aware of the chill,
utterly ignoring it as he spoke, he said that, when he was a
young man, he used to go to a café not far away: was it still
there? Stiffly, Francis said that he ought to get back to Cambridge. No, said Roger, come and have tea. Again they refused. "I want to talk to you," said Roger—not with official
authority, but his own. In a sullen silence, we sat at a table
in the café window, the December mists thick in the street
outside. It was one of those anonymous places, neither a
rackety one for the young nor a tea-room for the elderly:
the atmosphere was something between that of a respectable
pull-up for carmen and a coffee-room for white-collar
workers.

Roger said: "You disapproved of what I've just done."

"I'm afraid I did," Francis replied.

"I think you're wrong," said Roger.

Francis said curtly that he had given Brodzinski too much
encouragement. Walter Luke, more violent, asked if he didn't
realise that the man was a mad Pole, whose only uncertainty
was whether he hated Russians as Russians more than Russians as Communists, and who would cheerfully die himself
along with the entire population of the United States and
Great Britain, so long as there wasn't a Russian left alive.
If that was the sort of lunacy we were going to get mixed
up in, he, Luke, for one, hadn't bargained on it.

Roger said that he knew all that. But Walter was wrong

on just one point. Brodzinski was not mad. He had a touch of paranoia. But a touch of paranoia was a very useful part of one's equipment. On far more people than not, it had a hypnotic effect.

"I wish I had it," Roger added, with a grim smile. "If I had, I shouldn't have to spend time telling you I am not deserting. No, your colleague Brodzinski is a man of power. Don't deceive yourselves about that. My bet is that his power is likely to influence quite a number of people before we're through. He's going to require very careful handling. You see, he's got one great advantage. What he wants, what he's saying, is very simple and it's what a lot of people want to hear. What *you* want—and what I want quite as much as you do, if I may say so—is very difficult and not in the least what a lot of people want to hear. That's why we're going to need all the luck in the world if we're going to get away with it. If you think it's going to be easy and painless, then my advice to you is to cut all your connections with Government as fast as you possibly can. It's going to be hell, and we may easily lose. As for me, I'm committed. But I'm taking bigger risks than any of you, and you've got to let me do it in my own way."

Yes, I thought then, and in cooler blood afterwards, he was taking risks. Just as he had done, talking to me at the Carlton Club. He was taking risks in speaking in that tone to Getliffe and Luke. And yet, he knew they were both, in spite of Luke's raucous tongue, men trained to discretion. He also knew, what was more significant, that they were "committed" in the sense he had used the word. For years before Hiroshima, they had foreseen the technological dangers. They could be relied upon as allies.

Luke was still grumbling. Why had Roger taken them there? What did he think he had achieved?

Roger explained that he wanted to shower Brodzinski with

attentions: he wouldn't be satisfied, but it might for the time being keep him quiet.

That reply satisfied Walter Luke. It would not have satisfied me.

It was part of Roger's technique to seem more spontaneous than he was. Or rather, it was part of his nature which he had developed into a technique. His spontaneity was genuine, it gave him some of his bite: but he could govern it. He had not given Luke and Getliffe the slightest indication of what, I was now certain, was his strongest reason for buttering up Brodzinski.

The reason was simple. Roger was set on easing Lord Gilbey out and getting the job himself. He wanted Brodzinski to do the opposite of keeping quiet, to shout his discontent. I had seen too many examples of this process not to recognize it now.

Roger was less hypocritical than most men. He would have made the same moves without excuse. Yet, I was coming to believe that, as he had just said, he was committed. Old Thomas Bevill used to lecture me, in his Polonius-like fashion, on the forces driving the great politicians he had known. He rolled out his Victorian phrases: one force, Bevill used to say, was a consciousness of powers. Another, and a rarer one, was a consciousness of purpose. For men seeking excuses for themselves, that was the best of all.

Neither Getliffe nor Luke realised what Roger was up to. Yet, if they had, they would not have minded much. It seemed strange, but they would have minded less than I did. For I had an affection for Lord Gilbey. Sometimes my affections ran away with me. They had done so years before, I now believed, in a struggle on a pettier scale when I had been voting for a Master of my college. They had made me forget function, or justice, or even the end to be served. Now I was getting older, I could realise those mistakes in the past, mistakes which a man like Francis, high-principled as he was, would never have made. For him, this issue would be simple. Lord Gilbey never ought to have been in this job in the first place: the sooner he was removed the better. Roger had to be rough. Gilbey would cling like a mollusk, in distinguished incompetence. If Roger was not prepared to be rough, then he was no good to us.

Getliffe and Luke would be right. Yet they might not know that Roger was a more deeply forested character than they were. I believed in his purpose, but it would have comforted me to know why he had it. Perhaps, I thought once or twice that autumn, it would have comforted him too.

CHAPTER VI

A WEEKEND IN
THE COUNTRY

During the winter, the gossip began to swirl out from the clubs and the Whitehall corridors that Lord Gilbey was "getting past it." At the same time, Roger's name crept into the political columns in the Sunday papers, as the first junior Minister in the new government to be talked about for promotion. It looked as though he were handling the press, or rather the political link-men who added to their incomes through leaking secret information to the press, with skill and nerve. About whether these link-men really existed, administrators like Hector Rose went on speculating, as though they were some species still in doubt, like the yeti, or the plesiosaur in Loch Ness. Rose, with his rigid propriety, could not easily believe in them. My guess was that Roger not only believed in them, but knew them. If so, he got himself liked, but never let out that he had a policy already formed, much less what it was. In fact, the political commentators, while agreeing that he was coming to the front, gave diametrically different reasons why he should do so.

Early in February, Roger told me that he was spending the weekend at Basset, Diana Skidmore's house in Hampshire. It was not a coincidence that Margaret and I had just received the same invitation. Diana had an intelligence network of her own, and this meant that the connection between

Roger and me was already spotted. So far as Roger went, it meant more. Diana was a good judge of how people's stock was standing, whatever their profession was: upon stock prices within the government, her judgment was something like infallible. Since Diana had a marked preference for those on the rise, the frequency of a man's invitations to Basset bore a high correlation to his political progress.

People said that about her, and it was true. But, hearing it before one met her, one felt one had been misled. Driving down the Southampton road, the wiper skirling on the windscreen, the wind battering behind us, Margaret and I were saying that we should be glad to see her. The road was dark, the rain was pelting, we lost our way.

"I like her really," said Margaret, "she's so relaxing."

I questioned this.

"One hasn't got to compete, because one can't. *You* wouldn't know. But I should never buy a special frock to go to Basset in."

I said it would be nice to get there, in any garments whatsoever. When at last we saw the lights of the Basset lodge, we felt as travellers might have done in a lonelier and less domesticated age, getting a glimpse of light over the empty fields.

It was a feeling that seemed a little fatuous once we had driven up from the lodge through the dark and tossing parkland and stood in the great hall of Basset itself. The façade of the house was 18th Century, but this enormous hall was as warm as a New York apartment, smelling of flowers, flowers spread out in banks, flowers dominating the great warm space as though this were a wedding-breakfast. It was a welcome, not only of luxury, but of extreme comfort.

We went across the hall, over to the guest-list. The order of precedence had an eloquence of its own. Mr. Reginald Collingwood got the star suite: Collingwood was a senior Cabinet Minister. The Viscount and Viscountess Bridgewater got the next best. That designation marked the transformation of an old acquaintance of mine, Horace Timberlake, not a great territorial magnate but an industrial boss, who had since become one of the worthies of the Tory Party. We came third, presumably because we had been there a good many times. Then Mr. Roger Quaife and Lady Caroline Quaife. Then Mr. Montagu Cave. He had become a junior Minister at the same time as Roger. We noticed that, as had happened before, he was alone, without his wife. There were rumours that she was enjoying herself with other men. Then Mrs. Henneker. I made a displeased noise and Margaret grinned. Finally Mr. Robinson, by himself and unexplained.

Diana's brisk, commanding voice rang out from a passageway. She came into the hall, kissed us, led us into one of her sitting-rooms, brilliant, hung with Sisleys and Pissarros. She remembered what we drank, gave orders to the butler without asking us, said, "Is that right?"—knowing that it was right—and looked at us with bold, sharp, appraising eyes.

She was a woman in her early fifties, but she had worn well. She was slender, but wiry, not delicate. She had never been beautiful, so I had heard, perhaps not even pretty, and it was possible that her looks, which in middle-age suggested that she had once been lovely, were now at their best. She had a dashing, faintly monkey-like attractiveness, the air of a woman who had always known that she was attractive to men. As she herself was fond of saying, "Once a beauty, always a beauty," by which she didn't mean that the flesh was permanent, but that the confidence which underlay it was. Her great charm, in fact, was the charm of confidence. She was not conceited, though she liked showing off. She knew, she was too worldly not to know, that some men were frightened away. But for many she had an appeal, and she had not doubted it since she was a child.

She was wearing a sunblaze of diamonds on her left shoulder. I looked a little apologetically at my wife, who had put on my latest present, a peridot brooch. Margaret's taste did not run to ostentation, but face to face with Diana, she would not have minded a little more.

The curious thing was that the two of them came from the same sort of family. Diana's father was a barrister, and her relatives, like Margaret's, were academics, doctors, the upper stratum of professional people. Some of them even penetrated into the high Bloomsbury into which Margaret had been born. Nevertheless, despite her family, Diana had taken it for granted, from her childhood, that she belonged to the smartest of smart worlds. Taking it for granted, she duly got there, with remarkable speed. Before she was twenty-one, she had married Chauncey Skidmore, and one of the bigger American fortunes. Seeing her in middle-age, one couldn't help thinking that it was she, not the Skidmores, not her friends in the international circuit, who had been made for just that world.

It seemed like the triumph of an adventuress: but it didn't seem so to her, and it didn't seem so when one was close to her. She was self-willed and strong-willed; she was unusually shrewd: but she had the brilliance and, yes, the sweetness, of one who had enjoyed everything that happened to her. When she married Chauncey Skidmore, she loved him utterly. She had been widowed for over a year, and she still mourned him.

At dinner that night, there were—although the Quaifes were not arriving till the next day—eighteen at table. Diana had a habit of commanding extra guests from people to whom she let houses on the estate, or from masters at Winchester close by. I looked up at the ceiling, painted by some 18th Century Venetian now forgotten. The chatter had gone up several decibels, so that one could hear only in lulls the rain slashing against the windows at one's back. Confidentially, the butler filled my glass; the four footmen were going round soft-footed. For an instant it seemed to me bizarre that all this was still going on. It was, however, fair to say that it did not seem bizarre to others present. A spirited conversation was proceeding about what, when Diana's son inherited the house, would need doing to the structure: or whether she ought to start on it, bit by bit. In her ringing voice, Diana turned to Collingwood on her right: "Reggie, what do you think I ought to do?" Collingwood did not usually utter unless spoken to. He replied: "I should leave it for him to worry about."

That seemed to show the elements of realism. It occurred to me that, a quarter of a century before, I had sat in rich houses, listening to my friends, the heirs, assuming that before we were middle-aged, such houses would exist no more. Well, that hadn't happened. Now Diana's friends were talking as though it never would happen. Perhaps they had some excuse.

I was watching Collingwood. I had met him before, but only in a group. He struck me as the most puzzling of political figures—puzzling, because politics seemed the last career for him to choose.

He was a handsome man, lucky both in his bone-structure and his colouring. His skin tone was fresh and glowing, and he had eyes like blue quartz, as full of colour, as opaque. For his chosen career, however, he had what one might have thought a handicap; for he found speech, either in public or private, abnormally difficult. As a public speaker he was not only diffident and dull, but gave the impression that, just because he disliked doing it so much, he was going to persevere. In private he was not in the least diffident, but still the words would not come. He could not, or did not care to, make any kind of conversation. It seemed a singular piece of negative equipment for a politician.

And yet, he had deliberately made the choice. He was a well-to-do country gentleman who had gone into merchant banking and made a success of it. But he had broken off that career; it was politics that he could not resist; if it meant making speeches, well then, it meant making speeches.

He carried weight inside the Cabinet, and even more inside his party, far more than colleagues of his who seemed to have ten times his natural gifts. That was why, that night at dinner, I was anxious when I heard, or thought I heard, a reply of his to Diana, which sounded like dubiety about the Quaifes. I could not be sure; at such a table, listening to one's partner, who in my case turned out, with an absence of surprise on my part, to be Mrs. Henneker, one needed a kind of directional hearing-sense to pick up the gossip flowing by. If Roger had Collingwood against him, it was serious for us all—but I was captured again by Mrs. Henneker, who was thinking of writing a life of her dead husband, who had been a Rear Admiral, monstrously treated, so she explained to me, by the Board of Admiralty.

Across the table, Cave, who was a gourmet, was eating without pleasure; but, since for him quantity could be made to turn into quality, he was also eating like a glutton, or a hungry child.

Once more, maddeningly, a whiff of disapproval from the top of the table. A person whose name I could not catch was in trouble. I caught a remark from Lord Bridgewater, plethoric, pineapple-headed: "He's letting us down, you know what I mean." To which Collingwood replied, "It won't do." And a little later, mixed with a clarification about the Rear Admiral, I heard Collingwood again: "He's got to be stopped." I had no idea who the man was. I had no idea, either, what kind of trouble he was in—except that I should have been prepared to bet that it wasn't sexual. If it had been, Diana would have been flashing signals of amusement, and the others would not have been so condemnatory and grave. Whatever they said in public, in private they were as sexually tolerant as people could be. They could not forgive public scandals, and sometimes they made special rules. In private, though, and within their own circle, or any circle which touched theirs, no one cared what anyone "did." Divorces—there had been several round this table, including

Margaret's. A nephew of Diana's had been run in while picking up a guardsman in the Park: "That chap had hard
luck," I had heard them say.

Nevertheless, there was constraint in the air. Margaret and
I, when we were alone, told each other that we were puzzled.

Next morning, in mackintosh and Wellingtons, I went for
a walk in the rain with Monty Cave. Until we turned back
to the house, he was preoccupied—preoccupied, so it seemed,
with sadness. I wished I knew him well enough to ask. Suddenly he burst out in darts of flashing, malicious high
spirits: wasn't Diana showing strange signs of a taste in
modern music? wasn't Mr. Robinson a connoisseur?
wasn't she capable of assimilating any man's tastes? And
then: why did people have absurd pet-names? Sammikins—
Bobbity—how would I like to be Lewikins? "Or perhaps,"
said Cave, with a fat man's sparkle, "that's what your friends
do call you."

He wasn't restful; his mood changed too fast for that,
until we talked politics. Then he was lucid, imaginative, un-
expectedly humane. For the first time, I could understand
how he was making his reputation.

Back in the house, I felt the constraint tightened again, as
soon as the Quaifes arrived. I caught Margaret's eye: in the
midst of the party we couldn't talk. Yet soon I realised that,
whatever the reason, it was not that which had worried me
most: for just before lunch, I found Caro and Diana drinking
whiskey, and agreeing that Gilbey must be got rid of.

"You're in on this, Lewis!" cried Diana. "Old Bushy"
(Gilbey) "has never been the slightest bit of good to us, has
he?"

I sat down. "I don't think this is his line," I said.

"Don't be pie-faced," said Diana. "He's a nice, smart
cavalry officer, and he'd have married an actress if they'd
let him, but that's his ceiling and you know it."

"He'd never have married an actress, he's the biggest snob of the lot of them," said Caro.

"Do you think the priests would have got to work?" said Diana. Gilbey's family was Catholic, and to these two he seemed to have lived in the backwoods. There was much hooting hilarity, which did not disguise the truth, that Diana and Caro understood each other and meant business.

"The point is," said Diana, "he's no good. And we can't afford him."

She glanced at Caro with appraising eyes, at a pretty woman twenty years younger than herself, at a pretty woman as tough as herself, at an ally.

"I can tell you this," Diana added sharply, "Reggie Collingwood is certain that we can't afford him."

It ought to have been good news. After an instant, Caro frowned.

"I'm afraid I've got no special use for Reggie," she said.

"Listen," said Diana, "you have got to be careful. And Roger, of course. But *you* have got to be very careful."

If I had not been there, she would have said more. A few minutes later we went in to lunch.

As for me, until after dinner on the Sunday night, I remained half-mystified. The hours seeped away, punctuated by meals; I might have been on an ocean crossing, wondering why I hadn't taken an aircraft. The rain beat down, the windows streamed, the horizon was a couple of fields away; it was, in fact, singularly like being on a ship in gloomy, but not rough, weather.

I did not get a word with Roger alone. Even with Margaret, I managed to speak only in our rooms. She was having more than her share of the philosophy of Lord Bridgewater, while in the great drawing-room of Basset, in various subsidiary drawing-rooms, in the library, I found myself occupied with Mrs. Henneker.

She was nothing like so brassy as I had previously known

her. When she discovered me alone in the library on Saturday afternoon, she still looked dense, but her confidence had oozed away. The curious thing was, she was outfaced. Through the misted window, we watched Diana and Caro stepping it out along the drive in mackintoshes and hoods, taking their exercise in the drenching rain.

"The rich think they can buy *anything*," said Mrs. Henneker heavily. The *mana* of Diana's wealth was too much for her, just as it might have been for my relatives or my old friends or others really poor. There was a certain irony, I thought. Mrs. Henneker herself must have been worth a hundred thousand pounds or so.

Mrs. Henneker did not listen to any repartee of mine. But she had a use for me. Perhaps under the provocation of the Basset opulence, her purpose had crystallised. She was going to write that biography of her husband, and I could be of minor assistance.

"Of course," she said, "I've never done any writing, I've never had the time. But my friends always tell me that I write the most amusing letters. Of course, I should want a bit of help with the technique. I think the best thing would be for me to send you the first chapters when I've finished them. Then we can really get down to work."

She had obsessive energy, and she was methodical. On the Sunday morning, while most of the house-party, Roger among them, went to church, cars squelching on the muddy gravel, she brought me a synopsis of her husband's life. After the drawn-out luncheon, Diana's neighbours staying until after tea, Mrs. Henneker got hold of me again, and told me with triumph that she had already written the first two paragraphs, which she would like me to read.

When at last I got up to my dressing-room, light was streaming in from our bedroom and Margaret called out. I'd better hurry, she said. I replied that I had been with Mrs. Henneker: she found my experience funnier than I did. As

I pulled off my coat, she called out again: "Caro's brother seems to have stirred up the dovecotes."

She had been hearing about it after tea. At last I understood one of Cave's obliquities the morning before. For Caro's brother was called, not only by his family but by acquaintances, "Sammikins." He was also Lord Houghton, a Tory M.P., young and heterodox. Recently, Margaret and I recalled, he had published a short book on Anglo-Indian relations. Neither of us had read it, but the newspapers had splashed it about. From the reviews, it seemed to be anti-Churchill, pro-Nehru, and passionately pro-Gandhi. It sounded a curious book for a Tory M.P. to write. That was part of his offence. "He's not exactly their favourite character, should you say?" said Margaret. She was frowning at herself, and her dress, in the glass. She was not quite so uncompetitive, these days, as she would have had me think.

I could guess what Diana had said to Caro. At dinner the topic was not mentioned, and I began to hope that we were, for the time being, safely through. The conversation had the half-intimacy, the fatigue, the diminuendo, of the close of a long weekend. Since there was no host, the men did not stay long round the dining-table, and in the drawing-room afterwards, we sat round in a semi-circle, Diana, impresario-like, placing herself between Collingwood and Roger, encouraging them to talk across her.

Suddenly Lord Bridgewater, open-faced, open-eyed, cleared his throat. We knew what was coming. He hadn't been born in this society, but he had taken its colour. At home he was an amiable man, but he had a liking for unpleasant jobs. He spoke across the width of the room to Caro. "I hope we shan't hear any more of Sammikins, you know what I mean." For once, almost for the first time, I saw Caro put out. She flushed. She had to control herself: she hated doing so. It was in her nature not only not to give a damn, but to say that she didn't. After a pause, she replied, a little feebly: "Horace,

I'm sorry, but I'm not my brother's keeper." Sammikins was a couple of years younger than she was, and, listening, I was sure that she loved him.

"Some people," said Collingwood, "would say that he could do with one."

"They'd better say that to him," said Caro, "that's all."

"He's not doing any good to the Party," said Lord Bridgewater, "he's not doing any good at all."

Collingwood looked at Caro. His eyes brightened in women's company, but his manner did not change and he said straight at her:

"It's got to be stopped."

"What do you mean?"

"I mean, that if Sammikins won't stop it himself, we shall have to stop him."

In Collingwood's difficult, senatorial tone, the nickname sounded more than ever ridiculous. Caro was still just keeping her temper.

"I don't think," she replied, "that any of you have the slightest idea what he's like."

"That doesn't enter," said Collingwood. "I mean, that if he writes anything like this again, or makes any more speeches on the same lines, we can't have anything more to do with him."

On the other side of Diana, I saw Roger's frowning face. He was gazing at his wife. She, dark with shame, was shaking her head as though telling him to keep quiet. Up to now, she knew—better than anyone there—that he had not made a false move, or one not calculated, since he entered the Government. This wasn't the time to let go.

Caro gave Collingwood a social smile.

"You mean," she said, "you're ready to take the whip away?"*

"Certainly."

---

* I.e., cease to regard him as a member of the Parliamentary Party.

"That wouldn't matter much, for him."

I believed that, for an instant, she was talking professional politics in the sense Collingwood would understand. Her brother, as heir to his father's title, could not reckon on a serious political career.

"That's not all," said Collingwood. "No one likes—being right out of things."

There was a pause. Caro thought successively of things to say, discarded them all.

"I utterly disagree with nearly everything you've said." It was Roger's voice, not quietened, addressed to the room as well as to Collingwood. He must have been enraged by the choice he had to make: now he had made it, he sounded spontaneous and free.

Like Caro, I had been afraid of this. Now that it had happened, I felt excited, upset, and at the same time relieved.

"I don't know how you can." Collingwood looked lofty and cold.

"I assure you that I do. I have the advantage, of course, of knowing the man very well. I don't think many of you have that advantage, have you?" Roger asked the question with a flick, his glance moving towards his wife. "I can tell you, if a few of us had his spirit and his idealism, then we should be doing a lot better than we are."

Caro had flushed right up to her hair-line. She was anxious for Roger, she knew he was being unwise: but she was proud of him, proud because he had put her first. She had not known what to expect, had tried to persuade herself that she hoped for his silence. But he had not been silent: and she was filled with joy. I saw Margaret flash her an exhilarated glance, then flash me a worried one.

"Aren't you forgetting judgment, Quaife?" asked Lord Bridgewater.

Roger swept on. "No, I'm not forgetting judgment. But we're too inclined to talk about judgment when we mean the ability to agree with everyone. That's death. Let's have a look at what this man has really done. He's stated a case— pretty roughly, that I'll grant you: he hasn't taken the meaning out of everything he said, which is another gift we tend to over-value. In one or two places he's overstated his case. That I accept, and it's a fault you're always going to find in sincere and passionate men. But still, the major points in his book are substantially true. What is more, everyone in this room, and almost everyone competent to express an opinion, knows they are substantially true."

"I can't agree," said Collingwood.

"You know it. You may disagree with the attitudes, but you know the points are true. That's why you're all so angry. These things are true. The sin this man has committed is to say them. It's quite all right for people like us to know these things. But it's quite wrong for anyone to say them —outside our charmed circle. Aren't we all coming to take that for granted more and more? Isn't it becoming much more desirable to observe the etiquette rather than tell the truth? I don't know whether it frightens you, but it certainly frightens me. Politics is too serious a business to be played like a private game at a private party. In the next ten years, it's going to be more serious than anything we've ever im- agined. That's why we need every man who's got the spine enough to say what he really thinks. That's why we need this man you're all so bitter about. That's why—" he finished, in a conversational tone, speaking to Collingwood—"if there is any question of his being pushed out, I shouldn't be able to sit quietly by."

"I'm sure you wouldn't," Collingwood replied, in his own awkward kind of conversational tone. He was quite composed. There was no sign of what effect Roger had made on him, or whether he had made any effect at all. "I'm sure you wouldn't."

CHAPTER VII

ANOTHER HOME

The next night, Monday, Margaret and I were due to dine at the Osbaldistons'. As our taxi drew up, we could not help reflecting that it was something of a change from Basset; for the Osbaldistons lived in a house, detached, but only just detached, on the west side of Clapham Common. It might have been one of the houses I had visited as a boy, feeling that I was going up in the world, in the provincial town where I was born, the houses of minor professional men, schoolmasters, accountants, solicitors' clerks.

We went up the path between two rows of privets; the front door had a panel of coloured glass, leaded, in an acanthus design, and the passage light shone pinkly through.

Inside the house, I was thinking that there was no need for Douglas Osbaldiston to live like that. The decoration and furnishing had not been changed from the fashion of the early 'twenties: beige wallpaper with a satin stripe and a discreet floral dado: some indifferent romantic landscapes, water-colours, in wooden frames, gate-legged tables, a sideboard of fumed oak with green handles. At the top of the Civil Service, he could have done much better for himself. But, just as some men of Douglas's origins or mine set themselves up as country gentlemen, Douglas did the reverse. It was done out of deliberate unpretentiousness, but, as with the bogus country gentlemen, it was becoming a little of an act. When, over dinner, we told him that we had been at Basset for the weekend, he whistled cheerfully, in excellent imitation of a clerk reading the gossip columns and dreaming of social altitudes inaccessible to him. Yet Douglas knew— for he was the most clear-headed of operators—that just as he suspected that places like Basset still had too much effect on government decisions, so Diana Skidmore and her friends had an identical, and perhaps a stronger, suspicion about his colleagues and himself. Neither side was sure where the real power rested. In the great rich house, among the Christian names of the eminent, there were glances backwards, from the knowledgeable, in the direction of suburban villas such as this.

In the tiny dining-room, we were having an excellent dinner, cooked by Mary Osbaldiston: clear soup, a steak and kidney pie, lemon soufflé. It was much better than anything to be found at Basset. When I praised the meal, she flushed with gratification. She was a fine-featured woman, intelligent and undecorated as Douglas himself; she had no style and much sweetness. Margaret and I were fond of her, Margaret especially so, both of us knowing that they had a deprivation we had been spared. They had longed for children, and had had none.

Douglas had the pertinacity and precision of a boss administrator; he wanted to know exactly why and how I had come to know Diana Skidmore. He was not in the least envious of my extra-official life; he was not asking entirely through inquisitiveness, through needing another piece of information about how the world ticks.

He listened, with the direct concentration of a detective. Anything about business, anything that might affect Ministers, was a concern of his. In particular, when I told him about Roger's outburst, he regarded that as very much a concern of his.

"I must say," said Douglas, "I thought he was a cooler customer."

His face had ceased to look like a scholar's.

"Why in God's name did he choose this time of all times to blow his top? Lord love me, we don't have much luck in our masters—"

I was saying that I thought we had been lucky in Roger, but Douglas went on:

"I suppose he did it out of chivalry. Chivalry can be an expensive luxury. Not only for him, but for the rest of us."

His wife said that we didn't know the relations of Caro Quaife and her brother. Perhaps that was the secret.

"No," said Douglas. "I don't see how that could be much excuse. It was an irresponsible thing to do. I can't imagine indulging in that sort of chivalry if anything hung on it—" He grinned at his wife. It sounded bleak, but it was said with trust. Douglas knew precisely what he wanted; he was tough and, in his fashion, ruthless; he was going to the top of his own tree, and his dégagé air wasn't enough disguise; but his affections were strong, and he was a passionate man, not a cold one.

"Mind you, Lewis," said Douglas, "if this man Quaife gets away with this performance, he's in a very strong position. The best way to arrive is to arrive with no one to thank for it. He must know that as well as we do."

Douglas had his full share of a man of action's optimism. The optimism which makes a gulf between men of action and purely reflective men, which makes a man insensitive to defeat until it has really happened. He was telling us that he himself had some news on the brighter side: he would cheer us up with it, after we had all moved together into the "front room."

As soon as I heard that phrase, I was amused. To talk about the "front room," as his mother or mine might have done, was going a bit too far in the direction of modesty, even for

Douglas. This house, though small, was not as small as that, and the so-called "front room" was in fact a study. On the desk lay a black official brief case. Round the walls, in bookshelves which ran up to the ceiling, was packed one of the most curious collections of 19th and 20th Century novels that I had seen. Douglas allowed himself something between a luxury and an affectation. He liked to read novels in much the state in which they had first been read. So in the shelves one could find most of the classical English, Russian, American and French novels in editions and bindings not more than a few years away from their original publication.

We sat within sight and smell of those volumes, while Douglas told us the hopeful news. He was not exaggerating. The news was as promising as he had said, and more unexpected. It was—that several influences, apparently independently, were lobbying against Gilbey and for Roger. They were influences which "had the ear" of senior Ministers, who would be bound at least to listen. The first was the aircraft industry, or that part of it represented by my old boss, Lord Lufkin, who had extended his empire since the war. The second was a group of vociferous Air Marshals. The third, more heterogeneous, consisted of scientists. Lufkin had been to see the Chancellor: a couple of Air Marshals had lunched with the Prime Minister, the scientists had been talking "at Ministerial level."

"It's one of the slickest campaigns I've ever seen," said Douglas.

"Who sparked it off?"

"You won't believe it, but some of the lines seem to go back to a chap of no consequence at all."

"Who?"

"The man Brodzinski."

Douglas added,

"Of course, if it hadn't been him, it would have been someone else." Like most high-class administrators, Douglas did not believe much in personal flukes. "But I must say, he seems to have a pretty good eye for the people who cut ice in our part of London."

We were each working out the chances. Personality for personality, Gilbey's backers were powerful, and had the social pull: but in the long run, big business, with the military and the scientists, usually won.

"Unless he did himself in irretrievably with your *very* smart friends," said Douglas with an amiable jeer, "I bet Quaife is in the job within twelve months."

He passed the decanter round again. Then he asked: "Tell me, Lewis, if he does get there, have you any idea what he's going to try to do?"

I hesitated. He suspected, or had guessed, that I was in Roger's confidence. In return, I had guessed that he was not. I knew for sure that some of the forces propelling Roger into power were just the forces that, once there, he would have to fight. Douglas had said earlier that the best way to arrive was to arrive with no one to thank for it. Had he now a shrewd idea that Roger might be more cluttered up than that?

Mary Osbaldiston had taken out a piece of needlework, a tray-cloth, or something of the kind: she was working daisies round the edge of it, with finical care. Margaret, who could not sew a stitch, remarked on it, and asked her something about the pattern: but she was not missing a word of the conversation, and her gaze flickered up in my direction.

"Look, there are some peculiar features about the situation," Douglas pressed on. "It isn't only Brodzinski and the wild men who are clamouring for Quaife, you know. There's your old chum, Francis Getliffe and his friends. Now whatever sleight of hand Quaife goes in for, and I fancy he's pretty good at that, he's not going to please both gangs. Tell me, do you know what he's really going to do?"

I nearly came out into the open. I had one clear and conscious reason for not doing so. I knew that Douglas, like nearly all his colleagues, was deeply conservative. He was too clever not to see the arguments for Roger's policy, but he would not like them. Yet that was not the reason which kept me quiet. There was another, so worn into me that I did not notice it was there. I had lived too long in affairs; I had been in too many situations like this, where discretion was probably the right, and certainly the easiest, course. Sometimes in the past I had got into trouble, and that had happened when I followed my impulse and blasted discretion away.

So that night it was second nature to say something noncommittal. Douglas gazed at me, his face for an instant more youthful. Then he smiled, and passed the decanter over.

We made something of a night of it. In the taxi going home, Margaret, holding my hand against her cheek, said:

"You made a mistake, you know." She went on to say that he was a man one could trust completely. She did not say, but she meant, that we all four liked each other, and that it was a mistake to deny affection. I was angry with her. I had a sharp sense of injustice, the sense of injustice which is specially sharp when one knows one is in the wrong.

CHAPTER VIII

KNIGHT ON

A TOMBSTONE

In March, three weeks after the Basset and Clapham combination, there was more news, which none of us could have allowed for. One morning at the office, Douglas Osbaldiston rang me up: Gilbey had been taken ill during the night, and they were not certain that he would live.

The story ran round Whitehall all that morning, and reached the clubs at lunch-time. It was announced in the evening papers. Everyone that I met assumed from the start, just as I did myself, that Gilbey was going to die. A friend of mine was busy adding a hundred words about Gilbey's political achievements to an account of his career; the chief of the obituary department of a morning paper had appealed in distress, saying that he was in "an impossible situation" with his editor, having been "caught short about a man like Gilbey."

As usual, at the prospect of a death, everyone else was a little more alive. There was a tang of excitement in the air. As usual, also, the professional conversations were already beginning: Douglas was invited to have a drink with a Cabinet Minister, Rose spent the afternoon with our own Minister, talking about a scheme for redistributing the work between the two departments. I had seen the same in a smaller world twenty years before, when I was living in a college. How many deaths mattered, really mattered, mattered like an illness of one's own, to any individual man? We pretended they did, out of a kind of biological team-spirit; in some ways, it was a valuable hypocrisy. But the real number was smaller than we dared admit.

As I heard men talking about Gilbey during the next day or two, I could not help remembering what Thomas Bevill, that cunning, simple old man, used to tell me was the first rule of politics: *Always be on the spot. Never go away. Never be too proud to be present.* Perhaps, after all, that was only the second rule, and the first was: *Keep alive.*

Another person seemed to have a similar thought that week. That other person was Lord Gilbey. Four days after the first news, I received a telephone call from his private secretary. The rumours of the illness, came a chanting Etonian voice, were very much exaggerated. It was utter nonsense to suggest that he was dying. All that had happened was a "minor cardiac incident." Lord Gilbey was extremely bored, and would welcome visitors: he very much hoped that I would call upon him at the London Clinic some afternoon the following week.

A similar message, I discovered, had been sent to politicians, senior officers, Douglas Osbaldiston and Hector Rose. Rose commented: "Well, we may have to agree that the noble Lord is not precisely a nonpareil as a departmental Minister, but we can't reasonably refuse him marks for spirit, can we?"

When I visited him at the Clinic, no one could have refused him marks, though it was a spirit we were not used to. He was lying flat, absolutely immobile—the sight recalled another invalid I used to visit—like the effigy of a knight on a tomb, a knight who had not gone on crusade, for his legs were thrust straight out. The bed was so high that, as I sat by its side, my face was on a level with his, and he could have whispered. He did not whisper: he enunciated, quietly,

but in something like his usual modulated and faintly histri-
onic tone.

"This is very civil of you," he said. "When I'm safely out
of here, we must meet somewhere pleasanter. You must let
me give you dinner at the In and Out." I said I should like it.

"I ought to be out of here in about a month. It will be
another two months, though—" he added in a minatory
manner, as though I had been indulging in over-optimism—
"before I'm back in the saddle again." I replied with something banal, that that wouldn't be very long.

"I never thought I was going to die." He did not move at
all: his cheeks were beautifully shaven, his hair was beautifully trimmed. Looking at the ceiling as he asked a question,
he permitted himself one change of expression: his eyes
opened into incredulous circles, as he said: "Do you know,
people have sat in this very room and asked me if *I* was
afraid of death?"

There was the slightest emphasis on the pronoun. He
went on: "I've been close to death too often to be frightened
of it now."

It sounded ham. It was ham. He began talking about his
life. He had lost most of his closest friends, his brother
officers, "on the battlefield," in the first war. Every year he
had been given since, he had counted as a bonus, he said.
He had seen more of the battlefield in the second war than
most men of his own age. Several times he thought his hour
had come. Had he enjoyed war? I asked. Yes, of course he
had enjoyed it. More than anything in life.

I asked him, after all this, what virtues did he really admire?

"That's very simple. There's only one virtue for me, when
it comes down to the last things."

"What is it, then?"

"Physical courage. I can forgive anything in a man who has
it. I can never respect a man without it."

This seemed to me at the time, and even more later, the

oddest conversation I had ever had with a brave man. I had met others who took their courage as a matter of course, and who were consoling to anyone who did not come up to their standard. Not so Lord Gilbey. He was the only soldier I knew who could refer, with poetic enthusiasm, to *the battle-field*.

It occurred to me that all his life Lord Gilbey had been in search of glory. Glory in the old pre-Christian sense, glory such as the Mycenaeans and Norsemen fought for. Put him in with a shipload of Vikings, and he would have endured what they did, and boasted as much. True, he was Catholic-born: he did his religious duties, and that morning, so he had told me, he had been visited by his "*con*-fessor." But it was not salvation that he prayed for, it was glory.

Looking at him prostrate, so handsome, so unlined, I wondered if that was why this attack had knocked him out. It must have been—one didn't need to be a doctor to see it —graver than we had officially been told. Was it the kind of attack that comes to men who have been taught to suppress their own anxieties? No one could be less introspective; but even he must have known that he had made a mess of his political job, which needed, by a curious irony, a variety of courage that he did not begin to possess. He must certainly have known that he was being criticised, conspired against, threatened with being kicked upstairs. He had shown no sign of it. He had sat among the colleagues who thought least of him, and remained charming, vain, armoured. Probably he didn't let himself think what their opinion of him was, or what they intended. Was this the price he paid?

Next afternoon, I went to see Roger in the House. I sat in the civil servants' box, within touching distance of the government benches, while he answered a question. It was a question put down by one of the members whom Lufkin used for these purposes, to embarrass Gilbey. "Was the Minister aware that no decision had yet been announced on—" There followed a list of aircraft projects. Roger would, in any case, have had to answer in the Commons, but with Gilbey ill, he was in acting charge of the department. The questioner pointedly, and, I suspected, under instructions, demonstrated that he was not making difficulties for Roger himself. When Roger gave a dead-pan, stonewalling reply, neither the member nor any of the aircraft spokesmen followed with a subsidiary. There were one or two half-smiles of understanding. After questions, Roger took me along to his room. It struck me that, although I often called on him now, he almost never took me to the tea-room or the bar. I had heard it mentioned that he spent too little time in casual mateyness among crowds of members, that he was either too arrogant, or too shy. It seemed strange, when he was so easy with anyone in private.

The room was cramped, unlike his stately office in the Ministry across Whitehall. Beyond the window, mock gothic, the afternoon sky was sulphurous.

I asked him if he had visited Gilbey yet. Yes, of course, he said, twice.

"What do you think?" I said.

"Don't you think he's probably lucky to be alive?"

I said yes. Then I told him what I had thought in the Clinic the day before, that it might be a psychosomatic illness. Or was I psychologising too much?

"You mean, if I hadn't put on the pressure, and we'd all said he was wonderful, he might still be on his feet? You may very well be right."

"I meant a bit more than that," I said. "Presuming the old man gets better and comes back to the job: then what?"

I did not need to go further. I meant, a man in Gilbey's condition oughtn't to have to live among the infighting. If he did, there was a finite danger that he wouldn't live at all.

Roger had missed nothing. His eyes met mine in recognition. He was smoking a cigarette, and he did not answer for a time.

"No," he said at last, "I'm not going to take any more responsibility than I'm bound to. This isn't very real."

"Isn't it?"

"He's out," said Roger, "whatever I do now. He'll never come back."

"Is that settled?"

"I'm sure it is," he said. He broke off.

"Do you want an answer to the question you're really asking?"

I said, "Leave it."

"I'm prepared to answer," he said. "I should go on regardless."

He had been speaking without smoothness, as though he were dredging up the words. Then he said, in a brisk tone: "But this isn't real. He's out."

He went on, with a sarcastic smile, "I'm sure he's out. I'm not so sure I'm in."

"What are the chances?"

Roger answered, with matter-of-fact precision: "Slightly better than evens. Perhaps 6–4 on."

"Did you do yourself harm," I put in, "at Basset? That last night?"

"I may have done." He went on, with a baffled frown, like a short-sighted child screwing up his eyes: "The trouble was, I couldn't do anything else."

A couple of days later, I arrived at the London Clinic immediately after lunch. Gilbey might not have moved a millimetre in seventy-two hours. Eyes staring at the ceiling, hair shining, face unblemished. He spoke of Roger, who had visited him that morning. Affably, with friendly condescension, Gilbey told me, what I knew myself, that Roger had had a distinguished record in the last war.

"You wouldn't think it to look at him," said Gilbey, harking back to our previous conversation. "But he's *all right.* He's quite *all right.*"

Gilbey proceeded to talk, enjoying himself, about his own campaigns. Within a few minutes, however, he received a reminder of mortality. His secretary busily entered the quiet, the marmoreally-composed sickroom, Gilbey static except for his lips, me unmoving beside him, the trees motionless in the garden outside.

"Sir," said the secretary. He was an elegant young man with a Brigade tie.

"Green?"

"I have a telegram for you, sir."

"Read it, my dear chap, read it."

Since Gilbey's eyes did not alter their upward gaze, he did not know that the telegram was still unopened. We heard the rip of paper.

"Read it, my dear chap."

Green coughed. "It comes from an address in S.W.10—I think that's Fulham, sir." He gave the signatory's name. "Someone called Porson."

"Please read it."

Momentarily, I caught a glance from Green's eyes, pale, strained, hare-like. He read: "All the trumpets will sound for you on the other side."

Just for a second, Gilbey's mouth pursed, then tightened. Very soon, the modulated voice said to the ceiling: "How nice!"

In a voice even more careful, unemphatic, clipped and trim, he added:

"How *very* nice!"

CHAPTER IX

TWO KINDS OF

ALIENATION

As soon as I could, after the telegram had been read, I said goodbye to Gilbey. I indicated to Green that I wanted a word with him outside. Nurses were passing by, the corridor was busy, it was not until we reached the waiting-room that I could let my temper go.

In the panelled room, with its copies of the *Tatler*, the *Field, Punch* on the console table, I said: "Give me that telegram."

As I glanced at it—the words shining out as though innocent of trouble—I said: "You bloody fool!"

"What?" said Green.

"Why in God's name don't you read telegrams before you bring them in? Why hadn't you got the wit to invent something, when you saw what you'd got in front of you?"

I looked at the telegram again. Porson. It might be. In this lunacy, anything was possible. An old acquaintance of mine. For the sake of action, for the sake of doing anything. I rushed out of the room, out of the Clinic, shouted for a taxi, gave the address, just off the Fulham Road.

The taxi chugged through the afternoon traffic, southwest across London. I was so angry that I did not know why I was going there. I had lost touch with my own feelings. Guilt, concern, personal fates, public ends—I hadn't the patience

72

to think of any of them. Nothing except pushing the taxi on.

At last, after the driver had made false shots, trying squares, places, mews, we drove up a street of tall terraced houses, shabby, unpainted. In front of one, I looked at the slips of cardboard by the bells. The other names were handwritten, but against the top floor bell was a soiled visiting card: Mr. R. Porson, Barrister-at-Law.

Empty milk bottles stood on the steps. Inside the door, which was on the latch, letters and newspapers lay in the unlit hall. I climbed upstairs. On the second landing, the door of a bathroom opened, the only one, it seemed, in the house. I went up to the top floor and knocked. A thick, strident voice answered, and I entered. Yes, it was the man I used to know—twenty years older, more than half drunk. He greeted me noisily, but I cut him short by giving him the telegram.

"Did you send this?"

He nodded.

"Why?"

"I wanted to cheer him up."

In the attic flat, which had a skylight and a high window, Porson peered at me. "What's the matter, old boy? You look a bit white. I insist on prescribing for you. What you need is a good stiff drink."

"Why did you send this?"

"The poor chap hasn't got long to go. It's been all over the papers," said Porson. "I've got a great respect for him. We don't breed men like him nowadays. He's a bit different from all these young pansies. So I wanted him to know that some of us were thinking about him. I wasn't prepared to let him go out alone."

Fiercely he cried out: "Well, is there anything the matter with that?"

He lurched back into his chair. He said:

"I don't mind telling you, I don't run to telegrams unless I have to. Four bob. But I thought it was the least I could do."

"What in Heaven's name," I shouted, "do you imagine it was like for him—"

He was too drunk to understand. I was shouting for my own benefit alone. In time I gave it up. There was nothing to do. I accepted his drink.

"Well," he said, examining me with a critical, patronising air, "from all I hear, you haven't done so badly, young man. I've always insisted you'd have done better, though, if you had listened to me more in the old days."

"What about you?" I asked.

"I've got a great many talents. You know that as well as anybody. Somehow they haven't done as much for me as they should. There's still plenty of time to pull something off. Do you realise," he said in a threatening tone, "that I'm only sixty-two?"

He had gone many steps downhill since I last saw him before the war. This tiny room, furnished with a divan bed, a table, one easy chair and one hard one, showed still the almost pernickety, aunt-like tidiness that I remembered, but it must have been the cheapest he could find. Even then, the rent must have come out of his bit of capital. So far as I knew, he had done no work for years. On the mantelpiece he kept a picture of Ann March, his symbol of unrequited love, his *princesse lointaine*. There were also photographs of two young men. In himself he looked broken-down, his face puce, flecked with broken veins. The tic down his left cheek convulsed it more than ever. Yet at some moments he appeared—in his expression, not only in his spirit—much younger than he was, instead of older: as though unhappiness, discontent, frustration, failure, drink, had been a preservative during which time stood still, as it could not for luckier and stabler men. All his old hatreds came boiling out, just as fresh as they had always been—the Jews, the Reds, the Pansies. He was particularly violent about the pansies, much more so than in the past. I couldn't pretend that Lord Gilbey was any of those things, could I? "He's a man after my own heart, I insist on that," he cried belligerently. "Do you understand why I had to send a personal message? Because if you don't now, my boy, you never will."

The outburst died down. He seemed glad to have me there; he took it without surprise, as though I had seen him the day before and had just called in again. In a tone both gentle and defiant he said: "You may not believe it, but I'm very comfortable here."

He went on: "There are a lot of young people round this neighbourhood. I like the young. I don't care what anyone says against them, I like the young. And it's very good for them to have an older man with plenty of experience to come to for advice."

He was impatient for me to meet them. But we had to wait until the pub opened, he said. He was restless, he stumped over to the whiskey bottle several times, he kept looking at his watch. As the afternoon light edged through the high window, he got to his feet and gazed out.

"Anyway," he said loudly, "you can't deny that I've got a nice view."

Porson's acquaintances came to the pub at the corner of his street, where he installed us both at the crack of opening-time. They were mostly young, not many over thirty. Some of them were living on very little; one or two might have some money from home. There were painters there, there were one or two writers and schoolteachers. They were friendly, and gave Porson what he wanted. They made him a bit of a figure. They treated me amiably, as though I were someone of their age, and I liked them. It might have been a sentimentality, the consequence of my abortive anger and this resurrection of the past in Porson, an old acquaintance become not more respectable, but considerably less so. It might have been a sentimentality, but I was speculating whether there was a higher proportion of kind faces there than in the places I nowadays spent my time. It might have been a sentimentality, and probably was. But theirs was a life which, if one has ever lived it or been close to it, never quite relinquishes its last finger-hold upon one. I could think of contemporaries of mine, middle-aged persons with a public face, who dreamed a little more often than one would think likely of escaping back to places such as this.

Some of the people in that pub seemed to live in a present which to them was ideal. They could go on, as though the future would always be like this. It was a slap-happy March evening. They kept standing Porson drinks. I was enjoying myself: and yet, at the same time, I was both softened and shadowed. I knew well enough what anyone of political insight would say, whether they were Marxists, or irregulars like Roger Quaife, or hard anti-communists from the *Partisan Review*. They would agree about the condition, though they fought about the end. They would say that there was no protest in this pub. Not that these people shared Porson's fits of crazed reaction. They had good will, but except for one or two picked causes, they could not feel it mattered. Nearly everyone there would have joined in a demonstration against hanging. Otherwise, they shrugged their shoulders, lived their lives, and behaved as though they were immortal.

Was this their version of the Basset house-party, which also talked as though there would never be a change again?

They would have had no use for Roger Quaife. To them, he would be part of an apparatus with which they had no connection, from which they were alienated, as completely as if it were the governing class of San Domingo. So was he alienated from them. How could he reach them? How could he, or any politician, find a way through?

They were not going to worry about Roger Quaife, or the scientists, or the civil servants, or anybody else who had to take a decision. They did not thank anybody for worrying about them. Yes, there were unhappy people in the pub, now it was filling up. A schoolmaster with an anxiety-ridden face, who lived alone: a girl sitting at the bar, staring with schizoid stillness at a glass of beer. For them, there were friends here prepared to worry. Even for old Porson, drunken, boastful, violent, a little mad.

I should have liked to stay. But somehow, the fact that they were so un-anxious, so island-like, had the reverse effect on me. In the noisy and youthful pub, they were rooting up a half-memory, buried somewhere in my mind. Yes! It was another evening, another part of London, Roger questioning David Rubin, the uninflected replies.

This was not the place for me. I finished my drink, said goodbye to Porson who "insisted" on inviting me there another time. I pushed through the crowd, affable, cordial and happy, and went out into the street, lights from the shops doubled in the moist pavements of the Fulham Road.

CHAPTER X

NEWS IN SOUTH STREET

By the early summer, gossip was bubbling and bursting. Gilbey had left the Clinic and gone home. One political columnist was prophesying that he would soon be back. Elsewhere, rumours appeared that he had already accepted a Government post abroad. As for his successor, names were being mentioned, Roger's usually among them, but not prominently, except in one Sunday paper.

Nearer the point of action, we were mystified. Some of the rumours we knew to be nonsense, but not all. Men like Douglas Osbaldiston and Hector Rose, or even Roger himself, were not sure where they came from. Diana Skidmore and Caro's relatives, people who made an occupation out of being in the know, could pick up nothing, or at least what they did pick up was useless. It was one of those occasions, commoner than one might think, when the "insiders" were reading their newspapers for enlightenment as inquisitively as anyone else.

Of us all, Roger put on the most impassive front. He did his job in the office without any fuss; he answered questions in the House: he made a couple of speeches. In all this, he was behaving like a competent stand-in. As I watched him, through those weeks, I realised that he had one singular natural advantage, besides his self-control. He had the knack of appearing more relaxed, far less formidable, than he really was. One night, after a debate which Douglas and I were attending, a young member took us all to Pratt's. In the tiny parlour, round the kitchen fire, there were several hard, able faces, but Roger's was not among them. He sat there, drinking pints of beer, a heavy, clumsy man, looking amiable, idealistic, clever, simple, rather like an impressive innocent among card-sharpers. Among hard-featured faces, his stood out, full of enjoyment, full of feeling, revealing neither ambition nor strain.

One afternoon in June, I received another summons from Lord Gilbey. This time I was asked to call, so my personal assistant said, at his "private residence." What for? No, the invitation had come, not from Green, but from some humbler person, who was unwilling to say. Had anyone else been asked? My P.A. missed nothing. She had already rung up Hector Rose's office, and Douglas's. Each had been summoned also: Rose was busy at a meeting, Douglas was already on his way.

It was a short distance to Gilbey's, for he had a flat, one of the last in private occupation, in Carlton House Terrace. It was a short distance, but it took some time. Cars were inching, bonnet to tail, along the Mall, cars with crosses on their wind-screens, on their way to a Palace garden party. It must have been a Thursday.

The flat, when I finally got there, was at the top of the building. A smart young woman came to greet me. I enquired, "Mr. Green?"

Mr. Green was no longer working for Lord Gilbey.

Lady Gilbey was out for tea, but Lord Gilbey would like to see me at once. He and Douglas were standing by the drawing-room window, from which one looked, in the gusty, sparkling sunshine, right across St. James's Park, across the glitter of the lake, to the towers and turrets of our offices, away above the solid summer trees. Below, the roofs of cars, hurrying now the Mall was thinning, flashed their sema-phores in the sun. It was a pleasant London vista: but Lord

Gilbey was regarding it without enthusiasm. He welcomed me gracefully, but he did not smile.

He moved to a chair. As he walked, and as he sat down, he seemed to be deliberating how each muscle worked. That must have been the result of his illness, automatic now. Otherwise he had forgotten it, he was preoccupied with chagrin and etiquette.

"Sir Hector Rose isn't able to join us, I hear," he said, with distant courtesy. "I should be grateful if you would give him my regrets. I wanted to speak to some of you people who have been giving me advice. I've already spoken to some of my colleagues." He gazed at us, immaculate, fresh-faced, sad. "I'd rather you heard it from me first," he went on. "I don't suppose you'll believe it, but this morning, just before luncheon, I had a letter from the Prime Minister."

Suddenly he broke out: "He ought to have come himself. He *ought* to have!"

He lifted a hand carefully, as though not exerting himself too jerkily, and pointed out of the window in the direction of Downing Street.

"It's not very far," he said. "It's not *very* far."

Another aspect of etiquette struck him, and he went on:

"I must say it was a very decent letter. Yes. It was a decent letter, I've got to give him that."

Neither of us knew when to begin condoling. It was some while before Gilbey got to the bare facts. At last he said:

"The long and the short of it is, they're getting rid of me."

He turned his gaze, absently, from Douglas to me: "Do you know, I really can't believe it." He was having fugues, as one often does under the impact of bad news, in which the bad news hadn't happened and in which he was still planning his return to the department. Then the truth broke through again.

"They haven't even told me who my successor is going to be. They ought to have asked my advice. They ought to have."

He looked at us: "Who is it going to be?" Douglas said none of us knew.

"If I believed what I saw in the papers," said Gilbey, outrage too much for him, "they're thinking of replacing a man like me—" very slowly he raised his right hand just above the height of his shoulder—"by a man like Grigson." This time his left hand descended carefully, palm outwards, below his knee.

He got on to a more cheerful topic. "They" (after his first complaint he could not bring himself to refer to the Prime Minister in the singular, or by name) had offered him a "step-up" in the peerage. "It's civil of them, I suppose."

It was the only step-up the Gilbeys had had since they were ennobled in the 18th Century, when one of them, a Lancashire squire, had married the daughter of a wealthy slave-trader. "Rascals. Awful rascals," said Lord Gilbey, with the obscure satisfaction that came over him as he meditated on his origins. When anyone else meditated so, he did not feel the same satisfaction. I had heard him comment on a scholarly work which traced the connection of some English aristocratic families with the African slave-trade—"I should have thought," he had said in pain, "that that kind of thing is rather *unnecessary*."

Gilbey was dwelling on the consequences of the step-up. Place in ceremonies, change in the coronet. "I don't suppose I shall see another coronation, but you never know. I'm a great believer in being prepared."

Gilbey was lonely, and we stayed for another half-hour. When at last we left, he said that he proposed to attend the Lords more regularly, not less. "They can do with an eye on them, you know." His tone was simple and embittered.

Out in the open, crossing the path beside the Park, Douglas, black hat pulled down, gave a grin of surreptitious kindness. Then he said: "That's that."

Ministers came, Ministers went. On his side, Douglas

wouldn't have expected his Minister to mourn for him if he were moved to a dim job, or rejoice if he clambered back to the Treasury.

"Now perhaps," he said, "we can get down to serious business."

He did not speculate on who would get Gilbey's job. He might have been holding off, in case I knew more than I actually did. Whereas in fact, the moment I regained my own office, I rang up Roger and was asked to go round at once. He was in his Whitehall room, not across the way. When I got there, I looked at the clock. It was just after half-past four.

"Yes," said Roger, sitting loose and heavy behind his desk, "I know all about it."

"Have you heard anything?"

"Not yet." He added evenly: "Unless I hear tonight, of course, it's all gone wrong."

I did not know whether that was true, or whether he was placating fate by getting ready for the worst.

"I didn't go to the House this afternoon. I thought that was asking a bit much."

He gave a sarcastic grin, but I thought he was playing the same trick.

He would not mention his plans, or the future, or any shape or aspect of politics at all. We talked on, neither of us interested, finding it hard to spin out the time, with the clock ticking. A man from his private office came in with a file. "Tomorrow," said Roger roughly. As a rule he was polite with his subordinates.

Through the open window came the chimes of Big Ben. Half-past five.

"This is getting pretty near the bone," said Roger.

I asked if he wouldn't have a drink. He shook his head without speaking.

At nineteen minutes to six—I could not help but watch the clock—the telephone buzzed. "You answer it," said Roger. For an instant his nerve had frayed.

I heard an excited voice from his own office. The call was from Number 10. Soon I was speaking to the Prime Minister's principal private secretary, and passed the telephone to Roger.

"Yes," said Roger, "I can come along. I'll be with you at six."

He looked at me without expression.

"This looks like it," he remarked. "I don't know, there may be a catch in it yet."

I took a taxi home, with the whole afternoon's story, except for the dénouement, ready to tell Margaret. But she was dressed ready to go out, and laughing at me because my news was stale. Diana Skidmore had been tracking the day's events and had rung Margaret up, asking us round for drinks at her house in South Street.

Park Lane was full of party frocks, morning suits, grey top hats, those who had stuck out the Royal garden party to an end and were now walking to buses and tubes. One or two top hats and frocks turned, a little less humbly, into South Street, and into Diana's house.

It was, by the standards of Basset, small, the rooms high but narrow; yet, because it was more crowded with valuable objects, it gave an even greater sense of opulence, opulence compressed, each of its elements within arm's reach. At Basset, one could walk by a bank of flowers between one precious acquisition and the next: space itself gave some effect of simplicity, of *plein air*. But here in South Street, despite Diana's efforts, the effect was not unlike that of an auctioneer's saleroom or a display of wedding-presents.

When Margaret and I arrived, Diana, with an air of concentrated sincerity, was explaining to a guest what an extremely *small* house it was. She was giving her explanation with a depth of architectural expertness which I didn't know she possessed: which she hadn't possessed until a month or two before. It sounded as though she had passed from the influence of her musician under the influence of an architect, and got delight out of showing it off—just as a young girl, first in love, gets delight out of mentioning the man's name.

It was very foolish, I felt sometimes in the presence of Diana, to imagine that worldly people were cynical. Born worldlings, like herself, were not in the least cynical. They were worldlings just because they weren't, just because they loved the world.

Seeing Margaret and me, Diana slid her guest on to another group, and became her managing self, all nonsense swept away. Yes, she had found out that Roger was with the Prime Minister. He and Caro had been invited to come when they could, and if they felt like it.

"No one in politics here," said Diana briskly. "Is that right?"

She wasn't going to expose them, if the prize had been snatched away at the end.

We mingled among the party, most of them rich and leisured. Probably the majority had not so much as heard of Roger Quaife. Margaret and I were sharing the same thought, as we caught each other's eye: he ought to be here by now. I noticed that Diana, who did not easily get worried, had taken an extra drink.

Then they came, Caro on one side of Roger, and on the other her brother Sammikins, all of them tall, Roger inches taller than the other man, and stones heavier. We had only to look at Caro to know the answer. She was glowing with pleasure, with disrespectful pleasure, that she wanted to cast over us all. They each took a glass of champagne on their way towards us.

"That's all right," Roger said. It sounded unconcerned, in the midst of kisses and handshakes. It sounded ludicrously tight-lipped. A stranger might have thought he looked the same as he had looked a couple of hours before. Yet, beneath a social smile, reserved, almost timid, his eyes were lit up, the lines round his mouth had settled—as though triumph were suffusing him and it was a luxury not to let it out. Beneath the timid smile, he gave an impression both savage and youthful. He was a man, I was thinking, who was not too opaque to suffer his sorrows or relish his victories.

"The old boy hasn't done too badly, has he?" said Caro to Margaret. Sammikins was trumpeting with laughter.

At close quarters he looked like an athlete, light on his feet with animal spirits. He had eyes like Caro's, large, innocent and daring. He had her air, even more highly developed, of not giving a damn. He showed more open delight at Roger's appointment than anyone there. Talking to me, he was enumerating in a resounding voice all the persons whom it would most displease.

Joining our group, Diana was avid for action. "Look," she said to Roger, "I want to give you a real party. We can clear the decks here and lay it on for later tonight. Or have it tomorrow. Which would you like?"

Sammikins would have liked either. So would Caro, but she was looking at Roger.

Slowly he shook his head. He smiled diffidently at Diana, thanked her, and then said: "I don't think it's the right time."

She returned his smile, as though she had a soft spot for him, not just a political hostess's. With a rasp, she asked: "Why isn't it the right time?"

"There have been thousands of Cabinet Ministers before me. Most of them didn't deserve a party."

"Oh, rubbish. You're you. And I want to give a party for *you.*"

He said: "Wait till I've done something."

"Do you mean that?" cried Diana.

"I'd much rather you waited."

She did not press him any further. Somehow she, and the rest of us, partly understood, or thought we did. What he said might have been priggish. It was not that, so much as superstitious. Just as he had been placating fate in his own office, so, in a different fashion, the job in his hands, he was doing now. It was the superstitiousness of a man in spiritual training, who had set himself a task, who could not afford to let himself be softened, who was going to feel he had wasted his life unless he brought it off.

II

"IN THE PALM OF MY HAND"

CHAPTER XI

INTRODUCTION
OF AN OUTSIDER

Once or twice during the next few months, I found myself wondering whether Roger and his associates would qualify for a footnote in history. If so, what would the professionals make of them? I did not envy the historians the job. Of course there would be documents. There would be only too many documents. A good many of them I wrote myself. There were memoranda, minutes of meetings, official files, "appreciations," notes of verbal discussions. None of these was faked.

And yet they gave no idea, in many respects were actually misleading, of what had really been done, and, even more, of what had really been intended. That was true of any documentary record of events that I had seen. I supposed that a few historians might make a strong guess as to what Roger was like. But how was a historian going to reach the motives of people who were just names on the file, Douglas Osbaldiston, Hector Rose, the scientists, the back-bench M.P.s? There would be no evidence left. But those were the men who were taking part in the decisions and we had to be aware of their motives every day of our lives.

There was, however, another insight which we didn't possess, and which might come easily to people looking back on us. In personal terms we knew, at least partially, what we were up to. Did we know in social terms? What kind of social forces were pushing together men as different as Roger, Francis Getliffe, Walter Luke, and the rest of us? What kind of social forces could a politician like Roger draw upon? In our particular society, were there any? Those were questions we might ask, and occasionally did: but it was in the nature of things that we shouldn't have any way of judging the answers, while to a future observer they would stand out, plain as platitudes.

One peaceful summer afternoon, soon after he had taken office, Roger had called some of the scientists into his room. Once, when he was off-guard, I had heard him say at Pratt's that he had only to open his door to find *four knights* wanting something from him. There they all were, but there were more than four, and this time he wanted something from them. He was setting up a committee for his own guidance, he said. He was just asking them for a forecast about nuclear armaments to cover the next ten years. He wanted conclusions as brutal as they could manage to make them. They could work as invisibly as they liked. If they wanted Lewis Eliot as *rapporteur* at any time, they could have him. But above all, they had got to take the gloves off. He was asking them for naked opinions, and he was asking for them by October.

Deliberately—it was part of his touch with men like these —he had let the blarney dissolve away. He had spoken as harshly as any of them. He looked round the table, where the faces stood out, moulded in the diffused sunlight. On his right, Walter Luke, who had just become the chief scientist of Roger's department, tough, cube-headed, prematurely grey. Then Francis Getliffe: then Sir Laurence Astill, smooth-faced, contented with himself: then Eric Pearson, scientific adviser to my own department, youthful and cocky, like a bright American undergraduate: three more, drawn in from universities, like Getliffe and Astill, and so back to me.

Walter Luke grinned. He said: "Well, as H.M.G. pays me my keep, I've got to play, haven't I? There's no need to ask me. It's what these chaps say that counts." He pointed a stiff, strong arm at Astill and the others. As his reputation for scientific judgment grew, his manners had become more off-hand.

"Sir Francis," said Roger, "you'll come in?"

Francis hesitated. He said: "Minister, of course it's an honour to be asked—"

"It's not an honour," said Roger, "it's an intolerable job. But you can bring more to it than most men."

"I should really rather like to be excused—"

"I don't think I can let you. You've had more experience than any of us."

"Minister, believe me, everyone here knows all that I know—"

"I can't accept that," said Roger.

Francis hesitated again; courteously, but with a frown, he said: "There doesn't seem any way out, Minister. I'll try to do what I can."

It sounded like the familiar minuet, as though no one would have been more disappointed than Francis if he had been taken at his word. But that was the opposite of the truth. Other men, wanting flattery or a job, talked about their consciences. Francis was one of the few whom conscience drove. He was a radical through conscience, not through rebellion. He had always had to force himself into personal struggles. He would have liked to think that for him they were all over.

Just over a year before, he had puzzled his friends at our old college. They assumed that he would be a candidate for the Mastership, and they believed that they could get him elected. At the last moment, he had refused to stand. The reason he gave was that he wanted all his time for his research, that he was having the best ideas of his life. I believed that was part of the truth, but not all. His skin was wearing even thinner as he grew older. I fancied that he could not face being talked about, the gossip and the malice.

Incidentally, instead of electing my old friend Arthur

Brown, the college had managed to choose a man called G. S. Clark, and was becoming more factious than anyone could remember.

All Francis wanted for himself was to live in Cambridge, to spend long days in his laboratory, to watch, with worried, disapproving love, how his second and favourite daughter was getting on with an American research student. He wanted no more struggles. That afternoon, as he said yes, he felt nothing but trapped.

Sir Laurence Astill was speaking firmly: "If in your judgment, Minister, you feel that I have a contribution to make, then I shall consider myself obliged to accept."

"That's very good of you," said Roger.

"Though how you expect us to fit in these various kinds of service and look after our departments at the same time—" Sir Laurence had not finished. "Sometime I'd like a word with you, on the position of the senior university scientist in general."

"Any time," said Roger.

Sir Laurence nodded his head with satisfaction. He liked being in the company of Ministers: talk with Ministers was big stuff. Just as Francis was sated with the high political world, Astill was insatiable.

The others, without fuss, agreed to serve. Then Roger came to what, in his mind and mine, was the point of the meeting. What he was going to suggest, we had agreed between ourselves. I was as much behind it as he was; later on, I had to remind myself of that. "Now that we've got a committee together, and a quite exceptionally strong one," said Roger, blandishment coming into his tone for the first time that afternoon, "I should like to know what you'd all feel if I added another member."

"Minister?" said Astill acquiescently.

"I'm bringing it up to you, because the man I'm thinking of does present some problems. That is, I know he doesn't see

eye to eye with most of us. He might easily make you waste
a certain amount of time. But I have a strongish feeling that
it might be worth it."

He paused and went on: "I was thinking of Michael Brodzinski."

Faces were impassive, the shut faces of committeemen. After
an interval, Astill took the lead. "I think I can probably speak
for our colleagues, Minister. Certainly I should have no ob-
jection to working with Dr. Brodzinski."

Astill liked agreeing with a Minister. This wasn't time-serv-
ing, it wasn't even self-seeking: it was just that Astill believed
that Ministers were likely to be right. "I dare say we shall have
our points of difference. But no one has ever doubted that
he is a man of great scientific quality. He will have his own
contribution to make."

Someone said, in a low voice—was it Pearson?—"If you
can't beat them, join them. But this is the other way round."

The other academics said that they could get on with Brodzinski. Francis was looking at his watch, as though anxious to
be back in Cambridge. He said: "Minister, I agree with the
rest. I'm inclined to think that he'd be more dangerous outside than in."

"I'm afraid that doesn't quite represent my attitude," said
Astill.

"Still," Roger said, "you're quite happy about it, Astill?"

"I'm not. I think you're all wrong," Walter Luke burst out.
"As bloody wrong as you can be. I thought so when I first
heard this idea, and I think so now."

Everyone looked at him. I said quietly, "I've told you, you
can watch him—"

"Look here," said Walter, "you're all used to reasonable
ways of doing business, aren't you?"

No one replied.

"You're all used to taking people along with you, aren't
you?"

Again, silence.

"So am I, God help me. Sometimes it works, I grant you that. But do you think it's going to work in anything as critical as this?"

Someone said we had to try it.

"You're wiser old bastards than I am," said Walter, "but I can't see any good coming out of it."

The whole table was stirring with impatience. Walter's outburst had evoked the group-sense of a meeting. Getliffe, Astill, everyone there, wanted him to stop. Technical insight they all gave him credit for; but not psychological insight. He gave himself no credit for it, either. Battered-looking he might be, but he still often thought of himself as younger than he was. That strain of juvenility, of deliberate juvenility—for he was proud of this, and in his heart despised the "wise old bastards"—took away the authority with which he might have spoken that afternoon.

Roger was regarding him with hard eyes.

"Would you take the responsibility, if I gave you your head and left Brodzinski outside?"

"I suppose so," Walter said.

Roger said: "You needn't worry. I'm going to overrule you."

A week later, at the same place, at the same time, Michael Brodzinski was making his first appearance on the committee. The others were standing round, before the meeting, when a secretary came to tell me that Brodzinski had arrived. I went out to welcome him, and, before we had shaken hands, just from the joyful recognition on his face, I was certain that he had received some account of the first discussion, that he knew I was partly responsible for getting him there, and so gave me his trust.

I led him into Roger's room. Approaching the knot of scientists, who were still standing, Brodzinski looked very powerful physically. He was much the most heavily muscled, more so than Walter, who was a strong man.

Once more I was certain that he had heard precisely how he had been discussed. "Good afternoon, Sir Laurence," he said to Astill, with great politeness and qualified trust. To Francis Getliffe the politeness was still great, the trust more qualified. To Walter the politeness became extreme, the politeness of an enemy.

Roger called out a greeting. It was a hearty, banal bit of cordiality, something like how grateful Roger was to have his help. At once Brodzinski left Walter, and listened as though he were receiving a citation. With his splendid, passionate, luminous eyes, he was looking at Roger as more than a supporter, as something like a saviour.

CHAPTER XII

AN EVEN BET

Twice that month, I was invited out by Caro's brother. It seemed a little taxing, but on the second occasion, when my wife was staying with her sister, I said yes. It seemed more taxing still, face to face with Sammikins—a name I found increasingly unsuitable for this loud-voiced, untameable man —in one of the military clubs.

He had given me dinner, and a good one. Then, sitting in the library, under the oil-paintings of generals of the Crimean War, the Mutiny, fierce-looking generals of the late-Victorian peace, we had gone on to the port. I was lying back relaxed in my chair. Opposite me, Sammikins sat straight up, wild and active as a hare. He was trying to persuade me to bet.

It might have been because he couldn't resist it. Earlier that evening he had been inviting me to a race-meeting. Like his sister, he owned race-horses, and he thought it was unnatural, he thought I was holding something back, when I professed boredom in the presence of those romantic animals. But if I wouldn't bet on horses, surely I would on something else? He kept making suggestions, with cheerful, manic, loud-voiced glee. It might have been just the addiction. Or it might have been that he was provoked by anyone like me. Here was I, fifteen years older, my manner restrained by the side of his (which didn't differentiate me too sharply from most of the human race). Did he want to prove that we weren't all that unlike?

I took him on. I said that, if we were going to bet, he had one advantage; he was, at any rate potentially, richer than I was. I also had an advantage: I understood the nature of odds, and I doubted if he did. If I were ready to bet, it was going to be on something which gave us each precisely an even chance.

"Done," he said.

Finally we settled that Sammikins should order more glasses of port, and afterwards not touch the bell again. Then, for the period of the next half hour, we would mark down the number of times the waiter's bell was rung. He would bet on an odd number, I on an even. How much? he said.

"Ten pounds," I replied.

Sammikins put his watch on the table between us. We agreed on the starting and finishing time, and watched the second hand go round. As it came up to the figure twelve, Sammikins cried: "They're off!"

On a sheet of club writing-paper, I kept the score. There were only half a dozen men in the library, one of whom kept sniffing in an irritated fashion at Sammikins' barks of laughter. The only likely orderers appeared to be a party of three senior officers. Immediately after the start, they rang for the waiter, and I heard them asking for large whiskeys all round. With decent luck, I was reckoning, they ought to manage another.

Watching them with bold, excited eyes, Sammikins, who knew two of them, discussed their characters. I was embarrassed in case his voice should carry. Like his sister's, his judgments were simple and direct. He had much more insight than staider men. He told stories about those two in the last war. He liked talking about the military life. Why hadn't he stayed in the army? I asked him. Yes, he had loved it, he said. With his fierce, restless look, he added that he couldn't have stood being a peace-time officer. It occurred to me that, in different times, he might have been happy as a soldier of fortune.

No, he couldn't have stood being a peace-time officer, he said: any more than he could stand the thought of keeping up the estate when his father died.

"I suppose," said Sammikins, with a laugh loud even for him, "that I shall have to dodder about in the Lords. How would *you* like that? Eh?"

He meant that he would detest it. He was speaking, as usual, the naked truth. Though it didn't seem to fit him, he had all his family's passion, which Caro shared, for politics. No one could possibly have less of a political temperament than Sammikins had: yet he loved it all. He loved the House of Commons, it didn't matter how many enemies he made there. He was talking about his Party's leaders, with the same devastating simplicity with which he had talked about the generals, but with his eyes popping with excitement. He didn't think any better of the politicians, but they entranced him more.

One of the generals pressed the button by the fireplace, and the waiter came in. Sixteen minutes had passed. They ordered another round. I made a stroke on the writing-paper and smiled.

"Soaking," said Sammikins, who was not a specially abstemious man, with disapproval.

No movement from anyone else in the room. The man whom Sammikins's laugh made wretched was reading a leather-bound volume, another was writing a letter, another gazing critically at a glossy magazine.

"They want stirring up," said Sammikins, in a reproving tone. But he was surveying the room with a gambler's euphoria. He began speaking of the last appointment of a junior Minister—who was Roger's Parliamentary Secretary, occupying the job which Roger had filled under Gilbey.

"He's no good," said Sammikins. The man's name was

Leverett-Smith. He was spoken of as a safe appointment, which to Sammikins meant that there was no merit in it.

"He's rich," I said.

"No, he's pretty well-off, that's all."

It occurred to me that Sammikins did not have an indifference which, in my provincial youth, we should have expected of him. Romantically, we used to talk about the aristocratic contempt for money. Sammikins was rough on ordinary bourgeois affluence: but he had no contempt at all for money, when, as with Diana Skidmore, there was enough of it.

"He's no good," cried Sammikins. "He's just a boring little lawyer on the make. He doesn't want to do anything, blast him, he doesn't even want the power, he's just pushing on, simply to puff himself up."

I suspected that Leverett-Smith had been put in as a counterweight to Roger, who scarcely knew him and had not been consulted. I said that such men, who didn't threaten anyone and who were in politics for the sake of the charade (for I believed Sammikins was right there), often went a long way.

"So do clothes-moths," said Sammikins, "that's what he is —a damned industrious clothes-moth. We've got too many of them, and they'll do us in."

Sammikins, who had a store of bizarre information, most of which turned out to be accurate, had two addenda on Leverett-Smith. A, that he and his wife were only keeping together for social reasons; B, that she had been a protegée of Lord ——, who happened to be a *voyeur*. Then, with an insistence that I didn't understand, he returned to talking of government appointments, as though he had appointments on the brain. At that moment, when twenty-seven minutes had gone, I saw with surprise and chagrin one of the generals get up with long, creaking movements of the legs, and go to the bell.

"Put down one more, Lewis," cried Sammikins, with a cracking laugh, "three! That's an odd number, you know."

The waiter was very quick. The general called for three pints of bitter, in tankards.

"That's a very good idea." Sammikins gave another violent laugh. He looked at the watch. Twenty-nine minutes had passed, the second hand was going round.

"Well," he said, staring at me, bold and triumphant.

I heard a sniff from close by. With a glance of hate towards Sammikins, the man who had been registering protest about his noisiness soberly put a marker into his book, closed it, and went towards the bell.

"Twenty seconds to spare," I said. "My game, I think."

Sammikins swore. Like any gambler I had ever known, he expected to make money out of it. It didn't seem an addiction so much as a process of interior logic. Both he and Caro lost hundreds a year on their horses, but they always thought of them as a business which would pull round. However, he had to write me out a cheque, while his enemy and bane, in a gravelly voice, still with a hostile glare at Sammikins, ordered a glass of tonic water.

Without any preamble, his cheque passed over to me, Sammikins said:

"The trouble with Roger is, he can't make up his mind."

For an instant I was at a loss, as though I had suddenly got mixed up in a different conversation.

"That's why I've been chasing you," he said, so directly, so arrogantly, so innocently, that it didn't seem either flattering or unflattering: it just sounded like, and was, the bare truth.

"*That's* what I wanted to talk to you about."

By now I was ready for anything, but not for what he actually said. Noisily he asked me: "Roger hasn't picked his P.P.S.* yet, has he?"

---

* Another of the confusing uses of "Secretary" in British Government. P.P.S. means Parliamentary Private Secretary. A P.P.S. is not a Minister, and is not paid. He devils for his Minister in Parliament, collects information, makes himself generally useful. For a young member, such a job is often his first connection with Ministers.

It was a question to which I had not given thought. I assumed that Roger would choose one of a dozen young backbenchers, glad to get their first touch of recognition.

"Or has he, and we haven't heard?" Sammikins insisted.

I said I had not heard the matter so much as mentioned.

"I want the job," said Sammikins.

I found myself curiously embarrassed. I didn't want to meet his eyes, as though I had done something shady. Didn't he realise that he was a public figure? Didn't he realise that he would be a political liability? A good many people admired his devil-may-care, but not the party bosses or other solid men. No politician in his senses would want him as an ally, much less as a colleague, least of all Roger, who had to avoid all rows except the big ones.

I thought that I had better try to speak openly myself.

"He's taken one big risk for you already," I said.

I was reminding him of the time Roger had defended him in Collingwood's face.

Yes, he knew all about that. "He's a good chap," said Sammikins. "He's a damned clever chap, but I tell you, I wish he could make up his mind."

"Has Caro told you anything?"

"What the hell can she tell me? I expect she's doing her best." He took it for granted that she was persuading Roger on his behalf, working for him as she had done all their lives. I wondered whether she was. She must know that she would be doing her husband harm.

"She knows what I want. Of course she's doing her best," he said with trust, with dismissive trust. It was a younger brother's feeling—with all the responsibility and most of the love on the sister's side.

"I want the job," said Sammikins, speaking like a man who is saying his last word.

It was not his last word, however. In his restless fashion, he arranged for us to go round to Lord North Street for a night-cap, shamelessly hoping that his presence would act like blackmail. As he drove me in his Jaguar—it was getting late, Piccadilly was dark and empty under the trees, even after a vinous night he was a beautiful driver—he repeated his last word. Yes, he wanted the job. Listening to him as he went on talking, I was puzzled that he wanted it so much. True, he might be tired of doing nothing. True, his entire family assumed that political jobs were theirs by right, without any nonsense about qualifications. They were not intellectuals, he had scarcely heard intellectual conversation in his life, but since he was a child he had breathed day by day politics in the air, he had heard the familiar, authoritative gossip about who's in, who's out, who's going to get this or that. But it still seemed strange: here was the humblest of ambitions, and all his energies were fixed on it.

In Caro's drawing-room, he did not get a yes or no, or even an acknowledgment of suspense. Caro knew why he was there; she was protective, but gave nothing away. Roger also knew why he was there. He was friendly and paternal, himself having a soft spot for Sammikins. Roger was skilled in keeping off the point, and even Sammikins was over-awed enough not to force it. Watching the three of them—Caro looked flushed and pretty, but subdued, and was drinking more than usual —I thought I could guess what had happened. I believed she had, in fact, mentioned Sammikins' hopes to Roger, full of the sneaking shame with which one tries to pull off something for a child one loves, and knows to be unsuited. I did not think that she had pressed Roger: and I didn't think that he had told her that the idea was mad.

All the time, Roger was certain of what he was going to do. He did it within a week of Sammikins'—blackmail? appeal? It looked prosaic. Roger appointed Mrs. Henneker's son-in-law, Tom Wyndham, who, at the dinner-party when Roger was interrogating David Rubin, had protested about the American scientists "kicking us downstairs." It was a commonplace choice: it was also a cool one.

Roger knew, as bleakly as anyone, that Tom Wyndham was a stupid man. That didn't matter. Roger was securing his base. He had calculated the forces against him—the Air Staff, the aircraft industry, the extreme right of his own party, some of the forces which had helped him into power, as Douglas Osbaldiston, another cool analyst, had pointed out in his own "front room."

Roger was making sure of his own forces, and one of them was the Admiralty. It was good tactics, he had decided, to get "channels," private "channels," to them from the start. That was where Wyndham came in. He had been a naval officer himself, his mother-in-law would have her uses. It was worth while making sure of your potential friends, said Roger. As a rule you couldn't win over your enemies, but you could lose your friends.

The more I saw of him, the sharper-edged he seemed. Now that he was making his first decisions, in private he threw off some of the tricks and covers of his personality, as though they had been an overcoat. When I saw him so, I thought we had a chance.

One morning, though, he did not seem sharp-edged at all. He was wearing a morning-coat, grey waistcoat, striped trousers. He was absent-mindedly nervous. I had watched him when he was anxious, but in nothing like this state. I asked him what was the matter. When I heard the answer, I thought he was joking. He was going to the Palace that morning—to have an audience with the Queen, and to be sworn into the Privy Council.

I had seen dignitaries, industrialists, academics, waiting in the queue at a Palace investiture, with their hands shaking, as though, when they entered into the Presence, they expected some sinister courtier to put out a foot and trip them up. It seemed absurd that Roger should feel as frightened in the shadow of *mana*. It was easy to feel with him as a detached modern soul—while in fact he concealed a romantic, or better, a superstitious, yearning for an older world. It was not for show, nor for propriety's sake, that he was a church-goer. When I asked him why he was Conservative, he had given me a rationalisation, and a good one; but he had left an obstinate part of his nature out of it. It was not an accident, perhaps, that he married into a family with an historic name: or at least, when he first met Caro, that her name had its own magic for him.

He was fond of laughing off those who were in politics simply for the sake of the *charm of Government,* of the charm of being in the inner circle. Sammikins's "charade," the charmed circle—people who were lured by it, said Roger, were useless, and he was right. But, for him, there may have been another charm, deeper, subtler, less rational than that.

I felt relieved when he came back from the Palace, looking jaunty again, and produced brisk plans about how we might seduce Lord Lufkin away from the rest of the aircraft industry.

CHAPTER XIII

IN HONOUR OF
LORD LUFKIN

That summer, Roger judged that we were doing a little better than we had calculated. As carefully as a competent Intelligence officer, he was keeping track of his enemies. Not that they were enemies yet, in any personal sense: so far he had fewer of them than most politicians. The "enemies" he watched were those who just because of what they wanted, or because of the forces behind them, could not help trying to stop him.

About those, he was as realistic as a man could be. Yet, like most realistic men, he detested having the hard truth brought to him by another. I had to tell him, early in the scientists' series of meetings, that Brodzinski was not budging by an inch. It was news we had both feared, but for an afternoon Roger regarded me as though I were an enemy myself.

Soon he was in action again. Before the House rose in July, he had talked to the Party's defence committee, which meant fifty back-bench members, some of whom he knew were already disquieted. Right from the beginning, he had made his calculation. He could live with disquiet on the extreme right, in the long run it would boil over: but if he lost the solid centre of his own party, then he was finished. So he talked—in what language I didn't know, though I could guess —to the respectable county members, the "Knights of the

Shire." According to Wyndham, who was moved to unusual lyricism, the meeting went "like a dream."

During August, Roger asked Osbaldiston to convene a group of top civil servants, to get some administrative machinery ready in time for the scientists' report. Since this was an inter-departmental group, and Rose was the senior member, it met in his room. A vase of chrysanthemums on the desk, as usual, the window open on to the Park, as usual, and as usual Rose welcoming us with a courtesy so exaggerated that it sounded faintly jeering.

"My dear Douglas, how extremely good of you to spare the time! My dear Lewis, how very good of you to come!" Since my office was ten yards away, and since the summons was official, it was not in fact a benevolent exertion on my part.

As we sat round the table, Rose's opposite numbers in the Service departments, Douglas, a Second Secretary from the Treasury, and me, Rose was just perceptibly tart. He didn't mean this to be a long meeting. He was irritated at having to hold it at all. He did not indulge his mood. He merely said: "I take it that we've all seen Lewis Eliot's memorandum on the scientists' first few meetings, haven't we? I believe they've been instructed to report to your Minister by October, Douglas, or have I got that wrong?"

"Quite right," said Douglas.

"In that case, I'm obliged to confess that in the meantime even this distinguished gathering can only hope to produce a marginal result," said Rose. "We don't know what they're going to say. Nor, unless I seriously misjudge our scientific colleagues, do they. All that we can be reasonably certain about is that they can be relied upon to say several different, and probably contradictory, things."

There were grins. Rose was not alone in that room in having a generalised dislike of scientists.

"No, Hector, we can go a bit further than that," said Douglas, neither piqued nor over-borne. "My master isn't asking you to do anything quite useless."

"My dear Douglas, I should be the last person to suggest that your admirable department, or your admirable Minister, could ever ask anyone such a thing."

Rose found it hard to forget that Douglas had once been a junior civil servant, working under him.

"Right," said Douglas. "I agree we shan't actually receive the report until October, but—"

"By the way," Rose broke in, getting down to business, "I take it there are remote chances we shall get the report by then?"

"We ought to," I said.

"But before that comes along, we've got a pretty shrewd idea what it's going to say, in general terms. This paper—" Douglas tapped it—"gives us enough. Some of the scientists are producing arguments at one extreme, and some at the other. There's this chap Brodzinski, and you ought to know that he's got some backers, who's trying to push us into investing a very sizeable fraction of our defence budget, and an even higher fraction of our total scientific manpower, on this pet scheme of his. I ought to say, and Lewis will correct me if I'm wrong, that none of the scientists, even those who think he's a national danger, have ever suggested this scheme is airy-fairy."

They had studied the first estimates of the cost. Several would have liked to believe in the scheme. They had, though, to shake their heads. The Air Ministry man said his department wished for an opportunity of "another look at it," and Rose said:

"Of course, my dear Edgar, of course. But I'm afraid we should all be mildly surprised if your ingenious friend can really persuade us that we can afford the unaffordable."

"That's our view," said Douglas. "It's just not on."

Someone, who was taking note of the meeting, wrote a few words. Nothing more formal was said, and there was no formal decision. From that moment, however, it would have been innocent to think that Brodzinski's scheme stood a good chance.

Douglas said, "The other extreme view—and this isn't such an easy one—is that the country hasn't got the resources, and won't have within foreseeable time, to have any genuine kind of independent weapon at all. That is, we shan't be able to make do without borrowing from the Americans: and the scientists think the balance of advantage is for us to be honest and say so, and slide out of the nuclear weapons business as soon as we conveniently can. As I said, this is the other extreme. But I ought to say that it seems to be held by chaps who are usually level-headed, like Francis Getliffe and our own scientific adviser, Walter Luke."

"No," said Rose, "this isn't such an easy one. They know as well as we do that this isn't just a scientific decision. It's an economic decision, and, I should have thought, even more a political one."

Rose was speaking carefully. He knew precisely what Douglas was aiming at. Rose had not yet declared himself, but he was inclined to think that Douglas was right. Not that he liked him. Douglas was tipped to have the final professional success denied to himself, and he was envious. But liking mattered less than one might have thought, in these alliances.

Douglas, tilting back his chair like an undergraduate, speaking with his casual, lethal relevance, was arguing that the Luke-Getliffe view also wasn't really "on." Furthermore, it might be attractive to the public, and we ought to be prepared to "damp it down." It might be a practicable policy ten or fifteen years ahead, but it wasn't a practicable policy now. The scientists thought it was easy to find absolute solutions; there weren't any. None of the great world pundits, no one in the world—for once Douglas showed a trace of irritation—knew the right way, or whether there was a way at all.

Rose began to speak, massive, precise, qualified. I was

thinking that until Brodzinski had been disposed of, Douglas had spoken like a correct departmental chief, representing his Minister's view. But what he had just said was nowhere near his Minister's view, and Douglas must have known it. I was sure that he did not feel either irregular or conspiratorial. This wasn't intrigue, it was almost the reverse. It was a part of a process, not entirely conscious, often mysterious to those taking part in it and sometimes to them above all, which had no name, but which might be labelled the formation, or crystallisation, of "official" opinion. This official opinion was expected to filter back to the politicians, so that out of the to-ing and fro-ing a decision would emerge. Who had the power? It was the question that had struck me, moving between Basset and Clapham Common. Perhaps it was a question without meaning—either way, the slick answers were all wrong.

I wanted to play for time. The longer it took for official opinion to crystallise, the better. But I was in an awkward position. Officially, I was junior to these heads of departments; further, I had to take care that I didn't speak as though I knew Roger's mind.

The talk went on. Someone had just said, "We mustn't try to run before we can walk." Douglas cocked an eyebrow at me, as he heard that well-judged remark—as though indicating that, though we might be on opposite sides, our literary comradeship was not impaired.

I thought this was my best time.

"I wonder if I could say something, Hector?" I put in. "Just as a private person?"

Hector Rose was irritated. We had never got on, our natures gritted on each other: but he had known me a long time, in this kind of situation he knew me very well, and he could guess that I was going to break the harmony. He wanted me to be quiet. He said: "My dear Lewis. Anything you have to tell us, in any of your various capacities, we shall all be delighted to hear. Please instruct us, my dear Lewis."

"I just wanted to raise a question, that's all." I was as used to his techniques as he to mine.

"I'm sure that would be equally illuminating," said Rose.

I asked my question: but I asked it in several different ways. Wasn't Douglas pre-judging the issue when he talked about Getliffe's view as the "other extreme?" Wasn't this view, in fact, deliberately conceived as a means of taking one first step? Did they assume that no first step could ever be taken? Were they all accepting that the entire process had got out of conscious control?

Osbaldiston spoke first. "I don't think it's possible, you know, to look too far ahead."

"We're all grateful to you, Lewis," said Rose, "for a most interesting piece of exegesis. We're very, very grateful. But I suggest, with great respect, that we've got to deal with immediate situations. The problem really is, isn't it, what our masters can actually perform in the course of the present Parliament? The point at issue is how much, in that time, they could alter their present defence policy, or whether they can alter it at all. We do appreciate, believe me, your taking the trouble to give us—what shall I call it?—a more uninhibited point of view. Thank you very, very, very much."

I didn't mind. I had taken none of them with me, but I didn't expect to. I had done what I intended; that is, warn them that others were thinking flat contrary to them, that official opinion might not be altogether homogeneous. They knew now, since they were far from fools, that those other opinions must have reached Roger, and that I had intended most of all.

Other people were trying to nobble the civil servants, I thought, a night or two later, when Margaret and I were sitting in the stalls at Covent Garden. I looked at the lower right-hand box and there saw, in white tie, white waistcoat,

Hector Rose. That was surprising, for Rose was tone-deaf and hated music. I didn't care for it myself, but had gone to please Margaret: and, as she had pointed out to me, opera at least had the benefit of words. It was even more surprising to see him as a guest of honour, with one of the most forceful of aircraft manufacturers on his right, the aircraft manufacturer's wife on his left, and two pretty daughters behind him.

It was absurd to suppose that Rose could be bought by dinner and a ticket to the opera. It was absurd to suppose that Rose could be bought by any money under Heaven: it would be like trying to slip Robespierre a five pound note. And yet, though he could not have wanted to, he had accepted this invitation. I remembered the instructions he used to give me during the war: that a civil servant ought not to be too finicky about accepting hospitality, but should take it if he felt it natural to do so, and, if not, not. I wondered how natural Hector Rose felt in the box at Covent Garden.

It was equally absurd to suppose that, when Roger made a counter-move, Lord Lufkin could be bought by a dinner, even by a lavish dinner in his honour. Lord Lufkin was financially capable of paying for his own dinners, even lavish ones. Yet he too, who disliked being entertained, accepted the invitation. He was one of the hardest and most austere of men, as I had known for years, having worked for him long before. He would be about as easy to bribe as Rose himself. I had never heard a bribe, in the crude sense, so much as hinted at, anywhere near these people, much less offered. In my own life, I had been offered exactly one bribe, flat, across the table—but that had happened when I was a don at Cambridge. Nothing of the sort was thinkable with the Roses and the Lufkins, although enormous contracts flowed from Rose and Osbaldiston towards Lufkin, and enormous influence flowed back. If Roger got his policy through, one enormous contract would cease to flow to Lufkin. That was a reason why Roger invented a pretext for fêting him—and the pretext was, rather improbably, the occasion of his sixty-first birthday.

The point was, Lufkin came. A crowd was waiting for him in the penthouse of the Dorchester. In the hot flowery room, door opened to the corridor so that men could watch for Lufkin himself, stood Hector Rose, Douglas, Walter Luke, Laurence Astill, Monty Cave, Leverett-Smith (the new Parliamentary Secretary), Tom Wyndham, M.P.s, civil servants, scientists, the whole of Roger's entourage, businessmen, even some of Lufkin's competitors. At last he was seen, sighted like the first sail of the Armada, turning out of the main passage, walking along the soundless corridor, flanked by two of his own staff and two hotel servants, like so many security men.

He had got lost on the penthouse floor, he said, as Roger greeted him. Lufkin spoke as though his getting lost was much to his credit, but even more to everyone else's discredit. He stood there, drinking tomato-juice, surrounded by people absorbing the radiations of power. There was one man whom I had seen absorbing such radiations before; he loved them for their own sake, he was an executive, something like a sales manager, of a rival organisation. Bald, rosy-cheeked, faintly Pickwickian, he stayed happy in the presence of the great man, smiling when the great man spoke. I remembered that his name was Hood.

When we moved into the dining-room, Lufkin sat on Roger's right, neat-headed, skull-faced, appearing younger than most of the company, although he was the oldest man present. He was also the most successful man present, in the terms of that world. He was a nonconformist Minister's son who had made a big fortune. But it wasn't his money which made him so important to Roger: it was partly the concentration of industrial power he had in his hands, partly because he was the most unusual of tycoons. He had taken a peerage from a Labour Government, but he was so powerful,

so indifferent, that his fellow tycoons had by now to forgive
him even that. Able, technically far-sighted, bleak, he sat
by Roger's side, like one who is above the necessity to talk.
If I knew him, there would be only one subject on which
he would discover the necessity to talk: he would not be above
probing the Minister's intention about the contract. When he
knew, which would not be tonight, that the contract might
be cancelled, he would then discover the necessity to talk
about which alternative contract the Minister was proposing
to give him in exchange. I was certain that Roger was prepared for these bargains months ahead. With Lufkin placated, the other tycoons in the industry would have lost their
hardest voice. This was one of the oldest tactics of all.

Lufkin's birthday party—the great table, the flowers,
the glass, the miscellaneous crowd—looked a singular fes-
tivity. Lufkin himself, who was spare and ascetic, ate almost
nothing—the caviar passed him, the pâté passed him. He
allowed himself two strong whiskeys, which he drank along
with his fish, and let the rest of the meal go by. Meanwhile,
as I heard, sitting opposite them, Roger was getting to
work with flattery.

To an outsider, it would have sounded gross, the flattery
squeezed out like toothpaste. My own fear was, not that
Roger was overdoing it, but that he was not doing it enough.
Lufkin was one of the ablest men, and certainly one of the
most effective, that I had known. He was tough, shrewd,
curiously imaginative, and for his own purposes a first-rate
judge of men. But none of that, none of it at all, conflicted
with a vanity so overwhelming that no one quite believed it.
In days past, when he had paid me as a legal consultant, I
used to hear his own staff chanting his praises like so many
cherubim; yet even they, he felt, missed important points
in his character and achievements. I remembered hearing
spinster-aunts of mine telling me in my childhood that great
men never cared for flattery. Well, Lufkin would have been

a shock to my aunts. It would have been even more of a shock for them to discover that among my most gifted acquaintances, he liked flattery more than the others—but not all that much more.

Lufkin showed no pleasure as he listened to the eulogies. Occasionally he corrected Roger on points of fact—such as when Roger suggested, in stretching his interests from the chemical industry to aircraft, that he had taken a risk. Lufkin commented: "It wasn't a risk if you knew what you were doing."

"It must have taken nerve as well as judgment," said Roger.

"That's as maybe," Lufkin replied. Perhaps from the set of his small, handsome head, one might have told that he was not displeased.

Once or twice they were exchanging serious questions. "Don't touch it. You'll be throwing good money after bad," said Lufkin, as though he couldn't be wrong. Roger knew, as I did, that he was not often wrong.

I could not guess how they were feeling about each other. I hoped that Lufkin, whose vanity did not fog his cold eye for ability, could scarcely miss Roger's. I was encouraged when, after Roger had proposed the guest of honour's health, Lufkin got up to reply. He began to tell the story of his life. I had heard it a good many times, and it was always a sign of favour.

He was a very bad speaker, following a very good one. He had no sense of an audience, while Roger's tone had been just right. None of that worried Lufkin. He stood, erect and bony as a young man, as confident of his oratory as Winston Churchill in one of his less diffident moods. He began by a few bleak words about governments in general, and Ministers in particular. He would have been a richer man, he informed us, if he had never listened to any Minister. Then, with his characteristic gift of getting the moral edge both ways, he added that money had never mattered to him.

He just wanted to do his duty, and he was glad Roger Quaife had understood him.

There was nothing oblique or hypocritical about Lufkin. Like a supreme man of action, he believed in what he said and the obvious goodness of his intention. He proceeded to illustrate this by his own story. It was always the same. It bore a curious family resemblance to *Mein Kampf.* It consisted of about six highly abstract anecdotes, most of which had happened, so far as they had a historical origin at all, before he was twenty. One consisted of the young Lufkin being taken by the family doctor—it was not clear why—to see a factory working at half-strength. "I decided there and then that when I had factories of my own, they were going to be full. Or they weren't going to be open at all. Period." Another, which I specially liked, told of a slightly older Lufkin being warned by some anonymous wiseacre—"Lufkin, you'll *fail,* because you won't remember that the best is the enemy of the good." Lufkin's skull-face looked impassive, and he added ominously: "Well, I had to make that chap an allowance in his old age." The story of Lufkin's life always ended in his early twenties. It did so now, which meant that he had reached a date when many of the dinner-party were scarcely born. That did not concern him. Abruptly he sat down, with a grim smile of satisfaction, and folded his arms on his chest.

There was great sycophantic applause, Hood clapping his hands higher than the hands of the rest, his face radiant, as if he had been swept away by the performance of a world-famous soprano, and thought a standing ovation would be in order. Roger patted Lufkin on the back. Yet, I was becoming pretty sure, neither of them underrated the other. Roger had seen too much of powerful men to be put off by the grotesque aspect of Lufkin. It looked as though they might reach a working agreement, and, if so, Roger had scored his first tactical success.

CHAPTER XIV

HUMILIATION
AMONG FRIENDS

A week after Lufkin's birthday, I was standing in a crowded drawing-room at the American Ambassador's house, deafened by the party's surge and swell. Margaret and I had been exchanging a word or two with the wife of J. C. Smith, Collingwood's nephew. I had not met her before. She was a short, slender woman, dark, attractive in a muted way, not very talkative. I wondered incuriously why I hadn't seen her husband's name in Hansard for so long. She passed away from us. Someone else called out to Margaret, and in the huddle I found myself against David Rubin.

Soon I was shaking my fingers to restore the circulation while he looked at me with sombre-eyed *Schadenfreude*. I had asked for whiskey with plenty of ice, and had got it: the glass was so thin that my hand had become numbed with cold. Just then, one of the embassy counsellors came towards Rubin, looking for him, not drifting in the party's stream. Although he knew me well, his manner was constrained. After a few cordialities, he apologised and took Rubin aside.

For an instant I was left alone in the ruck of the party. Over the heads of the people nearby I could see the flaxen hair of Arthur Plimpton, the young American who was going round with Francis Getliffe's daughter. I caught his eye and beckoned him: but before he could make his way through the crowd, Rubin and the diplomat were back.

"Lewis had better hear this," said Rubin.

"It'll be all over town in an hour or so, anyway," said the diplomat.

"What is it?"

"I don't know whether you're in the picture already," he replied, "but your people and the French are going into Su-*ez*."

He pronounced the name in the American manner, with the accent on the second syllable.

I was not occupied with phonetic niceties. I cursed. Both of them were used to me as a man with an equable public face. Suddenly they had seen me lose my temper and were uncomfortable.

"Didn't you expect it?"

From the summer onwards I had heard forecasts and thought they were irresponsible. "Good God Almighty," I said, "don't you think I believed that we had the faintest residue of sense? Do you think any sane man would have taken it seriously?"

"I'm afraid you've got to now," said the diplomat.

Just then Arthur Plimpton joined us. He greeted the other two, then looked at me and asked straight out: "Is there anything wrong, sir?"

"Yes, Arthur, there is. We've gone off our blasted heads."

He was a great favourite of mine. He was a craggily handsome young man of twenty-three. When he got older, the cheekbones would protrude and the bright blue eyes sink in: he already looked harder than an Englishman of the same age. He was capable, arrogant, and had a pleasant touch of cheek. He was also considerate, though at that moment the most he could think of doing was reach me another drink.

Within half an hour, he and David Rubin had drawn my

wife and me away from the party and had established us in a pub in St. John's Wood. They were surprised, I realised as I became cooler, that we were so much outraged. But they were both kind and tactful men. They wanted to see us happier. For a time they kept off the evening's news, but finding that made us more preoccupied, Arthur, the younger and more direct, plunged in. He asked what was worrying us most.

Margaret burst out, "What isn't?"

Just for a second, Arthur smiled.

Her eyes were bright, she had flushed down her neck. Then he realised that she was more violent, more intransigent, than I was.

"They've learned nothing and they're no good," she said. "I've never liked playing along behind them, and I wish we never had!"

"All I hope," said David Rubin, with a sad, sardonic smile, "is that if you must do something immoral, you manage to make it work."

"How can we bring it off?" I cried. "What century do you think we're living in? Do they think we can hold the Middle East with a couple of brigade groups?"

"I don't know how this'll go over in our country," said Arthur.

"How will it?" I said angrily.

Rubin shrugged his shoulders.

I said: "Countries, when their power is slipping away, are always liable to do idiotic things. So are social classes. You may find yourselves in the same position some day."

"Not yet," said Arthur, with confidence.

"No, not yet," said David Rubin.

Margaret and I were humiliated, and the others went on trying to cheer us up. When I had glimmers of detachment, which was not often that night, I thought that their attitudes were diametrically opposite to what one might expect.

David Rubin was a man of deep and complex sophistication. His grandparents had been born in Poland, he had no English genes in him at all. Yet it was he who loved England more uncritically, which was strange, for he was one of the most critical of men. He did not like being patronised by English pundits, but he still had a love-affair with England, just a little like that of Brodzinski, who was a scientific enemy of his. He loved the pretty, picture-book England— far more than Margaret and I could have loved it. And at first sight surprisingly, far more so than Arthur Plimpton, who was as Anglo-Saxon as we were, who had the run of Basset and Diana Skidmore's smart friends, who knew the privileged in our country as well as his own, and who had no special respect for any of them.

If Arthur had been an English boy, I should, when I first met him a couple of years before, have been able to place him within five minutes. As it was, it was apparent that he was well-off. But it had taken Diana to enlighten me that that was putting it mildly. Diana did not show enthusiasm for the idea that he might marry Penelope Getliffe. Diana considered that marriage with the daughter of a scientist, however eminent, would be a come-down. She was laying plans for something more suitable.

Despite, or perhaps because of, all this, Arthur was not over-impressed by England. On that night of Suez, he was full of idealism, genuine idealism, damning the British Government. I distinctly recalled that when he spoke of capitalist enterprises, particularly of methods of adding to his own fortune, he showed an anti-idealism which would have made Commodore Vanderbilt look unduly fastidious. Yet that night, he talked with great hope and purity.

It heartened Margaret, whose nature was purer than mine. Myself, I was discouraged. I was remembering the outbursts of idealism that I had listened to, from young men as good as this one, back in my own group in a provincial town, when our hopes had been more revolutionary than Arthur could have believed, but still as pure as his. I fell silent, half-hearing the argument, Arthur and Margaret on one side, David Rubin on the other, Rubin becoming more and more elaborate and Byzantine. I was signalling to Margaret to come away. If I stayed there, I should just become more despondent, and more drunk.

There was one glint of original sin, as Arthur saw Margaret and me getting ready to go. He might have been talking with extreme purity; but he was not above using his charm on Margaret, persuading her to invite Penelope to stay at our flat, and, as it were coincidentally, him too. I supposed he was trying to get her out of the atmosphere of the Cambridge house. But I was feeling corrupt that night, and it occurred to me that, like most of the very rich people I had known, he was trying to save money.

CHAPTER XV

SELF-DEFENCE

On the Sunday afternoon, Margaret and I walked down, under the smoky, blue-hazed autumn sky, to Trafalgar Square. We could not get nearer than the bottom of the Haymarket. Margaret was taken back, high-coloured, to the "demo's" of her teens. For her, more than for me, the past might be regained; she could not help hoping to recapture the spirit of it, just as she hoped that places we had visited together in the past might always hold a spark of their old magic. She was not as possessed by time lost as I was, yet I believed she could more easily possess herself of it. The speeches of protest boomed out. We were part of a crowd, we were all together. It was a long time since I had been part of a crowd, and, that day, I felt as Margaret did.

During the next few days, wherever I went, in the offices, clubs and dinner-parties, tempers were more bitter than they had been in this part of the London world since Munich. As at the time of Munich, one began to refuse invitations to houses where the quarrel would spring up. This time, how-ever, the divide took a different line. Hector Rose and his colleagues, the top administrators, had most of them been devoted Municheers. Now, conservative as they were, dis-posed by temperament and training to be at one with Gov-

ernment, they couldn't take it. Rose astonished me when
he talked.

"I don't like committing my own future actions, my dear
Lewis, which in any case will shortly be of interest to no one
but myself—but I confess that I don't see how I'm going to
hypnotise myself into voting Conservative again."

He was irked because for once he had known less than
usual about the final decision: but also, he was shocked. "I
don't mind these people—" he meant the politicians, and
for once did not use the obsequious "our masters"—"failing
to achieve an adequate level of intelligence. After all, I've
been trying to make them understand the difference between
a precise and an imprecise statement for nearly forty years.
But I do mind, perhaps I mind rather excessively, when they
fail to show the judgment of so many cockatoos." Bitterly,
Rose considered the parallel, and appeared to find it close
enough.

He was sitting in his room behind the bowl of flowers.
He said: "Tell me, Lewis, you are rather close to Roger
Quaife, is that true? Closer, that is, than one might expect a
civil servant, even a somewhat irregular civil servant, to be
to a politician, even a somewhat irregular politician?"

"That's more or less true."

"He must have been in it, you know. Or did you hear?"

"Nothing at all," I said.

"The rumour is that he put up some sort of opposition
in Cabinet. I should be mildly curious to know. I have seen
a good many Ministers who were remarkably bold outside,
but who somehow were not quite so intransigent when they
got round the Cabinet table."

There was a new rasp in Rose's tone. He went on: "In
any case, my dear Lewis, it wouldn't do any harm, and it
might conceivably do a trivial amount of good, if you
dropped the word to Quaife that a number of comparatively
sensible and responsible persons have the feeling that they

suddenly find themselves doing their sensible and responsible work in a lunatic asylum. It can't do any harm, if you communicate that impression. I should be very, very grateful to you."

Even for Rose, it took an effort of discipline that afternoon to return to his duties, to his "sensible and responsible work."

Meanwhile, Tom Wyndham and his friends of the back benches were happy. "I feel I can hold my head up at last," said one of them. I did not see Diana Skidmore during those days, but I heard about her: the whole of the Basset circle was solid for Suez. Just as the officials seemed slumped in their chairs, the politicians became brilliant with euphoria. Sammikins, for once not odd man out, exuded more euphoria than any of them. In his case, there was a special reason. He happened, alone among his right-wing group, to be pro-Zionist. Whether this was just a whim, I did not know, but he had applied for a commission in the Israeli Army, and he was riotously happy at the prospect of getting in one more bout of fighting before he grew too old.

In the clubs, the journalists and political commentators carried the rumours along. We were all at the pitch of credulity or suspiciousness—because in crises these states are the same, just as they are in extreme jealousy—when anything seemed as probable as anything else. Some supporters of the Government were restive, we heard. I had a conversation myself with Cave and a couple of his friends, who were speaking the same bitter language as the officials, the professional men. "This is the last charge of Eton and the Brigade of Guards," said one young Conservative. How could we stop it? How many members of the Cabinet had been against it? Was ——— going to resign? Above all, what had Roger done?

One morning, during a respite from Cabinet meetings, Roger sent for me to give some instructions about the scientists' committee. He did not volunteer a word about Suez. I thought that, just then, it would do no good to press it. Soon a secretary came in: Mr. Cave had called. Would the Minister see him?

On the instant, as soon as the name was mentioned, Roger's equable manner broke. "Am I never going to get a minute's peace? Good God alive, why don't some of you protect me a bit?"

He relapsed into sullenness, saying he was too busy, too pestered, she must make some excuse. The girl waited. She knew, as well as Roger did, that Cave was the most talented of Roger's party supporters. She knew he ought not to be turned away. At last Roger, with a maximum of ill-grace, said he supposed she had better send him in.

I made to go out, but Roger, frowning, shook his head. When Cave entered, his head was thrown back from his slack, heavy body, eyes flickering under the thick arches of brow. Roger had made himself seem matey again. It was Cave who came to the point.

"We can't grumble about things being dull, can we?"

There were a few remarks, affable, half-malicious, to which Roger did not need to reply. All of a sudden, Cave ceased being devious.

"Is there really any bit of sanity in this affair?" he said.

"What am I expected to say to that?"

"I'm speaking for some of your friends, you know," said Cave. "Is there anything which you know and we don't, that would alter our opinion?"

"I shouldn't think so, should you?"

"No, Roger," said Cave, who, having thrown away side-digs or any kind of malice, was speaking with authority. "I was asking you seriously. Is there anything we don't know?"

Roger replied, for a second friendly and easy:

"Nothing that would make you change your minds."

"Well, then; you must know what we think. This is stupid. It's wrong. On the lowest level, it won't work."

"This isn't exactly an original opinion, is it?"

Neither Cave nor I knew then, though I was able to check the date later, that on the night before the Cabinet had heard of the veto from Washington.

"I'm quite sure it's your own. But how much have you been able to put it across?"

"You don't expect me to tell you what's happened in the Cabinet, do you?"

"You have been known to drop a hint, you know." Cave, his chin sunk down, had spoken with a touch of edge.

At that remark, Roger's temper, which I had not seen him lose before, except as a tactic, broke loose. His face went white: his voice became both thick and strangulated. He cried: "I'll tell you one thing. I've not lost my senses. I don't believe this is the greatest stroke of English policy since 1688. How in hell can you imagine that I don't see what you see?" His anger was ugly and harsh. He did not relish the voice of conscience, perhaps most of all, when it came from a man as clever, as much a rival, as Monty Cave: but that wasn't all. That was only the trigger.

"I'll tell you another thing," Roger shouted. "You're wondering what I said in Cabinet. I'll tell you. I said absolutely nothing."

Cave stared at him, not put off by violence, for he was not an emotional coward, but astonished. In a moment he said, steadily:

"I think you should have done."

"Do you? Then it's time you learned something about the world you're living in." He rounded on me. "*You* pretend to know what politics is like! It's time you learned something, too. I tell you, I said absolutely nothing. I'm sick and tired of having to explain myself every step of the way. *This* is the politics you all talk about. Nothing I could have said would make the slightest difference. Once these people had got the bit between their teeth, there was no doubt what was going to happen. Yes, I let it go on round me. Yes, I acquiesced in something much more indefensible than you've begun to guess. And you expect me to explain, do you? Nothing I could have said would have made the faintest difference. No, it would have made one difference. It would have meant that one newcomer would have lost whatever bit of credit he possessed. I've taken risks. You've both seen me take an unjustified risk."

He was referring to his defense of Sammikins. He was speaking with extreme rancour, as though denouncing the folly, and worse, of somebody else. "If I were any good at what I'm trying to do, I never ought to allow myself to take risks for the sake of feeling handsome. I only ought to take one risk. I've got a fifty per cent chance of doing what I set out to do."

He snapped his fingers, less unobtrusively than usual. "If I can't do what we believe in, then I reckon no one is going to do it. For that, I'll make a great many sacrifices you two would be too genteel to make. I'll sacrifice all the useless protests. I'll let you think I'm a trimmer and a time-server. I'll do anything. But I'm not prepared for you two to come and teach me when I've got to be noble. It doesn't matter whether I look noble or contemptible, so long as I bring this off. I'm fighting on one front. That's going to be hard enough. Nothing that any of you say is going to make me start fighting on two fronts, or any number of fronts, or whatever you think I ought to fight on." There was a pause.

"I don't find it as easy as you do," said Monty Cave. "Isn't it slightly too easy to find reasons for doing nothing, when it turns out to be advantageous to oneself?"

Roger's temper had subsided as suddenly as it had blown up.

"If I were going to fall over backwards to get into trouble, whenever there are decent reasons for keeping out of harm's way, then I shouldn't be any use to you, or in this job."

For a man of action—which he was, as much so as Lord Lufkin—Roger was unusually in touch with his own experience. But as he made that reply, I thought he was speaking like other men of action, other politicians that I had known. They had the gift, common to college politicians like my old friend Arthur Brown, or national performers like Roger, of switching off self-distrust, of knowing when not to be too nice about themselves. It was not a romantic gift: but it was one, as more delicate souls like Francis Getliffe found to their disadvantage, the lack of which not only added to the pain of life, but cost one half the game.

CHAPTER XVI

PRETEXT FOR
A CONVERSATION

The days of Suez were over. Monty Cave, with two other junior Ministers, had resigned from the Government. There were still dinner-parties from which it was advisable to excuse ourselves. But I could not excuse myself from Gilbey's speech in the House of Lords.

It was not an occasion made for drama. There were perhaps forty men lolling on the red benches, under the elaboration of stained glass, the brass and scarlet of the galleries, the chamber more flashy than the Commons, the colours hotter. If Roger had not asked me, I should not have thought of listening. The Government spokesman was uttering generalities, at the tranquillising length which Douglas Osbaldiston judged suitable, about the defence programme after Suez. The Opposition was expressing concern. One very old peer muttered mysteriously about the use of the camel. A young peer talked about bases. Then Gilbey rose, from the back of the Government benches. He was looking ill, iller than he really was, I thought. It occurred to me that he was doing his best to emulate the elder Pitt. But I hadn't realised what he was capable of. Speaking to an official brief, he was fumbling, incompetent, and had embarrassed us for years. On his own, he was eloquent, and as uninhibited as an actor of his own generation playing Sydney Carton.

"I should have liked to speak before your lordships in the uniform which has been the greatest pride and privilege of my life," he told them in his light, resonant, reedy tenor. "But a man should not wear uniform who is not well enough to fight." Slowly he put his hand on his heart. "In recent days, my lords, I have wished devoutly that I was well enough to fight. When the Prime Minister, God bless him, decided, with a justice and righteousness that are as unchallengeable as any in our history, that we had to intervene by force of arms to keep the peace, and our own inalienable rights in Suez, I looked the world in the face as I have not been able to do these last ten years. For a few days, true Englishmen were able to look the whole world in the face. Is this *the last time* that true Englishmen will have that privilege, my lords?"

As usual with Lord Gilbey, it was ham. As usual with his kind of ham, it was perfectly sincere.

But Gilbey, despite his sincerity, was not so simple as he seemed. This speech began as a threnody for his own England: but it turned into an opportunity for revenge on those who had kicked him out. He was not clever, but he had some cunning. He had worked out that the enemies of Suez within the Government had been his own enemies. As the rumours that Roger was anti-Suez went round the clubs, Gilbey had decided that these were the forces, this man the intriguer, who had supplanted him. Like other vain and robust men, Gilbey had no capacity for forgiveness whatsoever. He did not propose to forgive this time. Speaking as an elder statesman, without mentioning Roger by name, he expressed his doubts about the nation's defences, about "intellectual gamblers" who would let us all go soft. "This is a *knife in the back,*" an acquaintance in the gallery wrote on an envelope and passed to me.

Gilbey was finishing. "My lords, I wish for nothing more than that I could assure you that the country's safety is in the best possible hands. It is a long time since I lay awake at night. I have found myself lying awake, these last bitter nights, wondering whether we can become strong again. That is our only safety. Whatever it costs, whether we have to live like paupers, this country must be able to defend itself. Most of us here, my lords, are coming to the end of our lives. That matters nothing to me, nothing to any of us, if only, at the hour of our death, we can know that the country is safe."

Again, slowly, Gilbey put his hand on his heart. As he sat down, he took from his waistcoat pocket a small pillbox. There were hear-hears, and one or two cheers from the benches round him. Gilbey took a capsule, and closed his eyes. He sat there with eyes closed, hand on heart, for some minutes. Then, bowing to the Woolsack, leaning on the arm of a younger man, he left the Chamber.

When I had to report this performance to Roger, he took it better than other bad news. "If it comes to playing dirty," he said, "aristocrats have got everyone else beaten, any day of the week. You should see my wife's relatives when they get to work. It's a great disadvantage to be held back by middle-class morality."

He spoke with equanimity. We both knew that the enemies, both as people and as groups, would become visible from now on. The extreme right, he was saying, was bound to be ten times more powerful in any society like ours, or the American society, than the extreme left. He had been watching them before this. It was not only Gilbey who would be talking, he said.

No, it was not only Gilbey who would be talking, as Caro proved to me a few days later, when she came to have a drink at our flat. She herself, like all her family, had been pro-Suez. At the dinner-table in Lord North Street, she had been outspoken for it, while Roger had not said much. Had they arranged this between themselves, or did they know the moves so well that they did not need to? It was good tactics for Roger to have a wife, and a Seymour, who was talking the party line. Good tactics or not, prearranged or not, Caro believed what she said. Once again, people were not clever enough to dissimulate. When Caro talked to me with a bold, dashing, innocent stare, I was furious with her, but I did not doubt that she was honest. She was as much pro-Suez as Lord Gilbey, and for the same reason. What was more, she insisted that Roger's constituents were pro-Suez too, including many of the poor.

She pressed me to visit them, wanted so urgently to take me, that I suspected she might have another motive. She wore me down. One afternoon in November, she drove me down to what she called her "office." We had not far to go, for Roger held one of the safe Kensington seats. Caro drove through the remnants of gentility in Queen's Gate, the private hotels, the flats, the rooming-houses, the students' hostels, past the end of Cromwell Road and Earl's Court—crowded with the small-part actresses, the African students, the artists, all displaying themselves in the autumn sun, and (I remarked to Caro) as remote from Lord Gilbey's concerns as if he were a Japanese *daimyo*. Caro just said: "Most of them don't vote anyway."

Her "office" turned out to be in one of the back-streets close by Olympia, a back-street of terrace houses, like those I used to walk past in my childhood on the way home. Each Monday afternoon, Caro used, so I gathered, to sit from two to six in the "front room" of one of her constituency "chums," a big woman with a glottal Cockney accent, who made us a pot of tea, was on hearty, patting, egalitarian terms with Caro, and cherished her delight at calling a woman of title by her Christian name.

That room, that street, seemed un-businesslike for Caro. It was at the wrong end of the constituency. The seat was safe, the Kensington end would go on returning Roger, if

he turned into a gorilla. But down here she was surrounded
by the working-class. Among the knockabout poor, the
lumpen proletariat, she might pick up a vote or two; but
the rest, with similar English impartiality and phlegm, would
go on voting for another gorilla, provided he was Roger's
opponent.

There Caro sat, in the tiny, close-smelling front room,
ready to talk to any caller for hours to come. Through the
window, the houses opposite stood near and plain, so near
that one could see the wood-pocks on the doors. The first of
Caro's visitors—perhaps clients was a better word—were
Conservative supporters, elderly people living on small private
means or pensions, who had made the trip from Courtfield
Gardens or Nevern Square, from single rooms in the high
19th Century houses, who had come out here—for what?
Mostly to have someone to talk to, I thought.

A good many of them were lonely, pointlessly lonely, cook-
ing for themselves, going out to the public library for books.
Some wanted to speak of their young days, of gentilities past
and gone. They were irremediably lonely in the teeming
town, lonely, and also frightened. They worried about the
bombs: and though some of them would have said they had
nothing to live for, that made them less willing to die.
"Dying is a messy business anyway," said an old lady who
had thirty years before taught at a smart girls'-school, putting
a stoical face on it. I couldn't have comforted her: dying
was a messy business, but this was a hard way to die, frightened, neglected and alone. I couldn't have comforted her,
but Caro could, not through insight, not even through
sympathy, for Caro was as brave as her brother—but through
a kind of comradeship, unexacting, earthy, almost callous,
as though saying: We're all dirty flesh, we're all in the same
boat.

Those genteel clients, some eccentric and seedy, some
keeping up appearances, were pro-Suez all right. That wasn't

a surprise. It was more of a surprise when I listened to the
later ones. They came from the streets round about, working
people finished for the day; they were the sort of mixture
you could pick up anywhere, just beyond the prosperous
core of the great, muddled, grumbling town; they worked
on the underground and in small factories, they filled in their
Pools coupons and bet with a street bookmaker. They were
members of Trade Unions and voted Labour. Their reasons
for coming along were matter-of-fact—mostly to do with
housing, sometimes with schools. In her turn, Caro was
brisk and matter-of-fact: yes, that could be taken up, no,
that wasn't on.

She gave one or two a tip for a race next day—not *de haut
en bas,* but because she was, if possible, slightly more obsessed with horse-racing than they were themselves. She was
playing fair, but once or twice she mentioned Suez, sometimes the others did. It was true what she had stated: there
were several who would never have voted for "her people,"
they would have said they were against the bosses—but just
then, in a baffled, resentful fashion, they were on her side
and Lord Gilbey's, not on mine.

When she had said her goodbyes, and we went outside
into the sharp night, the stars were bright for London. Behind the curtains, lights shone pallid in the basement rooms.
At the corner, the pub stood festooned with bulbs, red,
yellow and blue. The whole street was squat, peaceful, prosaic,
cheerful. Caro was insisting that I should go back to Lord
North Street for a drink. I knew that Roger was in the country making a speech. I knew she was not so fond of my
company as all that. She still had something on her mind.

She was driving fast, the eastward traffic was slight on the
way home to Westminster.

"You see," she said. She meant that she had been right.

I wasn't pleased. I began arguing with her; this was a tiny
sample which showed nothing, not the real midland or

northern working-class. But I wasn't sure. Some politicians brought back from their constituencies the same report as hers.

"I hope they're all pleased with the result," I said. "I hope you are, too."

"We ought to have gone through with it," said Caro.

"You're all clinging with your fingernails onto the past," I said. "Where in God's name do you think that is going to take us?"

"We ought to have gone through with it."

Out of patience with each other, tempers already edged, we sat in her drawing-room. She had been talking all the afternoon, I was tired with having just sat by: but she was restless and active. She mentioned the two boys, both at preparatory schools. Neither of them was "bright," she said, with an air of faint satisfaction. "My family was never much good at brains."

I fancied that when I left she would go on drinking by herself. She was looking older that night, the skin reddened and roughened round her cheekbones. But it made no difference to her prettiness, and she walked about the room, not with grace, but with the spring, the confidence in her muscles, of someone who loved the physical life.

She went back to the sofa, curled her legs under her, and gazed straight at me.

"I want to talk," she said.

"Yes?"

"You knew, did you?" She was staring at me as boldly as her brother had done in his club. She went on: "You know that Roger has had his own line on this?" (She meant Suez.) "You know it, I *know* you know it, and it's dead opposite to the way I feel. Well, that's all down the drain now. It doesn't matter a hoot what any of us thought. We've just got to cut our losses and start again."

Suddenly she asked me: "You see Roger quite a lot nowadays, don't you?" I nodded.

"I suppose you realise that *no one* has any influence on him?"

She gave her loud, unconstricted laugh.

"I don't mean he's a monster. He lets me do anything I want round the house, and he's good with the children. But when it comes to things outside, it's a different kettle of fish. When it comes to where he's going and how he's going to get there, then *no one* has a scrap of influence on him."

She said it with submission. Gossips at Basset, and places like it, often said confidently that she ran him. Partly because she was splendid to look at, partly because, as in the incident of Sammikins, Roger behaved to her with deference and chivalry. She's the master in that set-up, the gossips said in knowledgeable whispers, particularly in Caro's smart, rich world.

Caro had just told me who the master was. She said it as though with surprise at her own submission. Also, as she spoke, there was a jab of triumph at my expense, for she was insisting that I was a subordinate also. She liked insisting on it—because Caro, who seemed as dashing and as much a gambler as her brother, whom other women grumbled had had all the luck, was jealous of her husband's friends.

"No one's going to push him where he doesn't want to go," she said, "it's just as well to get that straight."

"I've done a certain amount of business with him, you know," I said.

"I know about the business you've been doing. What do you take me for?" she cried. "That's why I've got to talk to you. What is it all going to add up to?"

"I should guess," I said, "that he's a better judge of that than I am."

"I've not said so to him"—Caro's eyes were fierce—"because one never ought to say these things or even think them, once he's made up his mind, if one's going to be any help—but I doubt if he's going to get away with it."

"It's a risk," I replied. "But he's gone into it with his eyes open."

"*Has* he?"

"What do you mean? Don't you believe in what he's doing?" I asked.

"I've got to believe in it."

"Well?"

"I can't argue with you. I don't know enough," she said. "But I'd follow my instincts, and I don't think he's got an even chance of getting away with it. So I want to ask you something." She was speaking, not in a friendly tone, but with passion.

"What is it?"

"He'll do what he wants in the long run. I've given you fair warning. But you and your friends can make it more difficult for him. *Don't.* That's what I'm asking you. I want you to give him room to maneuver. He may have to slide gracefully out of this whole business. That doesn't matter, if he does it in time. But if he gets in it up to the neck, then he might ruin himself. I tell you, you and your friends mustn't make it too difficult for him."

She was no more intellectual than Sammikins. She rarely read anything, except fashionable memoirs. But she knew this game of high politics better than I did, perhaps better than Roger did himself. She knew it *as* a game, in which one won or lost. It did not count whether Roger had to abandon a policy. What did count was whether his chances of a higher office were going up or down. To that, she was utterly committed, utterly loyal, with every cell of her flesh.

Previously, I had been getting colder to her. But suddenly the passion of her loyalty moved me.

I said the whole campaign was in his hands. He was too good a politician not to smell the dangers.

"You've got to make it easy for him."

"I don't think you need worry—"

"How do you expect me not to? What's going to happen to him if this goes wrong?"

"I should have thought"—I was now speaking gently—"that he was a very tough man. He'd come back, I'm sure he would."

"I've seen too many future P.M.s," she said, the edge having left her voice also, "who've made a mess of something, or somehow or other taken the wrong turn. They're pretty pathetic afterwards. It must be awful to have a brilliant future behind you. I don't know whether he could bear it."

"If he had to bear it," I said, "then of course he would."

"He'd never be satisfied with second prizes. He'd eat his heart out. Don't you admit it? He's made for the top, and nothing else will do."

As she gazed at me with great open guiltless eyes, she was immersed in him. Then, all of a sudden, the intimacy and tension broke. She threw her head back in a hearty, hooting laugh, and exclaimed: "Just imagine him giving up the unequal struggle and settling down as Governor-General of New Zealand!" She had cheered up, and poured herself another drink.

I was amused by Caro's picture of ultimate failure and degradation.

Soon I said that it was time I went home. She tried, insistently, naggingly, to keep me there for another quarter of an hour. Although we were on better terms by now, she was not fond of me. It was simply that, with husband away, children away, she was bored. Like Diana, and other rich and pretty women, she was not good at being bored, and the person nearest to her had to pay for it. When I refused to stay she sulked, but began thinking that she would enjoy gambling her time away. As I left the house, she was ringing round her friends, trying to arrange for a night's poker.

CHAPTER XVII

THE SWITCH
OF SUSPICION

I had said to Caro that Roger was too good a politician not to smell the dangers. In fact, a nose for danger was the most useful single gift in the political in-fighting: unless it stopped one acting altogether, in which case it was the least. That winter, while others were still vertiginous about Suez, Roger was looking out for opponents, critics, enemies, a year ahead. His policy would be coming into the open then. It was better tactics to let powers like Lufkin get the first taste of it from Roger direct. Patiently he set himself to dine out with them, telling them a little, occasionally letting out a burst of calculated candour.

Moving round Whitehall and the clubs, I got some of the backwash of all this. I even heard a compliment from Lord Lufkin, who said: "Well, considering that he's a politician, you can't say that he's altogether a fool." This evaluation, which in both form and content reminded me of the New Criticism, was the highest praise I remembered Lufkin bestowing on anyone, with the solitary exception of himself.

Towards the end of December, Roger passed one of these forestalling operations on to me. The scientists had fallen behind with their report, but we knew it was going to be delivered early in the New Year; we knew also what it was going to contain. There would be differences in detail be-

tween Laurence Astill and Francis Getliffe, but by and large
they would all be saying the same thing, except for Brodzinski. He had retained an implacable confidence throughout,
absolutely assured both that he was right and that he must
prevail. It was clear that he would insist on writing a minority
report.

My job, said Roger, was to give him a hint of the future,
to pacify him, but to warn him that for the present he
couldn't bank on much support, that Government couldn't
do much for him.

My own nose for danger twitched. I still reproached myself for not having been open with Douglas Osbaldiston
from the start, when he had invited me to do so. I thought
it was right to be open with Brodzinski now. But I felt sure
that Roger ought to do it.

Roger was vexed and overtired. When I said that I
shouldn't have any success, Roger replied that I had been
doing these things all my life. When I said that Brodzinski
was a dangerous man, Roger shrugged. No one was dangerous,
he replied, unless he represented something. He, Roger, was
taking care of the industry and the military. Brodzinski was
just a man out on his own. "Are you afraid of a bit of temperament? We're going to run into worse than that, you
know. Are you going to leave everything to me?"

It was as near a quarrel as we had had. After I left him,
I wrote him a letter saying that he was making a mistake,
and that I wouldn't talk to Brodzinski. Feeling superstitious,
I went over to the window and then returned to my desk
and tore the letter up.

After the next meeting of the scientists, a few days before
Christmas, I took my chance to get Brodzinski alone. Walter
Luke had walked away with Francis Getliffe and Astill; Pear-
son was going off, as he did phlegmatically each fortnight,
to catch the evening plane to Washington. So I could ask
Brodzinski to come across with me to the Athenaeum, and

we walked along the edge of the pond in the shivery winter
dark. A steam of mist hung over the black water. Just after
I had heard the scurry, glug and pop of a bird diving, I said:

"How do you think it is going?"

"What is going?" In his deep, chest-throbbing voice,
Brodzinski as usual addressed me in style.

"How do you think the committee is going?"

"Let me ask you one question. Why did those three" (he
meant Luke, Getliffe, Astill) "go away together?"

He was almost whispering in the empty park. His face was
turned to mine, his great eyes luminous with suspicion.
"They went away," he answered himself, "to continue drafting without me being there to intervene." It was more than
likely. If it had not been likely, he would still have imagined it.

"Do you think that I am happy about the committee,
————?" Once more, the bass, unyielding courtesy.

We walked in silence. It was not a good start. In the club,
I took him upstairs to the big drawing-room. There, on the
reading desk, was the Candidates' Book. I thought it might
mollify him to pass by. His name was entered: we had all
signed our names in support, Francis, Luke, Astill, Osbaldiston, Hector Rose, the whole lot of us. Somehow everyone
knew that he craved to be a member, that he was passionately
set on it. We were doing our best. Not merely to soften
him, to keep him quiet: but in part, I thought, for an entirely different reason. Despite his force of character, despite
his paranoia, there was something pathetic about him.

No, not despite his paranoia, but because of it. Paranoia
had a hypnotic effect, even on tough and experienced men.
I had come across a first intimation of this earlier in my life,
in the temperament of my earliest benefactor, George Pas-
sant. It was not entirely, or even mainly, his generosity, his
great balloon-like dreams, that drew the young: it was not
the scale of his character or his formidable passions. It was

that, in his fits of suspicion, of feeling done down and persecuted, he was naked to the world. He called for, and got,
sympathy in the way most of us could never do. We might
behave better: we might need help out of proportion more:
we might even be genuinely pathetic. And yet, by the side
of the George Passants, we could never suggest to those round
us that revelation, that insight into pathos, which came from
seeming innocent, uncorrupt, and without defence.

It was like that with Brodzinski. I had told Roger that
Brodzinski was a dangerous man: that was a workaday comment, the sort of warning I could keep in the front of my
mind. Sitting by him at the end of the Athenaeum drawing-
room, watching his eyes stray to the Candidates' Book, I
wasn't thinking about warnings: I could feel how once more
he was exposed to the brilliance of suspicion, this naked
sense of a group of privileged persons, whom he wanted
above all to belong to, conspiring together to push him out.
One's impulse, even mine, was to make it easier. He ought
to be shown that there were no plots against him; one ought
to lend a hand. I found myself hoping that the committee
would elect him out of turn.

When I offered him a drink, he asked for half a glass of
sherry and sipped at it, looking doubtfully at me while I
put down a whiskey. For a man so massive and virile, he
was curiously old-maidish in some of his habits—or perhaps
it was that he expected to find in all Anglo-Saxons the signs
of incipient alcoholism. I said: "The Minister is extremely
grateful for all you've done on his committee. You know how
grateful he is, don't you?"

"He is a fine man," said Brodzinski, with deep feeling.

"I am sure," I went on, "that before long the Government
will want to give you some recognition."

I knew that it was being arranged for him to get a C.B.E.
in the June Honours List. I had settled with Roger that I
should hint at this.

Brodzinski stared at me with lambent eyes. He understood some of Whitehall politics much better than most Englishmen: but on these matters of honorific etiquette, he was mystified. He could not have guessed where Roger or Douglas Osbaldiston, or anyone else, came in. On the other hand, he gave a very English reply.

"It doesn't matter whether I get recognised. All that matters is that we do the right thing."

"The Minister is extremely grateful for the advice you have given. I know he'll want to tell you so himself."

Brodzinski sat back in the leather-covered chair, his great chest protruding like a singer's. His face, wide and shield-shaped, was hard with thought, the flap of dusty hair fell to his eyebrows. He was still preoccupied, I guessed, with the thought of drafting going on without him. Yet he was happy. Roger he had spoken of as a trusted, powerful friend. He was sitting with me as though I were another friend, lesser, but still powerful.

"It will soon be time," he said, "for the Minister to assert himself."

I was having to feel my way.

"Of course," I said, "what any Minister can do on his own is pretty limited."

"I am afraid I do not understand you."

"I mean," I said, "you mustn't expect miracles. He's a very able man, as I'm sure you realised a long time ago, and he's prepared to do things that most Ministers wouldn't. But, you know, he can't do much without the support of his colleagues at all levels. He can only do what a great many people think ought to be done—not just himself."

There was a rim of white all round his irises. His gaze was fixed on me, and stayed so. He said:

"I still do not understand you, ———" Once more he addressed me in full. "Or, at least I *hope* I do not understand you."

"I am saying that the area of freedom of action for a Minister is smaller, a great deal smaller, than most people can ever understand."

"I can see that could be so." He seemed exaggeratedly reasonable, and once more he was optimistic. "But let us come to practical examples. There are questions—we have been trying to discuss them this afternoon—where there is not unanimity of opinion. There *cannot* be unanimity of opinion. There will be differences, with some scientists taking Getliffe's view, and some scientists taking mine. Am I correct?"

"There hasn't been unanimity so far, has there?" I was trying the effect of sarcasm, but he went on, set-faced, as though we were already agreed:

"Well then, in such circumstances, the Minister can use his authority on one side or the other: am I correct again?"

"In some circumstances," I replied, "he could."

"In *these* circumstances, then?" He was throwing in all the weight of his nature, bearing me down. Yet his expression looked as though all was simple, as though difficulties did not exist, and his friends, including me, would give him what he longed for: as though disappointment did not exist on this earth.

I was searching for the words. At last I said: "I don't think you must count on it."

"Why not?"

"I've been trying to explain, the Minister is bound to listen to his advisers. You've been giving him one kind of advice. But—you know this, don't you?—the overwhelming majority of opinion is dead against you. The Minister can't say that the pros and cons are about equal, and then just decide."

"I think I understand. I think I understand clearly." His heavy hands on his thighs, Brodzinski stared at me. His face had not altered, but his eyes had flared up. The transition was complete, as if the switch of suspicion had, between one instant and the next, been turned on in his mind. A second before, beautiful, expectant clarity: now, the sight of an enemy.

"What do you understand?"

"It is very easy. The Minister is not to be allowed to make up his own mind. These scientists have been carefully picked by other officials. Of course they have. They advise one thing, I advise another. Then other officials surround the Minister. They pick and choose, they are not willing to let the matter be discussed. Of course they are not. I see what I am expected to understand."

"You mustn't look for sinister explanations."

"I do not look for them. I am obliged to see them."

"I am not prepared," I said, my voice getting harder, "to listen to suggestions that you have not been treated fairly. Do you really believe that my colleagues have been trying to do you down?"

"I am not speaking about your colleagues."

"You mean me?"

"I believe there is a saying—if the cap fits, wear it."

I had become the spider in the web, the origin of persecution. No one likes being hated: most of us are afraid of it: it jars to the bone when we meet hatred face to face. But it was better that I should be the enemy, not Roger.

I had to sound as if I didn't mind being insulted, as though I had no temper of my own. I wanted to lash out and do it better than he did. Temperaments like his clashed right at the roots with mine: even if he were not being offensive, he would have tempted me to say something hard. But I was doing a job, and I couldn't afford luxuries, certainly not the luxury of being myself. I said, sounding like a middle-aged public man: "I repeat, the Minister is very grateful for all the effort you've put into this work. I think I ought to say that he has an exceptionally high opinion of you."

"I hope you are right."

"He has made it perfectly clear—"

"I hope you are right." Suddenly his face was full of illumination, as though he were looking over my shoulder. "Then I shall go straight to him in the future."

"That may not be possible, when he's occupied—"

"That," said Brodzinski, "is for the Minister to say."

With ritual courtesy, he enquired what I should be doing for Christmas. With dignity he thanked me for entertaining him. When I took him to the top of the stairs, he gripped my hand in his immense one. I returned to the drawing-room, and stood preoccupied, not noticing acquaintances about the room, with my back to the fire. I was thinking angrily of Roger. He should have broken the news himself.

A cheerful little old man patted my arm. "I saw you caballing down there—" he pointed to the end of the room "—with that scientist chap."

"Oh yes?" I said.

"Talking a bit of shop?"

"Talking a bit of shop," I said.

I was wondering just how I could have done it better. One thing was clear: I could hardly have done it worse. I was wondering what Brodzinski would do next.

I was letting myself get worn down by one man. It seemed foolish, right out of proportion, as I stood there by the fire, in the drawing-room of the Athenaeum.

It seemed even more foolish, half an hour later, in the drawing-room of my own flat. Francis Getliffe was there before me, having come for dinner before he got the late train back to Cambridge. He was talking to Margaret, who liked him best of my old friends, who shone at him as if, in different circumstances, he might have been her choice. This was not so, and he knew it was not. She was fond of him, both because she recognised his reciprocal affection, and because she admired what his life had been. Like hers, it had been signally without equivocation. They knew how to talk to each other simply, without parentheses.

The room was bright, the pictures were lively on the walls, it was a home such as in my young manhood I thought I should never have. I mentioned that I had had a scene with Brodzinski. Margaret was smiling, because of the place where it had happened. Francis was impatient. The sooner he delivered the report to Roger, the better: as for this man, he could not see that he mattered. Nor could I, drinking before dinner in my own home.

Francis had quite a different concern. Soon after I arrived, a young man and a girl came into the room, both of them flushed. The young man was Arthur Plimpton, who immediately took charge of the drinks. He made Margaret lie back, and went round with a tinkling tray, re-filling our glasses, calling Francis and me "Sir," with his mixture of respect and impudence. The girl was Penelope, Francis's younger daughter.

She was nineteen, but looked older. She was taller than her father, Junoesque and, in a rosy, flowering fashion, beautiful. She did not much resemble either of her parents. Where that particular style of beauty came from, no one could explain; if I had not known, it would not have occurred to me that her mother was Jewish.

Arthur had managed to get his way. It had been easy to coax Margaret into inviting them to stay with us for a week. It had not been so easy for Penelope to accept. Francis, who usually rejoiced in his children's love-affairs and marriages, did not seem to rejoice in this. The fact was that someone had let him know, after Arthur had got inside the family, how rich the young man was. Francis did not like it: or rather, he would have liked them to get married, but could not let anyone see it, even his oldest friends. He would not, even by an ordinary invitation, appear to be encouraging his daughter to marry a fortune. His sense of punctilio was getting stiffer as he grew older: he had all the hard pride of the English professional classes, plus something added of his own.

It amused me, having known Francis since we were both young. I had seen him, less orthodox than now, marrying for love, but also marrying into a rich family. I had seen him defying taboos, a Gentile carrying off a Jewish girl. I had seen him less respectable than now. Other people, meeting him in his middle fifties, regarded him as he and I regarded the dignitaries of our own youth—Sir Francis Getliffe, high-principled, decent, full of *gravitas,* a little formal and, yes, a little priggish. I could not regard him so. Even when he was behaving stiffly, I could still hear, as none of us can help hearing with the friends of our youth, the chimes of another time: the "chimes of midnight," in the empty, lonely streets we had once walked together.

That did not prevent Margaret and me from twitting him, saying that he was showing ridiculous decorum, and ourselves opening our house to Arthur. I was fond of Penelope, who happened to be my goddaughter, but of the pair it was Arthur who was the more fun.

That night at dinner, he had two objectives. One was to absorb the conversation. He could not get over his discovery that Sir Francis, so eminent, so strait-laced about domestic behaviour, was, when he talked about the world, by American standards wildly radical. Arthur could not have enough of it. It shocked him, and gave him a thrill of guilt. Not, I thought, that anything Francis, Margaret or I said would affect him by as much as one per cent. But I thought also, with a certain grim satisfaction, that it would do him no harm to hear us talk about Communists as though they were human beings.

Arthur's second objective was less intellectual. It was to get Penelope to himself. Towards the end of the meal, Francis was looking at his watch. He would soon have to leave for Liverpool Street. If Arthur waited half an hour, he and Penelope could slip out without a word. But Arthur was a young man of spirit.

"Sir Francis," he said, "we will have to be going ourselves. I must say, it's been a very fine evening."

"Where are you going?" said Margaret, since Francis did not reply.

"Penny and I are going to dance someplace."

They were both waiting. Penelope, who was not talkative, had an inward-turning smile.

They might be late, Arthur went on, and asked Margaret if they could have a key.

"I'll get her back safe and sound," Arthur said to Francis. Francis nodded.

"And I'll send her back to Cambridge in time for Christmas," Arthur went on, a little lordly, and knowing it.

I joined in, to stop Arthur teasing Francis any more. I said we would all travel to Cambridge together. We were taking our children, as we did each year, to spend Christmas with my brother Martin.

Francis, back in authority again, asked us all to come to his house on Boxing Day. There was to be a great party of Francis's children, a couple of grandchildren, Martin's family and ours.

Just for an instant, Arthur looked appealing. He wanted to be invited. Francis knew it, and glanced at him from under high, quixotic eyebrows. Arthur might be obstinate, but he had met another obstinate man. This time Francis held the initiative. He did not budge. He gave no invitation. He said politely that in five minutes he must be off.

Resilient, Arthur was on his feet.

"We have to go too. Come on, Penny. It's been a very fine evening, Sir Francis."

They told Margaret they wouldn't want breakfast, and would see her later in the morning. Arthur said good-night to Francis, and Penelope kissed him. Then they went out, a handsome couple, cherishing their secrets, disclosing nothing except happiness, full of the pride of life, full of joy.

CHAPTER XVIII

THE EUPHORIA OF
TOUCHING WOOD

On a bright January morning, the telephones kept ringing in my office. Did I know, did anyone know, who was going to be the new Prime Minister? Had anyone been summoned to the Palace? All over Whitehall, all through the maze of the Treasury Building, men were gossiping. To some, in particular to Ministers like Roger, the answer mattered. To one or two, it would be decisive. No one in Roger's circle knew what it was going to be. They had not been ready for the resignation. Now the Chancellor was being backed: so was the Home Secretary. Moral sentiments were being expressed, and a good deal of damage being done.

After lunch, we heard that Charles Lenton had been sent for. There had not been such a turnover of fortune for over thirty years. By the end of the afternoon, people in high places were discovering virtues in Lenton that had not before been so vividly perceived. He was a middle-ranking Minister who had, for a short time after the war, been in charge of Hector Rose's department. He was now fifty-five, young to be Prime Minister. He was a lawyer by profession, and people commented that he must be the first Conservative Prime Minister since Disraeli without substantial private means. He was hearty, healthy, unpretentious: he looked amiable and slightly porcine, except that, as a political cartoonist and a smart photographer happily observed, he was born with bags under his eyes. Rose said: "At any rate, my dear Lewis, we shan't be dazzled by coruscations of brilliance."

Roger said nothing. He was waiting to see where the influence lay. In the London network, messages about the Prime Minister began flashing like the bulbs on a computer. Whom he listened to, where he spent the weekend, whom he had a drink with late at night.

Within three months, Roger and his friends were certain of one thing. The Prime Minister had set himself up with a confidant. This was not in itself surprising: most men in the "first place" (as some liked to call the Prime Ministership) did so. But it was more surprising when they realised who the confidant was. It was Reggie Collingwood.

From the outside, the two of them had nothing in common. Collingwood was arrogant, unsocial, in a subfusc fashion grand—whereas the Prime Minister was matey and deliberately prosaic, as though his ambition was to look natural in a bowler hat, coming in on the underground from Purley.

Yet there it was. At once the gossips were tipping Ministers whom Collingwood appeared to fancy. They all agreed that Roger's stock was on the way down.

It sounded too near the truth. I had heard from Caro herself that Collingwood had never got on with her family. They were too smart, too much in the high world, for him. Collingwood might have spent a lot of time in the high world, but he did not approve of it. As for Roger, Collingwood had had nothing to do with him. They had not had so much as a drink together. At Basset, during that weekend twelve months before, they had met like remote acquaintances: and then Roger had found himself in, or forced, a quarrel.

Before long, the gossips began to hedge. Monty Cave was brought back into the Government, and promoted to full Ministerial rank. The commentators got busy once more.

Was this a gesture towards Roger? Or was the P.M. playing both ends against the middle? Or, a more ingenious gloss, was he showing the left-wing of the party that he had nothing against them, before he eased Roger out?

A few days after Cave's appointment, I was sitting in the barber's in Curzon Street when I heard a breathy whisper near my ear. "Well, what's going to happen tomorrow night?"

As soon as I got out of the chair, I heard some more. Apparently Roger had been summoned to one of those private dinners which busybodies like my informant were beginning to know about: dinners with the Prime Minister, and Collingwood and a single guest, which took place, because Collingwood didn't like the Tory clubs, in his own suite at an old-fashioned hotel.

"Well, what are they going to say to him?"

I didn't know. I didn't even know whether the story was true. My informant was a man with a selfless passion for gossip. As I walked down the street in the sunshine, I was thinking bleakly of the old Dostoievskian phrase, that I had heard something "on not specially reliable authority."

But it was true. In forty-eight hours we knew, when Caro telephoned Margaret to ask if they could come to dinner that night, with no one present but the four of us.

They arrived very early. The sun was still high over the Park, blinding Caro as she sat down opposite the window. She screwed up her eyes, hooted, told Margaret that she wanted a drink but that Roger needed one first. Roger had scarcely spoken, and Caro's voice, as in her own house, took charge. But Margaret liked her more, and got on with her better, than I did.

Soon they were sitting side by side on the sofa, all of us suddenly quiet.

I said to Roger: "So you saw them last night, did you?"

"Why do you think," said Caro, "that we've parked ourselves on you like this?"

From his armchair, Roger was gazing, eyes blank, at the picture over the fireplace.

"How did it go?" I asked.

He muttered, as though he were having to force himself to talk.

I was at a loss. He was not inhibited because Margaret was there. He knew that she was as discreet as I was, or more so. Both he and Caro felt safe with her, and trusted her.

Roger brushed both hands over his eyes, forehead and temples, like a man trying to freshen himself.

"I don't know," he said. He leaned forward. "Look here," he said, "if I said what the position seemed like tonight— I should have to say that I've got it in the palm of my hand."

He sounded realistic, sober, baffled. He sounded as though he didn't want us to see, didn't want himself to see, that he was happy.

"Isn't that good news?" said Margaret.

"I can't quite believe it," said Roger.

"You can, you know," said Caro gently.

"You've all got to remember"—Roger was speaking with care—"that things change very fast at the top. I'm in favour now. It may not last twelve months. Things may begin to go the other way. Remember your uncle and what happened to him. *You* ought to know what to expect," he said to Caro. "So ought Lewis and Margaret. They've seen enough. For all we know, I'm at the top of the hill tonight. I may start moving downwards tomorrow. Or perhaps I've already started. We've all got to remember that."

It was the sort of solemn warning that a sanguine man gives to others, because he feels he ought to give it to himself. Roger sounded so cautious, statesmanlike and wise; he was trying to be all those things; but in his heart he didn't believe a word of it. Behind his puzzled, twisted expression, he was lit up with hope—or almost with hope realised. There were times that evening when he felt that what he wanted to do was already done. There were also times when he was thinking of his next office, and of his next office but one.

Yet, all through the evening, he spoke with self-knowledge, as though he were putting pretensions to one side, almost as though he had been deflated. It was a curious result of success, or the foretaste of success.

We stayed for a long time drinking before dinner. Yes, he had had a reception the night before that he hadn't dared imagine. The P.M. had been cordial; of course the P.M. was professionally cordial, so it didn't mean much. What did mean something was that he had assured Roger of support. As for Collingwood, he had gone out of his way to be friendly; which, from him, who never troubled to be friendly, or couldn't be, had been something no one could have expected.

"The extraordinary thing is," said Roger, his face puzzled and simple, "he seems to like me."

"Why not?" said Margaret.

"Why should he?" said Roger.

He went on:

"You know, it's the first time anyone at the top has crooked his finger at me and said in effect—'My boy, your place is up here.' Up to now they've let me crawl up and fight every inch of the way. I'm not the sort of man people feel inclined to help, you know."

He had spoken with a trace of passion. To others, I was thinking, even to me, that complaint rang strangely. He was too formidable a man for one to think of him as being "promising," as needing patronage or protection. To most men, to the Collingwoods and their kind, he must have seemed mature and dominant, even before he was forty, long before he had in any sense "arrived." Yet Roger did not see himself like that. Perhaps no one saw himself as beyond question formidable, mature, dominant. Roger knew that, when other men had been helped up, he had been left alone. He spoke as though this had been a wound: as though, years before, it had made him harden his will.

"Never mind," said Caro, "they like you, they're telling you you're in."

Roger said, "They've left it pretty late."

As we sat at dinner, he was amiable but absent-minded, until Caro, looking prettier than I had seen her, had been talking about her brother. He broke into a conversation. Across the table, he said to his wife: "It doesn't matter much being liked, for this kind of life."

We might have been back in the drawing-room, still discussing the Prime Minister and Collingwood. We hadn't realised, while we talked, that he was daydreaming contentedly away.

For a second, Caro didn't take the reference. Then she misjudged him. She said: "But they do like you."

She went on telling him that Collingwood was sincere. She seemed to be reassuring Roger that he got liked as easily as most men. But that wasn't a reassurance he needed. With a grin, part shame-faced, part sarcastic, he said: "No, that's neither here nor there. I meant, it doesn't matter much being liked. For serious purposes, it doesn't really count. Nothing like so much as your relatives have always thought."

She hesitated. His tone had not escaped her. He had spoken of "your" relatives as though he had not accepted them, would never accept them, as being his. Yet that was reversing the truth. It had not been easy for him, I had been told, at the time of his marriage. She had loved him to the highest pitch of obstinacy and they had had to put up with her decision. He was not wholly unacceptable, it wasn't as though she had been a wild young girl and he something like a dance-band leader: he was presentable, he would "do." But

he was not "one of them." They would have made him into
"one of them," if will had been the only element involved;
but they could not do it. Years later, there were times when
they still couldn't help behaving as though he were the local
doctor, or the parson, whom Caro happened to have invited
to a meal.

"That's how most of them got on," said Caro.

"Not in the real stuff," Roger replied. "What you want is
someone who believes what you do. It's preferable if he
doesn't want to cut your throat."

He was speaking as he had once done, when we were dining
at the Carlton Club. It was a theme his mind kept digging
into. Personal relations, so Roger went on saying, didn't
decide anything in the "real stuff." Being one of a group,
as with the Whig aristocrats from whom Caro's family
descended, decided much more. But in the long run, his job
didn't depend on that. In the real issues he wasn't going to
get support, just because Reggie Collingwood enjoyed
splitting a bottle with him. These things weren't as easy:
they weren't as romantic. "If they like me, and it seems that
they may do, they'll take a little longer to kick me out.
They might even kick me upstairs. But that's all the benefit
I should get out of being liked. While as for support—that's
a different cup of tea. They're going to support me for a bit
—because it fits in with what they want to do. Because they
believe we're on the same side. Up to a point. They're watching me, you know. I tell you, real politics isn't as personal as
people think."

Margaret said: "Doesn't that make it worse?"

Roger replied: "Don't you think it's probably better?"
His tone was not bantering. It wasn't even specially wise. It
was eager. Suddenly I felt in him—what was often hidden,
because of his will, his tricks, even the power of his nature—
something quite simple. He knew the temptations, the charm
of politics, the romantic trappings—but there were times

when he wanted to throw them right away. There were times when he could tell himself, and be full of faith, that there was something he wanted to do. Then he could feel that there was a justification for his life. He wanted that grace more than most men: the lumber dropped away from him, he seemed to himself light, undivided, at one.

In the drawing-room, drinking after dinner, tired, content, Roger went on talking about politics. One story had come up the night before, which Collingwood had said he ought to know. A rumour was running round about Cave's appointment. It had reached the clubs; they could expect it in the political columns next Sunday, said Collingwood, who didn't appear to know that in Whitehall we had heard it already. It was that this appointment had been the pay-off for Roger and his associates. Roger had struck a bargain with Charles Lenton when the Prime Ministership fell vacant. He and his friends would support Lenton for the place, but they had fixed the price, and the price was a Ministry for Cave.

"What do you think of that?" asked Roger. He, like Collingwood, seemed to have been surprised by the rumour. Collingwood was an unsociable widower, but I thought there was less excuse for Roger.

"Well," I said, "it's not the most terrible accusation I've ever heard." I was laughing at him. He had been enjoying himself, talking without humbug. All night his mood had been realistic, modest, almost chastened: that was the way he faced the promise of success. And yet, at this mild bid of slander, he felt indignant and ill-used.

"But it's not true!" Roger raised his voice.

"They'll say worse things than that, which won't be true either," I said.

Roger said: "No, the point is: *politics are not like that.* God knows, I've played it rougher than that before now. If necessary I shall play it rough again. But *not like that.*" He was speaking with complete reasonableness. "Of course politics can be corrupt. But not corrupt in that fashion. No one makes that kind of bargain. It's not that we're specially admirable. But we've got to make things work, and they couldn't work like that, and they don't. I've never seen anyone make a deal of that kind in my life. It's only people who don't know how the world ticks who think it ticks like that."

I was thinking I had once, twenty years before, seen someone propose such a deal. It had happened in my college. The college politicians had turned it down at sight, outraged, just as Roger was, by a man who didn't know "how the world ticks," by a man who made the world look worse than it was because he had all the cynicism of the unworldly.

We had not drawn the curtains, and through the open windows a breeze was blowing in. For an instant I leaned out. There was a smell of petrol from the Bayswater Road, mixed with the smell of spring. It was a clear night for London, and above the neon haze, over the trees in the park, I could make out some stars.

I turned back to the room. Roger was stretched out, quiet, and happy again, on the sofa. Margaret had asked him a question I did not catch. He was replying without fuss that the decisions had to be taken soon. He might soon cease to be useful. He would be lucky if he had ten years.

CHAPTER XIX

SUDDEN CESSATION
OF A NUISANCE

It puzzled me, not that Brodzinski kept pressing for a
private talk with Roger, but that all of a sudden he left off
doing so. Once he had given me up, letters came into Roger's
office. Brodzinski begged for an interview on a matter of
grave public concern. He wished to explain his disagreement
with his scientific colleagues. He had been alarmed by the
attitude of the secretary of the committee.

It was a nuisance, but Ministers' offices were used to
nuisances. Roger asked Osbaldiston to see Brodzinsky. Douglas, more guarded and official than I had been, gave a reply
as though to a Parliamentary Question: no, the Minister had
not reached a conclusion: he was studying both the majority
report and Brodzinski's minority report. For a few days, this
seemed to reassure Brodzinski. Then the letters began again.
Once more I told Roger not to underestimate him.

Roger asked, what could he do? Write to the *Times?* Talk
to the Opposition military spokesmen? There were
safeguarded. We had, through Francis Getliffe and others,
our own contacts. Francis and I had, for years, been closer
to them than to Roger's colleagues. What could the man do?
I had to agree. After the talk in the Athenaeum, I had come
away apprehensive. Now the anxiety had lost its edge. As out
of habit, I repeated that Roger ought to have a word with
him.

On the Thursday which followed his dinner with the Prime Minister, Roger had been invited to a conversazione of the Royal Society. The day after, he mentioned that he had spent a quarter of an hour with Brodzinski alone.

It looked as though Roger had spread himself. The next letter from Brodzinski said he had always known that the Minister understood. If they could continue the conversation undisturbed, he, Brodzinski, was certain that all the obstacles would be removed. In a few days Roger replied politely. Another letter arrived by return. Then telephone calls. Would the Minister's Private Secretary arrange a meeting? Could the Minister be told that Brodzinski was on the line? Could he be put straight through?

Suddenly it all stopped. No more telephone calls. No more letters. It was bewildering. I took what precautions I could. We knew his points of influence in the Air Ministry, in the House. Was he pressing them, instead? But no: he seemed not to have been near them. There was no disquiet anywhere, there were not even any rumours hissing round.

The patient young men in Roger's private office allowed themselves a shrug of relief. He had got tired of it at last, they said. Four months of commotion: then absolute silence. From their records, they could date when silence fell. It was the third week in May.

In that same week, I happened to have been enquiring whether certain invitations to accept Honours had been sent out. My question had nothing to do with Brodzinski, though I thought mechanically that his invitation must have gone out too. It did not occur to me, not remotely, to connect the two dates.

As the summer began, all of us round Roger were more confident than we had yet been. First drafts of the White Paper were being composed. Francis Getliffe came from Cambridge twice a week to confer with Douglas and Walter Luke. Papers passed between Douglas's office and Rose's. Roger had issued an instruction that the office draft must be ready for him by August. Then he would publish when he guessed the time was right. In private, he was preparing for the month after Christmas, the beginning of 1958.

While we were drafting, Diana Skidmore was going through her standard summer round. On the last day of Ascot Week, she invited some of us to a party in South Street. She had heard—as though she had a ticker-tape service about American visitors—that David Rubin was in England. She had not met him: "He's brilliant, isn't he?" she asked. Yes, I assured her, he was certainly brilliant. "Bring him along," she ordered. There had been a time when the Basset circle was supposed to be anti-Semitic. That, at least, had changed.

When Margaret, David Rubin and I stood at the edge of Diana's drawing-room, about seven o'clock on the wet June evening, not much else seemed to have changed. The voices were as hearty as ever: the champagne went round as fast: the women stood in their Ascot frocks, the men in their Ascot uniforms. There were a dozen Ministers there, several of the Opposition front bench, many Conservative members, and a few from the other side.

There was a crowd of Diana's rich friends. She welcomed us with vigour. Yes, she knew that David Rubin was talking to the English nuclear scientists.

"People over here being sensible?" she said to him. "Come and tell me about them. I'll arrange something next week." She was peremptory as usual, and yet, because she took it for granted that it was for her to behave like a prince, to open England up to him, he took it for granted too.

How was it, I had sometimes wondered, that, despite her use of her riches, she didn't attract more resentment? Even when she put a hand, with complete confidence, into any kind of politics? She had been drawn back into the swirling, meaty, noisy gaggle: there she was, listening deferentially to a handsome architect. Even in her devoted marriage, she had had a hankering for one *guru* after another. Just as she took it for granted that she could talk to Ministers, so she loved being a pupil. If it seemed a contradiction to others, it seemed natural to her, and that was all she cared about.

Margaret had been taken away by Monty Cave. I noticed Rubin being shouted at hilariously by Sammikins. I walked round the party, and then, half an hour after we came in, found myself by Rubin's side again. He was watching the crowd with his air of resignation, of sad intelligence.

"They're in better shape, aren't they?" He meant that these people, or some of them, had lost their collective confidence over Suez. Now they were behaving as though they had found it again. Rubin knew, as well as I did, that political sorrows did not last long. Political memory lasted about a fortnight. It did not count beside a new love-affair, a new job, even, for many of these men, the active glow after making a good speech.

"No country's got a ruling class like this." David Rubin opened his hands towards the room. "I don't know what they hope for, and they don't know either. But they still feel they're the lords of this world."

I was fond of Rubin and respected him, but his reflections on England were irking me. I said he mustn't judge the country by this group. Being born in my provincial town wasn't much different from being born in Brooklyn. He ought to know the boys I grew up among. Rubin interrupted, with a sharp smile:

"No. You're a far-sighted man, I know it, Lewis. But you're just as confident in yourself as these characters are." Once more he shrugged at the room. "You don't believe a single thing that they believe, but you've borrowed more from them than you know."

People were going out to dinner, and the party thinned. Gradually those who were left came to the middle of the room. There stood Diana and her architect, Sammikins and two decorative women, Margaret and Lord Bridgewater, and a few more. I joined the group just as David Rubin came up from the other side with Cave's wife, who was for once out with her husband. She was ash-blonde, with a hard, strained, beautiful face. Rubin had begun to enjoy himself. He might have a darker world view than anyone there, but he gained certain consolations.

No one could talk much, in that inner residue of the party, but Sammikins. He was trumpeting away with a euphoria startling even by his own standards. Just as Diana had lost money at Ascot, he had won. With the irrationality of the rich, Diana had been put out. With the irrationality of the harassed, which he would remain until his father died, Sammikins was elated. He wanted to entertain us all. He spoke with the luminosity of one who saw that his financial problems had been settled forever. "All the time I was at school," he cried, "m' tutor gave me one piece of advice. He said, 'Houghton, never go in for horse-racing. They suck you in.'" Sammikins caught sight of David Rubin, and raised his voice once more. "What do you think of that, Professor? What do you think of that for a piece of advice? Not à *point*, eh?"

David Rubin did not much like being called Professor. Also, he found Sammikins's allusions somewhat esoteric. But he grappled. He replied: "I'm afraid I have to agree with your friend."

"M' tutor."

"Anyway, he's right. Statistically, he must be right."

"Horses are better than cards, any day of the week. Damn it all, Professor, I've proved it!"

David Rubin was getting noise-drunk. Sammikins, in a more conciliatory tone, went on: "I grant you this, Professor, I don't know about roulette. I've known men who made an income at roulette."

The scientific truth was too strong for Rubin.

"No. If you played roulette for infinite time, however you played, you'd be bound to lose." He took Sammikins by the arm. We had the pleasant spectacle of Rubin, Nobel-Laureate, most elegant of conceptual thinkers, not quite sober, trying to explain to Sammikins, positive that he had found the secret of prosperity, distinctly drunk, about the theory of probability.

Diana said, in her clear, military rasp, that racing was a mug's game. On the other hand, she was sharp with happiness. She wanted to have dinner with the architect. It was only out of duty, as we were all ready to go, that she mentioned the Government.

"They seem to be getting on a bit better," she said.

There were murmurs of agreement all round her.

"Roger's doing all right," she said to me. She was not asking my opinion, she was telling me.

She went on: "Reggie Collingwood thinks well of him." We were getting near the door. Diana said: "Yes. Reggie says he's a good listener."

Diana had passed on the good news, and I went away happy. Objectively, Collingwood's statement was true; but, from a man who could hardly utter about one of the most eloquent men in London, it seemed an odd compliment.

CHAPTER XX

EVENING IN
THE PARK

In September, with the House in recess, Roger kept coming to his office. It was what the civil servants called the "leave season." Douglas was away and so, in my department, was Hector Rose. Nevertheless, Roger's secretaries were arranging a set of meetings to which I had to go. As I arrived in his room for one of them, Roger asked in a matter-of-fact tone if I minded staying behind after it was over. He had something he wanted to talk to me about, so he said.

He seemed a little preoccupied as he took the meeting. When he spoke, he was fumbling for the words, as a man does when he is tired and strained. I did not take much notice. The meeting was purring efficiently on. There were some unfamiliar faces, deputy secretaries, under-secretaries, appearing instead of their bosses. The competent voices carried on, the business was getting done.

The cups of tea were brought in, the weak and milky tea, the plates of biscuits. The meeting was doing all that Roger wanted. He might be tired, but he was showing good judgment. He did not hurry them, he let the decisions form. It was past six o'clock when the papers were being packed in the brief cases. Practised and polite, Roger said his good-evenings and his thanks, and we were left alone.

"That went rather well," I said.

There was a pause, as though he had to remember what I was speaking about, before he replied: "Yes, it did, didn't it?"

I was standing up, stretching myself. He had stayed in his chair. He looked up without expression, and asked:

"Do you mind if we go for a stroll in the Park?"

We went down the corridors, down the stone stairs, out through the main entrance. We crossed over the Park by the lake; one of the pelicans was spreading its wings. The trees were creaking in a blustery wind; on the grass, the first leaves had fallen. It was a dark evening, with clouds, low and grey, driving across from the west. Roger had not spoken since we left the office. For an instant, I was not thinking of him. The smell of the water, of the autumn night, had filled me with a sense, vague but overmastering, of sadness and joy, as though I were played on by a memory which I could not in truth recall, of a place not far away, of a time many years before, when my first love, long since dead, had told me without kindness that she would come to me.

We walked slowly along the path. Girls, going home late from the offices, were scurrying in front of us. It was so windy that most of the seats by the lakeside were empty. Suddenly Roger said:

"Shall we sit down?"

Miniature waves were flecking the water. As we sat and watched them, Roger, without turning to me, said in a curt, flat and even tone:

"There may possibly be trouble. I don't think it's likely, but it's possible."

I was shocked out of my reverie. My first thought was to ask if any of his supporters, high or low, Collingwood or the back-benchers, had turned against him.

"No. Nothing like that. Nothing like that at all."

Was he trying to break some news affecting me? I had

nothing on my mind, I could not think what it might be. I
gave him a chance to tell me, but he shook his head.

Now it had come to the point, the confidence would not
flow. He stared at the water. At last he said:

"I have a young woman."

For the instant, I felt nothing but surprise.

"We've kept it absolutely quiet. Now she's been threatened. Someone's found out."

"Who has?"

"Just a voice she didn't know, over the telephone," he
said.

"Does it matter?"

"How do we know?"

"What are you frightened of?"

There was a pause before he said:

"If it came out it might do some harm."

I was still surprised. I had thought his marriage happy
enough. A man of action's marriage, not all-excluding; but
strong, a comfort, an alliance. Some of his worry was infecting
me. I felt an irritation, an impatience, that I could not keep
quiet. What more did he want? I was asking myself, as
simply, as uncharitably as my mother might have done.
A good-looking wife, children, a rich home: what was he taking risks for? Risks, he seemed to think, which might damage
his plans and mine. I was condemning him as simply as that,
not in the least like one who had seen people in trouble, not
like one who had done harm himself.

At the same time, I could not help feeling a kind of
warmth, not affection so much as a visceral warmth. In the
midst of his anxiety, he had been half-pleased to confess. Not
with just the pleasure displayed by men higher-minded than
he was, as they modestly admit a conquest—no, with a
pleasure deeper than that, something more like joy. Looking
at him as he sat, still gazing at the lake, not meeting my eyes,
I should have guessed that he had not had much to do with

women. But his emotions were powerful and, perhaps, so could his passions be. As he sat there, his face heavy, thinking of the dangers, he seemed comforted by what had happened to him—like a man for whom the promise of life is still there. I set myself to ask a practical question. What were the chances of it coming out?

"She's worried. I've never known her lose her nerve before."

I said probably she had never had to cope with a scandal. But the technique was all worked out. Go to a good tough lawyer. Tell everything.

"You've no reason to think that any rumours have gone round already, have you? I certainly haven't."

Roger shook his head.

"Then it ought to be fairly easy to stop the hole."

He did not respond, or look at me. He stared into the distance. In a moment, knowing that I was giving him no comfort, I broke off.

I said: "I'm sure this can be handled. You ought to tell her that. But even if it couldn't be, and the worst came to the worst—is it the end of the world?" I meant, as I went on to say, that the people he lived amongst were used to scandals out of comparison more disreputable than this.

"You're fooling yourself," he said harshly. "It isn't so easy."

I wondered, was he holding something back? Was she very young? "Is there something special about it?" I said. "Who is she?"

It seemed that he could not reply. He sat without speaking, and then in a burst of words put me off.

"It isn't important what's done. It is important who does it. There are plenty of people—you know as well as I do—who want an excuse to knife me. Don't you accept that this would be a reasonable excuse?"

"You haven't told me how."

"There's an old maxim in the Anglican church. You can

get away with unorthodox behaviour. Or you can get away with unorthodox doctrine. But you can't get away with both of them at the same time."

For an instant, his spirits had flashed up. In the same sharp, realistic, almost amused tone, he added:

"Remember, I've never been one of the family. Perhaps, if I had been, I could get away with more."

What was "the family?"

The inner circle of privilege, the Caves, Wyndhams, Collingwoods, Diana's friends, the Bridgewaters, the people who, though they might like one another less than they liked Roger, took one another for granted, as they did not take him.

"No," I said, "you've never been one of them. But Caro is."

I brought in her name deliberately. There was a silence. Then he answered the question I had not asked. "If this thing breaks, Caro will stand by me."

"She doesn't know?"

He shook his head, and then broke out with violence: "I won't have Caro hurt." It sounded more angry than anything he had said. Had he been talking about one worry, about the practical risk that still seemed to me unreal, in order to conceal another from himself? What kind of guilt did he feel, how much was he tied? All of a sudden, I thought I understood at last his outburst on Sammikin's behalf at Basset. It had seemed uncomfortable, untypical, not only to the rest of us but to himself. Yes, it had been chivalrous, it had been done for Caro's sake. But it had been altogether too chivalrous. It had the strain, the extravagant self-abnegation, of a man who gives his wife too many sacrifices, just to atone for not giving her his love.

"Isn't Caro going to be hurt anyway?" I said.

He did not reply.

"This affair isn't ready to stop, is it?"

"Not for either of us. Not for—" He hesitated. He still

had not told me the woman's name. Now he wanted to, but at last brought out the pronoun, not the name.

"Can you give her up?"

"No," said Roger.

Beneath the layers of worry, there was something else pressing him. Part joy: part something else again, which I could feel in the air, but to which I could not put a name—as though it were a superstitious sense, a gift of foresight.

He leaned back, and did not confide any more.

To the left, above the trees, the light from a window shone out—an office window, perhaps in Roger's Ministry, though I could not be sure—a square of yellow light high in the dark evening.

III
PRIVACY

CHAPTER XXI

BREAKFAST

It was the morning after Roger had talked to me in the Park, and Margaret and I were sitting at breakfast. From the table, I could look down at the slips of garden running behind the Tyburn chapel. I glanced across at my wife, young-looking in her dressing-gown, fresh, not made up. Sometimes I laughed at her for looking so fresh in the morning: for in fact it was I who woke up easily, while she was slumbrous, not at her best, until she had sat beside the window and drunk her first cups of tea.

That morning, she was not too slumbrous to read my expression. She knew that I was worrying, and asked me why. At once I told her Roger's story. I didn't think twice about telling her; we had no secrets, I wanted to confide. She wasn't intimate with Roger as I was, nor with Caro either, and I didn't expect her to be specially concerned. To my surprise, her colour rose. Her cheeks flushed, making her eyes look bluer still. She muttered: "Damn him."

"He'll be all right—" I was consoling her; but she broke out:

"Never mind about him. I was thinking of Caro."

She said:

"You haven't given her a thought, have you?"

"There are two other people as well—"

"He's behaved atrociously, and she's the one who's going to face it."

As a rule, she was no more given to this kind of moral indignation than I was myself. Already her temper was high and mine was rising. I tried to quieten us both, and said, in the shorthand we were used to, that Roger wasn't the first person in the world to cut loose: others had done the same.

"If you mean that I damaged someone else to come to you," she flared up, "that's true."

"I didn't mean that."

I had spoken without thinking.

"I know you didn't." Her temper broke, she smiled. "You know, I'd behave the same way again. But I haven't much to be proud of in that respect."

"Nor have I."

"You didn't betray your own marriage. That's why I can't brush off Roger betraying his."

"You say I'm not giving Caro a thought?" Once more we were arguing, once more we were near to quarrelling. "But how much are you giving him?"

"You said yourself, he'll be all right, he'll come through," she said scornfully. Just then she had no feeling for him at all. "Do you know what it's going to be like for her—if they break up?" She went on with passion. "Shock. Humiliation. Loss."

I was forced to think, Caro had been happy, she had paraded her happiness. She had done much for him—perhaps too much? Had he ever accepted it, or the way her family looked at him?

All that I had to admit. And yet, I said, trying to sound reasonable, let's not make it over-tragic. If it came to losing him, wouldn't she recover? She was still young, she was pretty, she wasn't a delicate flower, she was rich. How long would it take her to get another husband?

"You're making it too easy for yourselves," said Margaret.

"Who am I making it too easy for?"

"For him. And for yourself." Her eyes were snapping.

"Losing him," she said, "that might be the least of it. It will be bad enough. But the humiliation will be worse." She added:

"You've always said Caro doesn't give a damn. Any more than her brother does. But it's people who don't give a damn who can't bear being humiliated. They can't live with it, when they have to know what it means."

I was thinking, Margaret was speaking of what she knew. She too, by nature, by training, made her own rules: they were more refined rules than Caro's, but they were just as independent. Her family and all her Bloomsbury connections cared no more what others thought than Caro's did, in some ways less. She knew just how vulnerable that kind of independence was.

She knew something deeper. When she and I first married she had sometimes been frightened: should we come apart? I might think that I had come home. In her heart, knowing mine, she had not been as sure. She had told herself what she must be ready to feel and what it would cost.

Hearing of Roger and Caro, she felt those fears, long since buried, flood back. Suddenly I realised why the argument had mounted into a quarrel. I stopped my next retort, I stopped defending Roger. Instead, I said, looking into her eyes:

"It's a bad thing to be proud, isn't it?"

The words meant nothing to anyone in the world except ourselves. To her, they were saying that I had been at fault and so had she. At once there was nothing between us. The quarrel died down, the tingle of rancour died from the air, and across the table Margaret gave an open smile.

CHAPTER XXII

"THE KNIVES ARE SHARPENING"

One evening in the week that Roger made his confidence, Hector Rose sent his compliments to my office and asked if I could find it convenient to call upon him. After I had traversed the ten yards along the corridor, I was, as usual, greeted with gratitude for this athletic feat. "My dear Lewis, how very, very good of you to come!"

He installed me in the chair by his desk, from which I could look out over the sun-speckled trees, as though this were my first visit to his room. He sat in his own chair, behind the chrysanthemums, and gave me a smile of dazzling meaninglessness. Then, within a second, he had got down to business.

"There's to be a Cabinet committee," he said, "by which our masters mean, with their customary happy use of words, something to which the phrase is not appropriate. However, there it is."

The committee was to "have an oversight" of some of Roger's problems, in particular the White Paper. It consisted of Collingwood in the chair, Roger himself, Cave, and our own Minister. According to present habit, there would be a floating and varying population, Ministers, civil servants, scientists, attending on and off, which was why Rose had produced his jibe. "In fact," he said, "you and I will no doubt have the inestimable privilege of attending some of the performances ourselves."

For an instant, Rose's tidy mind was preoccupied with the shapelessness of new-style administration; but I broke in:

"What does this mean?"

"By itself,"—he came back to business with a bite—"it doesn't mean anything. Or at least anything significant, should you say? The membership seems to be designed to strengthen Mr. Quaife's hand. I seem to have heard, from sensible sources, that the Lord President" (Collingwood) "is a moderately strong backer of Quaife. So, on the face of it, there ought to be certain advantages for policies which Mr. Quaife and others appear to have at heart."

He was baiting me, but not in his customary machine-like manner. He seemed uncomfortable. He folded his arms. His head did not move, but his light eyes fixed themselves on mine. "You asked me an implied question," he said curtly. "I can't be certain, but I have a suspicion the answer is yes." He added: "I fancy you do, too. I may be wrong, but I think I ought to warn you that the knives are sharpening."

"What evidence have you got?"

"Not much. Nothing very considerable." He hesitated. "No, I shouldn't feel at liberty to worry you with that."

Again he had spoken with discomfort, as though—I could neither understand, nor believe it—he was protecting me.

"Do you mean that I'm personally involved?"

"I don't feel at liberty to speak. I'm not going to worry you unnecessarily."

Nothing would budge him. At last he said:

"But I do feel at liberty to say just one thing. I think you might reasonably communicate to your friends that a certain amount of speed about their decisions might not come amiss. In my judgment, the Opposition is going to increase the more chance it gets to form. I shouldn't have thought that this was a time for going slow." As deliberately as another man might light a cigarette, he smelled a flower. "I confess, I should rather like to know exactly what our friend Douglas Osbaldiston expects to happen. He has always had a remarkably shrewd nose for the way the wind is blowing. It's a valuable gift. Of course, he's a great friend of both of us, but I think it's fair comment to say that this particular gift hasn't exactly been a handicap to him in his career."

I had never known Hector Rose behave like this. First, he had told me, not quite "in terms" (as he would have said himself) but still definitely, that he was supporting Roger's policy. That was surprising. I had assumed that he started, like Douglas and his colleagues, suspicious of it. He might have become convinced by reason: with Rose, more than most men, that could conceivably happen: or else the events of Suez were still working changes in him. Still, it was a surprise. But far more of a surprise was his outburst about Douglas.

I had known Hector Rose for nearly twenty years. In all that time, I had not heard him pass a judgment on any of his equals. Not that he did not make them—but keeping them quiet was part of the disciplined life. I had known for years that he probably disliked, and certainly envied, Douglas. He knew that I knew. Yet I was astonished, and perhaps he was too, that he should let it out.

Just then the telephone rang. It was for me: Francis Getliffe had called at my office. When I told Rose he said:

"I think, if he wouldn't mind, I should rather like him to spare me five minutes."

After I had given the message, Rose regarded me as though, for the second time that evening, he could not decide whether to speak or not. He said: "You'll have a chance to talk to him later, will you?"

"I should think so," I said.

"In that case, I should be grateful if you passed on the substance of what I've been telling you."

"You mean, there's going to be trouble?"

"There are certain advantages in being prepared, shouldn't you say?"

"Including personal trouble?"

"That's going further than I was prepared to go."

Yet he wanted Francis Getliffe to know about it, and he also wanted to avoid telling him.

When Francis came into the room, however, Rose was so polite that he seemed to be caricaturing himself. "My dear Sir Francis, it really is extraordinarily good of you! I didn't expect to have this pleasure—" All the time he was brandishing Francis's title; while Francis, who was not undisposed to formality himself, insisted on calling him "Secretary." They sounded, I thought impatiently, used to it as I was, like two 17th Century Spaniards: but that wasn't fair. They really sounded like two official mid-20th Century Englishmen. In fact, they respected each other. Rose liked Francis much more than he did me.

Rose did not keep us long. He asked Francis if he were happy about the work of the scientific committee. Yes, said Francis. Was he, if it came to a public controversy—"and I'm sure you don't need me to tell you, but there may be mild repercussions"—willing to put the weight of his authority behind it?

"Yes," said Francis, and added, what else could he do?

There were thanks, courtesies, goodbyes, more thanks and courtesies. Soon Francis and I were walking across the Park to the Duke of York's Steps. "What was that in aid of?" Francis asked.

"He was telling you that there's going to be a Godalmighty row."

"I suppose we had to expect it, didn't we?"

"More than we bargained on, I fancy." I repeated what Rose had said to me. I went on: "He can be so oblique that it drives you mad, but he was suggesting that I'm going to be shot at."

On the grass, couples were lying in the sunshine. Francis walked on, edgy, preoccupied. He said that he didn't see how that could happen. It was more likely to happen to himself.

I said: "Look, no one wants to bring bad news. But I've got a feeling, though Rose didn't say a positive word, that he thinks that too."

Francis said, "I'm tired of all this."

We went a few yards in silence. He added:

"If we get this business through, then I shall want to drop out. I don't think I can take it any more." He began to talk about the international situation: what did I think? Intellectually, he still stuck to his analysis. The technical and military arguments all pointed the same way: peace was becoming much more likely than war. Intellectually he still believed that. Did I? Yet when Quaife and the scientists tried to take one tiny step, not dramatic, quite realistic, then all Hell was ready to break loose.

"Sometimes I can't help thinking that people won't see sense in time. I don't mean that people are wicked. I don't even mean they're stupid. But we're all in a mad bus, and the only thing we're all agreed on is to prevent anyone getting to the wheel."

We were climbing up the steps. He said sharply:

"Lewis, I could do with some advice."

For a second, I was afraid he was thinking of resigning. Instead he went on:

"I just don't know what to do about Penelope and that young man."

His tone had become even more worried and sombre. On the way across the Park he, who knew more about it than most men, had been gloomy over the military future. Now he spoke as though his daughter had really been the problem on his mind. He spoke exactly as a Victorian parent might have spoken, as though all the future were predictable and secure except for his daughter's marriage, and the well-being of his grandchildren.

He was on his way, he said, to meet her in the Ladies' Annexe of the club (the Athenaeum). Would I come too? It might help him out. He hadn't the slightest idea of what had been happening, or what she planned. He did not know whether she and Arthur were secretly engaged, or had even thought of getting married. Arthur had, that summer, returned home to America. Francis did not know whether they had quarrelled.

He did not know—but this he didn't say, for she was his daughter, and both of us were talking more prudishly than if she had been another girl—whether she had been sleeping with Arthur. For myself, in private, I thought it highly probable.

As we sat in the drawing-room of the Annexe, waiting for her, Francis looked more baffled than I had known him. Both he and his wife were lost. Penelope was more obstinate than either of them, and she wasn't given to explaining herself. She had never been an academic girl: she had taken some sort of secretarial course, and she showed about as much interest in Francis's scientific friends as she would have done in so many Amazonian Indians. At present, however, she was prepared to recognise their existence. It had occurred to her that some of them lived in the United States; no doubt one could be persuaded to give her a job.

"I've got to stop it," said Francis, as we went on waiting. "I can't have her going over." He spoke resolutely, like King Lear in the storm, and about as convincingly. He had already ordered a bottle of champagne, with the air of a man trying to keep an exigent girl-friend in a good temper.

At last she came in, with her flouncing walk, flushed, handsome, frowning. "I thought it was number twelve," she said.

She gazed at us firmly, giving us the blame for her own mistake.

"As you see," I replied, "you thought wrong."

"It used to be number twelve."

"Never."

"I remember *going* to number twelve." She spoke with an extreme display of mumpsimus, persisting confidently in error.

"In that case, either you remember wrong, or you went to the wrong place before."

She stopped lowering, and gave me an open, happy grin. I could imagine what Arthur and others saw in her.

With a healthy thirst, she put down two glasses of champagne.

Francis's manner to her was courteous but uneasy, very much as when he was talking to Hector Rose. He told her that ———— from Oxford was dining with them. "How old is he?" Penelope sat up.

"Forty-seven or -eight."

Penelope sank back.

"Now if you'd ever seen him," I remarked, "you'd certainly have put on a new dress."

"Of course I shouldn't." Then a thought struck her. "Does he know people in America?"

"Why America?" I said, trying to help Francis out.

"Oh, I'm going there this fall or next spring."

Francis cleared his throat. Screwing himself up, he said:

"I'm sorry, Penny, but I wish you'd get that out of your mind."

"Why?"

"Because I'm afraid it can't happen."

"We'll see."

Francis took the plunge.

"I don't mean that we couldn't find a way for you to earn your keep. I expect we could—"

"Then let's get going!" said Penelope, with enthusiasm.

"That isn't the point. Don't you see it isn't?"

Francis paused: then rushed on:

"Don't you see, we can't let you deposit yourself on young Plimpton's doorstep?"

"Why not?"

Penelope stretched herself luxuriously, with the poised expression of one who has said her last word for the evening.

Francis continued a one-sided conversation, without answers. Didn't she see that they couldn't let her? Didn't she realise that they had to behave like responsible persons?

Suddenly his tone became gentler, and even more embarrassed. He said: "All that's bad enough, but there's something worse."

This time she responded:

"What's that?"

"My dear girl, I'm not going to ask you what your feelings are for young—Arthur, or what his are for you. I don't think any of us is entitled to ask that."

She gazed at him with splendid grey eyes, her face quite unreadable.

"But suppose you do care for him, and something went wrong? You're both very young, and the chances are that something will go wrong. Well, if you've gone over to be with him, and then you're left alone—that's a risk I just can't think of your taking."

Penelope gave a gnomic smile and said:

"When I go to America I may not see Arthur at all."

CHAPTER XXIII

VISIT TO A SMALL
SITTING-ROOM

It was still September. In the middle of the morning, the telephone rang on my desk. My personal assistant was speaking: someone called Ellen Smith was on the line, asking to talk to me urgently. The name meant nothing: what did she want? No, said the P.A., she had refused to say. I hesitated. This was one of the occupational risks. Then I said, "All right, put her through."

"My name is Ellen Smith." The voice was brisk and cultivated. "I've met you once before."

I said "Yes?" But I did not remember.

"I think Roger—Roger Quaife—has told you, hasn't he?"

Now I understood.

"He's given me permission," she went on, "to talk to you myself. Do you mind?"

Would I call at her flat one evening, when she had got back from her job? That would be better than saying anything on the telephone, didn't I agree? She didn't want to impose on me, but she was worried. She hoped I could bear it.

She sounded precise, nervous, active. I had no impression of her at all. On the way to her flat in Ebury Street, I thought to myself that it was well-placed for Westminster—chance or not. But about her, I did not know whether she was single or married, nor anything else.

When she opened the door to me, the first thing I felt was the obvious, the banal irony. She seemed familiar, yet I could not place her. She shook hands with an expression both diffident and severe. She was small and slender, but not at all frail, dark-haired, wearing a white jersey over a black skirt. She was no younger than Caro. By the side of Caro, the confident, the splendid, she would have looked insignificant. One memory, though not about herself, came back with the relevance of someone telling one the time, and I remembered Caro, gay in the drawing-room at Lord North Street, roaring with laughter and saying the woman a wife needs to fear isn't the raving beauty, but that little grey mouse in the corner. It seemed the most cut and dried of ironies to remember that, and then to follow Ellen Smith into her chic, small sitting-room. I still could not recall meeting her, or anything about her.

She poured me a drink. She drew her legs onto the sofa, the tumblers on the table between us.

"It's kind of you to come," she said.

"Nonsense," I replied, a little over-heartily.

"Is it nonsense?" She looked at me. For an instant I had Caro's eyes in mind, bold, full, innocent. These eyes were not bold, but deeper-set, lit up with attention, lit up with insight. Then the contrast faded out. I was studying her face, not beautiful, not pretty, but fine and delicate. The delicacy, the acuteness of her expression, struck one more when one looked up from her strong shoulders. She smiled, diffidently and honestly. "This is damned awkward," she said.

Suddenly a memory flashed back—was it because my fingers were cold against the glass? The Ambassadorial house in Regent's Park, the night of Suez, the wife of J. C. Smith.

So this was she. Yes, it was awkward, though that was not what she meant. Smith, Collingwood's nephew, fanatical, dedicated, so people said about him: I had read some of his speeches and articles: they had a curious gritty violence. They were shot through with a conspiratorial feeling of history and politics: and yet I had met young Conservative members who worshipped him. The wife of J. C. Smith. Yes, it was awkward. I said something muted, such as, the less she fretted the better.

This time her smile was brilliant.

"That's easier said than done, you know."

I tried to take the edge off both of us. I asked what she had been doing that day. She told me that she had been out as usual at her job. She seemed to be working in a reference library. We mentioned the names of acquaintances, among them Lord Lufkin. I said that I had once worked for him. "I'm sure that was good for you," she said with a faint flash of mischief. Strained as she was, her spirits did not take much to revive them. She did not forget about my comfort, either. The glass was refilled, the cigarette-box was open. She broke out: "I am not fretting about him and me. You do believe that, don't you?"

She went on: "I'm happy about us. I'm happier than I've ever been in my life. And I think he's happy too. It sounds too conceited to live, but I think he's happy too."

She had no conceit at all, I was thinking, far too little for her own good.

She had spoken so directly that I could do the same. I asked, where was her husband, what had happened to her marriage? She shook her head.

"I've got to tell you," she said. "It sounds ugly. If I heard it about someone else, I should write her off. I know I should." She said that, besides Roger, only her husband's parents knew the truth about him. It was to be kept a dead secret. Then she said, flat and hard: "He's in a mental home." It wasn't certain that he would get better, she said. His constituency had been told that he was ill and might not contest his seat at the next election.

"It's been coming on for years. Yes, and that hasn't stopped me. I saw the chance to be happy, and I took it." She looked at me with an expression honest, guilty and stern. "I'm not going to make excuses. But you might believe this. It sounds disloyal, but if he hadn't been getting unbalanced I should have left him long ago. I tried to look after him. If it hadn't been for that, I should have left him long before Roger came along." She gave a sharp-eyed smile, not merciful to herself. "There's something wrong with a woman who falls for a man she can't endure and then for one she can't marry, isn't there?"

"It could be bad luck."

"It's not all bad luck." Then she said, without pretence: "But, do you know, just now I can't feel that there's much wrong with me. You can understand that, can't you?"

She laughed out loud. One couldn't doubt her warmth, her ardour, her capacity for happiness. And yet I felt that this was not a life for which she was made. Plenty of women I knew in London made the best of this sort of bachelor life in flats like this—though hers was brighter, more expensive, than most of theirs. Plenty of women came back from offices as she did, looked after their little nests, waited for their men. Some of them could take it: light come, light go. Some even felt their blood run hotter because they had to keep a secret, because the curtains were drawn and they were listening—alone—for the snap of the lift-door. Looking at Ellen, I was sure that, though she would bear it in secrecy if she couldn't get him any other way, she was paying a price, maybe higher than she knew.

I asked how long had their affair been going on.

"Three years," she said.

That set me back. Three years. All the time I had known him well. For an instant I was piqued, at having noticed nothing.

There was a silence. Her eyes, dark blue, painfully honest, were studying me. She said:

"I want to ask you something. Very seriously."

"Yes?" I replied.

"Ought I to get out of it?"

I hesitated.

"Is that a fair question?" I asked.

"Isn't it?"

I said: "But could you get out of it?"

Her eyes stayed steady. She did not reply. After a moment she said: "I couldn't do him harm. We've been good for each other. You'd expect him to be good for me, of course, but somehow it isn't all one-sided. I don't know why, but sometimes I think I've been good for him." She was speaking simply, tentatively: then she broke out: "Anyway, it would be the end for me if I let him go."

Her voice had risen; tears had come. With a rough, schoolgirlish gesture, she brushed her cheeks with the back of her fingers. Then she sniffled, and made herself go on in a braver tone. "But I couldn't do him harm, you know that, don't you?"

"I think I do."

"I believe in what he's doing. You believe in it, isn't that true?" She said she wasn't "political," but she was shrewd. She knew where his position was weak.

She gave a sharp smile: "I'm not fooling you, am I? I'm not the sort of person to make gestures. Naturally I couldn't do him harm. I couldn't bear to damage his career, just because it's him. But I couldn't bear to damage him—because I'm pretty selfish. If he suffered any sort of public harm because of him and me, he'd never really forgive me. Do you think he would?"

I noticed, not for the first time, her curious trick of throwing questions at me, questions about herself which I could not have enough knowledge to answer. In another woman, it would have seemed like an appeal for attention—"Look at *me*!"—an opening gambit to intimacy, to flirtation. But she was not thinking of me at all as a man, only as someone who might help her. This was her method, not precisely of confiding so much as of briefing me, so that if the chance came I could be some use.

I said something non-committal.

"No," she said, "it would be the end."

In an even, realistic, almost sarcastic tone, she added: "So I get the rough end of the stick, however I play it."

I wanted to comfort her. I told her the only use I could be was practical. What was happening now? Had she been to a lawyer? What else had she done?

Up till then, she had been too apprehensive to get to the facts. And yet, was that really so? She was apprehensive, all right, but she had spirit and courage. In theory, she had asked me there to talk about the facts. After the years of silence, though, it was a release to have a confidant. Even for her, who had so little opinion of herself—perhaps most of all for her— it was a luxury to boast a little.

The facts did not tell me much. Yes, she had been to a law- yer. He had got her telephone calls intercepted: once or twice the voice had broken through. Always from call-boxes, noth- ing to identify it. The same voice? Yes. What sort? Not quite out of the top drawer, said Ellen, just as Mrs. Henneker would have said it, as only an Englishwoman would have said it. Rough? Oh no. Like someone fairly refined, from the outer suburbs. Obscene? Not in the least. Just saying that her liaison with Roger was known, telling her the evenings when he visited her, and asking her to warn Roger to be careful.

Since the check on telephone calls, she had received a couple of anonymous letters. That was why, she said when it was nearly time for me to leave, she had begged me to call that night. Yes, she had shown them to the lawyer. Now she spread them out on the table, beside the tumblers.

I had a phobia about anonymous letters. I had been exposed to them myself. I could not prevent my nerve-ends tingling, from the packed, paranoid handwriting, the psychic smell, the sense of madness whirling in a vacuum, of malice one could never meet in the flesh, of hatred pulsating in lonely rooms. But these letters were not of the usual kind. They were written in a bold and normal script on clean quarto paper. They were polite and businesslike. They said that Roger had been known to visit her between five and seven in the evening, on the dates set down. ("Correct?" I asked. "Quite correct," said Ellen.) The writer had documentary proof of their relation. ("Possible?" "I'm afraid we've written letters.") If Roger continued in the public eye, this information would, with regret, have to be made known. Just that, and no more.

"Who is it?" she cried. "Is it some madman?"

"Do you think," I said slowly, "it sounds like that?"

"Is it just someone who hates us? Or one of us?"

"I almost wish it were."

"You mean—?"

"It looks to me," I said, "more rational than that."

"It's something to do with Roger's politics?" she added, her face flushed with fighting anger. "I was afraid of that. By God, this is becoming a dirty game!"

I was glad that she was angry, not just beaten down. I said I wanted to take the letters away. I had acquaintances in Security, I explained. Their discretion was absolute. They were good at this kind of operation. If anyone could find out who this man was, or who was behind him, they could.

Ellen, an active woman, was soothed by the prospect of action. Bright-eyed, she made me have another drink before I left. She was talking almost happily, more happily than she had done all the evening, when she said out of the blue, a frown clouding her face: "I suppose you know her?"

All of a sudden she got up from the sofa, turned her back on me, rearranged some flowers—as though she wanted to talk about Caro but wasn't able to accept the pain.

"Yes, I know her."

She gazed at me: "I was going to ask you what she was like." She paused. "Never mind."

At the lift-door, when we said goodbye, she looked at me, so I thought, with trust. But her expression had gone back to that which had greeted me, diffident, severe.

CHAPTER XXIV

DESPATCH BOXES
IN THE BEDROOM

Basset in October, a week before the new session: the leaves falling on the drive, the smoke from the lodge chimney unmoving in the still air, the burnished sunset, the lights streaming from the house, the drinks waiting in the flower-packed hall. It might have been something out of an eclogue, specially designed to illustrate how lucky these lives were, or as an advertisement composed in order to increase the rate of political recruitment.

Even to an insider, it all looked so safe.

It all looked so safe at dinner. Collingwood, silent and marmoreal, sat on Diana's right: Roger, promoted to her left hand, looked as composed as Collingwood, as much a fixture. Caro, in high and handsome spirits, was flashing signals to him and Diana across the table. Caro's neighbour, a member of the Opposition shadow cabinet, teased her as though he fitted as comfortably as anyone there, which in fact he did. He was a smooth, handsome man called Burnett, a neighbour of Diana's whom she had called in for dinner. Young Arthur Plimpton was sitting between my wife and a very pretty girl, Hermione Fox, a relative of Caro's. It didn't take much skill to deduce that this was one of Diana's counter-measures against Penelope Getliffe. Arthur, looking both bold and shifty, was in England for a week, intent upon not drawing too much of my attention and Margaret's.

But there was at least one person who was putting on a public face. Monty Cave's wife had at last left him for good; to anyone but himself it seemed a release, but not to him. The morning he received the final note, he had gone to his department and done his work. That was three days ago. And now he was sitting at the dinner-table, his clever, fat, subtle face giving away nothing except interest, polite, receptive—as though it were absurd to think that a man so disciplined could suffer much, could ever have wished for death.

He was a man of abnormal control, on the outside. Mrs. Henneker did not know what had happened to him.

When Margaret and I came into the house out of the Virgilian evening, Mrs. Henneker had been lurking in the hall. I was just getting comfortable, we were having our first chat with Diana, when Mrs. Henneker installed herself at my side. She was waiting for the other two to start talking. The instant they did so, she said, with her sparkling, dense, confident look: "I've got something to show you!"

Yes, it was my retribution. She had finished a draft of her "Life," as she kept calling it, the biography of her husband. There was no escape. I had to explain to Margaret, who gave a snort of laughter, then, composing her face, told me sternly how fortunate I was to be in on the beginning of a masterpiece. I had to follow Mrs. Henneker into the library. Would I prefer her to read the manuscript aloud to me? I thought not. She looked disappointed. She took a chair very close to mine, watching my face with inflexible attention as I turned over the pages. To my consternation, it was a good deal better than I had expected. When she wrote, she didn't fuss, she just wrote. That I might have reckoned on: what I hadn't, was that she and her husband had adored each other. She did not find this in the least surprising, and as she wrote, some of it came through.

This was a real love-story, I tried to tell her. The valuable things in the book were there. So she ought to play down the

injustices she believed him to have suffered, her own estimate
of what ought to have happened to him. I didn't say, but I
thought I might have to, that she wasn't being over-wise in
telling us that as a fighting commander he was in the class of
Nelson, as a naval thinker not far behind Mahan, as a moral
influence comparable with Einstein—if she wanted us to believe that as a husband, he was as good as Robert Browning.

I had spoken gently, or at least I had intended to. Mrs.
Henneker brooded. She stared at me. It was near dinner-time,
I said, and we had left ourselves only a quarter of an hour
to dress. In a stately fashion, Mrs. Henneker inclined her
head. She had not thanked me for my suggestions, much
less commented upon them.

At the dinner-table, she was still brooding. She was too
much preoccupied to speak to me. When Arthur, accom-
plished with elderly matrons, took time off to be polite to
her, he did not get much further. At last, after the fish,
she burst out, not to either of us, but to the table at large:

"I suppose I must be old-fashioned!"

She had spoken so loudly, so furiously, that everyone attended.

In her briskest tone, Diana said:

"What is it, Kate?"

"I believe in happy marriages. I was happy with my husband and I don't mind anyone knowing it. But my neighbour—" she meant me, she was speaking with unconcealed
distaste "—tells me that I mustn't say so."

For an instant I was put out. This was what came of
giving literary advice. I should never persuade her, nor presumably anyone else, that I had said the exact opposite.

She was put out too. She was indifferent to anyone round
her. She said, "Doesn't anyone nowadays like being married,
except me?"

The table was quiet. Roger knew about Monty's state:
so did Caro. So did Margaret. I could not prevent my glance

deviating towards him. Nor, in that quiet and undisciplined instant, could others. He was sitting with his eyes open and meaningless, his mouth also open: he looked more childlike than clever, foolish, a bit of a clown.

It was Caro who cracked the silence. Her colour had risen. She called out, just like someone offering a bet: "Damn it, most of us do our best, don't we?" She was teasing Margaret and me, each of whom had been married twice. She laughed at Arthur and Hermione Fox. They had plenty of time ahead, she said, they probably wouldn't do any better than we had all done.

Arthur gave a creaking laugh. If Caro had been his own age, she would have known exactly how much he fought shy of getting married; she would have had it out of him. He wouldn't have cared. For some, the flash of sympathy between them was a relief.

Except that, for some moments yet, Monty Cave sat with his clown's face. Then his expression, and those of the rest of us, became disciplined again.

With one exception, that Margaret and I speculated about. At the head of her own table, Diana was crying. Even when she gave us orders about how long to stay over the port, the tears returned. When we were alone in our bedroom, Margaret and I talked about it. Yes, she had behaved much as usual after dinner; she still sounded like a curious mixture of Becky Sharp and a good regimental officer keeping us all on our toes. We both knew that her marriage to Skidmore was supposed to have been an abnormally happy one. Was that why she had cried?

Next morning, meeting me in the hall, she told me that she was too tired to go out with the guns. It was the first time I had known her energies flag. She was still enough herself to give me instructions. I didn't shoot, I might be bored, but I was to keep Monty Cave company in her place. "He's not to be left by himself just now," she said. It sounded matter-of-fact and kind. Actually it was kind, but not entirely matter-of-fact. Diana was providing against the remotest chance of a suicide.

Soon the shooting parties were setting out, with me among them. Reggie Collingwood, Caro and Roger walked along together through the golden fields. So far as Collingwood had any casual pleasures, shooting was the favourite one. He approved of Roger for sharing it: while Roger, who had taken on the pastimes of Caro's family when he married her, lolloped tweedily along between them, looking as natural as an Edwardian statesman.

Monty and I veered to the left. When I spoke to him, he answered me, quite sweet-temperedly, but that was all. By the side of the other party, we were funereal. Then quick steps came padding up behind us. I looked round. It was Arthur Plimpton, dressed no more fittingly than I was, but carrying a gun. I did not understand why he had sacrificed a day with a comely young woman, but I was glad to see him. It was possible that he had come out of good nature. He was no fool, and he couldn't have been in Basset for twenty-four hours without picking up the story of Monty's wife.

"Do you like hunting, sir?" he said cheerfully to Monty.

"No, I never hunt," said Monty, who had just brought down two birds with a right and left.

"If I may say so, sir, you're doing pretty well for a beginner." Arthur knew as well as I did that the English did not refer to this form of avicide as "hunting." He had used the word out of mischief. He turned out to be a competent shot, about as good as Collingwood or Roger. Of the four of them, Monty was far and away the best. He might be a clever, sad, fat man, whom women were not drawn to: but his eyes and limbs worked like a machine.

At about one o'clock, we all gathered on a mound, eating out of the picnic-baskets. The morning mist had cleared, the light was mellow, clear as Constable's. Caro stretched herself on the turf with the sensuous virtue of one who has taken exercise; she took a swig from a brandy flask and passed it to Roger. The party looked like a tableau out of someone's attempt to present a simpler age.

Collingwood gazed at the shining countryside. "It's a nice day," he said.

When, in the dying afternoon, we were sitting in the library up at the house, having just got back for tea, Collingwood felt the phrase could not be much improved. He and Roger and Cave sat in their tweeds round Diana, who was pouring out. "It's been a nice day," said Collingwood.

Though it would have taken a great expert in Collingwoodian dialogue to detect this, he was not so patriarchally content as he had been at mid-day in the sunshine. During the afternoon, the difference between the bags had mounted. By the time we walked home, Collingwood and Roger had had the worst of the day. Collingwood was inclined to blame it onto Roger.

"You seem to have been in good form, Cave," said Collingwood in the library, with manly frankness, with oblique reproach.

Monty Cave muttered politely, but without interest.

Arthur joined in: "He was good all day," and began talking to Cave himself. Arthur was suggesting a two-handed shoot, just the two of them, first thing the next morning.

Collingwood was surveying them. He approved of attempts to "take his mind off it." He approved of young men making efforts with their elders. Most of all, he approved of able, rich young men. Drinking whiskey instead of tea, he stretched out stockinged legs and gave a well-disposed sigh. Turning to his hostess, he remarked: "Diana, I must say, it's been a nice day."

When the despatch boxes arrived, both Diana and he made their routine grumbles, just as they had been doing since the 'twenties, when he got his first office, and she was starting to run a political house. As Margaret and I were strolling in the courtyard, in the bluish twilight, a Government car drove up. A secretary descended, carrying one of the boxes, red and oblong, which we were all used to. We followed him in: this one was for Monty Cave. Within minutes, two other secretaries, carrying two identical boxes, walked through the great hall of Basset, on their way to Collingwood and Roger Quaife.

In the library, Diana, revived, her face less drawn, went through the minuet of grumbles, while she had the satisfaction of seeing three boxes being opened on three pairs of knickerbockered knees.

"I'd better put dinner off till nine?" she said.

"I'm afraid it looks like it," replied Collingwood. His tone was grave and ill-used: yet he couldn't, any more than Diana, conceal a kind of pleasure, the pleasure, secretive but shining, that they got from being at the centre of things.

Diana had the drill laid on. Dinner to be late, drinks to be sent up at once to the Ministers' rooms. Soon Collingwood was lumbering up the wide staircase, with the step of a man who has to bear too much. The other two followed. I wasn't wanted, and it was some time before I went up to my room. There, as I dressed, Margaret was baiting me through the door, hilarious at the stately ritual downstairs. Did all men in power behave like this? Why? Because otherwise, I replied, they wouldn't reach power, enjoy it, or keep it.

Just then, there was a knock on the door. It was one of the menservants, bearing an envelope, addressed to me in Collingwood's bold Edwardian hand. Inside was a sheet of Basset writing-paper, covered by more of Collingwood's elephantine writing. It said:

"I should be grateful if you could spare us a few minutes of your time. It would be a convenience if you could come without delay."

I took in the note to Margaret without a word, and left her laughing.

Inside Collingwood's bedroom, which was the biggest in

the house, the boxes gaped open on a table, and the great fourposter bed was strewn with papers. All three men were still wearing their outdoor suits, though Collingwood had taken off his jacket. He was sitting on the bed, and the other two had drawn up chairs nearby, each holding a glass in his hand.

"Oh, there you are," said Collingwood. "We want to get something fixed up."

Roger explained that they had received a Cabinet paper. He said to Collingwood: "I assume Eliot can see it? He'll get it in his own office on Monday."

Collingwood nodded.

I ran through it. It was only a couple of pages, typed in triple spacing on one of the large-letter machines, as though specially designed for long-sighted elderly men. It came from the Minister of Labour. It said that if a change in weapons policy was at any time contemplated, the Minister wished the Labour position to be established from the beginning. That is, a sudden stop, even in a single isolated project, such as ———, would mean unemployment for seven thousand men, of whom three thousand were specialists, and difficult to assimilate. This would be embarrassing for the Minister. Any more fundamental change in weapons policy would produce large pockets of unemployment. Unless the changes were spread over several years, they would be unacceptable.

It sounded official, cautious, reasonable. But everyone in the room knew that it meant more. It was a sighting-shot: and it was a sighting-shot, as it were, by proxy. It was not really this Minister who was testing Roger's intentions. It was a set of other interests, who were still keeping quiet. Service-groups? Big firms? None of us knew, but all of us were guessing.

"They've been getting at him," said Collingwood.

"It's very easy, as I said before," Roger leaned back, "for them to overplay their hands."

He looked confident, full of weight, springy with resource. Collingwood turned his handsome head and watched him in silence. So far as I could feel it in the air, there had been no argument.

"Well, then, Quaife, I'm with you. I agree, the committee" (he meant the Cabinet committee on defence policy, about which Rose had given me the first news) "ought to meet tomorrow or Tuesday. That's where we want you to help us—" He spoke to me. He gave, as usual, the impression that he was ill at ease and that he didn't care whether he was at ease or not. Everyone at Basset called him Reggie, but he still found it an effort not to speak to those two Cabinet colleagues of his as Mr. Quaife and Mr. Cave. He just managed to use their surnames. As for me, though I had met him a dozen times in the house, he could not become as familiar as that.

He assumed that I was at his disposal for a modest task. They wanted the committee convened over the weekend. As Douglas Osbaldiston was the Secretary, that was his job. Would I telephone him and get that in motion before dinner?

It was barely polite. It was certainly not adroit. Yet, within the next ten minutes, I saw, or thought I saw, how he kept his power. Before I arrived, they had been talking about three big firms: how much influence could they pull out? By this time, Roger and Cave spoke of "pressure groups," or "lobbies," as though they were Americans.

"If they were solid together, they might be more of a menace," said Roger. "But they're not, we haven't given them a chance to be. There are always going to be some Government contracts. For some of our friends, that prospect carries its own simple logic."

By the side of Roger, braced for the struggle, his voice taking on its taunting edge, Cave looked slack and gone to seed. But he was more at home than he had been all the weekend. He didn't see, he said, any lobby being effective by itself. "But I should make two qualifications. First, Government must know its own mind. Second, and this isn't quite a platitude, lobbies may be important if they happen to touch opinion deeper than their own. That is, if they touch opinion which hasn't their own axe to grind."

"Fair comment," said Roger.

Collingwood stirred, and put one arm round the bed-post. "I see." He was speaking to neither of them in particular, making pauses like one reading from a script: but the authority was there. "If I understand you both right, there isn't much between us. I take it Cave means that we've got to feel our way. I agree to that. We've got to watch whether any of these forces are having any effect on the Party. We can't push the Party further than it's prepared to go. I'm not presuming to give Quaife any advice. I never give anyone any advice." He said this as though it were the most exalted claim a man could make. "But, if I were Quaife, I should wrap up some of his intentions. I shouldn't let them get down to particular consequences until we've carried most of them with us. Carried them further than they thought. But not further than some of us are ready to go. I shouldn't let the White Paper give them much idea which weapons were being struck off straight away. I should wrap it up." He was still addressing the wall. "If I were Quaife, I should remember one other thing. I've got a feeling that the Party needs a lead. And by the Party, I mean the country as well. They need to feel that they're doing something new. I've got a feeling that, if anyone gives them a lead, they'll forgive him a lot. They may not like everything he's doing, but they'll be ready to forgive him."

It was a curious speech, I thought, as I listened, and even more so later. A good deal of it was common form, not specially ominous, but carefully uncommitted. The last part was not such common form. He seemed to be inviting Roger to take a risk. As he did so, I had felt for the first time that he was, in his own right, a formidable man. Was he inducing

Roger to take one risk too many? He had sounded, in a stony way, sincere. What did he wish for Roger? He had done him good turns. Did he like him? Men like Collingwood did not like or dislike freely. I was still uncertain about his feelings for Roger, or whether he had any feelings for him at all.

Next day, Margaret and I had to leave the house after tea. The weather had not changed. Just as when we arrived, it was an evening so tranquil that the chimney smoke seemed painted on the sky, and in the air there was a smell of burning leaves. Diana stood by herself in the courtyard, waving us off.

It had been a weekend in the country, with unhappiness in the house, and foreboding. As we settled down in the car, though, I felt, not relief to get away, but disquiet. For some of the disquiet I could find reason; but it was still there, swelling, nagging, changing, as though I were back in my childhood after a holiday, returning home, not knowing what I should find nor what I feared.

CHAPTER XXV

A SPEECH TO
THE FISHMONGERS

The committee room looked inwards to the Treasury yard: the rain sloshed down. Past Collingwood's head, on the two sides of the window, quivered the turning plane-leaves. In the chair, Collingwood behaved as he had done before, sitting on the bed at Basset. He was formal with the Ministers: Douglas Osbaldiston he treated like a servant, which Douglas showed no sign of noticing, must less of minding. But Collingwood got what he wanted. Arguments did not continue, except on lines which he approved, and there were not many. He had come to inspect the skeleton of the White Paper. In his view, it ought to be what he called "a set of balances."

This suited Roger. It was not the way in which, that summer, before the Opposition began to crystallise, we had been making drafts. This way left him some tactical freedom. It sounded as though he and Collingwood, after the bedroom conference, had made a deal. Yet I knew for certain that, since half-past eight on the Saturday night, two and a half days before, they had not exchanged a word in private. Enough had been said. They each understood what would follow, and so did Monty Cave and I. This was the way business got done, very rarely with intrigue, not as a rule with cut and dried agreements: quite different from the imaginative picture of the cynical and unworldly.

Osbaldiston, who was neither cynical nor unworldly, would have understood it without even a comment, if he had been present on Saturday night. As it was, he was momentarily surprised. He had expected something more dramatic from his Minister, and had been uneasy. Douglas did not approve of anything dramatic, on paper. Now he realised that the White Paper was going to be filled with detail. He was more comfortable with it so.

While Hector Rose, sick with migraine, when I reported to him that afternoon, smelled compromise in the air:

"I think I remember, my dear Lewis, mentioning to you that the knives were sharpening. Has it ever crossed your mind that our masters are somewhat easily frightened off?" He looked at me with sarcastic satisfaction in his own judgment. I told him more about the meeting, which he would have attended himself if he had been well. I said that the Air Minister had reserved his position at much too great length. Rose nodded. It would be a month or two before the White Paper could be finished, they had agreed. By that time, Roger had told them casually, just before the end of the meeting, he would have his "winding-up" ready for them to see. "That went down?" Rose raised his eyebrows. "It sounds like a very neat job of papering-over-the-cracks, shouldn't you say?"

But Rose and a good many others were puzzled when, within a fortnight, Roger next spoke in public. Long before the Basset weekend, Lufkin had made him commit himself to the actual engagement. Whether he had changed his mind about what to say, after Collingwood's allocution, I did not know. Whether he had decided to use this occasion, instead of going on to the television screen, I did not know also. It may have been the chance conjunction of Collingwood and Lufkin that led him to give what became known, a little bizarrely, as the Fishmongers' Hall Speech.

Lord Lufkin was a Fishmonger. Not that he had ever sold

a fish: not even in the Hamletian sense. Lufkin had a singular gift for getting it both ways. He disapproved of the hereditary peerage, and had become a hereditary peer. In just the same way, he had nothing but scorn for the old Livery Companies. It was grotesque, said Lufkin, with acid scorn, for business-men to take on the names of honest trades they had not a vestige of connection with: and to stand themselves good dinners out of money earned by better men. It was mediaeval juju, said Lufkin. It was "atavistic," he said mysteriously, with the spirit that John Knox might have shown when he was less well disposed than usual to Mary Queen of Scots. None of that prevented him taking all the honours in his own Livery, which, by some fluke, was the Fishmongers. That year, he had risen to be the Prime Warden of the Fish-mongers. Most of his colleagues enjoyed each honorific job as it came, and would have enjoyed this. Lufkin showed no sign of pleasure: except, I sometimes fancied, at the thought of doing someone else out of it.

He went through his duties. That was why he had in-vited Roger to the Michaelmas dinner and had arranged for him to speak. That was why Lufkin stood in a great drawing-room at the Hall, that November night, dressed in a russet Tudor gown tipped with fur, surrounded by other officials of the Livery, dressed in less grand gowns tipped with less grand fur. Above the fancy dress protruded Lufkin's small, neat, handsome 20th Century head, as he shook hand after hand with an impersonation of cordiality.

With maces carried before him, he led the procession into the Hall for dinner. It was a hall not unlike, though larger than a college hall: and the dinner was not unlike, though larger than, a college feast. Roger sat at the High Table, on Lufkin's right hand. I was somewhere down the Hall, placed between a banker, cultivated and reactionary, and a Labour M.P. less cultivated, but not much less reactionary. I did not know many men there, though across the room I caught sight of Sammikins, leaning back with a glass in his hand. The food and drink were good, but not good enough to go out for. I knew that Roger was going to use the occasion to "fly a kite." I had not seen the script, and did not expect much. I was not at all keyed-up. I got the banker off the subject of South Africa, on which he sounded like an unusually illiberal Afrikaner, on to German translations of Dostoievsky, where I knew nothing, and he a great deal.

Speeches. A long, and very bad one, by the chairman of an insurance company. I drank another glass of port. A short and very bad one by Lufkin, who sat down among dutiful plaudits as though he both expected them and was impervious.

Then the toastmaster cried: "Pray silence for your guest, the Right Honorable Roger Quaife, one of Her Majesty's Privy Councillors, holder of the Distinguished Service Order, Member of Parliament for ———."

In the candlelight, looking at the table before me, I saw the sheen of glass, of gold and silver plate. I turned as Roger rose. He looked enormous, after the image left by Lufkin. He began the incantation: "My Lord and Prime Warden, your Grace, my Lords, Members of the Honorable Livery Company of the Fishmongers, gentlemen—."

He stopped short, and stood there in silence. He went on in a quiet tone: "We have, all of us here, a good deal to be thankful for. This is an autumn night, and there is no war. An autumn night, and no war. For ten years out of the lives of almost every man here, we could not have said as much. We are lucky now, tonight. We have to make sure that that luck lasts. Some of us have fought in two wars. Most of us have fought in one. I don't need to tell anyone who has fought, that war is hell. We have seen better men than ourselves killed beside us. We have seen the way they died. We have seen our dead. But that is not the worst of it. In the wars we fought, there were times when we could still admire our friends: one was terrified oneself, but others were brave. War was stink, and rot, and burning, but human beings were often fine. Individual men still counted. It is hard to imagine how, in any major war which we can now foresee, they can count much again."

At that point, Roger had to break off into official language and point out how the armed services were still all-important. But soon he was talking in his own voice again. That was the knack—it was more than a knack, it was a quality which had drawn some of us to him—which held his audience. The hall was quiet. He went on:

"We all think, from time to time, of thermo-nuclear war. Of course we do. We should be foolish, as well as wicked, if we didn't. We can dimly imagine what such a war would be like. By its side, any horrors that men have so far contrived to inflict upon other men would look like a tea-party. So we know that this must never happen. Yet, though we know that, we do not know the way to stop it. I have met men of good will, who don't easily give up hope, thinking to themselves that we are all—all mankind—caught in a hideous trap. I don't believe that. I believe that with courage and intelligence and a little luck, we shall find a way out. I don't pretend it will be easy. I doubt whether there is any total solution. Perhaps we've got to hack away here and there, trying to do comparatively small things, which may make war that much less likely. That is why I am taking the opportunity tonight to ask a few questions. No one in the world, I think, knows the answer to all of them, perhaps not to many. That is a reason why we should at least ask them. Most of all, in this country. Ours is a country which has been as stable as any in the world for the longest time. We are an experienced people. We have been through many dangers. It happens, through no fault of our own, that this new danger, this change in the nature of war, this thermo-nuclear breakthrough, threatens us more vitally and completely than any major power. Simply because, by world standards, we are no bigger than a pocket-handkerchief, and live so close together. This degree of danger, of course, ought not to affect our judgment. I know there are some—most of all, old people living alone, and some of the young, who feel this predicament as unfair—who quite naturally, in their own hearts, occasionally feel frightened."

There had been no noise, almost no coughing, in the hall. I had been aware of the faces round me, some naked with interest, the banker's reflective and morose. Just then, a voice down the end of the opposite table shouted, thick with drink: "Speak for yourself!"

Sammikins was on his feet, berserk, calling to the interrupter.

"Shut up, you blasted swine!"

"Speak for yourself!" came a drunken voice.

Sammikins's neighbours were pulling him down, as he cried, "Where have you fought? This man has, you pig!"

Roger held up his hand. He stood, impassive, immobile, without a flicker. He said: "I'm prepared for anyone to accuse me of being cowardly. That doesn't matter. It's hard, I sometimes think, for a man with young children not to be. But I'm not prepared for anyone to accuse the people of this country of being cowardly. They've proved the opposite quite enough for any reasonable man. Anything we decide, now or in the future, about our military position, will be done because it seems to us moral and sensible, not because we're frightened, or because, on the other hand, we have to prove that we're not." He drew the first rumble of hear-hears. He let them run, then held up his hand again.

"Now, after this bit of pleasantry, I'm going to ask the questions. As I say, no one knows the answers. But if all of us think about them, we may some day be able to say something that decent people, people of good will all over the world, are waiting to hear. First, if there is no agreement or control, how many countries are going to possess thermo-nuclear weapons by, say, 1967? My guess, and this is a political guess, and yours is as good as mine, is that four or five will actually have them. Unless it is not beyond the wit of man to stop them. Second, does this spread of weapons make thermo-nuclear war more or less likely? Again, your guess is as good as mine. But mine is sombre. Third, why are countries going to possess themselves of these weapons? Is it for national security, or for less rational reasons? Fourth, can this catastrophe—no, that is going further than I feel inclined; I ought to say, this extreme increase of danger— can it be stopped? Is it possible that any of us, any country or group of countries, can give a message or indication that will, in fact, make military and human sense?"

Roger had been speaking for ten minutes, and he continued for as long again. In the whole of the second half of his speech, he went off again into official language, the cryptic, encyclical language of a Minister of the Crown. The effect was odd, but I was sure that it was calculated. He had tried them deep enough: now was the time to reassure them. They would be glad of platitudes, and he was ready to oblige them.

He did not make much of a peroration, and sat down to steady, though not excessive, applause. There was an amiable and inept vote of thanks, and the Prime Warden's procession, maces in front, Roger alongside Lufkin, left the hall.

When I recalled the evening, I thought that few of the people round me realised that they had been listening to what would become a well-known speech. I was not certain that I realised it myself. There was a sense of curiosity, in some a sense of malaise, in some of let-down. I heard various speculations on my way out. Most of them were respectful but puzzled.

In the press of men jostling towards the cloakroom, I saw

Sammikins, his eyes flaring, his face wild as a hawk's. He was not far from me, but he shouted: "I'm sick of this mob! Come for a walk."

I had a feeling that the invitation was not specially calculated to please his neighbours, who stood stolid and heavy while he pushed through them, lean, elegant, decorations on his lapel.

We had neither of us brought overcoats or hats, and so got straight out before the others, into the night air.

"By God!" cried Sammikins.

He had drunk a good deal, but was not drunk. Yet it would have been an error to think that he was tractable. He was inflamed with his grievance, his vicarious grievance of the interruption.

"By God, he's" (he was talking of Roger) "a better man than they are. I know men in his regiment. I tell you, he's as brave as a man can reasonably be."

I said that no one doubted it.

"Who the hell was that bloody man?"

"Does it matter?" I asked.

"I expect he was a colonel in the Pay Corps. I'd like to ram the words down his fat throat. What in God's name do you mean, 'Does it matter?' "

I said being accused of something one knows oneself to be ridiculous, and which everyone else knows to be ridiculous, never hurt one. As I said it, I was thinking: Is that true? It pacified Sammikins for the time being, while I was brooding. No, I had sometimes been hurt by an accusation entirely false: more so than by some which were dead accurate.

In silence we walked to a corner and paused there for a moment, looking across the road at the bulk of the Monument, black against the moonlight blue of the sky. It was not cold; a southwest wind was blowing. We turned down Arthur Street and into Upper Thames Street, keeping parallel with the wharves. Beyond the ragged bomb-sites, where the willow herb was growing still, since the air raids nearly twenty years before, we saw the glitter of the river, the density of warehouses, the skeletal cranes.

"He's a great man, isn't he?" said Sammikins.

"What is a great man?"

"By God, are you turning on him now?"

I had spoken carelessly, but his temper was still on the trigger.

"Look," I said. "I've thrown everything I could behind him. And I'm taking more risks than most of his friends."

"I know that, I know that. Yes, damn it, he's a great man."

He gave me a friendly smile. As we walked along what used to be a narrow street, now wide open to the moonlight, he said: "My sister did well for herself when she married him. I suppose she was bound to make a happy marriage and have a brood of children. But, you know, I always thought she'd marry one of us. She was lucky that she didn't."

When Sammikins said that he thought she would marry "one of us," he spoke as unselfconsciously as his great-grandfather might have done, saying he thought that his sister might have married a "gentleman." Despite his hero-worship of Roger, that was exactly what Sammikins meant. As he spoke, however, there was something which took my attention more. Caro was more concerned about him, loved him more than he loved her. Nevertheless, he was fond of her; and yet he saw her marriage in terms of happiness, exactly as the world saw it. Diana, seeing them walking in the grounds at Basset, or as allies at a Government dinner-table, might have seen it so. This despite the fact that both Diana and, even more, Sammikins had lived all their lives in a raffish society, where the surface was calm and the events not so orderly. Listening to Sammikins talking of his sister's marriage, I thought of Ellen, alone in her flat in the same town.

"Yes, she's got her children." He was going on about Caro. "And I am a barren stock."

It was the only self-pity I had known him indulge in, and, incidentally, the only literary flourish I had ever heard him make.

There was plenty of gossip as to why he had not married. He was in his thirties, as handsome as Caro in his own fashion. He was chronically in debt, partly because of his gambling, partly because his money, until his father died, was tied up in trusts he was always trying to break. But sooner or later, as well as inheriting the earldom, he would become a very rich man. He was one of the most eligible of bachelors. Diana commented briskly, with the mercilessness of the 20th Century, that there must be "something wrong with him." It was said that he liked young men.

All that might easily be true. I suspected that he was one of those—and there were plenty, often among men of his spectacular courage—who didn't find the sexual life straightforward, but who, if left to themselves, came to terms with it as well as simpler men. Half-sophistication, I was convinced as I grew older, was worse than no sophistication: half-knowledge was worse than no knowledge. Label someone a homosexual too quickly, and he will believe you. Tell him he is predestined to keep out of the main stream, and you will help push him out. The only service you can do him—it was a very hard truth—was to keep quiet. So the last thing I wanted that night was to force a confidence. I did not even want to receive it. I was glad (though faintly cheated, my inquisitiveness unsatisfied) when, after a few more laments at large, he gave a strident laugh and said: "Oh, to hell with it."

Immediately he wanted me to accompany him to ———'s (a gambling club). When I refused, he pressed me at least to come to Pratt's and make a night of it. No, I said, I must be getting home. Then let's walk a bit, he said. He said it scornfully, as though despising my bourgeois habit of going to bed. He did not want to be left alone.

We walked through the streets of the old City. From the bottom of Duck's Foot Lane, we caught sight of the dome of St. Paul's and, as if adjacent to it, the pinnacles of Dick Whittington's church, white as sugar icing in the moonlight. The City of London, in its technical sense, as opposed to the great incomprehensible town, meant little either to him or to me. It evoked no memories, I had never worked there, all it brought back were taxi-rides on the way to Liverpool Street Station. Yet something played on us—the sight of the vast cathedral? The bomb-sites? The absolute loneliness, not another person in the streets? The false-romantic memory of the past, the history which is not one's own but lives in the imagination? Something played on us, not only on him but on me, who was more sober and less adrift.

We had passed Great Trinity Lane and had turned right: St. Paul's sprang now into open view before us, soot and whitewash.

Sammikins said:

"I suppose Roger is right. If there is another war, it'll be the end of us, won't it?"

I said yes.

He turned to me:

"How much does it matter?"

He was speaking in earnest. I couldn't make a sarcastic reply. I answered: "What else matters?"

"No. I'm asking you. How much do any of us believe in human life? When it comes to the point?"

"If we don't, then there's no hope for us."

"Perhaps there isn't," he said. "I tell you, aren't we being hypocritical? How much do any of us care, really care, for human life?"

I was silent. And in a clear tone, neither fierce nor wild, he went on:

'How much do you care? Except for the people round you? Come on. What is the truth?"

I could not answer straight away. At last I said:

"I think I do. At any rate, I want to."

He said: "I doubt if I do. I've taken life before now, and I could do it again. Of course I care for a few lives. But as for the rest, I don't believe—when you strip away the trappings—that I give a rap." And that's truer of more people than any of us would like to think."

CHAPTER XXVI

PARLIAMENTARY
QUESTION

The headlines, on the morning after the dinner in Fish-mongers' Hall, had a simple but pleasing eloquence. ARMED SERVICES ALL-IMPORTANT: then, in smaller letters, "No Substitute for Fighting Men. Minister's Strong Speech," said the *Daily Telegraph* (Conservative). SE-CURITY COMES FIRST, "Mr. R. Quaife on World Dangers," said *The Times* (moderate Conservative). SPREAD OF ATOMIC WEAPONS, "How Many Countries Will Possess the Bomb?" said *The Manchester Guardian* (Centre). CHANCE FOR THE COMMONWEALTH, "Our Lead in Atomic Bomb," said the *Daily Express* (irregular Conservative). TAGGING BEHIND THE U.S., said the *Daily Worker* (Communist).

The comments were more friendly than I had expected. It looked as though the speech would soon be forgotten. When I went over the press with Roger, we were both re-lieved. I thought he felt, as much as I did, a sense of anti-climax.

In the same week, I noticed a tiny news item, as obscure as a *fait divers*, in the "Telegrams in Brief" column of *The Times*.

"Los Angeles. Dr. Brodzinski, British physicist, in a speech here tonight, attacked 'New Look' in British defence policy as defeatist and calculated to play into hands of Moscow."

I was angry, much more angry then apprehensive. I was sufficiently on guard—or sufficiently trained to be careful— to put through a call to David Rubin in Washington. No, he said, no reports of Brodzinski's speech had reached the New York or Washington papers. They wouldn't carry it now. He thought we could forget about Brodzinski. If he, Rubin, were Roger, he'd play it rather cool. He would be over to talk to us in the New Year.

That sounded undisquieting. No one else seemed to have noticed the news item. It did not arrive in the departmental press-cuttings. I decided not to worry Roger with it, and put it out of mind myself.

A fortnight later, in the middle of a brilliant, eggshell blue November morning, I was sitting in Osbaldiston's office. We had been working on the new draft of the White Paper, Collingwood having contorted Douglas's first. Douglas was good-humoured. As usual, he took no more pride in author-ship than most of us take in the collective enterprise of travelling on a bus.

His personal assistant came in with an armful of files, and put them in the in-tray. Out of habit his eye, like mine, had caught sight of a green tab on one of them. "Thank you, Eunice," he said equably, looking not much older than the athletic girl. "A bit of trouble?"

"The P.Q. is on top, Sir Douglas," she said.

It was part of the drill he had been used to for twenty-five years. A Parliamentary Question worked like a Pavlovian bell, demanding priority. Whenever he saw one, Douglas, who was the least vexable of men, became a little vexed.

He opened the file and spread it on his desk. I could see the printed question, upside down: under it, very short notes in holograph. It looked like one of those questions which were rushed, like a chain of buckets at a village fire, straight up to the Permanent Secretary.

With a frown, a single line across his forehead, he read the question. He turned over the page and in silence studied

another document. In a hard, offended tone, he burst out,
"I don't like this." He skimmed the file across the desk. The
question stood in the name of the member for a South Coast
holiday town, a young man who was becoming notorious as
an extreme reactionary. It read:

> "To ask the Minister of ———" (Roger's department)
> "if he is satisfied with Security arrangements in his depart-
> ment, especially among senior officials."

That looked innocuous enough: but Douglas's juniors,
thorough as detectives, had noticed that this same member
had been making a speech in his own constituency, a speech
in which he had quoted from Brodzinski's at Los Angeles.
Here were the press-cuttings, the local English paper, the *Los
Angeles Times,* pasted onto the file's second page.

With a curious sense of *déjà vu,* mixed up with incredulity
and a feeling that all this had happened time out of mind, I
began reading them. Brodzinski's lecture at U.C.L.A.:
"Science and the Communist Threat": Danger, danger,
danger: Infiltration: Softening, Conscious, Unconscious: as
bad or worse in his own country (U.K.) as in the U.S.: People
in high positions, scientific and non-scientific, betraying defence; best defence ideas sabotaged; security risks, security
risks, security risks.

"This isn't very pleasant," said Douglas, interrupting me.

"It's insane."

"Insane people can do harm, as you have reason to know."
He said it with tartness and yet with sympathy. He knew
of my first marriage, and it was easy for us to speak intimately.

"How much effect will this really have—"

"You're taking it too easily," he said, hard and sharp.

It must have been years since anyone made me that particular reproach. Then I realised that Douglas had taken charge.
He was speaking with complete authority. Because he was so

unpretentious, so fresh, lean and juvenile in appearance, one fell into the trap of thinking him lightweight. He was no more lightweight than Lufkin or Hector Rose.

It was he who was going to handle this matter, not Roger. From the moment he read the question, he showed his concern. Why it should be so acute, I could not make out. At a first glance, Brodzinski was getting at Francis Getliffe, perhaps me, perhaps Walter Luke, or even Roger himself. It would be a nuisance for me if I were involved: but, in realistic terms, I thought, not much more. Douglas was a close friend: but his present gravity would have been disproportionate, if it had just been on my account.

No. Was he, as a high bureaucrat, troubled when open politics, in particular extremist open politics, looked like breaking out? He was both far-sighted and ambitious. He knew, as well as anyone in Whitehall, that in any dog-fight, all the dogs lose: you could be an innocent victim, or even a looker-on, but some of the mud stuck. If there were any sort of political convulsion, his Treasury friends and bosses would be watching him. His name would get a tag on it. It would be unjust, but he would be the last man to complain of injustice. It was his job to see that the fuss didn't happen. If it did, he might find himself cut off from the topmost jobs for life, a second Hector Rose.

There was another reason why he was disturbed. Though he was ambitious, he had high standards of behaviour. He could no more have made Brodzinski's speech than he could have knifed an old woman behind her counter. Although he was himself Conservative, more so even than his colleagues, he felt that the P.Q. could only have been asked— and he would have used simple, moral terms—by a fool and a cad. In a heart which was sterner than anyone imagined, Douglas did not make special allowances for fools, cads, or paranoids like Brodzinski. For him, they were moral outlaws.

"The Minister mustn't answer the question himself," he announced.

"Won't it be worse if he doesn't?"

But Douglas was not consulting me. Roger was himself "under fire a bit." He had to be guarded. We didn't want too many whispers about whether he was "sound." It was at just this point in politics where he was most vulnerable. No, the man to answer the question was the Parliamentary Secretary, Leverett-Smith. It was impossible to be sounder than Leverett-Smith.

What Douglas meant was that Leverett-Smith hadn't an idea in his head, was remarkably pompous, and trusted by his Party both in the House and at conferences. He would, in due course, make, Monty Cave had said with his fat man's malice, a quintessential Law Officer of the Crown.

Within a few minutes, Douglas had been inside Roger's office and had returned.

"He agrees," he said. Since Douglas must have spoken with the wrappings off, just as he had spoken to me, it would have been difficult for Roger not to agree. "Come on. You may have to speak for some of the scientists."

In Roger's room, Douglas had already written on the file the terms of a reply. When we called on Leverett-Smith, two doors down the passage, the pace of business became more stately.

"Parliamentary Secretary, we've got a job for you," Douglas had begun. But it took longer. Leverett-Smith, bulky, glossy-haired, spectacled, owlish, stood up to welcome us. Very slowly, he read the civil servants' comments as the question had made its way up, Douglas's draft, the newspaper clipping. Again very slowly, in his reverberating voice, he began to ask questions. What was the definition of "bad security risk" in British terms? What were the exact levels of security clearance? Had all members of the scientific committee been cleared for Top Secret, and for the information *none of us mentioned?*

Leverett-Smith went inexorably on. The method of slow talk, I thought, as Keynes used to say. Had all the civil servants been cleared? What were the dates of these clearances?

Like his colleagues, Douglas kept his relations with the Security organs obscure. He did not refer to documents, but answered out of his head—as accurately as a computer, but more impatiently. This was not the kind of examination a Permanent Secretary expected from a junior Minister—or, so far as that went, from a senior Minister either. The truth was, Leverett-Smith was not only cumbrous and self-important: he disliked Roger: he had no use for rough and ready scientists like Walter Luke, while men like Francis Getliffe or me made him uncomfortable. He did not like his job, except that it might be a jumping-off board. This mixture of technology, politics, ideology, moral conscience, military foresight, he felt odious and not quite respectable, full of company he did not choose to live his life among.

Actually, he lived his life in one of the odder English enclaves. He wasn't in the least an aristocrat, as Sammikins and his sister were: he wasn't a country gentleman, like Collingwood: to Diana's smart friends, he was stodgy middle-class. But the kind of middle-class in which he seemed never to have heard an unorthodox opinion—from his small boys'-school in Kensington, to his preparatory school, to his house at Winchester, to the Conservative Club of Oxford, he had moved with a bizarre absence of dissent.

"I don't completely understand, Secretary, why the Minister wishes me to take this question?"

After an hour's steady interrogation, he made this enquiry. Douglas, who did not often permit himself an expression of God-give-me-patience, almost did so now.

"He doesn't want to make an issue of it," he said. Then,

with his sweet and youthful smile, he added: "He thinks you would carry confidence with everybody. And that would kill this bit of nonsense stone-dead."

Leverett-Smith tilted his massive, cubical head. For the first time, he was slightly placated. He was interested to know if that was the Minister's considered judgment. He would, of course, have to consult him to make sure.

Douglas, still smiling sweetly, as though determined to prove that pique did not exist in public business, reminded him that they had only a few hours to play with.

"If the Minister really wishes me to undertake this duty, then naturally I should be unable to refuse," said Leverett-Smith, with something of the air of a peeress pressed to open a church bazaar. He had a parting shot.

"If I do undertake this duty, Secretary, I think I can accept your draft in principle. But I shall have to ask you to call on me after lunch, so that we can go over it together."

As Douglas left the room with me, he was silent. Pique might not exist in public business; but, I was thinking, if Leverett-Smith remained in political office at the time when Douglas became Head of the Treasury, he might conceivably remember this interview.

Yet although time might have been spent in Leverett-Smith's ceremonies, there had been no compromise. It was Douglas who had got his own way.

The question was down for Thursday. That morning, Roger asked me to go to the House, to see how Leverett-Smith performed. He also asked me, as though it were an absent-minded thought, to drop in afterwards at Ellen's flat for half an hour.

It was a raw afternoon, fog in the streets, ghostly residues of fog in the Chamber. About fifty members were settled on the benches, like an ill-attended matinee. As soon as prayers were finished, I had gone to the box behind the Speaker's

Chair. There were several questions before ours, a lot of backchat about the reprieve of a murderer whom a Welsh member kept referring to, with an air of passionate affection, as "Ernie" Wilson.

Then, from the back bench on the Government side, on my right hand, rose the man we were waiting for—young, smart, blond, avid. He announced that he begged to ask Question 22, in a manner self-assured and minatory, his head back, his chin raised, as if he were trying to get the maximum bark from the hanging microphones.

Leverett-Smith got up deliberately, as though his muscles were heavy and slow. He did not turn to the back-bencher in his rear: he stood gazing at a point far down on the opposite side below the gangway.

"Yes, sir," he said, as though announcing satisfaction, not only with security arrangements but with the universe.

The avid young man was on his feet.

"Has the Minister seen the statement made by Professor Brodzinski on November third, which has been widely published in the United States?"

Leverett-Smith's uninflected, confident voice came rolling out:

"My Right Honorable friend has seen this statement, which is erroneous in all respects. Her Majesty's Government has a defence policy which is the responsibility of Her Majesty's Government, and which is constantly being debated in this House. My Right Honorable friend acknowledges with gratitude the services of his advisers on the scientific committees and elsewhere. It does not need to be said that these men are one and all of the highest integrity and devoted to the national interest. As a matter of standard procedure, all persons including Her Majesty's Ministers having access to secret information are subjected to rigorous Security procedure. And this is the case with each person consulted, on any matter connected with Defence whatsoever, by my Right Honorable friend."

Subdued, respectful hear-hears. The blond young man was on his feet.

"I should like to ask whether all scientific advisers have gone through security vetting during this past year."

Leverett-Smith, standing once more, looked for an instant like an elephantine beast being baited. I was afraid that he would ask for notice of the question.

He stood there letting the seconds tick by. Then his voice resounded, once more impregnable.

"My Right Honorable friend regards the publication of the details of Security procedures as not being in the public interest."

Good, I thought. That was all we wanted.

Again, hear-hears. Again, the pestering, angry voice.

"Will the Minister produce the dates on which certain members of this scientific committee, the names of whom I am willing to supply, were last submitted to Security vetting? Some of us are not prepared to ignore Dr. Brodzinski—"

There were mutters of irritation from the Tory benches. The young man had gone too far.

This time, Leverett-Smith did not take so long to meditate. Solidly he announced to the middle distance: "This supplementary question is covered by my last answer. The question is also an unworthy reflection on gentlemen who, often at great sacrifices to themselves, are doing invaluable service to the country."

Vigorous hear-hears. Definite hear-hears, putting an end to supplementaries. Another question was called. Leverett-Smith sat broad-backed, basking in a job well done.

I was waiting for another question, further down the list, addressed to my own Minister. Douglas, who had been sitting beside me, left with a satisfied grin.

Sometime later, a debate was beginning. It was not yet time

for me to leave for Ebury Street. Then I saw Roger coming into the Chamber. He must have picked up gossip outside, for on his way to his seat on the front bench he stopped by Leverett-Smith and slapped him on the shoulder. Leverett-Smith, turning to him, gave a serious contented smile.

Roger lolled in his seat, reading his own papers, like a man working in a railway carriage. At some quip from the Opposition benches that raised a laugh, he gave a preoccupied, good-natured smile.

As another speech began, he looked up from his scripts, turned to the box, and caught my eye. With his thumb, he beckoned me to meet him outside. I saw him get up, whisper to another Minister and stroll out.

In the central lobby, full of visitors, of little groups chatting earnestly, of solitary persons waiting with passive resignation, much like Grand Central Station on a winter night, he came up to me.

"I hear Leverett was pretty good," he said.

"Better than you'd have been."

Roger drew down his lip in a grim chuckle. He was just going to speak, when I caught sight of Ellen walking past us. She must have come from the Strangers' Gallery, I thought, as she gave me the slight smile of a distant acquaintance. To Roger she made no sign of recognition, nor he to her. I watched her move away from us, through the lobby doors.

Roger said: "She'll be going straight home. We can follow in a few minutes. I think I'll come along with you."

In Palace Yard, the lamps, the taxi-lights, shone smearily through the fog. As we got near to the taxis, Roger muttered that it was better if I gave the address.

The click of the lift-door opening, the ring of the bell.

As Ellen opened the door, she was ready for me, but, seeing Roger, gave an astonished, delighted sigh. The door closed behind us, and she was in his arms. It was a hug of relief, of knowledge, the hug of lovers who know all the pleasure they can give each other. For her, perhaps, it was a little more. Meeting him only in this room, pressed in by this claustrophobia of secrecy, she was glad, this once, to throw her arms round him and have someone there to watch. They would have liked to go straight to bed. Nevertheless, it was a joy to her, as well as a frustration, to have me there.

At last they sat on the sofa, I in an armchair. "That wasn't so bad, was it?" she asked, enquiring about the incident in the House, but her tone so happy that she might have been asking another question. His eyes were as bright as hers. He answered, in the same sort of double-talk: "Not bad." Then he got down to business.

"Everyone seems to think that it passed off rather well."

I said I was sure it had.

She wanted us to tell her: would the question do any damage now? Difficult to say: possibly not, unless something bigger happened. She was frowning. She was shrewd, but she had not been brought up to politics and found the corridors hard to see her way through.

"Well, anyway," she said, "it must be the end of Brodzinski. That's something."

No, we said, that wasn't certain. Never underestimate the paranoid. I was mimicking Roger and also scoring off him, going back to his handling of Brodzinski. Often they stayed dangerous, while saner men went under. Never underestimate them, I said. Never try to placate them. It is a waste of time. They take and never give. The only way to deal with paranoids is to kick them in the teeth. If a chap has persecution mania, the only practical course is to give him something to feel persecuted about.

I was being off-hand, putting on a tough act to cheer her up. But she wasn't putting on a tough act when she said:

"I want him done in. I wish to God I could manage it myself." He had done, or was trying to do, Roger harm. That was enough.

"Can't you set some of the scientists on to him?" she asked me passionately.

"They're none too pleased," I replied.

"Hell, what good is that?"

Roger said that she needn't worry too much about Brodzinski. He would still have some nuisance value, but so far as having any practical influence, he might have shot his bolt. It wasn't a good idea, making attacks in America. It might create some enemies for us there, but they would have been enemies anyhow. As for this country, it would damage his credit, even with people who would have liked to use him.

"There'll be plenty more trouble," he said, "but as for Brodzinski, I fancy he'll stew in his own juice."

"You're not going to do anything to him?"

"Not if leaving him alone produces the right answer." He smiled at her.

"I want him done in," she cried again.

His arm was round her, and he tightened his hold. He told her that, in practical affairs, revenge was a luxury one couldn't afford. There was no point in it. She laughed out loud. "You speak for yourself. There would be some point in it for *me*."

I had been trying to cheer her up, but it was not easy. She was worried for Roger, more worried than either he or I were that night: yet she was full of spirit. Not just because she was with us. She was behaving as though a wound were healed.

At last I grasped it. This attack had nothing to do with her. She was suspicious that behind the telephone calls might be someone Roger had known. For a time, she had been ready to blame Brodzinski. The enquiries I had set moving had already told us that this was unlikely. Now she could believe it. It set her free to hate Brodzinski more. She was blazing with relief. She could not bear the danger to come through her. She would, I thought, have lost an eye,

an arm, her looks, if she could have lessened the danger for
Roger: and yet, that kind of unselfish love had its own egotism: she would have chosen that the danger were increased,
rather than it should have come from her.

I told her that the Intelligence people hadn't got anything
positive. They now had all her telephone calls intercepted.

"All that's done," she said, "is to be maddening when he—"
she looked at Roger—"is trying to get through."

"They've got their own techniques. You'll have to be patient, won't you?"

"Am I good at being patient?"

Roger said, "You're having the worst of this. You've got to
put up with it." He said it sharply, with absolute confidence.

She asked me, was there anything else she could do? Had
she just got to sit tight?

"It's pretty hard, you know," she said.

Roger said: "Yes, I know it is."

Soon afterwards, he looked at his watch and said he would
have to leave in another half-hour. On my way home, I
thought of them a little, free together, by themselves.

CHAPTER XXVII

PROMENADE BENEATH
THE CHANDELIERS

It needed no one to instruct Roger about gossip. He picked it up in the air: or more exactly, for there was nothing supernatural about it, he read it in the expressions of acquaintances, without a word spoken, as he walked about the House, his clubs, the offices, Downing Street. We all knew, in those November days, that it was boiling up: some of it sheer random gossip—malicious, mischievous, warm with human relish—some politically pointed.

I had not yet heard a whisper about Ellen, or any other woman. The P.Q. seemed to have fallen dead. One reason why he was being talked about was that he was getting precisely the support he could least afford. The Fishmongers' Hall speech, or bits of it, or glosses upon it, was passing round. It had made news. It was drawing the kind of publicity which, because no one understood it, the theatre people called "word of mouth." Roger had, within two or three weeks, become a favourite, or at any rate a hope, of liberal opinion. Liberal opinion? To some on the outside, certainly to the Marxists, it didn't mean much. It might use different language from the *Telegraph*, Lord Lufkin's colleagues, or the Conservative back-benchers, but, if ever there was a fighting-point, it would come down on the same side. Maybe. But this, inconveniently for Roger, was not how it appeared to the *Telegraph,* Lord Lufkin's colleagues, or the Conservative back-benchers. To them, the *New Statesman* and the *Observer* looked like Lenin's paper, *Iskra,* in one of its more revolutionary phases. If Roger got praise in such quarters, he was a man to be watched.

There was praise from other quarters, more dangerous still. Irregulars on the Opposition benches had begun to quote him: not the official spokesmen, who had their own troubles and who wanted to quieten the argument down, but the disarmers, the pacifists, the idealists. They were not an organised group; in numbers they might be less than thirty, but they were articulate and unconstrained. When I read one of their speeches, in which Roger got an approving word, I thought with acrimony, save us from our friends.

Roger knew all this. He did not speak of it to me; he held back any confidence about what he feared, or hoped, or planned to do. Once he talked of Ellen; and another time, in the bar of a club, he brought me a tankard of beer and suddenly said: "You're not religious, are you?"

He knew the answer. No, I said, I was an unbeliever.

"Curious," he said. His face looked puzzled, uncalculating, simple. "I should have thought you would have been."

He gulped at his own tankard. "You know, I can't imagine getting on without it."

"Of course," he went on, "there are plenty of people who like the Church, even though they don't really believe. I think I should still like the Church, if I didn't believe. But I do."

I asked: just what did he believe?

"I think," he said, "almost everything I learned as a child. I believe in God in Heaven, I believe in an after-life. It's no use telling me that Heaven isn't the place I used to think it was. I know that as well as they do. But I can't help believing."

He went on talking about faith. His tone was gentle, like

a man blundering on. He would have liked me to say, Yes, that's how I feel. He was utterly sincere: no one could confide like that and lie. And yet, half suspiciously, at the back of my mind I was thinking, it is possible for a man to confide, quite genuinely, one thing, because he wants to conceal another.

At the back of my mind I was thinking, this wasn't a device, it came to him by nature. Yet it would be just as effective in keeping me away from his next moves.

Up to now, I had shut up the doubt which Hector Rose had not spoken, but had, with acerbity, implied. I knew Roger as Rose didn't, and wouldn't have wanted to. Rose would have been totally uninterested in his purpose, his aspirations, or his faith. Rose judged men as functional creatures, and there he was often, more often than I cared to remember, dead right. He was asking one question about Roger, and one alone: What—when it came to the point— would he do?

Roger told me nothing. In the next week, I received only one message from him. And that was an invitation to a "bachelor supper" in Lord North Street, the night after the Lancaster House reception.

At Lancaster House, Roger was present, walking for a few minutes arm in arm with the Prime Minister, up and down the carpet, affable under the chandeliers. That did not distinguish him from other Ministers, or even from Osbaldiston or Rose. The Prime Minister had time for all, and was ready to walk arm in arm with anyone, affable under the chandeliers. It was the kind of reception, I thought as I stood on the stairs, that might have happened in much the same form and with much the same faces, a hundred years before, except that then it would probably have been held in the Prime Minister's own house, and that nowadays, so far as I remembered accounts of Victorian political parties, there was a good deal more to drink.

The occasion was the visit of some western Foreign Minister. The politicians and their wives were there, the civil servants and their wives. The politicians' wives were more expensively dressed than the civil servants', and in general more spectacular. On the other hand, the civil servants themselves were more spectacular than the politicians, so that a stranger might have thought them a more splendiferous race. With their white ties, they were wearing their crosses, medals and sashes, and the figure of Hector Rose, usually subfusc, shone and sparkled, more ornamented, more be-sashed, than that of anyone in the room.

The room itself was filling up, so was the staircase. Margaret was talking to the Osbaldistons. On my way to join them, I was stopped by Diana Skidmore. I admired her dress, her jewellery—star-sapphires. Underneath it all, she looked strained and pale. But she could assume high spirits; or else, they were as much part of her as the bones of her monkey face. She kept giving glances, smiling, recognising acquaint-ances as they passed.

She gazed at the Prime Minister, now walking up and down with Monty Cave. "He's doing it very nicely, isn't he?" she said. She spoke of the Prime Minister rather like a headmaster discussing the performance of the best thirteen-year-old in a gymnastic display. Then she asked me: "Where's Margaret?" I pointed her out, and began to take Diana towards her. Though Diana knew far more people at the reception than I did, she had not met the Osbaldistons.

She said she would like to, vivacious and party-bright. Before we had gone three steps, she stopped:

"No. I don't want to meet anyone else. I've met quite enough."

For an instant, I wondered if I had heard right. It wasn't like her breakdown at her own dinner-table. Her eyes were bright with will, not tears.

We were in the middle of the party. Yes, since that night at Basset, her backbone had stiffened again. She was miserable

when we talked of marriage. She wasn't used to being miserable without doing something about it. She couldn't go on
living alone in that great house. She wanted someone to talk
to her. The pupillages she went through, the times when,
like an adoring girl, she changed the colour of her thoughts
—they weren't enough. Love-affairs wouldn't be enough. She
wanted someone all the time.

"You're no good," she said, practical and open. "You've
got a wife."

In the great drawing-room, most of the faces looked happy.
Happier than in most gatherings, I thought. Then I saw Caro
walking out on Roger's arm, an impressive smiling couple,
unselfconscious, used to catching the public eye. Were there
others there with his kind of secret? There were bound to
be some: if one knew these lives, there would be some surprises. But not, perhaps, so many as one might think. In
this drawing-room the men and women were vigorous and
hearty. "Peach-fed" I had heard them called, though not by
themselves. There were some love-affairs floating around.
But most of them didn't chafe against the limits of the sexual
existence. Often they got more out of it than those who did.
But they didn't live, or talk, or excite themselves, as though
there were, there must be, a sexual heaven round the corner.
Perhaps, I sometimes thought, that was a pre-condition for
the active life.

Anyway, most of them were happy. That night, they seemed
to be getting a special happiness out of one another's reflected
glory: even the Prime Minister, though the glory reflected
was his own. It was one of their rewards. What others were
there?

In the hall, after Margaret and I had made our goodbyes,
we waited while car after car, Government car, firm's car,
were shouted for by name. Lord Bridgewater: Mr. Leverett-
Smith: the Belgian Ambassador: Sir Hector Rose. Margaret
asked me why I was smiling. I had just remembered that I

had once asked Lord Lufkin what rewards he thought he got, for a life which many people would have judged arduous beyond compare. Power, of course, I said. We took that for granted. The only other thing, I had suggested, was transport. He had not used a public vehicle in London for a generation: transport was always laid on. In the midst of his dog's life, he travelled as though on a magic carpet. Lord Lufkin had not been amused.

When I saw the other men, brought together for dinner in Lord North Street the following night, I thought Roger had made a tactical mistake. Monty Cave was there, Leverett-Smith, Tom Wyndham: both Rose and Osbaldiston, and also Francis Getliffe. It was easy to see the rationale. Cave was Roger's closest political ally, Leverett-Smith and Wyndham had had to know what was going on. The rest of us had all through been close to Roger's policy. But everyone there, except Francis, had attended the reception the night before. If I had been Roger, I should have waited for the afterglow from the charmed circle to fade: then they might not mind so much the risk of being out of it.

As I sat at the dinner-table, islamic except for Caro at the far end, I began to wonder what Roger's intentions were. He wasn't likely to speak openly, in front of Hector Rose or Douglas, or several of the others. He and Caro, who was working like an ally who has been rehearsed, seemed to be casting round for opinions: just how were the reactions coming in? They weren't asking specific questions. They were sitting back, waiting for any information that was collecting in the air.

Just as when Roger talked to me about religion, I could not rely on my judgment of him, or even be sure, because it was flickering, what my judgment was. Was this the way he would start, if he were looking for an opportunity to withdraw? Perhaps he was not making a tactical mistake after all.

Certainly—and this was clear and explicit—he was giving

everyone present the chance to come out with his doubts. He was not only giving them the chance, he was pressing them to do so.

After dinner, Caro did not leave. She was one of the junta, she sat over the port like the rest of us. Before the port was put on the table, something happened that I did not remember having seen in that house or anywhere else. The maids took off the tablecloth, then laid the wine-glasses on the bare and polished rosewood. It was, so she said, an old 19th Century custom which had been kept up in her father's house. The glasses, the silver, the decanters, the rounded pinkness from a bowl of roses, were reflected in the table-top: perhaps that was what her ancestors had enjoyed, perhaps that was how she imagined them sitting, forming Victoria's governments, handing out the jobs.

Sliding a decanter to Getliffe on his left, Roger said casually that everyone there knew pretty well who was for them and who against. For any sort of decision, one had to know that. Then he added, in the most detached of tones, rather like a research student at the Harvard School of Government: "I sometimes wonder how much freedom any of us have to make decisions? Politicians I mean. I wonder if the area of freedom isn't smaller than one's inclined to think."

Hector Rose must have been sure of what he had expected all along, that Roger was preparing a loophole of escape. But Rose took up the argument, as though he were being either judicious or perverse.

"With respect, Minister, I think it's even smaller than that. The older I grow and the more public decisions I have assisted at—in the French sense, I need hardly say—the more I believe that old Count Tolstoy was in the right of it."

Tom Wyndham looked stupefied but obstinate, as though Hector's opinions—obviously Russian-influenced—might well be subversive.

"It's slightly instructive to ask oneself"—it was rare for Rose to go out to dinner, but he seemed, as he aged, suddenly to be enjoying company—"exactly what would be the effect on public decisions, if the whole of your delightful party, Lady Caroline, were eliminated at one fell swoop? Or in fact, which I don't think is really very likely, if we extended the operation and eliminated the whole of Her Majesty's Government and the higher Civil Service? With great respect, I strongly suspect that the effect would be precisely nil. Exactly the same decisions would be taken within negligible limits, and they would be taken at almost exactly the same time."

Douglas joined in. He was not averse to disagreeing with Rose, and yet they shared their service solidarity. They did not want the talk to become too concrete: so Douglas took his cue from Rose. He didn't believe in predestination quite so much, he said. Perhaps other men could do the same jobs, make the same choices: but one had to act and feel as though that wasn't so. When one was at the centre of things, said Douglas, one did make the choices. No one believed in predestination when he was making a choice.

He looked round the table. For an instant, his dégagé air had quite gone. "And that's why we wanted to be at the centre of things."

"*We,* my dear Douglas?" asked Rose.

"I wasn't speaking only for myself," said Douglas.

Monty Cave, sitting opposite to me half-way down the table, had been watching Roger with quick eyes. His dinner-jacket rumpled, so that his body looked stubbier than it was, Monty caught everyone's attention. Turning away from Douglas and Rose, he asked Roger, in a quiet and confidential tone:

"Weren't you saying—something else?"

"What do you mean?"

"I mean," said Monty, and suddenly he could not resist the malicious fat grin, "weren't you saying something a little nearer home?"

"What do you think, Monty?"

"I thought you were telling us that in politics, what's going to be dead right ten years hence may be dead wrong now. That is unfortunately true. We all know that."

"Well?" Roger had no expression.

"I may have misunderstood you, but I thought you were asking us whether there was the faintest chance that mightn't be the present situation."

"Was that the impression I gave you?"

"In which case," said Monty, "wouldn't you be in favour of going into reverse? Wouldn't you tend to be just a little cautious?"

"Do you really think he's been so cautious?" Caro interrupted, from the end of the table. Her eyes were gleaming, her colour was high. She looked angry and splendid.

"I wasn't suggesting it was easy," said Monty.

"But you were suggesting that he was getting cold feet. Doesn't anyone realise that for months he's been playing his hand to the limit? It's possible that he may have been overplaying his hand. The only question is, where does he go from here?"

"Where does he?" said Monty.

There was a flash of hostility between them. He was attracted to her, afraid of her. On her part, he was too subtle, not virile enough. Her anger was genuine. She was fighting for Roger, she was ready to let fly; but she knew—as though by instinct—how to let fly in the way that did most good. She was leaving nothing to chance. She had seen plenty of disloyalties round dinner-tables such as this. She wanted to make sure of Leverett-Smith and Tom Wyndham: she was trying to prove to them that Roger was being pushed on by wilder men.

She was high-hearted, and her anger was genuine. How much so was this attack of Cave's? I didn't know whether he and Roger had an understanding. It had been convenient for Roger, it had suited his tactics, for the attack to be made.

"In my judgment—" Leverett-Smith began, with extreme pomposity.

"Yes, Horace?" Caro leaned towards him with two kinds of charm, the aristocratic embrace, the embrace of a pretty woman.

"In my judgment, we ought to remember that sometimes the more haste, the less speed." He produced this thought as though it contained the wisdom of the ages. Caro continued to smile admiringly.

"Have we been forgetting that?" she said.

"Do enlighten us," said Monty.

"I'm inclined to think that we've been moving perceptibly faster than opinion round us. It's right that we should move faster, otherwise we shouldn't be giving proper leadership. The problem as I see it," Leverett-Smith went on, "is to judge how much faster it is safe to go."

"Quite," Monty commented.

His contempt was palpable. I thought he was wrong to dismiss Leverett-Smith as a negligible man. He was as sententious as a man could reasonably be: but he wasn't budgeable. Thinking of the future, I wished he were more negligible, more budgeable. It might be a misfortune for Roger not to have someone malleable in that job.

Caro went on devoting herself to him and Tom Wyndham. She was good with them. She could sympathise with their doubts, the hesitations deep in their conservative flesh—partly because, though she would not have admitted it to anyone but Roger, and not to him, once he had committed himself, those hesitations were her own.

Tom Wyndham was still wistfully wishing that the battleship were the decisive weapon.

"I know it isn't, of course," he said.

"I'm so glad of that," said Monty Cave.

Tom persisted, red-faced and puzzled. Since the last war, everyone had gone on changing their minds on what you could fight with. He expected it was all right. But still, he said, "It takes the chaps" (he meant the serving officers, and also his friends in the House) "time to get used to things changing like this."

Francis Getliffe broke in, apologising to Wyndham and to Leverett-Smith with the aloof formality that was growing on him. But, just as he had become more formal, he had also become more impatient.

"There isn't much time," he said. "The time-scale of politics you know about, it's your business to. But the time-scale of applied science is something like ten times faster. If you're going to wait too long before everyone agrees, then the overwhelming probability is that there won't be anything left to wait for."

Roger stared at him. Hector Rose gave a grim smile. Then I put in my piece. If we got really stuck (I was deliberately identifying myself with Roger's policy) we still had one recourse. We had been trying to struggle through by the channels of "closed" politics—the corridors, the committees. If they got blocked, we could take it into the open. The only even quarter-way open statement had been the speech in Fishmongers' Hall. We all knew why this was so: the problems were, or at least we made them, technical: most of the facts were fogged by security: these were the decisions which in our country, in all countries, we had got used to settling by a handful of men, in secret. For many reasons, this was forced on us. But there might come a time when someone would have to break it. This mightn't be the time. But even the threat that it was, I said without emphasis, might have an interesting effect.

I didn't expect these remarks to be popular. They weren't. To Douglas, who loved me, they were shocking and best forgotten. To Rose, who didn't, they were the token of why I had never quite fitted in. Even Francis didn't like them much. As for the politicians, Cave was reflecting: he was the only man there who might have considered whether in fact there did exist—in a rich and comfortable country—the social forces to call upon.

Leverett-Smith said, "I can't associate myself with that suggestion."

Caro was frowning. There was no debate. Someone changed the subject, and it was a few minutes later that Roger said: "None of this is easy, you know."

Since his exchange with Cave he had not spoken. He had sat at the end of the table, sipping his port, pre-potent, brooding. Now he took charge. He showed his worry, he did not pretend. He knew, and he knew that we knew, that he had to carry everyone round that table with him. Listening, I thought I had never heard him put on a better performance. Performance? That was true and not true. This might not be all he intended, but it was a good deal. There were ambiguities which might be deliberate: there were also some that he didn't know himself.

As we said good-night, his influence was still pervasive. He seemed to have gained all he wanted.

On the way home, and in cooler blood next morning, I wondered what each man thought Roger had actually said. What you wanted to hear, you heard, even with people as experienced as these. Ask them to write down their accounts, and the answers would have a certain ironic interest. And yet, Roger had said nothing untruthful or even disingenuous.

As for myself, I was further from predicting his actions than I had been since Rose gave his first warning. Of course, Roger was leaving a channel of retreat: he would be crazy not to do so. Of course, he must have faced the thought— and Caro must have brought it into the open—that there was still time to back down, throw the stress of his policy just where solid men would be comfortable, then take another Ministry, and gain considerable credit into the bargain. So much was clear. I was sure of nothing else.

CHAPTER XXVIII

A NAME WITHOUT
MUCH MEANING

One morning in December, I received a report. It was brought by one of my acquaintances in Security. I was not allowed to see it, but I was used to their abracadabra. He gave me the name I wanted, and took the report away with him.

The name I wanted was that of Ellen's persecutor. When I heard it, I said: "Oh, yes?" It sounded matter-of-fact, like the name of a new housekeeper. It sounded—as facts tend to sound, whenever you are mixed up in a secret investigation—as probable or improbable as anything else. Yet, when I was left alone, it seemed very odd. Nothing like what I should have expected. Odd, but not melodramatically odd. I hadn't been told, as in an old-fashioned thriller, the name of Hector Rose or the Prime Minister, or Roger himself. Dully odd. Within five minutes, I rang up Ellen telling her I wanted to see her before one o'clock.

"What about?" But she did not need to ask.

Over the telephone, I made her give me a promise. I couldn't say anything, I told her, unless she did. When she had this information, she must do nothing with it, nothing of any kind, until we had agreed.

"I suppose so," she said, in a strong reluctant voice.

We had to find somewhere where we could safely meet. It was the Christmas holidays, and at my flat the children would be home. Hers? No, she said: for once, I thought, not practical.

Briskly, she fixed a rendezvous, in an art gallery off Burlington Gardens. There I found her, alone, in the middle of the inner room, on the single chair. Round the walls were slabs and flashes of colour on canvases of enormous size. It occurred to me, walking to her in the deserted gallery, that we might have been two solitary devotees of Action painting: or a middle-aged official, a smartly dressed, youngish woman, at a first assignation. As she saw me, her eyes were open, dark, apprehensive, waiting.

"Well?" she said.

I wasted no time.

"Apparently," I replied, "it's Hood."

For an instant, she couldn't believe that she had heard right, or that the Hood of whom I spoke was the man we both knew slightly, the little, pleasant-faced dispenser of drinks, cherry-cheeked, Pickwickian, who had a job, not one of the top jobs, but two or three down on the commercial side, with one of Lufkin's rivals. I told her I had met him last at Lufkin's birthday party, when he had been exhaling with admiration at each utterance that Lufkin made, and raising his hands high as if to applaud a *diva*.

"I've seen him in the library," she repeated several times. She went on: "But he can't can't have anything against me! I've hardly talked to him alone."

She was searching for something personal, a snub, a pass she hadn't noticed or had not responded to, but she couldn't flatter herself, she could not gain even that tiny bit of consolation.

"Perhaps seeing me there somehow put him on to us. How did he get on to us? Does anyone know?"

I said it didn't matter. To her, in that moment, it mattered so much that she could think of nothing else. Then she cried: "I've got to have it out with him."

"No."

"I've got to."

"That's why I made you promise," I said, "an hour ago."

She looked at me with violence, with something like hate. She was craving for action as though it were a drug. To be kept from it was intolerable. It was like a denial of the whole self, body and soul, body as well as soul.

Passionately she argued. It could do no harm, she said. It could do no good, I replied: it might be dangerous. Now that we had identified him, some of the menace was gone. If it was simply a personal grudge, which I said again that I didn't believe, he didn't count, except for nuisance value. She could live with that.

But if not a personal grudge, was he acting on his own? If not, for whom? Suddenly Ellen went into a brilliant fugue of paranoia. She saw some central intelligence marshalling enemies: enemies watching them, planning, moving in, studying each aspect of Roger's life and hers. This was one move, Brodzinski's was another. Who was directing it all?

I couldn't pacify her, or persuade her that it wasn't true. I didn't myself know what was happening. In that empty room, the reds in the pictures pushing out towards us, I began to feel in a web of persecution myself.

She wanted to shout, cry, fly out, make love to Roger, anything. Her colour was high—but, as though in a moment-by-moment change, just as a child changes when in illness, when I looked again I saw she had turned pale.

She went very quiet. The passion had died away. She was afraid. At last I got her to talk again: "If this goes on, I don't know whether I can stand it."

The truth was, she did not doubt her own fortitude, but his. "I don't know whether *he* can stand it." That was what the words really meant, deeper than she could express. Also, she could not bring herself to say that she had a new fear about why she might lose him. Some of those fears she could confess, as she had done at our first meeting, when she told me that if he lost his political career because of her, he would not forgive her. This was a new fear, which she could not confess, because it seemed a betrayal. But though she worshipped Roger, she knew him. She believed that these persecutions wouldn't stiffen him, but would drive him back into safety—back to the company of his colleagues, to the shelter of Lord North Street.

She could not stop herself from telling me:

"It's being away from him that matters now." She meant, not being with him every hour of every day. "When he comes to me he enjoys himself, you know. So do I." She said it with her usual realism, her lack of fuss. "But it's not enough now."

She said: "I'd give up everything, I tell you, I could live in the back-streets, I could live on nothing—I could do anything you like—if only I could be close to him the whole time. I could give up going to bed with him, if I had to, if I could just be near him, night and day, and day after day."

IV

TOWARDS A CHOICE

CHAPTER XXIX

MEMORIAL SERVICE

The bells of St. Margaret's Westminster tolled under the low cloud-lid, into the dark noon. It was three days after Christmas, the House was in recess, but the Prime Minister and Collingwood, top-hatted, in morning suits, walked under the awning into the porch. So did three other Ministers, a group of elderly peers, then Roger and Monty Cave. People on the pavement were not paying much attention; top-hats, a handful of bigwigs, some sort of service.

I sat in the middle of the church, where, by some optical illusion, the light seemed brighter than out of doors: over the altar, the stained glass gleamed and glowed, like the glass in the front door at home, when I was a child, or in the door at the Osbaldistons'. The vigorous, shining faces round me were composed into gravity, but there was no grief. It was part of the ceremonial, ceremonial which they enjoyed, part of the charm of their lives. Collingwood spent some time on his knees. The other Ministers and members sat in the two front rows, doing what was expected of them, doing what their successors would do for them, when their own memorial services came round.

In fact, the one they were commemorating that morning would not have considered that enough was being done. He had been a modest old man, but he had had the sharpest sense of the fitness of things. The church was only half-full. Not much of a turnout, he would have said. Much worse, he would have been baffled that the service wasn't being held in the Abbey. "Giving me a consolation prize," he would have said.

This was the Memorial Service to old Thomas Bevill, who had died before Christmas at the age of eighty-eight. When he was a Minister at the beginning of the war, I had been one of his personal staff. That had been my introduction to the official life, and I knew him better than most of the other mourners did. No one, least of all himself, could have called him a great man; and yet I had learned much from him. In a limited sense of the word, he was a politician, a born politician. He knew which levers to pull and how to pull them, more exactly than anyone I had met in Government, with a skill one meets more often in people working in a smaller world, such as Arthur Brown in my old college.

Bevill was an aristocrat, and it was part of his manner to appear like a bumbling amateur. He was as much an amateur as one of the Irish manipulators of the American Democratic machine. Bevill had a passion for politics. Like most devoted politicians, he was realistic about everything in them, except his own chances. He had been sacked, politely but firmly, in 1943, at the age of seventy-four. Everyone but himself knew it was the end. But he delayed taking his peerage, still hoping that another Conservative government would call him back. New Conservative governments came, but the telephone did not ring. At last, at eighty-four, he accepted his Viscounty, even then hating it, even then going round asking his friends whether, when the P.M. went, there mightn't be the chance of one more job. When he was told no, his blue eyes ceased to look mild, and became hot and furious. But he surrendered. For the last four years, Thomas Bevill had entered another avatar, under the style of Lord Grampound.

This was the end. He would get mentioned, as a very minor figure, in some of the official histories. He wouldn't rate a biography of his own. I looked at the order of the service—Thomas Bevill, First Viscount Grampound—and felt curiously sad. The dignitaries round me were mumbling the responses. Beside the Prime Minister and Collingwood stood Roger, assured among the assured, his fine voice audible.

I felt, yes, alienated as well as sad. Why, I should have been hard put to it to say. This was the kind of leave-taking any ruling society gave to one of their own. As for Thomas Bevill, I should not have said that I loved him much. He had been an ally of mine in days past, but that had been in the way of business. He had been kind to me, as he always was to his colleagues, out of instinctive policy, unless there were overmastering reasons for not being kind. That was about the size of it. He was a tough old Tory politician, patriotic to the core—and also, the nearer one got to the core, snobbish and callous. Yet I was not really thinking of him like that. Standing among the sound of confident official voices, I was out of it—just as he was out of it, because he was, like any one of us when our time comes, being so easily dismissed.

The service ended, and the congregation trooped out, euphoric, healthy-looking, duty done. I did not hear a word spoken about the old man. The Prime Minister, Collingwood and Roger got into the same car. As the car drove away, Monty Cave was watching it. He remarked to Sammikins, whom I had not noticed at the service: "We're going on again after lunch."

He meant, the Cabinet committee had been meeting that morning, and had not finished. This was, we already knew, intended to be their final meeting, and so none of their advisers, none of the scientists or civil servants, except Douglas, was present. Monty, with his clever, imbedded eyes, watched the car turn out of Parliament Square.

"Well-timed, don't you think?" he said to Sammikins.

Abruptly, as though he resented the invitation while he was giving it, he asked us whether we were doing anything for lunch. As we drove round to Cave's house in Smith Square, which I had not visited before, Sammikins was talking away in undiscouraged form, although both Cave and I were silent. Had he asked us just because he was lonely, I was thinking, or because there was something he intended, or felt obliged, to say?

The tall, narrow house sounded empty as we went in. In the dining-room I looked out of the window through the tawny winter air at the ruined church. It might have been part of a gothic fancy. Yet the room itself was bright and elegant; on one wall was a fine Sisley, of poplars and sunny water, on another a still life by Nicholas de Staël, pastel fruit in a white dish.

I asked him about another picture. He was vague: he didn't know the painter. He was better-read than most men, but he seemed not to have any visual sense. He was living in a museum of his wife's taste.

The maid brought in avocado pears, cold chicken, tongue, cheese. Cave ate greedily: Sammikins did not eat so much, or with such relish, but he appropriated the bottle of hock. Cave and I had adopted the habit, common among the younger administrators, of not drinking before the evening.

"This is the nicest sort of meal," Sammikins burst out, "why do we waste our time sitting down to bloody great set luncheons?"

Monty Cave smiled at him: yes, with affection: yes, perhaps with an envy for the dash, the abandon, he himself had never had. He said, as though casually, with his mouth full, "Well, we've had a not uneventful morning."

He said it more to me than to Sammikins. I knew that he was devious, subtle, cleverer than any of us. I suspected that he was not being casual. Certainly I wasn't. I asked:

"How did it go, then?"

"Oh, you know how these things usually go."

It wasn't exactly a snub, but it was maddening. It was deviousness carried to the point of perversity. I looked at him, the bones of his chin sunk into the flesh, his eyebrows like quarter moons, his eyes watchful, malicious and, in that slack face and body, disconcertingly bold. He said:

"Old Roger's taken to making jokes in meetings, nowadays. In Cabinets, as well as in this one. Rather good jokes, I must say, but I don't think Reggie sees them."

Sammikins gave his brazen laugh, but Cave had one sly eye on me, and went on:

"I sometimes wonder a little whether it's wise for politicians to make too many jokes. What do you think? I mean, it sometimes looks as though they're getting worried and are trying to put a bit too much of a face on it. Do you think that's possible?"

"Do you think Roger's getting worried?" I asked.

"I shouldn't have thought so. I can't for the life of me imagine why, can you?"

At that, even Sammikins, not listening so intently as I was, looked baffled.

We all knew that Roger was in his private crisis of politics. Cave knew it as well as any man alive. Suddenly I wondered whether, with extravagant indirectness, he was hinting at something which was not political at all. Was he really suggesting that Roger had another concern, different in kind? He was an observant and suspicious man, and he might have had his suspicions sharpened by unhappiness. Had he guessed that another marriage was in danger?

"No," I said to Cave, "I can't imagine why. Unless things went worse this morning than you've told us. And you're wondering if he's got to back down. And of course you too."

"Oh, no, no, no," Cave said rapidly. His whole face was transformed by a smile which seemed to come from within, evanescent, amused, youthful. "I assure you, it's all gone easier than I expected. Of course, the White Paper hasn't really got all that many teeth, has it? Unless someone is going to read it in a way Reggie Collingwood wouldn't approve."

He added: "Roger was exceptionally good. It was one of the times when he does look the biggest man among us— you know what I mean. It's true, he did just drop one hint, not very loudly and he threw it away—that, in certain circumstances, he conceivably might want to say a word or two in public. It was nothing like as vulgar as threatening to resign, you understand." Cave smiled again. "I may be wrong, of course, but I rather got the impression that some of our colleagues took the point."

With a glint in his eye, Cave said to me, in a very quiet tone: "So far as I remember that last party of Caro's, Roger might have learned that trick from you, mightn't he?"

It was just on two. The meeting was to start again in half an hour, and soon he would have to be going. We walked upstairs to the drawing-room, also bright, also hung with paintings. But what struck the eye was a large photograph of his wife. It made her look handsomer than she really was: clear-featured, vivid, strong. Not right for him, not conceivably right for him, as anyone studying that face would have guessed. But there it stood. He must have seen it every night when he came in alone. One had a feeling, both of pity and discomfort, that he was living, not only with, but on, his sorrow.

With a directness that I could not have matched, nor most of us, Sammikins marched up to the photograph and said:

"Have you heard from her?"

"Only through her solicitors."

"What about?"

"What do you think?" said Cave.

Sammikins turned on him and said, in a hard, astringent tone, "Look here, the sooner you say good-riddance, the better it'll be for you. I don't suppose you care about that. But the better it will be for her, too, and you do care about that, worse luck. And the better it'll be for everyone around you."

He might have been a regimental officer dealing with marital trouble in the ranks. Somehow it didn't sound like a wild young roisterer talking to an eminent man. It was not embarrassing to listen to.

"Never mind," said Cave gently, with a touch of gratitude, speaking quite genuinely, as Sammikins had spoken. Soon he was saying goodbye, on his way to Great George Street. I thought he was genuine again when, in sympathy and reassurance, he said to me: "Don't worry about this afternoon. It's all going according to plan."

But he could not resist one last twist, dig, or mystification: "The only question is, whose plan?"

CHAPTER XXX

A SENSE OF INSULT

On Sunday afternoon, a couple of days after the Memorial Service, Margaret and I were sitting at home. The children had gone out to Christmas parties and we were peaceful. Then the telephone rang. As she answered it, I saw her look surprised. Yes, he is in, she was saying. Apparently the other person was trying to make a date with me: Margaret, protective, suggested that we should be alone, so wouldn't it be better to come in for a drink? There was a long explanation. At last, she left the receiver off and came to me with a commiserating curse. "Hector Rose," she said.

Over the telephone, his voice sounded more than ever glacial. "I am most extremely sorry to disturb you, my dear Lewis, I wouldn't have done so if I hadn't a rather urgent reason. Do make my apologies to your wife. I really am very, very sorry."

When the polite wind-up had finished, it came out that he needed to see me that same afternoon. He would give me tea at the Athenaeum at half-past four. I didn't want to go, but he pressed me, all flah-flah dropped, clear and firm. Then, arrangements made, the apologies and thanks started over again.

Seeing our afternoon broken, Margaret and I were cross. I told her that I could not remember him doing this on a

Sunday, not even in the busiest time of the war: he must be coming in specially himself, from right beyond Highgate: it occurred to me that I had never been inside his house. Margaret, not placated, was scolding me for not saying no.

She took it for granted, as I did, that the summons had something to do with Roger's White Paper. Yet we had heard, on the Friday night, that Cave's prediction had been correct, and that the Cabinet committee had agreed. Margaret said: "Whatever it is, it could wait till tomorrow morning."

Leaving the comfortable room, leaving my wife, going out into the drizzling cold, I felt she was right.

It was not perceptibly more encouraging when my taxi drew up in front of the club. The building was in darkness: there, on the pavement, in the slush and the half-light, stood Hector Rose. He began apologising before I had paid my driver. "My dear Lewis, this is more than usually incompetent of me. I am most terribly sorry. I'd got it into my head that this was one of the weekends we are open. I must say, I'm capable of most kinds of mistake, but I shouldn't have thought I was capable of this." The courtesies grew more elaborate, at the same time more sarcastic, as though beneath them all he was really blaming me.

He went on explaining, with the same elaboration, that perhaps the consequences of his "fatuity" were not irretrievably grave: since "the club" was closed, the Senior would by agreement be open, and we could perhaps, without too much inconvenience, have our tea there. I was as familiar with these facts as he was. Fifty yards from us, just across the Place, the lights of what he called "the Senior" (the United Services Club) streamed through the first flutter of sleet. All I wanted to do was cut the formalities short and get into the warm.

We got into the warm. We sat in a corner of the club drawing-room and ordered tea and muffins. Rose was dressed in his weekend costume, sports jacket, grey flannel trousers.

Still the formalities were not cut short. This was so unlike him that I was at a loss. As a rule, after the ceremonies had in his view been properly performed, he got down to business like a man turning on a switch. His manner was so artificial, so sharply split from the personality beneath, that it was always difficult to pick up his mood. And yet, as he went on describing great labyrinthine curves of politeness, I had a sense, a distressing sense, that he was under strain.

We drank the tea, we ate the muffins. Rose was expressing a mannerly interest in the book reviews in the Sunday papers. He had noticed something on a subject that was bound to interest my wife, to whom, again, his regrets for intruding that day—

Usually I was patient: but I could wait no longer. I said: "What's all this about?"

He gazed at me with an expression I could not read.

"I suppose," I said, "that something has happened about Roger Quaife. Is that it?"

"Not directly," said Rose, in his brisk, businesslike tone. So at last he was engaged. He went on:

"No, so far as I know, that's all right. Our masters appear to be about to sanction what I must say is an unusually sensible White Paper. It's going to the Cabinet next week. It's a compromise, of course, but it has got some good points. Whether our masters stick to those when they get under shot and shell—that's quite another matter. Will our friend Quaife stick to it when they really get at him? I confess I find it an interesting speculation."

He was speaking from his active, working self: but he was still watching me.

"Well, then?" I said.

"I do think that's reasonably all right," he said, glad to be talking at a distance, like an Olympian god who hadn't yet decided on his favourite. "I don't believe you need have that on your mind."

"Then what do I need to have on my mind?" Again I could not read his expression. His face was set, authoritative, and, when he wasn't forcing smiles, without pretence.

"As a matter of fact," he said, "I've been having to spend some time with the Security people." He added sharply: "Far too much time, I may say."

Suddenly, comfortably, I thought I had it. Tuesday was New Year's Day. Each year, Rose sat in the group which gave out Honours. Was it conceivable that something had leaked, from our office? I asked: "Have some of the names slipped out?"

Rose looked at me, irritated. "I'm afraid I don't quite understand you."

"I meant, have some of the names in next week's list got out?"

"No, my dear chap, nothing like that. Nothing like that at all." It was rare for him to let his impatience show through. He had to make an effort to control it, before he spoke calmly, precisely, choosing his words:

"I didn't want to worry you unnecessarily. But I think I remember telling you, some months ago, about representations from various quarters, which I said then that I was doing my best to resist. When would that be?"

We both had good memories, trained memories. He knew, without my telling him, that it had been back in September, when he warned me that "the knives were sharpening." We could both have written a précis of that conversation.

"Well, I'm sorry to have to tell you, but I haven't been able to resist indefinitely. These people—what do they call them, in their abominable jargon? 'pressure groups?'—have been prepared to go over our heads. There's no remedy for it. Some of our scientists, I mean our most eminent scientists advising on defence policy—and that, I need hardly tell you, is our friend Quaife's policy—are going to be put through a new security investigation. I fancy the name for this procedure, though it is not specially elegant, is 'double checking.' "

Rose was speaking with bitter distaste, distaste apparently as much for me as for the pressure groups, as he went on with his exposition, magisterial, orderly, and lucid. Some of this influence had been set in motion by Brodzinski, working on the members whom he knew. Some might have got going independently. Some had been wafted over via Washington —prompted, perhaps, by Brodzinski's speeches, or his friends there, or possibly by a re-echo of the Question in the House. "We could have resisted any of these piecemeal," said Rose. "Though, as you may have noticed, our masters are not at —shall I say, their most Cromwellian?—when faced with a 'suggestion' from our major allies. But we could not resist them all combined. You must try to give us the benefit of the doubt."

Our eyes met, each of us blank-faced. No one apologised more profusely than Rose, when apologies were not needed: no one hated apologising more, when the occasion was real.

"The upshot is," he went on, "that some of our more distinguished scientists, who have done good service to the State, are going to have to submit to a distinctly humiliating experience. Or, alternatively, be cut off from any connection with the real stuff."

"Who are they?"

"There are one or two who don't matter much to us. Then there's Sir Laurence Astill."

I could not help smiling. Rose gave a wintry grin.

"I must say," I said, "I think that's rather funny. I wish I could be there when it happens."

"I have an idea," said Rose, "that he was thrown in to make things look more decent."

"The others?"

"One is Walter Luke. Between ourselves, since he's a chief Government scientist, I take that distinctly ill."

I swore.

"But still," I said, "Walter's a very tough man. I don't think he'll mind."

"I hope not." He paused. "Another is a very old friend of yours. Francis Getliffe."

I sat silent. At last I said:

"This is a scandal."

"I've tried to indicate that I don't regard it with enthusiasm myself."

"It's not only a scandal, but it's likely to be serious," I went on.

"That was one of my reasons for dragging you here this afternoon."

"Look," I said, "I know Francis very well. I've known him since we were very young men. He's as proud as a man can be. I doubt, I really do doubt, whether he'll take this."

"You must tell him he's got to."

"Why should he?"

"Duty," said Rose.

"He's only been lending a hand at all because of duty. If he's going to be insulted into the bargain—"

"My dear Lewis," said Rose, with a flash of icy temper, "a number of us, no doubt less eminent than Getliffe, but still reasonably adequate in our profession, are insulted in one way or another towards the end of our careers. But that doesn't permit us to abdicate."

It was almost the only personal complaint I had heard him make, and then half-veiled. I said:

"All Francis wants is to get on with his research and live in peace."

Rose replied:

"If I may borrow your own debating technique, may I suggest that, if he does so, there is slightly less chance that either he or any of the rest of us will live in peace?"

He continued sharply:

"Let's drop the nonsense. We all know that Getliffe is the scientific mind behind Quaife's policy. For military things, I think we're all agreed that he's the best scientific mind we've got. That being so, he's just got to swallow his pride. You've got to tell him so. I repeat, that was one of my reasons for giving you this news today. He'll probably hear of this unpleasantness tomorrow afternoon. You've got to soften the blow before he hears, and persuade him. If you believe in this policy so much—and I thought, forgive me, that there were certain indications that you did—you can't do any less."

I waited for a moment, then said, as quietly as I could:

"What I've only just realised—is that you believe in this policy so much."

Rose did not smile or blink, or show any sign of acquiescence.

"I am a civil servant," he said. "I play according to the rules." Briskly he asked me:

"Tell me, how embarrassing is this going to be for Francis Getliffe?"

"How sensibly do you think they'll handle him?"

"They will be told—they may just possibly even know —that he's an important man." He went on, the sarcasm left behind: "He has the reputation of being far to the Left. You know that?"

"Of course I know that," I replied. "He was a radical in the 'thirties. In some ways he still thinks of himself as a radical. That may be true intellectually. But in his heart, it isn't."

Rose did not answer for some instants. Then he pointed with his foot over to my right. I turned and looked. It was an oil-painting, like a great many in the drawing-room, of a Victorian officer, sidewhiskered, high-coloured, pop-eyed, period that of the Zulu Wars.

"The trouble with our major allies," he said, "is that they methodically read every speech Francis Getliffe has ever made, and can't believe that any of us know anything about him. One of the few advantages of living in England is that we do know just a little about one another, don't you agree? We know, for instance, the not entirely irrelevant fact that Francis Getliffe is as likely to betray his country as"—Rose read the name under the painting without emphasis, but with his bitterest edge—"Lieutenant-General Sir James Brudenell, Bart, C.B."

He was still speaking under strain. It had not got less, but greater, after he had broken the news about Francis. There was a jagged pause, before he said:

"There's something else you'll have to warn Getliffe about. I confess I find it offensive. But modern thought on this kind of procedure apparently requires what they like to call 're-search' into the subject's sexual life."

Taken unawares, I grinned. "They won't get much for their trouble," I said. "Francis married young, and they've lived happily ever after."

I added: "But what are they going to ask?"

"I've already suggested to them that it wouldn't be tactful to bring up the subject to Sir Francis Getliffe himself. But they'll feel obliged to scurry round his acquaintances and see if he's liable to any kind of blackmail. That is, I take it, to find out whether he has mistresses, or other attachments. As you know, there is a curious tendency to assume that any homosexual attachment means that a man is probably a traitor. I must say, I should like them to tell that to —————— and —————."

For once, Rose, the most discreet of men, was not at all discreet. He had given the names of a particularly tough Minister and of a high public servant.

"I must say," I echoed him, "I should like someone to tell Francis that it was being seriously investigated whether he had homosexual attachments or not."

The thought was not without humour.

But then I said:

"Look here, I don't think he's going to endure this."

"He's got to," said Rose, unyielding. "It's intolerable, but it's the way we live. I must ask you to ring him up to-night. You must talk to him before he hears from anyone else."

There was a silence.

"I'll do my best," I said.

"I'm grateful," said Rose. "I've told you before, this was one reason why I had to talk to you today."

"What's the other reason?" I had been dense, but suddenly I knew.

"The other reason, I'm afraid, is that the same procedure is to be applied to you."

I exclaimed. My temper boiled up. I was outraged.

"I'm sorry, Eliot," said Rose.

For years he had called me by my Christian name. Now, telling me this news, he felt as much estranged as when we first met. He had never really liked me. Over the years, we had established colleague-like relations, some sort of respect, some sort of trust. I had given him a little trouble, because, in an irregular position, I had taken liberties which a career civil servant could not, or would not, think of taking. Things I had said and written hadn't been easy for him. He had "picked up the pieces," not good-humouredly, but according to his obligation. Now, at last, he hadn't been able to protect me, as, by his sense of fitness, he should have protected a colleague. He felt something like dishonoured, leaving me exposed. As a consequence, he liked me less than he had ever done.

"It doesn't make it any more agreeable," he said stiffly, "but this has nothing to do with suggestions from our allies. They have asked questions about Getliffe, but nothing about you. No, you seem to have some enemies at home. I take it that isn't exactly a surprise to you?"

"Do you expect me to stand for it?"

"I've got to say to you what I said about Getliffe."

After a while, during which we sat mute opposite each other, he said, strained, cold, hostile:

"I think I ought to try to make it as smooth for you as I can. If you don't care to submit to this business, then I will make an excuse, which shouldn't be beyond human ingenuity, and someone they're less interested in can take over the defence work. Not of course"—with an effort, punctilio returned—"anyone else could be so valuable to us, my dear Lewis."

"Do you seriously think I could take that offer?"

"I made it in good faith."

"You knew I couldn't possibly accept?"

Rose had become as angry as I was. "Do you really believe that I haven't resisted this business for weeks?"

"But it has still happened."

Rose spoke with deliberate fairness, with deliberate reasonableness:

"I repeat, I'm sorry. As a matter of historical fact, I have been arguing your case and Getliffe's most of the autumn. But yesterday they gave me no option. I also repeat, I want to do anything in the department's power to make it smooth for you. If I were you, I think I should feel very much as you do. Please forget about telephoning Getliffe. It was inconsiderate of me to ask you that, when I had to talk about something which was even more unpleasant for you. And, incidentally, for me. There's no need to decide anything tonight. Let me know tomorrow what you would like done."

He had spoken with fairness. But I was a reproach, sitting there. All he wanted was for me to get out of his sight. As for me, I could not manage even the grace of his fairness.

"No, there's no choice," I said roughly. "You may as well tell these people to go ahead."

CHAPTER XXXI

RECOMMENDATION
BY A PRUDENT MAN

That night I did my duty, and rang up Francis in Cambridge. I was angry with him, just as Rose had been with me, because I had to persuade him. I was angry because he was so stiff-necked and hard to persuade. I was angry with Margaret, because out of love and her own high-principled temper she was saying what I wanted to say: that Francis and I should each of us resign and leave them to it.

But I felt something else, which I had not felt before, or not since I was a very young man—the intense, mescalin-vivid sense of being watched. When I picked up the receiver and asked for the Cambridge number, I was listening (was the line tapped?) to sounds on the aural threshold. The clicks and tinkles seemed to me as though they had been picked up by an amplifier.

It was the same for days to come. I remembered a refugee, years before, telling me one of the prices of exile. One had to think about actions which, before one left home, were as unconscious as dreaming. Now I knew what that meant. I found myself looking round before I took a taxi. Though the light was dim, the trees of the Park appeared to be preternaturally sharp; I felt I could have counted each twig. The top-light of another taxi shone like a beacon.

Early in the week, Ellen telephoned: she had that morning

received another anonymous letter: she and Roger wanted to talk to me together. Once more the world outside seemed over-brilliant. As we talked of where to meet, the spider-web of suspicion lit up, thread by thread. We sounded reasonable, to each other and to ourselves, but we weren't, quite. We had lost our sense of fact, just as people do when they are hypnotised by secrets: just as my brother and I had once done, when, in the war, worried by what we knew, we had gone into the middle of Hyde Park so as not to be overheard.

In the end—it was like being young and poor again, with nowhere to take one's young woman—we dropped in, one by one, into a pub on the Embankment. When I arrived, the lounge was empty and I sat at a table in the corner. Soon Roger joined me. I noticed that, despite all the photographs, no one behind the bar recognised him. Ellen came in: I went and greeted her, and brought her to the table.

She gave Roger her severe introductory smile, but her skin was glowing and the whites of her eyes were as clear as a child's. She looked as though strain and suspicion were good for her, as though energy was pumping through her. Of the three of us, it was Roger who seemed physically subdued. Yet, as I read the new letter Ellen had brought out of her bag, he was watching me with eyes as alert as hers.

The letter was in the same handwriting, but the words had run close together. The tone was threatening ("you haven't much longer to make him change his mind") and, for the first time, obscene. It was a curious kind of obscenity— as though the writer, setting out for a hard-baked business purpose, had gone off the track, had become as obsessed as someone scrawling in a public lavatory. The obsession slithered on, insinuating, sadistic, glassy-eyed.

I didn't want to go on reading, and pushed the letter away over the glass table-top.

"Well?" cried Ellen.

Roger sank back in his chair. Like me, he was shocked,

and at the same time didn't like being shocked. In a deliberately off-hand tone he said: "One thing is fairly clear.
He doesn't like us very much."

"I'm not going to stand it," she said.

"What else can we do?" Roger asked her, in a placating
voice.

"I'm going to do something." She appealed to me—no,
announced to me: "Don't you agree, this is the time to do
something?"

In the past minute, I had realised that for the first time
they were split. That was why I had been asked there that
night. She wanted me on her side: and Roger, as he sat back
in his chair, giving sensible, cautious reasons why they had
to go on enduring this in silence, believed that I had to be on
his.

He had spoken with caution, but without much authority.
The words came slowly. As for this man, there was no sign that
the threats would come to anything. Let it alone. Pretend
they were unmoved. It was a nuisance they could live with.

"That's easy for you," said Ellen.

He stared at her. It was nearly always wrong, he said
quietly, to take steps when you couldn't see the end.

"This man can be stopped," she insisted.

"You can't be sure."

"We can go to the police," she said sharply. "They'll protect you. Do you know that he could get six months for this?"

"I dare say so." Roger looked at her with a touch of
exasperation, as if she were a child being obtuse about her
sums. "But I am not in a position to appear in a witness-box
as Mr. X. One has to be singularly anonymous for that particular activity. You must see that. *I* can't be Mr. X."

She was silent for a minute. "No. Of course you can't."

He put his hand on hers for a second.

Then she flared up again. "But that isn't the only way. As
soon as I knew who he was, I knew he could be stopped. He'll

crumple up. This is my business, and I'm going to do it."
Her eyes were wide open with passion. She fixed her glance
on me.

"What do you think, Lewis?"

After a pause I replied, turning to Roger:

"It's a slight risk. But I fancy it's probably time to take
the offensive."

I said it with every appearance of reason, of deliberate
consideration, and perhaps as persuasively as I ever said anything.

Roger had been talking sense. Ellen was as gifted with
sense as he was: but she was made for action, her judgment
was always likely to leave her if she couldn't act. I ought to
have known that. Maybe, with half my mind, I did know.
But my own judgment had gone, for reasons more complex
than hers, and much more culpable. As I grew older, I had
learned patience. The influence I had on people like Roger
was partly because they thought me a tough and enduring
man; but this wasn't as natural as it seemed, nor so much all
of a piece. I had been born spontaneous, excessively so, emotional, malleable. The stoical public face had become real
enough, but the earlier nature went on underneath, and,
when the patience and control snapped, was still, in my
middle-age, capable of breaking through. This was dangerous
for me, and for those round me, since fits of temper, or
spontaneous affection, or sheer whims, filtered through the
public screen, and sounded as disciplined, as reliable, as
some part of my character had now become, and as I should
have liked the rest of it to be. It didn't happen often, because
I was on my guard: but occasionally it happened still, as on
that evening. No one but Margaret knew it, but for days,
since the dialogue with Rose, my temper had been smoulder-
ing. Like Ellen, I had gone into the pub craving for action.
Unlike her, though, I didn't sound as though I needed it.
The craving came out through layers of patience, mixed with

all the qualifications and devices of discipline, as though it were the reasonable, considered recommendation of a wise and prudent man.

Yes, I said, we were all being shot at. There were great advantages in absorbing the attacks, in showing passive strength. It made enemies worried about what one had in reserve. But one mustn't stay passive forever. If so, they ceased to worry, and treated one like a punchball. The whole art was to stay silent, to select one's time, and then pick them off. Perhaps the time had come, or was coming. This attack on Ellen—there the man was wide-open. If he had any connection with others, which we were no nearer knowing, it would interest them to hear that he had been coped with; anyway, this was the thing to do. Roger gave up, with only a token struggle. Except in little things, as Caro had once told me, he was the hardest of men to influence. In all our connection, I had scarcely once persuaded him: certainly not over-persuaded him. Sitting there, round the little table, it did not occur to me that I was over-persuading him. I felt as reasonable as I sounded. Almost at once, the three of us were talking, not of whether anything should be done, but of what.

Later on, when it was all over, I wondered what responsibility I had to accept. Perhaps I was being easy on myself—but had it made much difference, what I said that night? Surely it had been Ellen's will, or, more precisely, her desire, which had been decisive? For once, Roger had wanted to slump into acquiescence and let her have her way. He gave the impression, utterly unlike him, of being absent—not from strain so much as from a kind of comfort. He did not even speak much. When he did speak, he said, as though it were one of his most pointed reflections:

"I must say, it will make things smoother when we don't hear from him again."

Ellen hissed at him like a cat.

"By God, that's helpful!" she cried. She broke into a grin,

a lop-sided grin, furious and loving. As for him, he would be absent until he could take her in his arms.

The truth was, I now accepted, that the love was not one-sided. He loved her in return. It wasn't a passing fancy, such as a man of Roger's age and egotism might often have. He admired her, just as he admired Caro, and oddly enough for some of the same reasons: for these women were not so unlike as they seemed. Ellen was as upright as Caro, and as honourable: in her way, she was as worldly, though she had more grievances about the world. Perhaps she was deeper, nearer to the nerve of life. I believed Roger thought they were both better people than he was. And, of course, between him and Ellen there was a link of the senses, so strong that sitting with them was like being in a field of force. Why it was so strong, I should probably never know. It was better that I shouldn't. If one reads the love-letters that give the details of a grand passion, they make one forget that the passion can still be grand.

There was one other thing. Just as Ellen's judgment and mine had been distorted, so was his. He loved her. But in a fashion strange to him, he felt he had no right to love her. Not only, perhaps not mainly, because of his wife. People thought of him as a hard professional politician. There was truth in that. How complete the truth was, I still didn't know. I still wasn't sure which choices he would make. And yet I was sure that he had a hope of virtue. He wanted, perhaps more strongly than he himself could tell, to do something good. Somehow, as though he was dragged back to the priests and prophets, he would have felt more certain of virtue, more fit to do something good, if, like the greatest politicians, he could pay a price. It sounded atavistic and superstitious, as I looked at the two of them, the sharp, self-abnegating woman, the untransparent hulk of a man: yet, somewhere in my mind was nagging the myth of Samson's hair.

Ellen and I, with Roger mostly silent, were arguing what

was to be done. Private detectives? No, no point. Then I had an idea. This man was employed by one of Lord Lufkin's competitors. If Lufkin would talk to the other chairman —"Have you ever seen that done?" said Roger, suddenly alive.

Yes, I said, I had once seen it done.

It would mean telling Lufkin everything, Roger was saying.

"It would mean telling him a good deal."

"I'm against it," said Ellen.

Roger listened to her, but went on: "How far do you trust him?"

"If you gave him a confidence, he'd respect it," I said.

"That's not enough, is it?"

I said that Lufkin, cold fish as he was, had been a good friend to me. I said that he was, in his own interest, without qualification on Roger's side. I left them talking it over, as I went to the bar to get more drinks. As I stood there, the landlady spoke to me by name. I had used that pub for years, since the time during the war when I lived in Pimlico. There was nothing ominous in her addressing me, but her tone was hushed.

"There's someone I want to show you," she said.

For an instant I was alarmed. I looked round the room, the sense of being watched acute again. There weren't many people there, no one I knew or could suspect.

"Do you know who that is?" she whispered reverentially, pointing to the far end of the bar. There, sitting on a stool, eating a slice of veal and ham pie, with a glass of stout beside the plate, was a commonplace-looking man in a blue suit.

"No," I said.

"That," said the landlady, her whisper more sacramental, "is Van Heynegen's brother-in-law!"

It might have sounded like gibberish, or, alternatively, as if Van Heynegen were a distinguished public figure. Not a bit of it. Distinguished public figures were not in the land-lady's line. In that pub, Roger stayed anonymous and, if she had been told his name, she would have had no conception who he was. On the other hand, she had a clear conception who Van Heynegen was, and so had I. Van Heynegen had been, in fact, an entirely respectable South African, but an unfortunate one. About five years before, living, so far as I could remember, in Hammersmith, he had been murdered for the sake of a very small sum, about a hundred pounds. There had been nothing spectacular about the murder itself, but the consequences were somewhat gothic. For Van Heyne-gen had been, in an amateurish fashion, dissected, and the portions made into brown paper parcels, weighted down with bricks, and dropped, at various points between Blackfriars and Putney, into the river. It was the kind of bizarre crime which, unbeknownst to the landlady, foreigners thought typi-cal of her native town, the fate which waited for many of us, as we groped our way through the endless streets, in a never-ending fog. It was the kind of crime, true enough, which brought the landlady and me together. As she gave me this special treat, as she invited me to gaze, she knew that she was showing me an object touched by *mana*. It was true enough that this brother-in-law was another entirely respectable man, who had not had the slightest connection with the gothic occurrences. Did he, as an object of reverence, seem a little remote? Had the *mana* worn just a shade thin? The land-lady's whisper was in a tone which meant that *mana* never wore thin.

"That," she repeated, "is Van Heynegen's brother-in-law."

I went back to our table with a grin. Ellen had noticed me conferring with the landlady, she looked at me with appre-hensive eyes. I shook my head and said, "No, nothing."

They had decided against Lufkin. The straightforward method was to write a couple of lines to the man himself, saying without explanation that she wished to receive no further communications from him, and that any further letters would be returned. Nothing but that. It implicated no one but herself, and it told him that she knew.

At that we left it, and sat in the cheerful pub, now filling up, with the landlady busy, but her gaze still drawn by the magnet in the blue suit at the end of the bar.

CHAPTER XXXII

SYMPTOMS

The White Paper was published at last; the House had not reassembled. This concatenation was not just an amiable coincidence. We wanted official opinion to form, the more of it the better. There was our best chance. As soon as the Paper, Command 8964, came out, Roger's supporters were trying to read the signs.

The newspapers didn't tell us much. One paper cried: "Our Deterent To Go?" To our surprise, the slogan did not immediately catch on. Most of the comments of the defence correspondents were predictable: we could have written them ourselves. In fact, to an extent, we had written them ourselves, for two or three of the most influential correspondents were friends and disciples of Francis Getliffe. They knew the arguments as well as he or Walter Luke. They understood the White Paper, though it deserved fairly high marks for deliberate obscurity. They accepted that, sooner or later, there was only one answer.

The danger was that we were listening to ourselves. It was the occupational danger of this kind of politics: you cut yourselves off from your enemies, you basked in the echo of your own voice. That was one of the reasons why the real bosses stayed more optimistic than the rest of us. Even Roger, more realistic than other bosses, knowing that this was the moment, knowing that he had to be certain what the back-benchers were saying, had to force himself to visit the Carlton or White's.

The Cabinet had, as a compromise, accepted the White Paper. But Roger knew—inarticulate men like Collingwood could sometimes make themselves very clear—that they meant the compromise to be kept. If he tilted the balance, if he put his weight on the side of his own policy, he was in danger. The Prime Minister and his friends were not simple men, but they were used to listening to men simpler than themselves. If the back-benchers became suspicious of Roger, then simple men sometimes had grounds for their suspicions. It was by his own Party that he would be judged.

As for me, I liked hearing bad news no more than Roger did. But for the next fortnight, I called on acquaintances and used my clubs as I had not done since I married Margaret. I did not pick up many signs. With those I did pick up, I was not sure which way they pointed. Walking along Pall Mall, one wild windy January night, I was thinking that on the whole it was going a shade worse, but not decisively worse, than I reckoned on. Then I went up the steps of a club, where I was not a member, but was meeting a Whitehall colleague. He was the head of a service department, and after a few minutes with him I was encouraged. As he talked, one eye on his watch, needing to catch a train back to East Horsley for dinner, the odds seemed perceptibly shorter. I caught sight of Douglas Osbaldiston walking through the colonnades. My host said goodbye, and I stayed for a word, what I thought would be a casual word, with Douglas. As he came out into the light, I saw his face, and I was shocked. He looked ravaged.

Before I could ask him, he broke out: "Lewis, I'm nearly off my head with worry." He sat beside me. I said, "What is it?"

In reply, he said one word. "Mary." The name of his wife. Then he added that she might be very ill.

As though released, he told me of her signs and symptoms, hyperattentively, almost with fervour, just as a sick person tells one about his own. About two weeks before—no, Douglas corrected himself, with obsessive accuracy—eleven days before, she had complained of double vision. Holding her cigarette at arm's length, she had seen a replica alongside it. They had laughed. They were happy together. She had always been healthy. A week later, she said that she had lost feeling in her left arm. Suddenly they had looked at each other in distress. "We've always known, ever since we were married, when either of us was afraid." She had gone to her doctor. He couldn't reassure her. Forty-eight hours before, she had got up from a chair and been unable to control her legs. "She's been walking like a spastic," he cried. That morning she had been taken to hospital. He couldn't get any comfort. It would be a couple of days before they gave him any sort of answer.

"Of course," he said, "I've got the best neurologists in the place. I've been talking to them most of the day." It had been a consolation to use influence and power, to find out the names of the specialists, to have them brought in Government cars to his office. That day, Douglas had given up being unassuming.

"I suppose you know what we're afraid of?" he asked in a quiet tone.

"No." I failed him. All through his description I had been at a loss.

Even when he brought out the name of the disease, it was his manner that harrowed me most. "Disseminated sclerosis," he said. He added, "You must remember reading about Barbellion's disease."

Then, quite suddenly, he was full of an inexplicable hope.

"It may not be anything of the sort," he said robustly, almost as though it were for him to cheer me up. "They don't know. They can't know yet awhile. Don't forget, there are several possibilities which are more or less benign."

He had a surge of happiness, of confidence in the future. I did not know how soon his mood would change. Not liking to leave him in the club, I offered to take him home to my wife, or to go with him to his own house, deserted now. He gave an intimate smile, some of the freshness returning to his face. No, he wouldn't hear of it. He was perfectly all right, nothing could happen that night. He was staying at the club, he would go to bed with a good book. I ought to know he wasn't the man to take to the bottle by himself.

All he said in that patch of euphoria was, for him, curiously indirect, but when I said goodbye, he gripped my hand.

During the next few days, at meetings, in the office, speculations about Roger got sharper. Parliament would be sitting again in a week. Before Easter, there would, Rose and the others agreed, have to be a full-dress debate on the White Paper. But they did not agree either on the strength of Roger's position nor on his intentions. Rose, very distant from me at this time, merely gave a polite smile.

On the fourth morning after I had met Douglas at his club, his secretary rang up mine. Would I please go along at once?

As soon as I entered his room, I had no doubt. He was standing by the window. He gave me some sort of greeting. He said: "You were worried about her too, weren't you?" Then he burst out: "The news is bad."

What had they said?

He replied, no, it wasn't exactly what they had expected. It wasn't disseminated sclerosis. But that wasn't much improvement, he said, with a quiet and bitter sarcasm. The prognosis of what she had got was as bad or worse. It was another disease of the central nervous system, a rarer one. They could not predict its course with accuracy. The likelihood was, she would be dead within five years. Long before that, she would be completely paralysed. He said, his expression naked and passionate:

"Can you imagine how horrible it is to know that? About someone you've loved in the flesh?" He added: "About someone you still love in the flesh?"

For minutes I stayed silent, and he broke out in disjointed, violent spasms.

"I shall have to tell her soon.

"She's in very high spirits. That seems to be typical of these diseases. She hasn't any idea.

"I shall have to tell her.

"She's been kind all her life. Kind to everyone. Why should this happen to her?

"If I believed in God, I should throw Him back His ticket.

"She's good.

"She's got to die like this."

At last, when he fell silent, I asked whether there was anything I could do.

"There's nothing," he said, "that anyone can do." Then he said, in a level tone, "I'm sorry. I'm sorry, Lewis. She'll need her friends. She'll have a lot of time to see her friends. She'll want you and Margaret, of course she will."

There was a pause. He said:

"Well, that's all."

I could feel the effort of his will. His voice tightened and he added:

"Now I should like to talk some business."

He held up his copy of the White Paper, which had been lying on the blotter.

"I want your impression. How is this going down?"

"How do you think?"

"I've been occupied with other things. Come on, what is your impression?"

I replied: "Did anyone expect absolutely universal enthusiasm?"

"It hasn't got it, you mean?"

"There are some malcontents."

"From what I've been able to pick up," said Douglas, "that may be putting it mildly.

As he sat there unrelaxed, the nerve of professional expertness showed through. It was not the White Paper which worried him. It was the interpretation which he knew, as well as I did, Roger wished to make and to act upon. He had never liked Roger's policy: his instincts were too conservative for that. It was only because Roger was a strong Minister that he had got his way so far: or perhaps because Douglas wasn't unaffected by Roger's skills. But now Douglas neither liked the policy nor wanted to gamble on its chances. Just as he hadn't wished to be linked with a scandal when the Parliamentary Question came up, so he didn't wish to be linked with a failure.

As he shut out his suffering, his tormented thoughts of his wife, this other concern leaped out.

"It could be," I said. He was much too astute a man to be bluffed.

"It's no use deceiving ourselves," said Douglas. "Anyway, you wouldn't. There is a finite possibility that my Minister's present policy may be a dead duck."

"How finite?"

We stared at each other. I couldn't get him to commit himself. I pressed him. An even chance? That would, before this conversation, have been my secret guess. Douglas said:

"I hope he's sensible enough to cut his losses now. And start on another line. The important thing is, we've got to have another line in reserve."

"You mean—?"

"I mean, we have to start working out some alternative."

"If that became known," I said, "it would do great harm."

"It won't get known," he replied, "and it will have to be done at once. We shan't have long. It's a question of thinking out several eventualities and making up our minds which is going to be right."

"In this business," I said, "I've never had much doubt what is right."

"Then you're lucky."

For the moment, he was back in his off-hand form. Then he went on driving himself, clear, concentrated. He had said "which is going to be right" without any fuss, meaning which policies would, according to the climate of opinion, be both sensible and practicable. He proposed that afternoon to begin writing the draft of a new plan, "just to see how it looks." Then, if trouble came, the department would have something "up its sleeve."

In everything he said or intended, he was entirely straightforward. His code of behaviour was as rigid as that of Rose. He would inform Roger that afternoon of precisely what he intended to do.

In one respect, however, he differed from Rose. He did not indulge in any hypocrisy of formality or protocol. It never occurred to him to pretend—as Rose had always pretended, and sometimes managed to believe—that he had no influence on events. It never occurred to him to chant that he was simply there to carry out the policy of his "masters." On the contrary, Douglas often found it both necessary and pleasant to produce his own.

As I went down the corridors back to my own office, I was thinking of his interview with Roger that afternoon.

CHAPTER XXXIII

A MAN CALLED
MONTEITH

It was late that same afternoon when I received a note from Hector Rose—not a minute, but a note in his beautiful italic handwriting, beginning "My dear Lewis" and ending, "Yours ever." The substance was less emollient. Rose, who did not lack moral courage, and who was sitting three doors down the corridor, had shied away from telling it in person.

"Could you possibly make it convenient to come to my room at ten A.M. tomorrow? I know that this is both unpleasantly early and at intolerably short notice: but our friends in ———" (a branch of Security) "are apt to be somewhat pressing. They wish to have a personal interview with you, which is, I believe, the last stage in their proceedings. They have asked for a similar arrangement with Sir F. Getliffe in the afternoon. I take it you would not prefer to approach F. G. yourself, and we are acting on that assumption. I cannot tell you how sorry I am that the notice should be so short, and I have already had a word to say about this."

That night, as I let myself go to Margaret, taking comfort from her fury, I didn't find Rose's preoccupation with timing funny. I felt it was another dig, another jab of the needle. When I entered his room, at precisely five minutes to ten the next morning, he had something else to brood about and was as brusque as I was.

"Have you seen this?" he said, without any of his greetings. "This" was an editorial in one of the popular papers. It was an attack on the White Paper, under the heading: ARE THEY THROWING AWAY OUR INDEPENDENCE?

The paper went on asking: Do they intend to sell us out? Do they intend to stop us being a great power?

"Good God alive," cried Rose, "what kind of world are they living in? Do they think that if there were a single way in heaven or earth which could keep this damned country a great power, some of us wouldn't have killed ourselves to find it?"

Savagely, he went on swearing. I could scarcely remember hearing an oath from him, much less a piece of rhetoric. "Do these silly louts imagine," he burst out, "that it's specially easy to accept the facts?"

He looked at me, his eyes bleak.

"Ah, well," he said, "our masters will have a good deal on their plate. Now, before Monteith arrives, there is something I wanted to explain to you." Once more, smooth as a machine, he was on the track of protocol. "Monteith is going to conduct this business himself. We thought that was only fitting, both for you and Getliffe. But there was some difference of opinion about the venue. They thought it was perhaps hardly suitable to talk to you in your own room, as being your home ground, so to speak. Well, I was not prepared to let them invite you to their establishment, so we reached a compromise that Monteith should meet you here. I hope that is as much to your liking as anything can be, my dear Lewis, in these somewhat egregious circumstances."

He allowed himself that one flick. It was as near a token of support as he could manage. I nodded, and we gazed at each other. He announced, as though it were an interesting piece of social gossip, that he would soon vacate the room for the entire day.

Shortly afterwards, the private secretary brought in Monteith. This time Rose's greetings were back at their most profuse. Turning to me, he said: "Of course, you two must have met?"

In fact we hadn't, though we had been present together at a Treasury meeting. "Oh, in that case," said Rose, "do let me introduce you."

Monteith and I shook hands. He was a brisk, strong-boned man, with something like an actor's handsomeness, dark-haired, with drifts of white above the ears. His manner was quite unhistrionic, subdued and respectful. He was much the youngest of the three of us, probably ten years younger than I was. As we made some meaningless chat, he behaved like a junior colleague, modest but assured.

After Rose had conducted the ceremony of chit-chat for five minutes, he said: "Perhaps you won't mind if I leave you two together?"

When the door closed, Monteith and I were left looking at each other.

"I think we might sit down, don't you?" he said. Politely he showed me to an armchair, while he himself took Rose's. There was a bowl of blue hyacinths in front of him, fresh that morning, witness to Rose's passion for flowers. The smell of hyacinths was, for me, too sickly, too heavy, to stir up memories, as it might have done, of businesslike talks with Rose going back nearly twenty years. All the smell did was to give me a discomfort of the senses, as I sat there, staring into Monteith's face.

I did not know precisely what his function was. Was he the boss? Or a grey eminence, working behind another boss? Or just a deputy? I thought I knew: Rose certainly did. But, with a passion for mystification, including self-mystification, none of us discussed those agencies or their chains of command.

"You have had a most distinguished career—" Firmly, gracefully, Monteith addressed me in full style. "You will understand that I have to ask you some questions on certain parts of it."

He had not laid out a single note on the desk, much less produced a file. Throughout the next three hours, he worked from nothing but memory. In his own office, there must have been a dossier a good many inches high. I already knew that he had interviewed, not only scientists and civil servants who had been colleagues of mine during the war and after, not only old acquaintances at Cambridge, such as the former Master and Arthur Brown, but also figures from my remote past, a retired solicitor whom I had not seen for twenty-five years, even the father of my first wife. All this material he had stored in his head, and deployed with precision. It was an administrator's trick, which Rose or Douglas or I could have done ourselves. Still, it was impressive. It would have been so if I had watched him dealing with another's life. Since it was my own life, I found it at times deranging. There were facts about myself, sometimes facts near to the bone, which he knew more accurately than I did.

My earliest youth, my father's bankruptcy, poverty, my time as a clerk, reading for the Bar examinations—he had the dates at command, the names of people. It all sounded smooth and easy, not really like one's past at all. Then he asked: "When you were a young man in ———" (the provincial town) "you were active politically?" Speeches at local meetings, the I.L.P., schoolrooms, the nights in pubs: he ticked them off.

"You were then far out on the Left?"

I had set myself to tell the absolute truth. Yet it was difficult. We had few terms in common. I wasn't in complete control of my temper. Carefully, but in a sharpened tone, I said: "I believed in socialism. I had all the hopes of my time. But I wasn't a politician as real politicians understand the word. At that age, I wasn't dedicated enough for that. I was too ambitious in other ways."

At this, Monteith's fine eyes lit up. He gave me a smile, not humorous, but comradely. I was dissatisfied with my answer. I had not been interrogated before. Now I was beginning to understand, and detest, the pressures and the temptations. What I had said was quite true: and yet it was too conciliatory.

"Of course," said Monteith, "it's natural for young men to be interested in politics. I was myself, at the University."

"Were you?"

"Like you, but on the other side. I was on the committee of the Conservative Club." He said this with an air of innocent gratification, as though that revelation would astonish me, as though he were confessing to having been chairman of a nihilist cell.

Once more he was efficient, concentrated, ready to call me a liar.

The 'thirties, my start at the Bar, marriage, the first days of Hitler, the Spanish Civil War.

"You were strongly on the anti-Nationalist side?"

"In those days," I said, "we called it something different."

"That is, you were opposed to General Franco?"

"Of course," I replied.

"But you were very strongly and actively opposed?"

"I did what little came easy. I've often wished I'd done more."

He went over some committees I had sat on. All correct, I said.

"In the course of these activities, you mixed with persons of extreme political views?"

"Yes."

He addressed me formally again, and then—"You were very intimate with some of these persons?"

"I think I must ask you to be more specific."

"It is not suggested that you were, or have been at any time, a member of the Communist Party—"

"If it were suggested," I said, "it would not be true."

"Granted. But you have been intimate with some who have?"

"I should like the names."

He gave four—those of Arthur Mounteney, the physicist, two other scientists, R—— and T——, Mrs. Charles March.

I was never a close friend of Mounteney, I said. (It was irksome to find oneself going back on the defensive.)

"In any case, he left the Party in 1939," said Monteith, with brisk expertness.

"Nor of T——." Then I said: "I was certainly a friend of R——. I saw a good deal of him during the war."

"You saw him last October?"

"I was going to say that I don't see him often nowadays. But I am very fond of him. He is one of the best men I have ever known."

"Mrs. March?"

"Her husband and I were intimate friends when we were young men, and we still are. I met Ann at his father's house twenty odd years ago, and I have known her ever since. I suppose they dine with us three or four times a year."

"You don't deny that you have remained in close touch with Mrs. March?"

"Does it sound as though I were denying it?" I cried, furious at seeming to be at a moral disadvantage.

He gave a courteous, non-committal smile.

I made myself calm, trying to capture the initiative.

I said:

"Perhaps it's time that I got one or two things clear."

"Please do."

"First of all, though this really isn't the point, I am not inclined to give up my friends. It wouldn't have occurred to me to do so—either because they were communists or anything else. Ann March and R—— happen to be people of the highest character, but it wouldn't matter if they weren't.

If you extend your researches, you'll find that I have other friends, respectable politically, but otherwise disreputable by almost any standards."

"Yes, I was interested to find how remarkable your circle was," he said, not in the least outfaced.

"But that isn't the point, is it?"

He bowed his fine head.

"You want to know my political views, don't you? Why haven't you asked me? —Though I can't answer in one word. First of all, I haven't altered much as I've got older. I've learned a bit more, that's all. I'll have another word about that a little later. As I told you, I've never been dedicated to politics as a real politician is. But I've always been interested. I think I know something about power. I've watched it in various manifestations, almost all my working life. And you can't know something about power without being suspicious of it. That's one of the reasons why I couldn't go along with Ann March and R———. It seemed to me obvious in the 'thirties that the concentration of power which had developed under Stalin was too dangerous by half. I don't think I was being emotional about it. I just distrusted it. As a matter of fact, I'm not emotional about the operations of politics. That is why I oughtn't to give you any anxiety. I believe that, in the official life, we have to fall back on codes of honour and behaviour. We can't trust ourselves to do anything else."

He was gazing straight at me, but did not speak.

"But I want to be open with you," I said. "In terms of honour and behaviour, I think you and I would speak the language. In terms of ultimate politics, we almost certainly don't. I said that I'm not emotional about the operations of politics. But about the hopes behind them, I'm deeply so. I thought it was obvious that the Revolution in Russia was going to run into some major horrors of power. I wasn't popular with Ann March and R——— and some of my other friends for telling them so. But that isn't all. I always believed that the power was working two ways. They were doing good things with it, as well as bad. When once they got some insight into the horrors, then they might create a wonderful society. I now believe that, more confidently than I ever did. How it will compare with the American society, I don't know. But so long as they both survive, I should have thought that many of the best human hopes stand an excellent chance."

Monteith was still expressionless. Despite his job, or perhaps because of it, he did not think about politics except as something he had to give a secret answer to. He was not in the least a speculative man. He coughed, and said:

"A few more questions on the same subject, sir. Your first wife, just before the war, made a large donation to a certain communist?"

"Who was it?"

He mentioned a name which meant nothing to me.

"Are you sure?" I asked.

"Quite sure."

I knew absolutely nothing of him.

"If you're right," I said, "it wasn't for ideological reasons."

Just for an instant, he had stripped away the years. I was a youngish man, distraught, with a wife I had to look after: still capable of jealousy, but schooled to watching her in search of anyone who might alleviate the inner cold: still appalled because I did not know where she was or whom she was with, at the mercy of anyone who dropped news of her: still listening for her name.

There was a silence. With a stiff sensitivity he said: "I have informed myself about your tragedy. I need not ask you anything more about her."

He broke out sharply: "But you yourself. You attended meetings of ———?" He gave the title of what, not at the time but later, we had come to call a "Front" organisation.

"No."

"Please think again."

"I tell you no," I said.

"This is very curious." His manner throughout had been professional. He had kept hostility out: but now there was an edge. "I have evidence from someone who remembers sitting next to you. He remembers exactly how you looked. You pushed your chair back from the table and made a speech."

"I tell you, there is not a word of truth in it."

"My evidence is from someone reliable."

"Who is it?"

Monteith answered, "You ought to know that I can't reveal my sources."

"It is utterly and absolutely untrue." I was speaking harshly and angrily. "I take it you've got it from one of your ex-communists? I take it that most of your information comes that way?"

"You've no right to ask those questions."

I was suffused with outrage, with a disproportionate bitterness. After a moment I said:

"Look here, you ought to be careful about these channels of yours. This isn't specially important. So far as I know, this Front you're speaking of was quite innocuous. I had plenty of acquaintances far more committed than that. I've told you so, and I'm prepared to go on telling you so. But, as it happens, I never went anywhere near that particular group. I repeat, I never went to a meeting of theirs, or had any communication with them. That is flat. It has got to be accepted. Your man has invented this whole story. I also repeat, you ought to be careful of his stories about other people. This one doesn't matter much to me. But there may be others which could do more harm—to people who are more helpless."

For the first time, I had shaken him. Not, I later thought, by anger: he must have been used to that. More likely, because his technical expertness was being challenged. He had

had a good deal of experience. He knew that I, or any competent man, would not have denied a point so specific without being dead sure.

"I will look into it," he said.

"I suppose you'll give a report on this interview to Hector Rose?" I said.

"That is so."

"When you do, I should like you to mention this matter. And say that you are doing so at my request."

"I should have done that in any case."

Just then he was talking, not like an interrogator, but as though we were all officials together, getting to work on "a difficult one." "It's very curious." He was puzzled and distracted. When he went on with his questions, the snap had left him, like a man who is absent-minded because of trouble at home.

My record over the atomic bomb. Yes, I had known about it from the start. Yes, I had been close to the scientists all along. Yes, I had known Sawbridge, who gave away some secrets. Yes, he and my brother had been to school together. But Monteith was doing it mechanically; he knew that in the end it was my brother who had broken Sawbridge down.

Monteith was watchful again, as he talked of what I had done and thought about the dropping of the first bomb.

"I've made it public. You've only got to read, you know," I said. "And you'll find a certain amount more on the files."

"That has been done," replied Monteith. "But still, I should like to ask you."

Hadn't I, like many of the scientists, been actively opposed to the use of the bomb? Certainly, I said. Hadn't I met the scientists, just before Hiroshima, to see how they could stop it? Certainly, I said. Wasn't that going further than a civil servant should feel entitled to? "Civil servants have done more effective things than that," I said. "Often I wish I had."

Then I explained. While there was a chance of stopping

the bomb being dropped, we had used every handle we could pull: this wasn't improper unless (I couldn't resist saying) it was improper to oppose in secret the use of any kind of bomb at any time.

When the thing had happened, we had two alternatives. Either to resign and make a row, or else stay inside and do our best. Most of us had stayed inside, as I had done. For what motives? Duty, discipline, even conformity? Perhaps we had been wrong. But, I thought, if I had to make the choice again, I should have done the same.

After that, the interrogation petered out. My second marriage. Hadn't my father-in-law, before the war, before I knew either of them, belonged to various Fronts? asked Monteith, preoccupied once more. I didn't know. He might have done. He was an old-fashioned intellectual liberal. Official life—nothing there, though he was curious about when I first knew Roger. It was past one o'clock. Suddenly he slapped both palms on the desk.

"That is as far as I want to go." He leaped up, agile and quick, and gave me a lustrous glance. He said in a tone less formal, less respectful than when he began:

"I believe what you have told me." He shook my hand and went out rapidly through the outer office, leaving me standing there.

It had all been very civil. He was an able, probably a likeable, man doing his job. Yet, back in my office through the January afternoon, I felt black. Not that I was worrying about the result. It was something more organic than that, almost like being told that one's heart is not perfect, and that one has got to live carefully in order to survive. I did not touch a paper and did no work.

Much of the afternoon I looked out of the window, as though thinking, but not really thinking. I rang up Margaret. She alone knew that I should not shrug it off. She knew that in middle-age I was still vain, that I did not find it tolerable to account for my actions, except to myself. Over the telephone I told her that this ought to be nothing. A few hours of questions by a decent and responsible man. In the world we were living in, it was nothing. If you're living in the middle of a religious war, you ought to expect to get shot at, unless you go away and hide. But it was no use sounding robust to Margaret. She knew me.

I should bring Francis back to dinner, I said, after they had finished with him. This she had not expected, and she was troubled. She had already invited young Arthur Plimpton, once more in London: partly out of fun, partly out of matchmaking.

"I'd put him off," she said, "but I haven't the slightest idea where he's staying. Shall I try to get him through the Embassy?"

"Don't bother," I told her. "At best, he may lighten the atmosphere."

"And there might be something of an atmosphere," she replied.

No, it was no use sounding robust to Margaret—but it was to Francis. As we drove home, under the lights of the Mall, he did not refer to my interrogation, although he knew of it. He believed me to be more worldly, less quixotic, than he was: which was quite true. He assumed that I took what came to me as all in the day's work.

As for himself, he said: "I'm sorry that I let them do it."

He was very quiet. When we got into the flat, Arthur was waiting in the drawing-room, greeting us politely. He went on: "Sir Francis, you look as though you could use a drink." He took charge, installed us in the armchairs, poured out the whiskey. He was more adept than Francis' own son, I was thinking. Which didn't make him more endearing to Francis. But just then, Francis was blaming him, not only for his charm, but for his country. As Francis sat there, silent, courteous, hidalgo-like, he was searching for culprits on whom to blame that afternoon.

With Arthur present, I couldn't talk directly to Francis: nor, when Margaret came in, could she. She saw him, usually the most temperate of men, taking another drink, very stiff: she hated minuets, she longed to plunge in. As it was, she had to talk about Cambridge, the college, the family. Penelope was still in the United States—how was she? Quite well, when they last heard, said Francis, for once sounding not over-interested in his favourite daughter.

"I heard from her on Sunday, Sir Francis," said Arthur, dead-pan, like a man scoring an unobtrusive point.

"Did you," Francis replied, not as a question.

"Yes, she put in a transatlantic call."

Margaret could not resist it. "What did she say?"

"She wanted to know which was the best restaurant in Baltimore."

Arthur had spoken politely, impassively, and without a glint in his eye. Margaret's colour rose, but she went on. What was he going to do himself? Was he going back to the United States? Yes, said Arthur, he had settled on his career. He had arranged to enter the electronic industry. He talked about his firm-to-be with dismaying confidence. He knew more about business than Francis and Margaret and I all rolled together.

"So you'll be home again soon?" asked Margaret.

"It'll be fine," said Arthur. Suddenly, with an owlish look, he said: "Of course, I don't know Penny's plans."

"You don't?" said Margaret.

"I suppose she won't be back on this side?"

For once Margaret looked baffled. In Arthur's craggy face, the blue eyes shone dazzlingly sincere: but under the flesh there was a lurking grin.

When he left us—out of good manners, because, listening, he had picked up what was unspoken in the air—I felt saddened. I looked at Francis, and saw, not the friend I had grown up with, but an ageing man, stern, not serene, not at all at peace. I had first met him when he was Arthur's age. It had been pleasant—or so it seemed that night—to be arrogant and young.

"Francis," said Margaret, "you're being rather stupid about that boy."

Francis gave an unprofessorial curse.

There was a silence.

"I think," he spoke to her with trust and affection, as though it were a relief, "I've just about ceased to be useful. I think I've come to the limit."

She said that couldn't be true.

"I think it is," said Francis. He turned on me. "Lewis oughtn't to have persuaded me. I ought to have got out of it straight away. I shouldn't have been exposed to this."

We began to quarrel. There was rancour in our voices. He blamed me, we both blamed Roger. Politicians never take care of their tools, said Francis, with increasing anger. You're useful so long as you're useful. Then you're expendable. No doubt, said Francis bitterly, if things went wrong, Roger would play safe. In a gentlemanly fashion, he would go back to the fold: and in an equally gentlemanly fashion, his advisers would be disgraced.

"You can't be disgraced," said Margaret.

Francis began to talk to her in a more realistic tone. They would not keep him out just yet, he said. At least, he didn't think so. They wouldn't dare to say that he was a risk. And yet, when all this was over, win or lose, somehow it would be convenient for them not to involve him. The suggestion would go round that he didn't quite fit in. It would be better to have safer men. As our kind of world went on, the men had to get safer and safer. You couldn't afford to be different. No one could afford to have you, if you showed a trace of difference. The most valuable single gift was the ability to sing in unison. And so they would shut him out.

We went on quarrelling.

"You're too thin-skinned," I said, at my sharpest.

Margaret looked from him to me. She knew what in secret I had felt that day. She was wondering when, after Francis had gone, she could make a remark about the thinness of other skins.

CHAPTER XXXIV

THE PURITY OF BEING
PERSECUTED

The next evening, Margaret and I got out of the taxi on the Embankment and walked up into the Temple gardens. All day news had come prodding in, and I was jaded. The chief Government Whip had called on Roger. Some back benchers, carrying weight inside the Party, had to be re-assured. Roger would have to meet them. Two Opposition leaders had been making speeches in the country the night before. No one could interpret the public opinion polls.

Yes, we were somewhere near a crisis, I thought with a kind of puzzlement, as I looked over the river at the lurid city sky. How far did it reach? Maybe in a few months' time, some of the offices in this part of London would carry different names. Was that all? Maybe other lives stood to lose, lives stretched out under the lit-up sky. Roger and the others thought so: one had to think it, or it was harder to go on.

Those other lives did not respond much. A few did, not many. Perhaps they sent their messages to the corridors very rarely, when the dangers were on top of them: otherwise, perhaps, the messages came not at all.

Back towards the Strand, the hall of my old Inn blazed out like a church on a Sunday night. We were on our way to a Bar concert. In the Inn buildings, lighted windows were shining here and there, oblongs of brilliance in a bulk of darkness. We passed the set of chambers where I had worked as a young man. Some of the names were still there, as they had been in my time. Mr. H. Getliffe: Mr. W. Allen. On the next staircase, I noticed the name of a contemporary: Sir H. Salisbury. That was out of date: he had just been appointed Lord Justice of Appeal. Margaret, feeling that I was distressed, pressed my arm. This was a part of my life she hadn't known; she was apt to be jealous of it, and, as we walked past the building in the sharp air, she believed that I was homesick. She was wrong. I had felt something more like irritation. The Bar had never really suited me, I had not once thought of going back. And yet, if I could have been content with it, I should have had a smoother time. Like Salisbury. I shouldn't be in the middle of this present crisis.

The hall was draughty. Chairs, white programmes gleaming on them as at a church wedding, had been set in lines and then pushed into disorder, as people leaned over to talk. The event, though it didn't sound it, was an occasion of privilege. Several members from both front benches were there: Lord Lufkin and his entourage were there; so was Diana Skidmore, who had come with Monty Cave. As they shouted to one another, white-tied, bedecked, no one would have thought they were in a crisis. Much less that any of them resented, as I did, the moment in which we stood. They were behaving as though this was the kind of trouble politicians got into. They made jokes. They behaved as if these places were going to stay their own: while as for the rest—well, one could be reminded of them by the russet light of the city sky.

They weren't preoccupied with the coming debate, except to make some digs at Roger. What they were really interested in at this moment—or at least, what Diana and her friends were really interested in—was a job. The job, somewhat bewilderingly, was a Regius Professorship of History. Diana had recovered some of her spirits. There was a rumour that she had determined to make Monty Cave divorce his wife. Having become high-spirited once again, Diana had also, once again, become importunate. Her friends had to do what she told them: and what she told them was to twist the Prime Minister's arm. The P.M. had to hear her candidate's name from all possible angles. This name was Thomas Orbell.

It was not that Diana was a specially good judge of academic excellence. She would have been just as likely to have a candidate for a bishopric. She treated academic persons with reverence, as though they were sacred cows: but, though they might be sacred cows, they did not seem to her quite serious. That didn't stop her getting excited about the claims of Dr. Orbell, and didn't stop her friends getting excited for him or against. Not that they were wrapped up in the academic life. It was nice to toss the jobs around, it was nice to spot winners. This was one of the pleasures of the charmed circle. Margaret, who had been brought up among scholars, was uneasy. She knew Orbell and did not want to spoil his chances. She was certain that he wasn't good enough.

"He's *brilliant*," said Diana, herself resplendent in white, like the fairy on a Christmas tree.

In fact, Diana's enthusiasm, the cheerful, cherubim-chanting of a couple of her ministerial friends, Margaret's qualms, were likely all to be beside the point. True, the Prime Minister would listen; true, he would listen with porcine competence. Orbell's supporters might get words of encouragement. At exactly the same moment, a lantern-jawed young man in the private office, trained by Osbaldiston, would be collecting opinions with marmoreal calm. My private guess was that Tom Orbell stood about as much chance for this Chair as he did for the Headship of the Society of Jesus.

In the library after the performance, where we had herded for sandwiches and wine, I noticed Diana, her diamonds flashing, talk for a moment to Caro alone. Just before we left, Caro spoke to me and passed a message on.

Diana had been talking to Reggie Collingwood. He had said they would all have to "feel their way." It was conceivable that Roger would have to "draw in his horns" a bit. If so, they could look after him.

It sounded, and was meant to sound, casual and confident. But it was also deliberate. Collingwood wasn't given to indiscretion. Nor, when it came to confidences, was Diana. This remark was intended to reach Roger: and Caro was making sure that it reached me. As she told me, she took me by the arm, walking towards the door, and gazed at me with bold eyes. This was not a display of affection. She did not like me any better, she was no warmer to Roger's advisers, as she walked on my arm, her shoulders, because she was a strapping woman, not so far below my own. But she was making certain that I wasn't left out.

The Bar concert had taken place on a Thursday night. On the Saturday morning I was alone in our drawing-room, the children back at school, Margaret off for a day with her father, now both ill and valetudinarian, when the telephone rang. It was David Rubin.

This was not, in itself, a surprise. I had heard the day before that he was over on one of his State Department visits. I expected that he and I would find ourselves at the same meeting on Saturday afternoon. That turned out to be true, and David expressed his courteous gratification. But it was a surprise to hear him insisting that I arrange an interview with Roger. Apparently he had tried Roger's office the day before and had been rebuffed. It was odd enough for anyone to rebuff him: much odder for him to come back afterwards. "This isn't just an idea of visiting with him. I want to say something to him."

"I rather gathered that," I said. Over the phone came a reluctant cachinnation.

He was flying out next morning. The interview would have to be fixed for some time that night. I did my best. First of all, Caro would not put me through to Roger. When at last I made her, he greeted me as though I had brought bad news. Did I know that Parliament met next week? Did I by any chance remember that he was preparing for a debate? He wanted to see no one. I said (our voices were petty with strain) that he could be rude to me, though I didn't pretend to like it. But it was unwise to be rude to David Rubin.

When I saw Rubin that afternoon, for the first time in a year, he did not look so formidable. He was sitting at a table, between Francis Getliffe and another scientist, in one of the Royal Society's rooms in Burlington House. The room smelled musty, lined with bound volumes of periodicals, like an unused library. The light was dim. Rubin, lemur-like circles under his eyes, looked fastidious and depressed. When I passed a note along, saying that we were due at Lord North Street after dinner, he gave a nod, as from one who had to endure much before he slept.

He had to endure this meeting. He was by now too much of a Government figure to hope for a great deal. He was more pessimistic than anyone there. It was not an official meeting. Everyone in the room, at least in form, had attended as a private citizen. Nearly all were scientists who had been, or still were, concerned with the nuclear projects. They were trying to find a way of talking directly to their Soviet counterparts. Several men in the room had won world fame—there were the great academic physicists, Mounteney, who was chairman, Rubin himself, an old friend of mine called Constantine. There were also Government scientists, such as Walter Luke, who had demanded to take part.

All three Governments knew what was going on. Several officials, including me, had been invited. I remembered other meetings in these musty-smelling rooms, nearly twenty years before, when scientists told us that the nuclear bomb might work.

David Rubin sat like one who has listened often enough. Then, all of a sudden, he became interested. Scientific good will, legalisms, formulations—they vanished. For the door opened, and to everyone's astonishment, there came into the room Brodzinski. Soft-footed, for all his bulk, he walked to the table, his barrel chest thrust out. His eyes were stretched wide, as he looked at Arthur Mounteney. In his strong voice, in his off-English, he said, "I'm sorry to be late, Mr. Chairman."

Each person round the table knew of his speeches in America and knew that Getliffe and Luke had been damaged. Men like Mounteney detested him and all he stood for. For him to enter, and then make his little apology—it irritated them all, it was a ridiculous anticlimax.

"I don't understand," said Arthur Mounteney, "why you're here at all." His long and cavernous face was set. He couldn't produce a soft word among his friends, let alone now.

"I was invited, Mr. Chairman. As I suppose my colleagues were, also."

This I took to be true. Invitations had gone to the scientists on the defence committees as well as to the scientific elder statesmen. Presumably Brodzinski's name had remained upon the list.

"That doesn't mean there was any sense in your coming."

"I'm sorry, Mr. Chairman. Am I to understand that only those of a certain kind of opinion are allowed here?"

Walter Luke broke in, rough-voiced: "That's not the point, Brodzinski, and you know it. You've made yourself a blasted nuisance where we can't get at you. And every bleeding scientist in this game is having the carpet pulled from under him because of you."

"I do not consider your attitude is correct, Sir Walter."

"Come off it, man, who do you take us for?"

This was unlike the stately protocol of a meeting chaired by Hector Rose.

Francis Getliffe coughed, and with his curious relic of diffidence said to Mounteney: "I think perhaps I ought to have a word."

Mounteney nodded.

"Dr. Brodzinski," said Francis, looking down the table, "if you hadn't come here today I was going to ask you to call on me."

Francis was speaking quietly, without Mounteney's bleakness or Walter Luke's roughneck scorn. He had to make an effort, while they could quarrel by the light of nature. Nevertheless, it was Francis whom we all listened to, Brodzinski most of all.

Brodzinski, although nobody had thought, or perhaps wished, to invite him (since the normal courtesies had failed) to sit down, had found himself a chair. He sat in it, squarely, heavy as a mountain and as impervious.

"It's time you heard something about your behaviour. It's got to be made clear to you. I was going to do that. I had better do it now. You must realise there are two things your scientific colleagues hold against you. The first is the way you have behaved to some of us. This is not important in the long run: but it is enough to make us prefer not to have any personal dealings with you. You have made charges about us in public and, as I believe, more charges in private, that we could only meet by legal action. You have taken advantage of the fact that we are not willing to take legal action against a fellow scientist. You have said that we are dishonest. You have said that we have perverted the truth. You have said that we are disloyal to our country."

"I have been misrepresented, of course," said Brodzinski.

"Not in the least."

"I have always given you credit for good intentions, Sir

Francis," said Brodzinski. "I do not expect the same from you."

His expression was pure, persecuted, and brave. It was the courage of one who, even now, believed in his locked-in self that they would see how right he was. He felt no conflict, no regret nor remorse, just the certainty that he was right. At the same time, he wanted pity because he was being persecuted. He was crying out for pity. The more they saw he was right, the more they would persecute him.

Suddenly a thought came to me. I hadn't understood why, the previous summer, he had given up attempting to see Roger: as though he had switched from faith to enmity. It must have been the day the offer of his decoration arrived. He had accepted the decoration—but he could have felt, I was sure he could have felt, that it was another oblique piece of persecution, a token that he was not so high as the Getliffes of the world, a sign of dismissal.

"I had to make some criticisms," he said. "Because you were dangerous. I gave you the credit for not realising how dangerous you were, but, of course, I had to make some criticisms. You can see that, Dr. Rubin."

He turned with an open, hopeful face to David Rubin, who was scribbling on a sheet of paper. Rubin raised his head slowly and gazed at Brodzinski with opaque eyes.

"What you did," he said, "was not admissible."

"I did not expect any more from you, Dr. Rubin." This answer was so harsh and passionate that it left him mystified. Rubin believed that Brodzinski had remembered that he was a Gentile talking to a Jew.

"You said we were dangerous," Francis Getliffe went on. "I've finished now with your slanders on us. They only count because they're involved in the other damage you've done. That is the second thing you must hear about. It is the opinion of most of us that you've done great damage to decent people everywhere. If we are going to use the word dangerous, you are at present one of the most dangerous men in the world. And you've done the damage by distorting science. It is possible to have different views on the nuclear situation. It is not possible, without lying or irresponsibility or something worse, to say the things you have said. You've encouraged people to believe that the United States and England can destroy Russia without too much loss. Most of us would regard that suggestion as wicked, even if it were true. But we all know that it is not true, and, for as long as we can foresee, it never will be true."

"That is why you are dangerous," said Brodzinski. "That is why I have to expose myself. You think you are people of good will. You are doing great harm, in everything you do. You are even doing great harm in little meetings like this. That is why I have come where I am not welcome. You think you can come to terms with the Russians. You never will. The only realistic thing for all of us is to make the weapons as fast as we know how."

"You are prepared to think of war?" said Arthur Mounteney.

"Of course I am prepared to think of war. So is any realistic man," Brodzinski replied. "If there has to be a war, then we must win it. We can keep enough people alive. We shall soon pick up. Human beings are very strong."

"And that is what you hope for?" said Francis, in a dead, cold tone.

"That is what will happen."

"You can tolerate the thought of three hundred million deaths?"

"I can tolerate anything which will happen."

Brodzinski went on, his eyes lit up, once more pure: "You will not see, there are worse things which might happen."

"I have to assume that you are responsible for your actions," said Francis. "If that is so, I had better tell you straight away—I cannot sit in the same room with you."

Faces, closed to expression, looked down the table at Brodzinski. There was a silence. He sat squarely in his chair and said:

"I believe I am here by invitation, Mr. Chairman."

"It would save trouble if you left," said Arthur Mounteney.

With exaggerated reasonableness, Brodzinski said:

"But I can produce my invitation, Mr. Chairman."

"In that case, I shall adjourn the meeting. And call another to which you are not invited."

Later, that seemed to Rubin a masterpiece of Anglo-Saxon propriety.

Brodzinski stood up, massive, stiff.

"Mr. Chairman," he said, "I am sorry that my colleagues have seen fit to treat me in this fashion. But I expected it."

His dignity was absolute. With the same dignity, he went, soft-footed, strong-muscled, out of the room.

CHAPTER XXXV

A CHOICE

A few hours later, in David Rubin's bedroom, he and I were having a snack before we went on to Roger's house. The room was modest, in a cheap, genteel Kensington hotel: the snack was modest too. Rubin had the entrée to Heads of State, but, despite the "Tailor and Cutter" elegance of his clothes, he lived more simply than an Embassy clerk. He was a poor man, he had never earned money, apart from his academic salary and his prizes.

He sat without complaint in the cold bedroom, nibbling a stale sandwich, sipping at a weak and un-iced whiskey. He talked about his son at Harvard, and his mother who would scarcely have known what Harvard was, who had not spoken English in the home, and who had been ambitious for David—just as rapaciously as my mother for me. He spoke a little sadly. Everything had come off for him, spectacular achievement, happy marriage, the love of children. He was one of the men most venerated in the world. Yet there were times when he seemed to look back to his childhood, shrug his shoulders and think that he had expected more.

We had each been talking without reserve, like passengers at sea. He sat there, in elegant suit, silk shirt, hand-made shoes, shook his head, and looked at me with sad, kind eyes. It occurred to me that he had not given me a clue, not so much as a hint, why he was so insistent on talking to Roger that night.

When we arrived at Lord North Street, it was about half-past nine and Roger and Caro were still sitting in the dining-room. It was the place where Roger, nearly three years before, had interrogated Rubin. As on that evening, Rubin was ceremonious—bowing over Caro's hand: "Lady Caroline" —greeting Roger. As on that evening, Roger pushed the decanter round.

At Caro's right hand, Rubin was willing to drink his glass of port, but not to open a conversation. Caro looked down the table at Roger, who was sitting silent and impatient with strain. She had her own kind of stoicism. She was prepared to chat with Rubin, in a loud brassy fashion, about his flight next day, about whether he hated flying as much as she did. She was terrified every time, she said, with the exaggerated protestations of cowardice that her brother Sammikins went in for.

All four of us were waiting for the point to come. At last Roger could wait no longer.

"Well?" he said roughly, straight at Rubin.

"Minister?" said David Rubin, as though surprised.

"I thought you had something to tell me."

"Do you have time?" said Rubin mysteriously.

Roger nodded. To everyone's astonishment, Rubin began a long, dense and complex account of the theory of games as applied to nuclear strategy. Talk of over-simplification— this was over-complication gone mad. It was not long before Roger stopped him.

"Whatever you've come for," he said, "it isn't this."

Rubin looked at him with an expression harsh, affectionately distressed. Suddenly his whole manner changed from the incomprehensibly devious to a brutal-sounding snap.

"I came to tell you to get out while there's time. If not, you'll cut your own throat."

"Get out of what?"

"Out of your present planning, or design, or whatever you like to call it. You don't stand a chance."

"You think so, do you?" said Roger.

"Why else should I come?"

Then Rubin's tone became once more quiet and reasonable:

"Wait a minute. I couldn't make up my mind whether to let it go. It's because we respect you—"

"We want to hear," said Caro. This wasn't social, it wasn't to make him comfortable. It was said with absolute attention.

Roger and Rubin sat blank-faced. In the room, each sound was clear. To an extent they liked each other: but that didn't matter. Between them there was something quite different from liking or disliking, or even trust. It was the sense of actuality, the sense of events.

"First of all," said Rubin, "let me make my own position clear. Everything you've planned to do is sensible. This is right. Anyone who knows the facts of life knows that this is right. For the foreseeable future, there can only be two nuclear powers. One is my country, and the other is the Soviet Union. Your country cannot play in that league. As far as the economic and military side go, the sooner you get out the better. This is correct."

"You told us so," said Roger, "in this very room, years ago."

"What is more," said Rubin, "we will want you out. The way our thinking is shaping up, we will decide that these weapons ought to be concentrated in as few hands as possible. Meaning, us and the Soviets. This is right also. Before long, I'm ready to predict that you'll be under some pressure from us—"

"You're saying it in different terms, and for slightly different reasons." Roger spoke without either intransigence or suggestibility. "But you're saying what I've been saying, and what I've been trying to do."

"And what you can't do." Rubin's voice hardened as he added: "And what you must get out of, here and now."

There was a pause. Then, as though he were being simple, Roger asked:

"Why?"

Rubin shrugged his shoulders, spread his hands.

"I'm a scientist. You're a politician. And you ask me *that?*"

"I should still like to hear the answer."

"Do I have to tell you that a course of action can be right —and not worth a second's thought? It's not of importance that it's right. What is of importance is how it's done, who it's done by, and, most of all, when it's done."

"As you say," said Roger, "one's not unfamiliar with those principles. Now I wish you'd tell me what you know."

Rubin stared down at the table.

"I mustn't say that I know," he said at last. "But I suspect. A foreigner sometimes picks up indications that you wouldn't give such weight to. I believe you're swimming against the tide. Your colleagues will not admit it. But if you swim too far, they wouldn't be able to stay loyal to you, would they?"

Rubin went on: "They're not fools, if you don't mind me saying so. They've been watching you having to struggle for every inch you've made. Everything's turned out ten per cent, twenty per cent, sometimes fifty per cent, more difficult than you figured on. You know that better than any of us. Lewis knows." For an instant, under the hooded lids, I caught a glance, glinting with *Weltschmerz* and fellow-feeling. "Everything's turned out too difficult. It's my view of almost any human concern, that if it turns out impossibly difficult, if you've tried it every way, and it still won't go, then the time has come to call it a day. This is surely true of intellectual problems. The more I've seen of your type of problem the more I believe it's true of them. Your colleagues are good at keeping a stiff upper lip. But they're used to dealing with the real world. I suspect that they'll be compelled to think the same."

"Do you *know*?" Roger spoke quietly, and with all his force.

Rubin raised his head, then let his eyes fall again. "I've made my own position clear to everyone I know in Washington. They'll come round to thinking that you and I were right. But they haven't got there yet. They don't know what to think about your weapons. But I have to tell you something. They are worried about your motives for wanting to give them up."

"Do you think we ought to care about that?" cried Caro, with a flash of arrogance.

"I think you'll be unwise not to, Lady Caroline," said Rubin. "I don't claim they've analysed the situation. But as of this moment, they're not all that interested in what you do—as long as you don't seem to be sliding out of the Cold War. This is the one thing that they're scared of. This is the climate. This is the climate in which some of them are anxious about you now."

"How much have they listened to Brodzinski?" I said angrily.

"He hasn't helped," said Rubin. "He's done you some harm. But it's deeper than that."

"Yes," said Roger, "it's deeper than that."

"I'm glad you know." Rubin turned to Caro. "I told you, Lady Caroline, you'll be unwise not to care about this. Some of our people are in a state of tension about it. At various levels. Including high levels. Some of that tension is liable to be washed across to this side. Maybe some of it has been washed across already."

"That wouldn't be so astounding," said Roger.

"Of course, it's frustrating to disengage oneself," said Rubin. "But the facts are very strong. So far as I've observed anything on this side, you've only to play it cool and put it aside for five, ten years. Then you'll be right at the top here, unless my information is all wrong. And you'll be swimming with the tide, not against it. As for Washington, they'll be begging you to do exactly what you can't do now." Rubin gave a sharp, ironic smile. "And you're the one person in this country who will be able to do it. You're a valuable man. Not only to Britain, but to all of us. This is why I'm giving you this trouble. We can't afford to waste you. And I am as certain as I am of anything that if you didn't take one step backwards now, you would be wasted."

For an instant, none of us spoke. Roger looked down the table at his wife and said: "You hear what he says?"

"You have heard too, haven't you?" said Caro.

All the social clangour had left her voice. It held nothing but devotion. She was speaking as they did when they were alone. They had said very little, but enough. Roger knew what she thought, and what answer she wanted him to give. Their marriage might be breaking on his side, but it still had its shorthand. The message was simple. She was, though Rubin did not know it, his supporter.

Right through Roger's struggle, she had been utterly loyal. One expected nothing else: and yet, one knew what she was concealing. In her heart she couldn't give up her chauvinistic pride. Just as she had flared out against David Rubin, when he reminded them that the English power had sunk, so she couldn't accept that the great days were over. Her instincts were as simple as my mother's would have been.

But that wasn't the main force which drove her to Rubin's side, made her cheeks glow and eyes shine as she answered Roger. For Rubin had just offered Roger a prospect of the future: and that was her prospect too. It would have seemed to her absurd, finicky, hypocritical and above all genteel, not to want the top place for Roger. If he didn't want that, she would have said, then he ought not to be in politics at all. If she didn't want that for him, she ought not to be his wife.

"I agree with almost everything you've said." Roger spoke directly to Rubin. "You've made it very clear. I'm extremely grateful to you." His tone was subdued, reasonable, a little submissive. At that moment he sounded like one willing to be converted, or perhaps already converted, arguing for the sake of self-respect. "You know," he said, with an abstracted smile, "I've thought out some of these things for myself. You'll give me credit for that?"

Rubin smiled.

"Of course," Roger went on, "if you want to get anywhere in politics, you've got to be good at pushing on open doors. If you can't resist pushing on closed ones, then you ought to have chosen another job. That's what you're telling me, isn't it? Of course you're right. I shouldn't be surprised if you hadn't wasted some energy on closed doors in your time. Much more than I ever have. But then, of course, you're not a politician."

It might have been a jibe, I couldn't tell. If so, it was a gentle one. Roger was speaking without strain or edge. He said: "My one trouble is, I can't help thinking the present situation is slightly different. I think, if we don't bring this one off now, we never shall. Or we shan't until it's too late. Isn't that the only difference between us? Perhaps you can tell me that it isn't so."

"The honest answer is," said Rubin slowly, "that I don't know."

"You believe everything will drift along, with no one able to stop anywhere?"

"I don't know."

"Most of us understand the situation. None of us can affect it?"

"Does any one person matter very much? Can any one person do very much?"

"You're a wise man," said Roger.

There was a long pause. Roger spoke with complete relaxation, so that it was surprising to hear how strong his voice sounded. He said:

"You're saying, we're all caught. All the world. The position has crystallised on both sides. There's nothing for any of us to do. That's what you're saying, isn't it? All we can do is stick to our position, and be humble enough to accept that there's practically nothing we can do."

"In detail there may be a little," said Rubin.

"That's not much, is it?" Roger gave a friendly smile. "You're a very wise man." He paused again. "And yet, you know, it's pretty hard to take. In that case, one might as well not be here at all. Anyone could just wait until it's easy. I don't think I should have lived this life if that were all."

For a moment his tone had been passionate. Then it became curiously formal and courteous as he added:

"I'm most grateful for your advice. I very much wish I could accept it. It would make things easier for me."

He looked up the table and said to Caro, as though they were alone:

"I wish I could do what you want."

It seemed to me that had Caro known she was fighting for her marriage, she would not so openly have implied her opposition to Roger that night. He was guilt-ridden enough to welcome the smallest loophole of escape, just to feel to himself that it could not have gone on, anyway. Yet was that really so? He had known her mind, he had always known it. To her, loyalty to Roger would have seemed less if she had gone in for pretences. She had said nothing new that night. But I believed that her repetition, before Rubin, of what had already been said in private, might have given Roger some vestigial sense of relief, of which he was nevertheless ashamed.

He said, "I wish I could."

I wondered when Rubin had realised that Roger was going through with it? At what point, at what word? In intellect

Rubin was by far the subtler; in emotion, he was playing with a master.

There was another oddity. In private, Rubin was as high-principled, as morally fastidious, as Francis Getliffe. And yet —it was a disconcerting truth—there were times, and most important times, when the high-principled were not to be trusted—and perhaps Roger was. For to Roger there were occasions, not common, but not so rare as we all suspected, when morality grew out of action. In private, Rubin lived a better life than most men; and yet he would have been incapable of contemplating walking into obloquy, risking his reputation, gambling his future, as in clear sight Roger was doing now.

I wondered when I myself had realised that Roger was going through with it. In a sense, I had believed it soon after we became intimate, and I had backed my judgment. Yet simultaneously, I had not trusted my judgment very far. In the midst of his obfuscation, I had been no surer than anyone else that he would not desert us. And so, in that sense, I had not realised, or at least had not been certain, that he was going through with it until—until that night.

When did Roger realise it? He would not have known, or been interested to know. Morality sprang out of action, so did choices, certainly a choice as complex as this. Even now, he might not know in what terms he would have to make it: nor from what motives it would come.

How much part, it occurred to me again, had his relation with Ellen played?

"I can't accept your advice, David," said Roger, "but I do accept your estimate of my chances. You don't think I'm going to survive, do you? Nor do I. I'd like you to understand that I agree."

He added, with a hard and radiant smile:

"But it isn't absolutely cut and dried even now. They haven't quite finished with me yet."

Until that moment he had been speaking with total realism. Suddenly his mood had switched. He was suffused with hope, the hope of crisis, that hope which just before a struggle warms one with the assurance that it is already won. With the anxious pouches darker under his eyes, Rubin gazed at him in astonishment, and something like dismay.

He felt, we could all feel, that Roger was happy. He was not only happy and hopeful, he was also serene.

V
THE VOTE

CHAPTER XXXVI

SOMETHING OUT OF CHARACTER

The light on Big Ben was shining like a golden bead in the January evening; the House had reassembled. It was a season of parties. Three times that week my wife and I went out before dinner, to Diana's house in South Street, to a private member's flat, to a Government reception. The faces revolved about one like a stage army. Confident faces, responding to other confident faces, as though this parade was preserved forever, like a moment in time. Ministers and their wives linked themselves with other Ministers and their wives, drawn by the magnetism of office: groups of four, groups of six, sturdy, confident, confidential backs presented themselves (not impolitely, but because it was a treat to be together) to the room. Roger and Caro were there, looking as impregnable as the rest.

There was an hallucination about high places which acted like alcohol, not only on Roger under threat, but on whole circles. They couldn't believe they had lost the power till it had gone. Even when it had gone, they didn't always believe it.

That week and the next, mornings in the office were like wartime. Roger was sitting in his room, never looking bored, sending out for papers, asking for memoranda, intimate with no one, so far as I knew, certainly not with me.

Ripples of admiration and faith were flowing down the corridors. They reached middle-grade civil servants who, as a rule, wanted only to get home and listen to long-playing records. As for the scientists, they were triumphing already. Walter Luke, who had believed in Roger from the beginning, stopped me in a gloomy, lavatory-like passage in the Treasury where his uninhibited voice reverberated round: "By God, the old bleeder's going to get away with it! It just shows, if you go on talking sense for long enough, you wear 'em down in time."

When I mentioned Walter's opinion to Hector Rose, he said, with a frigid but not unfriendly smile: *"Sancta simplicitas."*

Even Rose was not immune from the excitement. Yet he found it necessary to tell me that he had been in touch with Monteith. The piece of false information, which I had protested about, had been checked. Rose had satisfied himself that it was an honest mistake. He told me this, as though the first imperative for both of us was that official procedures should be proved correct. Then he felt free to pass on to Roger's chances.

During those days I talked once or twice to Douglas, but only to try to comfort him about his wife. The prognosis had been confirmed: she would become paralysed, she would die within five years. At his desk he sat stoically writing upon official paper. When I went in, he talked of nothing but her.

February had come, it was warm for the time of year, Whitehall was basking in the smoky sunlight.

By the end of the month, Roger was due to make his speech on the White Paper. We were all lulling ourselves with work. All of a sudden, the lull broke. It broke in a fashion that no one had expected. It was a surprise to the optimistic: but it was even more of a surprise to the experienced. It didn't look much in the office. Just a note on a piece of paper. Harmless-looking, the words.

The Opposition had put down a motion to reduce the Navy vote by ten pounds.

It would have sounded archaic, or plain silly, to those who didn't know Parliament. Even to some who did, it sounded merely technical. It was technical, but most of us knew it meant much more. Who was behind it? Was it a piece of political chess? We did not believe it. Roger did not pretend to believe it.

Our maximum hope had been that, when the House "took notice" of the White Paper, the Opposition would not make much of the debate, or force a division. This hadn't seemed unrealistic. Some of them believed that Roger was as good— as near their line—as anyone they could expect. If he lost, they would get something worse. They had tried to damp down their own "wild men." But now the switch was sudden and absolute. They were going for him, attacking him before his White Paper speech. They were ready to give up two of their supply days for the job. They must have known something about Roger's side. They must have known more than that.

Roger had scarcely seen me, since the night at his house with Rubin. Now he sent for me.

He gave a smile as I entered his room, but it wasn't a comradely one. He had kept his command intact, and his self-control: but, so it seemed, at the price of denying that we knew each other well. We were talking like business partners, with years of risk behind us, with a special risk present now: no closer than that: his face was hard, impatient, over-clear.

What did I know about it? No more than he did, probably less, I said.

"I doubt if you can know less," he said. He broke out: "What does it mean?"

"How in God's name should I know?"

"You must have an idea."

I stared at him without speaking. Yes, I had an idea. I suspected we were fearing the same thing.

"We're grown men," he said. "Tell me."

I did so. I said it looked to me like a classical case of fraternisation behind the lines. That is, some of his enemies, on his own back benches, had been making a bargain with their Opposition counterparts. The Opposition back benchers had pressed their leaders to bring the vote. They would get support—how much support?—from the Government side. It was more decent that way. If Roger made a compromising speech, his colleagues and Party would stay with him. But if he were too unorthodox—well, if a Minister were too unorthodox to be convenient, there were other methods of dislodging him: this was one which gave least pain to his own Party.

"Yes," he said, "I think you're quite likely right. That may be it."

He had spoken neutrally. He went on, in an impatient, active tone: "Well, there's nothing for it. We've got to know."

He meant, we had to know, not only whether we were right, but, if so, who the enemy were. One or two dissidents in his own Party he could write off: but thirty or forty—and the more so if they were respected members—would mean the end. Unless he behaved as Collingwood and his colleagues would have done, and denied that he meant to do anything at all. For an instant the temptation flickered again. Then he shut it away. He was set.

He was estimating the odds, and also our sources of information. He would be talking to the Whips himself that day and to friends in the Party. The trouble was, he said, still talking cold sense, this didn't sound like a respectable revolt. He hadn't received a letter of regret, and no one had spoken to him face to face. We should have to go in for subterranean talking ourselves. Some of my Opposition friends might know something. So might the Press.

"You'd better find out," said Roger, as briskly as though he were himself only remotely concerned, but was advising me for my own good.

From two sources I learned much the same story. An Opposition front-bencher whom I had known at Cambridge told it to me: a journalist took me along to El Vino's to meet a couple of lobby correspondents. Next day, I had some news —not hard news, but more solid than a rumour—for Roger.

Yes, the correspondents had confirmed, our guess had something in it. There had been chaffering (one journalist claimed to know the place of the meeting) between a group of Opposition members and a few Conservatives. The Opposition members were mostly on the extreme right-wing of the Labour Party, though there were one or two pacifists and disarmers. I kept asking who the Conservatives were, and how many. There, just at the point of fact—the rumour got wrapped in wool. Very few, one of my informants thought —maybe only two or three. No one who counted. One was, they were sure, the young man who had asked the Parliamentary Question about Brodzinski's speech. "Oddballs," my acquaintance kept repeating in the noisy pub, as the drinks went round, as though he found the phrase satisfactory.

It wasn't bad news, so far as it existed. Considering our expectations, we might have been consoled. But Roger did not take it so. We were grown men, he had said. But it was one thing to face the thought of a betrayal, even a little one: another to hear that the thought was true. He was angry with me for bringing the news. He was bitter with himself. "I've never spent enough time drinking with fools," he cried. "I've never made them feel they're important. It's the one thing they can't forgive."

That evening, he did something out of character. Accompanied by Tom Wyndham, he spent hours in the smoking-room at the House, trying to be matey. I heard the story from Wyndham next day, who said in a puzzled fashion:

"It's the first time I've known the old boy lose his grip." The great figure, clumsy as a bear, standing in the middle of the room, catching acquaintances' eyes, downing tankards of beer, performing the only one of the personal arts at which he was downright bad. In a male crowd, he was at a loss. There he stood inept, grateful for the company of a colleague who was no use to him, until Tom Wyndham led him away.

He had lost his head. Within twenty-four hours he had regained it. He was outfacing me, daring me to suggest that he had been upset. This time, smoothly in charge, he was doing what ought to be done. One of his supporters had summoned a meeting of the private members' defence committee. No one at that meeting would have guessed that he had, even for a single evening, not been able to trust his nerve. No one would have guessed that he could stand inept, lost, among a crowd of acquaintances.

Reports came flicking through the lobbies that Roger was "holding them," that he was "in form," "back again." I saw one of my journalist informants talking, as though casually, with a smart, beaming-faced member fresh from the meeting.

Once, to most of us, it had merely been a matter of gossipy interest, to identify the leaks, the sources of news. Now we weren't so detached. This, as it happened, was good news.

I took the journalist back to El Vino's. He was so eupeptic, so willing to cheer me up, that I was ready to stand him many drinks. Yes, Roger had carried them with him. "That chap won't be finished till he's dead," said my acquaintance, with professional admiration. After another drink, he was speculating about Roger's enemies. Four or five, he said: anyway, you could count them on one hand. Men of straw. The phrase "oddballs" had a tendency to recur, giving him a sense of definition, illumination, perfection, denied to me.

CHAPTER XXXVII

THE USE OF MONEY

On the Sunday afternoon, my taxi drove through the empty, comfortable Cambridge streets, across Garret Hostel Bridge, along the Backs towards my brother's house. There he and Francis Getliffe were waiting for me. I hadn't come just to make conversation, but for a while we sat round the fire in the drawing-room: the bronze doors were not closed, and through the far window the great elm stood up against the cyclorama of sunset sky.

"I must say," I said, "it all looks remarkably placid."

Martin's controlled features broke into a grin.

"I must say," he jeered at me.

"What's the matter?"

"Do you realise that's exactly what used to infuriate you when big bosses came down from London and met you in the college, and told you what a peaceful place it was?"

His eyes were bright with fraternal malice. He told me one or two of the latest stories about the new Master's reign. Some of the college officers were finding it appropriate to write him letters rather than expose themselves to conversation. Martin gave a bleak smile. "You live in a sheltered world, you know," he said.

I wished that he had been with us in the Whitehall struggles. He was a harder man than Francis, tougher and more

apt for politics than most of us. Curiously, he was one of the
few scientists who had got out of atomic energy and made a
sacrifice for conscience' sake. He had chosen a dimmish career
as a college functionary: it seemed likely that that was where
he would stay. And yet, in his middle forties, his face set in
the shape it would remain until he was old, eyes watchful, he
gave out an air not only of detachment but content.

His wife, Irene, brought in the tea-tray. Once she had
been a wild young woman, and had made him live with
jealousy. But now time had played on her one of its pyknic
practical jokes. She had become mountainous, the flesh had
blown up as though she were a Michelin advertisement. She
must have weighed fifty or sixty pounds more than when I
first met her, before the war. Her yelp of a laugh was still
youthful and flirtatious. Her spirits had stayed high, he had
long ago won the battle of wills in their marriage, she had
come totally to love him, and also was content.

"Plotting?" she said to me. She behaved to me, she had
done for years, much as she did to Martin, as though knowing
one brother she knew the other: as though neither of us was
as sedate as he seemed.

"Not yet," I said.

As we drank our tea I asked Francis, just to delay my
mission, whether he had heard from Penelope.

"As a matter of fact," he replied, "I had a letter a couple
of days ago."

"What's she doing?"

He looked puzzled: "That's what I should like to know."

"What does she *say*?" Irene burst in.

"I'm not quite sure," said Francis.

He looked round at the three of us, hesitated, and then
went on: "Look here, what do you make of this?" He
pulled an envelope out of his pocket, put on his long-sighted
glasses, and began to read. He read, I couldn't help thinking,

as though the letter were written in a language like Etruscan, in which most of the words were still unknown.

" 'Dearest Daddy,

" 'Please do not *flap*. I am *perfectly* alright, and *perfectly* happy, working like a beaver, and all is fine with Art and me, and we haven't any special plans, but he may come back with me in the summer—he isn't sure. There's no need for you to worry about us, we're just having a lot of fun, and nobody's bothering about marriage or anything like that, so do stop *questioning*. I think you and Mummy must be *sex-maniacs*.

" 'I have met a nice boy called Brewster (*first* name), he dances as badly as I do so that suits us both. His father owns *three* night clubs in Reno but I don't tell Art that ! ! ! Anyway it is not at all serious and is only a bit of fun. I may go to Art's people for the weekend if I can raise the dollars. I don't always want him to pay for me.

" 'No more now. Brew is fuming (much I care) because he's double-parked and says he'll get a ticket if I don't hurry. Must go.

" 'Lots and lots of love,
" 'Penny.'

"Well?" said Francis, taking off his glasses. He broke out irritably, as though it were Penny's major crime: "I wish she could spell *'all right.'* "

The rest of us did not find it prudent to meet one another's eyes.

"What do you do?" said Francis. "What sanctions has one got?"

"You could cut off supplies," said Martin, who was a practical man.

"Yes," said Francis indecisively. After a long pause he went on: "I don't think I should like to do that."

"You're worrying too much," cried Irene, with a high, delighted laugh.

"Am I?"

"Of course you are."

"Why?" He was turning to her for reassurance.

"When I was her age, I could have written a letter just like that."

"Could you?" Francis gazed at her. She was good-natured, she wanted him to be happy. But he did not find the reassurance quite so overwhelming as she had expected; her youth wasn't perhaps the first model he would have chosen for his daughter.

When she left us, I got down at last to business. It was simple.

For Quaife to survive was going to be a close-run thing. Any bit of help was worth the effort. Could they whip up some scientific support for him—not from the usual quarters, not from the Pugwash group who had dismissed Brodzinski, but from uncommitted men? A speech or two in the House of Lords: a letter to the *Times* with some "respectable" signatures? Any demonstration might swing a vote or two.

I was still making my case at the moment that Irene returned, apologising, smelling a secret. There was someone on the telephone for me, a long-distance call. With a curse I went off into the lobby under the stairs: a voice came down the line that I didn't recognise, giving a name that I didn't know. We had met at Finch's, the voice was saying. That meant nothing. The pub on the Fulham Road, came the explanation, brisk, impatient. They had traced me to my home, and so to Cambridge. They thought I should know what to do. Old Ronald Porson had been arrested the night before. What for? Importuning in a lavatory.

I felt—first—sheer blind irritation at being distracted. Then a touch of pity, the black pity of the past. Then, most of all, the tiredness of the ties one couldn't escape, the accretion of the duties, the years, the acquaintanceships. I muttered something, but the brisk active male voice pressed on. They didn't know the ropes as well as I did.

I collected myself. I gave the name of a solicitor. If they hadn't got one already, they must make Porson listen to this man and do what he was told. Yes: this young friend of Porson's sounded efficient, they were all trying to look after him. The "old man" hadn't a penny, the voice said. Was I prepared to contribute? Of course, I said, anxious to be away: they must tell the solicitor that I would meet the bill. I felt tired, relieved, as I put the receiver down, trying to put the message out of mind.

As I went back to the hearth, Martin looked at me.

"Anything wrong?" he said.

"Someone in trouble," I replied. No, not anyone close. No one he knew.

I said impatiently, "Let's get on." I had made a proposal, we had been interrupted, there was not much time.

For a long time, as we sat round the fire, Martin did most of the talking. I knew, without our having spoken together, what he thought. He did not believe that we stood more than an outside chance. He did not believe that any government could bring off more than a poor compromise. He believed that any government would have to repudiate a man who tried to do more. But he did not tell me so. He had been close enough to decisions to know the times when it was better not to be told. Instead, he was ready to help: and yet, as he said, he wasn't eminent enough as a scientist to carry weight. Somehow, he remarked, the high scientific community had lost either its nerve or its will. There were plenty of people like himself, he went on, ready to be active. But the major scientists had retired into their profession—"There's no one of your standing," he said to Francis, "who's ready to take the risks you took twenty years ago." It wasn't that a new generation of scientists hadn't as much conscience or more: or as much good will: or even as much courage. Somehow the climate had changed, they were not impelled. Had the world got too big for them? Had events become too big for men?

Neither Martin nor I was willing to admit it. After sitting silent, Francis said, at any rate one had to go on acting as though it were not true.

Yes, he said, shrugging himself free, suddenly speaking as though he were a younger man, in command again, he thought my idea was worth trying. Yes, he agreed, it was no use Martin approaching the most senior scientists. He, Francis, would have to take on another job: he would do it himself. We were not to hope for much. He had used his influence too many times, and there was not much of it left.

As we went on talking, I was only half-thinking of the scientists. I could not get rid, completely or for long, of the thought of Porson. There was something I had heard in the voice over the telephone: something that the voice, confident as it sounded, hadn't uttered. They would have liked to ask me to come back, so that I could help him myself.

Years before, that was what I should have done. By now this kind of compulsion had grown dim. I was the worse for it. For most of us, the quixotic impulses might stay alive, but in time the actions didn't follow. I had used money to buy off my fellow-feeling, to save trouble, to save myself the expense of spirit that I was no longer impelled to spend.

CHAPTER XXXVIII

"A SMALL ROOM
AND A GAS-RING"

Lord Lufkin summoned Margaret and me to a dinner-party at twenty-four hours' notice, just as he summoned many guests. He had done the same for thirty years, long before his great success had come: he had done it during the years when he was hated: and still his guests had obeyed.

That February night—it was in the week after my visit to Cambridge—we trooped dutifully into Lufkin's drawing-room in St. James's Court. No one could have called it a cheerful room. Lufkin had had it panelled in dark pine, and there was not a picture on the walls except a portrait of himself. No one went to Lufkin's expecting a cheerful party. His gifts as a host were negative. Yet in that room there were standing a couple of Ministers, a Treasury boss, the President of the Royal Society, a fellow tycoon.

Lufkin stood in the middle, not making any small talk, nor any other size of talk; not shy so much as not feeling it worthwhile. He took it for granted that he was holding court. The interesting thing was, so did everyone round him. In the past, I had sometimes wondered why. The short answer was, the magnetic pull of power. Not simply, though that added, because he had become one of the top industrialists in England. Much more, because he had complete aptitude for power, had assumed it all his life, and now could back it with everything he had won.

He announced to his guests at large that he had taken over the suite adjoining this one. He ordered a door to be thrown open to show a perspective of tenebrous rooms.

"I decided we needed it," he said.

Lufkin's tastes were austere. He spent little on himself: his income must have been enormous, but he was pernicketily honest, he didn't use any half-legitimate devices for sliding away from taxes, and he had not made an impressive fortune. On the other hand, as though in revenge, he insisted on his firm giving him all the luxuries he had no liking for. This suite was already too big for him, but he had made them double it. He made them pay for his court-like dinner parties. He made them provide not one car, but half a dozen.

Even so, Lufkin had a supreme talent for getting it both ways. "I don't regard this flat as my own, of course," he was saying, with his usual moral certainty.

People near him, hypnotized into agreeing, were sagely nodding their heads.

"I regard it as the company's flat, not mine. I've told my staff that time and time again. This flat is for the use of the whole company."

If I had been alone with Lufkin, whom I had known much longer than had his other guests, I couldn't have resisted analysing that arcane remark. What would have happened if some member of his staff had taken him at his word, and booked the flat for the weekend?

"As for myself," he said, "my needs are very simple. All I want is *a small room and a gas-ring.*"

The maddening thing was, it was quite true.

Though Lufkin might have preferred a round of toast, we moved in to a dinner which was far from simple. The dining-room, through another inexplicable decree, was excessively bright, the only bright room in the flat. The chandeliers flashed heavily down above our heads. The table was over-flowered. The hierarchy of glasses glittered and shone.

Lufkin, himself content with a whiskey and soda for the meal, looked on with approbation as the glasses filled with sherry, hock, claret, champagne. He sat in the middle of his table, his skull-face still young, hair neat and dark in his sixties, with the air of a spectator at what he regarded as a well-conducted dinner. He did not trouble to speak much, though occasionally he talked in a manner off-hand but surreptitious to Margaret. He enjoyed the presence of women. Though he spent most of his time in male company, with his usual cross-grainedness he never liked it much. It was half-way through the meal when he addressed the table. His fellow-tycoon had begun talking of Roger Quaife and the White Paper. The Ministers were listening, attentive, deadpan, and so was I. Suddenly, Lufkin, who had been sitting back, as though utterly detached, his knife and fork aligned, three-quarters of his pheasant left uneaten, intervened.

In his hard, clear voice he said:

"What's that you were saying?"

"I said, the city's getting bearish about some of the long-term consequences."

"What do *they* know?" said Lufkin, with inspissated contempt.

"There's a feeling that Quaife's going to run the aircraft industry into the ground."

"Nonsense," said Lufkin, at his bleakest. He had caught my eye. Even Lufkin was not usually as rude as this without a purpose. I had suspected that this dinner wasn't such an accidental gathering as it seemed.

"There's nothing in that." He spoke as one who does not propose to say any more. Then he condescended to explain himself.

"Whatever happens, Quaife or no Quaife, or whether they throw you out at the next election—" he gave a sardonic smile at the Ministers "—and the other chaps come in, there's only room in this country for a couple of aircraft firms, at most. More likely than not, two is one too many."

"I suppose you mean," said the other industrialist with a show of spirit, "that you ought to be the only firm left in?"

Lufkin was the last man in existence to be worried about being *parti pris*: or to have qualms because he was safe with a major contract: or to question whether his own interests and the national interests must necessarily coincide.

"An efficient firm," he said, "ought to be ready to take its chance. Mine is."

That sounded like the cue. Again Lufkin, looking at no one in particular, caught my eye.

He said:

"I might as well tell you. I'm a hundred per cent pro Quaife. I hope you'll see—" he was speaking to the Ministers "—that *these people*" (by which Lufkin meant anyone he disapproved of) "don't make the job impossible for him. No one's ever done it properly, of course. With your set-up, there isn't a proper job to do. But Quaife's the only chap who hasn't been a hopeless failure. You might as well remember that."

Having given what, for him, was lavish praise, Lufkin had finished. Dinner proceeded.

The women left us, Margaret casting at me, over her shoulder, a look of one who is doomed. I had known Lufkin, in that room, keep the men talking over the port for two hours while the women waited. "You wouldn't suggest that I was conversationally inept, would you?" Margaret had said to me after one of these occasions. "But several times tonight *I dried*. We talked about the children, and then about the servant problem, and then about the cleaning of jewellery. I found it hard to be chatty about that. You'd better buy me a tiara, so I can join in next time." That night, however, Lufkin passed the decanter round twice and then remarked, as though it were self-evident, "I don't believe in segregating the sexes. Anachronistic."

As the Ministers, the tycoon, the Second Secretary, the P.R.S., were moving into the drawing-room, Lufkin called out sharply:

"Wait a minute, Lewis. I want a word with you."

I sat down opposite to him. He pushed a bowl of flowers aside so that he could stare at me.

There were no preliminaries. He remarked:

"You heard what I said about Quaife?"

"I'm grateful," I replied.

"It isn't a matter for gratitude. It's a matter for sense."

It wasn't getting easier to be on terms with Lufkin.

"I'd like to tell him," I said. "He can do with some moral support."

"You're intended to tell him."

"Good."

"I don't say something about a man in one place, and something else in another."

Like a good many of his claims for himself, this also was true.

His eyes, sunk deep in his neat, handsome head, swivelled round to me. "That's not the point," he said.

"What do you mean?"

"That's not why I sent them away."

For an instant there was a silence, a negotiator's silence. Like one tired of stating the obvious, he let out:

"Quaife's been a damned fool."

I did not reply. I sat, not showing excessive interest, gazing at him. He gave a sharp recognitory smile.

"I ought to tell you, I know about this woman of his," he said. "He's been a damned fool. I don't care what you think about his morals. A man doesn't want to get mixed up with a woman when he's trying something big."

Lufkin seldom missed an opportunity to apportion moral

blame. But his tone had become less aloof. I still did not reply, nor change my expression.

Once more, Lufkin smiled. "My information is," he said, "that the man Hood is going to blow the news wide open to Quaife's wife. And to Smith's connections. Any day now. This being, of course, the most helpful occasion."

This time, I was astounded. I showed it. All my practice at coping with Lufkin had failed me. I knew he sat at the centre of a kind of intelligence service; business and curiosity got mixed up; his underlings fed him with gossip as well as fact. But this seemed like divination. I must have looked like one of my aunts, confronted with a demonstration of spiritualist phenomena. Lufkin gave a grin of triumph.

Later on, I thought it was not so mysterious. After all, Hood was employed by a firm closely similar to Lufkin's. Between the two, there was contact, something like espionage, and personal intimacies at every level. There was nothing improbable in Hood's having a drinking companion, or even a confidential friend, on Lufkin's staff.

"It's likely to be true," said Lufkin.

"It may be," I said.

"This man," said Lufkin, "needs all his energy for the job in hand. I don't know, and I don't want to know, how his wife will take it. But it isn't the kind of trouble any of us would want hanging over us when we're fighting for our skins."

He was a tough ally. For his own sake, he wanted Roger to survive. But he was speaking with unusual sympathy, with something like comradely feeling. Once or twice in my own life, I had known him come out of his carapace and show something which was not affection, but might have been concern. It had happened only when one was in trouble with wife or children. No one knew much about his own marriage. His wife lived in the country and there was a rumour that she was afflicted. He could have had mistresses, but if so they had been concealed with his consummate executive skill. None of this we were likely to know for sure, until after he was dead.

My instructions were clear. I was to warn Roger, and then look after him. That being understood, the conference was over, and Lufkin got up to join his guests. As he did so, I asked about Hood. Was he being used by others? Were there people behind him?

"I don't believe in chance," said Lufkin.

As for the man himself, was he obsessed?

"I'm not interested in his psychology," said Lufkin. "I'm not interested in his motives. All I'm interested in is seeing him on the bread-line."

We did not speak again on our way to the drawing-room. There the party, in Lufkin's absence, had begun to sound a little gayer. He damped it down by establishing us in groups of three with no chance of transfer. For myself, I was pre-occupied, and I noticed Margaret glancing at me, a line between her eyes, knowing that something was wrong. In my trio, I heard, as though she were a long way off, the wife of one of the Ministers explaining analytically why her son had not got into Pop, a subject which, at the best of times, I should have found of limited interest.

One might have thought that Lufkin's dinner-parties broke up early. But they didn't, unless Lufkin broke them up himself. That night it was half-past eleven before, among the first uprising of departures, I managed to get in a word with Margaret. I told her that Lufkin had been warning me, and about what.

Looking at me, she did not need to ask much. "Ought you to go and see Roger?" she said.

I half-wanted to leave it till next day. She knew that I was tired. She knew that I should be more tired if I didn't act till next morning. She said, "You'd better go to him now, hadn't you?"

While Margaret waited with Lufkin, I telephoned Lord North Street. I heard Roger's voice, and began:

"Lufkin's been talking to me. There's something I've got to tell you."

"Yes."

"Can I come round?"

"You can't come here. We'll have to meet somewhere else."

Clubs would be closed by this time: we couldn't remember a restaurant nearby: at last I said, anxious to put down the telephone, that I would see him outside Victoria Station and was leaving straight away.

When I told Lufkin that I was going to Roger, he nodded with approval, as for any course of behaviour recommended by himself. "I can lay on transport," he said. "Also for your charming wife."

Two cars, two drivers, were waiting for us in the street. As mine drew up under the Victoria clock, I did not go into the empty hall, booking-offices closed as in a ghost station, but stayed outside on the pavement, alone except for some porters going home.

A taxi slithered from the direction of Victoria Street, through the rain-glossed yard.

As Roger came heavily towards me, I said:

"There's nowhere to go here." For an instant I was reminded of Hector Rose greeting me outside the darkened Athenaeum, months before.

I said there was a low-down coffee bar not far away. We were both standing stock-still.

Roger said, quite gently, "I don't think there is anything you can tell me. I think I know it all."

"My God," I said, in bitterness, "we might have been spared this."

I was angry, not with Hood, but with him. My temper had broken loose because of the risks we had run, of what we had tried to do, of the use he had made of me. He gave a grimace, of something like acquiescence.

"I'm sorry," he said, "to have got everyone into a mess."

Those were the kind of words I had heard before in a crisis: apathetic, inadequate, flat. But they made me more angry. He looked at me.

"Never mind," he said. "It's not lost yet."

As we stood there in front of the station, it was not I who was giving support and sympathy. It was the other way round.

In silence we walked across the station yard, through the dripping rain. By the time we were sitting in the coffee bar, under the livid lights, I had recovered myself.

We sipped tea so weak that it tasted like metal against the teeth. Roger had just said, "It's been very bad," when we were interrupted.

A man sat down at a table and remarked "Excuse me," in a voice that was nearly cultivated, not quite. His hands were trembling. He had a long, fine-drawn face, like the romantic stereotype of a scientist. His manner was confident. He told us a hard-luck story of considerable complexity. He was a lorry-driver, so he said. By a series of chances and conspiracies, his employers had decided to sack him. Not to put too fine a point on it, he was short of money. Could we see him through the night?

I didn't like him much, I didn't believe a word of it, above all I was maddened by his breaking in. Yet, as I shook my head, I was embarrassed, as though it were I who was doing the begging. As for him, he was not embarrassed in the least. "Never mind, old chap," he said.

Roger looked at him and, without a word, took out his wallet and gave him a ten-shilling note. The intruder took it civilly, but without any demonstration. "Always glad of a little encouragement," he said. He made polite goodbyes.

Roger did not watch or notice. He had given him money not out of fellow-feeling, or pity, or even to be rid of him. It had been the kind of compulsion that affects men who lead risky lives. Roger had been trying to buy a bit of luck.

Suddenly he told me straight out that Caro would "put a face on things," until the struggle was over. She would laugh off the rumours which would soon, if Lufkin's intelligence were correct, once more be sparking round all J. C. Smith's connections. Caro was ready to deny them to Collingwood himself.

But there was some other damage. Many people, including most of the guests at Lord North Street, and Diana Skidmore's friends, would have expected Caro—and Roger also —not to make much of the whole affair. Yes, Ellen had behaved badly, a wife ought to stick to her sick husband. Roger wasn't faultless either. Still, there were worse things. After all, Caro had lived in the world all her life. Her friends and family were not models of the puritan virtues. Caro herself had had lovers before her marriage. Like the rest of her circle, she prided herself on her rationality and tolerance. They all smoothed over scandals, were compassionate about sins of the flesh, by the side of which a man having a mistress— even in the circumstances of Roger and Ellen—was nothing but a display of respectability.

That day, since Caro first read the unsigned letter, none of that had counted, nor had ever seemed to exist. There was no enlightenment or reason in the air, just violence. They hadn't been quarreling about his public life, nor the morality of taking a colleague's wife: nor about love: nor sex: but about something fiercer. He was hers. They were married. She would not let him go.

He, too, felt the same violence. He felt tied and abject. He had come away, not knowing where to turn or what to do.

So far as I could tell, there had been no decision. Or rather, there seemed to have been two decisions which contradicted each other. As soon as the crisis was over, win or lose—Caro gave her ultimatum—he had to choose. She would not endure it more than a matter of weeks, months at the most. Then he had to look after his own career. It must be "this woman" or her. At the same time, she had said more than once that she would not give him a divorce.

"I don't know," he said. His face was blank and open. He did not look like a man a few days away from his major test.

For a while we sat, drinking more cups of the metallic tea, not saying much. Then he remarked:

"I told her" (he meant Ellen) "earlier in the day. I promised I'd ring her up before I went to bed. She'll be waiting."

Blundering, as though his limbs were heavy, he went off to look for a telephone behind the bar. When he came back he said flatly:

"She wants me to go and see her. She asked me to bring you too."

For an instant, I thought this was not meant seriously.

"She asked me," he repeated. Then I thought perhaps I understood. She was as proud as Caro: in some ways, she was prouder. She was intending to behave on her own terms.

The rain had stopped, and we went on foot to Ebury Street. It was well past one. At her door, Ellen greeted us with the severeness which I had long ago forgotten, but which took me back to the first time I saw her there. Once we were inside the smart little sitting-room, she gave Roger a kiss, but as a greeting, no more. It wasn't the hearty, conjugal kiss I had seen before, the kiss of happy lovers used to each other, pleased with each other, sure of pleasure to come.

She offered us drinks. Roger took a whiskey, so did I. I pressed her to join us. As a rule, she enjoyed her drink. But she was one of those who, in distress, refuse to accept any relief.

"This is atrocious," she said.

Roger repeated to her what he had told me. She listened with an expression impatient, strained and intent. She was hearing little new, most of it had been said already over the telephone. When he repeated that his wife would "see him through" the crisis, she burst out in scorn:

"What else could she do?"

Roger looked hurt, as well as angry. She was sitting opposite to him across the small table. She gave a laugh which wasn't a laugh, which reminded me of my mother when an expectation came to nothing or one of her pretensions was deflated, when she had, by laughing, to deny the moment in which we stood.

"I mean, you have to win. She couldn't spoil that!"

He said nothing. For a moment he looked desperately tired, fretted, drained, as if he had lost interest in everything but the desire to be alone, to switch off the light, turn his face into the pillow and sleep.

Shortly afterwards she cried:

"I'm sorry, I shouldn't have said that."

"I haven't the right to stop you."

"It was disloyal."

She meant, disloyal to him, not to Caro: and yet her emotions towards Caro were not simple. All three of them were passionate people. Under the high-spirited surface, she was as violent as Caro. If those two had met that night, I thought more than once, the confrontation might have gone any way at all.

She sat back and said: "I've been dreading this."

"Don't you think I know?" Roger replied.

There was a long silence. At last Ellen turned to me and said in a sharp, steady tone: "I'm willing to give him up."

"It's too late for that," said Roger.

"Why is it?" She looked straight at him. "You trust me, don't you? I've got that left, haven't I?"

"I trust you."

"Well, then, I meant what I said."

"It's too late. There were times when I might have taken that offer. Not now."

They were each speaking with stark honesty. On his side, with the cruelty of a love-relation which is nothing but a love-relation: where they were just naked with each other, with neither children, nor friends, nor the to-and-fro of society to console them, to keep them safe. On her side, she was speaking from loneliness, from the rapacity with which she wanted him, and, yes, from her own code of honour.

Their eyes met again, and fell away. Between them, at that instant, was not love: not desire: not even affection: but knowledge.

As though everything else was irrelevant, she said in a brisk, businesslike manner: "Well, you'd better settle how you're going to handle it next Thursday morning."

She meant the Cabinet, at which Roger's debate would, though possibly only perfunctorily, come up. Once she had been envious of Caro for knowing the political life as she did not. Now she had learned. Whom could he trust? Could he sound his colleagues before the meeting? Could I find out anything in Whitehall? Whom could he trust? More important, whom couldn't he trust?

We talked on for a couple of hours. The names went round. Collingwood, Monty Cave, the P.M., Minister after Minister, his own Parliamentary Secretary, Leverett-Smith. It was like sitting in Cambridge rooms twenty years before, counting heads, before a college election. It was like that. The chief difference was that this time the stakes were a little higher, and the penalties (it seemed to me that night) more severe.

CHAPTER XXXIX

POLITICAL

ARITHMETIC

During those days before the debate, Roger, whenever he went into the House or the Treasury Building or Downing Street, was under inspection: inspection often neither friendly nor unfriendly, but excited by the smell of human drama: the kind of inspection that I remembered my mother being subjected to, in the provincial back-streets, when we were going bankrupt—but it was also just as much a predilection of the old Norse heroes, who, on hearing that your house had been burned down, with you inside, were interested, not in your fate, but in how you had comported yourself.

As they watched him, Roger behaved well. He was a brave man, physically and morally, people were saying. It was true. Nevertheless, on those mornings he could not bring himself to read the political correspondents' gossip-columns. He listened to accounts of what they said, but could not read them. Though he walked through the lobbies, bulky and composed, cordial to men whom he suspected, he could not manage to invite the opinions of his own nearest supporters. He sat at his desk in the office, staring distantly at me, as though his articulateness and self-knowledge had both gone.

I had to guess what request he was making: yes, he would like to know where his Parliamentary Secretary, Leverett-Smith, stood, and Tom Wyndham too.

This was one of the jobs I fancied least. I had no detachment left. I also did not want to hear bad news. I did not want to convey it. It was easy to understand how leaders in danger got poor information.

In fact, I picked up nothing of much interest, certainly nothing that added to disquiet. Tom Wyndham was, as usual, euphoric and faithful. He had been one of Roger's best selections. He continued to carry some influence with the smart young ex-officers on the back benches. They might distrust Roger, but no one could distrust Tom Wyndham. He was positive all would turn out well. He did not even seem to understand what the fuss was about. As he stood me drinks at the bar of White's, I felt, for a short time, reassured and very fond of him. It was only when I got out into the February evening that it came to me, with displeasing clarity, that, though he had a good heart, he was also remarkably obtuse. He couldn't even see the chessboard, let alone two moves ahead.

With Leverett-Smith next morning—it was now five days before the Opposition motion—the interview was more prickly. It took place in his office and, to begin with, he showed mystification as to why I was there at all. Not unreasonably, he was put out. If the Minister (as he always called Roger) wished for a discussion, here was he, sitting four doors down the corridor, from 9:30 in the morning until he left for the House. His point was reasonable: that didn't make it more gratifying. He looked at me with his lawyer's gaze, and addressed me formally, like a junior Minister putting high civil servants in their place.

"With great respect—" he kept saying.

We should never have got on, not in any circumstances, least of all in these. We had hardly a thought or even an assumption in common.

I repeated that for Roger next week was the major crisis.

This wasn't an occasion for protocol. We were obliged to give him the best advice we could.

"With great respect," replied Leverett-Smith, "I am confident that neither of us needs to be reminded of his official duty."

Then he began something like a formal speech. It was a stiff, platitudinous and unyielding speech. He didn't like me any better as he made it. Yet he was revealing more sense than I gave him credit for. It was "common ground" that the Minister was about to undergo a supreme test. If he (Leverett-Smith) had been asked to give his counsel, he would have suggested *festina lente*. Indeed, he had so suggested, on occasions that I might conceivably remember. What might provoke opposition, if done prematurely, would be accepted with enthusiasm when the time was ripe. Nevertheless, in the Minister's mind the die was cast, and we all had to put away our misgivings and work towards a happy issue.

We should certainly have six abstentions, Leverett-Smith went on, suddenly getting down to the political arithmetic. Six we could survive. Twenty meant Roger was in peril unless he had reassured the centre of the party. Thirty-five, and he would, without any conceivable doubt, have to go.

"And you?" I asked quietly, and without hostility.

"I consider," said Leverett-Smith, formally but also without hostility, "that that question should not have been put. Except by the Minister himself. If he weren't overwrought, he would know that, if I had been going to disagree with my Minister, I should have done so in public before this, and I should naturally resign. So it oughtn't to need saying that now, if the worst comes to the worst, and the Minister has to go—which I still have good hopes is not going to happen—then as a matter of principle I shall go with him."

Spoken like a stick, I thought. But also like an upright man. The comparison with Roger, in the same position three years before, flickered like a smile on the wrong side of the face.

I was able to report to Roger that afternoon without needing to comfort him. He listened as though brooding: but when he heard of Leverett-Smith's stuffy speech, he shouted out loud. He sounded amused, but he wasn't really amused. He was in one of those states of suspicion when any piece of simple human virtue, or even decency, seems more than one can expect or bear.

He was wrapped up in his suspicions, in his plans for the counter-attacks, like a doctor confronted with the X-ray pictures of his own lungs. He did not even tell me, I did not know until I got home to Margaret, that Caro had invited me to their house the following night.

She had not telephoned, she had dropped in at our flat without notice.

"She obviously had to talk to somebody," Margaret said, looking upset, "and I suppose she didn't want to do it with her own friends, so she thought it had better be me."

I did not ask her what Caro had said, but Margaret wanted to tell me about it.

Caro had begun:

"I suppose you know?"—then had launched into a kind of strident abuse, half-real, half-histrionic, punctuated by the routine obscenities she would have heard round the stables at Newmarket. It was not so much abuse of Ellen, though there was some of that too, but of life itself. As the violence began to wear itself out, she had begun to look frightened, then terrified. She had said, her eyes wild, but with no tears in them, "I don't know how I shall bear being alone. I don't know how I am to bear it."

Margaret said, "She does love him. She says she can't imagine not hearing his key in the lock, not having the last drink with him at night. It's true: I don't know how she is going to bear it."

CHAPTER XL

AN EVENING OF
TRIUMPH

It was well after ten when we got out of the taxi in Lord North Street. We had been invited, not to dinner, but for an after-debate supper. The door shone open for another guest, light streaming across the lances of rain.

I felt Margaret's hand tighten in mine. When we had first entered this house, it had seemed enviable. Now it was threatened. Some of us, going up the stairs that night, knew, as well as Roger and Caro themselves, of both the threats.

She greeted us in the drawing-room, eyes flashing, jewels flashing, shoulders splendid under the lights. Her voice wasn't constricted; she hugged Margaret, perhaps a little more closely than usual, she brushed my cheek. I knew, as we kissed, that this was a performance, gallant as it was. She had never liked me much, but now, if it weren't for her obligation, she would have put me out of sight for good. She had either found out, or had decided for herself, that I had been in Roger's confidence. She might be generous and reckless, but she would not forget her wrongs. This one was not to be forgiven.

The clock was striking the half-hour. There were already three or four people in the drawing-room, including Diana Skidmore.

"They've not got back yet," said Caro, in her loud casual

tone, as though this were any other parliamentary night, "they" being the politicians.

"They've had quite a day, bless their hearts. I haven't seen Roger since he went to the Cabinet this morning. Have you seen any of them, Diana?"

"Not to speak of, you know," Diana replied, with a smile as bright, and as communicative, as her emeralds.

"Isn't Monty Cave making a great speech tonight?" Caro went on.

"I suppose he would have to say something, wouldn't he?" said Diana.

Caro told Diana that Monty would be along soon, in a tone which implied that Diana knew already. Diana responded with a question:

"Is the P.M. coming?"

Caro replied boldly: "I couldn't get him." She added, as though she wouldn't be outfaced:

"Reggie Collingwood promised to look in. If they're not too late."

It seemed clear—had the news reached Diana yet?—that Caro was trying to do her last service for Roger. She was not just seeing him through, she was doing more than that. She was calling up all her influence, until the debate. She was helping him to win, as thoroughly as if they had been happy.

And yet, though it was chivalrous, though she would truly have done it if she were losing him next week, did she expect, completely expect, to lose him? As I listened, she didn't seem as if she had quite let go. Did she still hope that if he won, if his career were once more assured, he would have to stay with her? On her own terms? Given a future as brilliant as it had looked the year before, how much of it would he risk or sacrifice?

It would be astonishing if at times, brilliant with certainty, she did not hope like that. For myself, I was at a loss to know whether she was right or wrong.

I wondered also what chances she believed he had of winning. She was radiant with fighting energy. She would go on beyond the last minute. But, though she wasn't subtle, she was shrewd and had seen much. She had been trying to get signals of encouragement from Diana and had received none. That must have been as patent to Caro as it was to Margaret and me. Not that Diana had finally given Roger up. She knew he was in extreme trouble, that was all. She was playing safe. Maybe she did not want to embarrass her closest political friends, like Collingwood; maybe she had heard from him the first whisper of a scandal: but, deeper than that, she was acting out of instinct.

The *beau monde* wasn't kind, Caro had once said to me on a carefree night. If it were kind, it would soon cease to be *beau*. It was tolerably good-natured, until you were really in trouble. Then you were on your own.

I wondered how many worlds were any better. If you were in trouble in the public eye, who was going to guard you? All the worlds I knew, not only the *beau*, but the civil servants, the academics, the industrialists, the scientists, huddled together to protect themselves. If you became exposed, they couldn't do much. It was the odd acquaintance, sometimes the wild, sometimes the sober who had concealed the fact that he was afraid of nothing and no one, who came out and took the risks and stood by one's side.

Car in the street below. Heavy footsteps on the stairs. Roger came in, came in alone.

I had an instant's anxiety, as though Caro's guests had let her down, as though her gesture had gone for nothing, and we were left with a useless supper-party, like so many Baltic Deputies.

Then, with a disproportionate relief, so that I gave a broad and apparently unprovoked grin in Diana's direction, I saw Cave at the door, with Collingwood's hand on his shoulder.

"Give Monty a drink," cried Roger, in his broadest, heartiest voice. "He's made the speech of a lifetime!"

"He'll make better speeches someday," said Collingwood with an air of the highest congratulation, rather like Demosthenes commenting on a hitherto tongue-tied pupil.

"Give him a drink!" cried Roger. He was standing by his wife. Their faces were open, robust, smiling. They might have been a serene couple, rejoicing, because they were so successful, in a great friend's success. Looking round, I should have liked to know how many of the others saw them so, and how much they knew.

As we sat down at the dinner-table downstairs, I was on edge and guessing. So were others. Some of the decisions— one could feel the crackle in the air—were not only not revealed, they were not yet taken. If Collingwood had heard the news about his nephew's wife, he showed no sign of it. His phlegm was absolute. Diana's self-control, Caro's flaming courage—they were tightened, because people round the table knew that nothing was settled; were waiting to see in what might pass as a convivial evening, where others would —the old phrase returned to me—"come down."

Cave held up a glass to the candlelight, viewed it with his round, sombre, acute eyes, and sat forward, the rolls of chin sinking into his chest. He kept receiving compliments, Collingwood's magisterial and not specially articulate, Roger's hearty but increasingly forced. Cave's glance darted towards them, his eyes sharply on guard, in the podgy, clown-like face. Diana was flattering him, with a brisk, hortatory rasp, as though irritated that he didn't know how good he was.

About his triumph in the House that evening, there was no ambiguity at all. It had no connection with Roger's policy or what was to come. Cave had, in a routine debate, wound up for the Government. To anyone outside the Commons, what he said would either be unnoticed or forgotten within days: but on the parliamentary stock exchange, the quotation in Cave had rushed up many points. On a normal evening, there would have been no more to it than that. Roger might have been expected to feel that particular blend of emotions appropriate to an occasion when a colleague, friend, rival and ally had just had a resplendent professional success.

As we listened that night, this wasn't all. There was no mystery about the triumph in the evening: but there was considerable mystery about the Cabinet a few hours before. Not that Collingwood or the others would in company have talked about Cabinet proceedings. Nevertheless, Caro and Diana, neither of them over-theoretical or over-delicate, were used to picking up the signs. Of course, they assumed, Roger's debate next week had been talked about that morning. Of course the Cabinet had taken steps. Caro asked Collingwood a question about the vote next Tuesday, with as much fuss as she would have asked about the prospects of a horse.

"We've been thinking about that, naturally," he said. He added gnomically: "Not that we're not always busy. We can't spend too much time on one thing, you understand."

He volunteered a piece of information. The proper operations had been set going. A three-line Whip had gone out.* Three or four dissidents were being worked on.

There was no side-talk round the table. Everyone was attending. Everyone knew the language. This meant that, in formal terms, the Government was not backing down. This was the maximum show of pressure on its Party. It could do no more.

But also, I was thinking, as I listened to Collingwood's grating, confident voice, it could do no less. They had gone too far not to bring out the standard procedure now. We were no nearer to knowing what had happened that morning.

Conceivably, Collingwood and the other Ministers could not have told us, even if they had wanted to. Not because of secrecy; not because some had their own different designs:

* I.e., the Government was ordering its supporters to attend.

but simply because of the way Cabinet business was done.

Word had come out from the Cabinet room that Lenton was, when he wanted to be, an efficient chairman. More than most recent Prime Ministers, he often let Ministers introduce topics, he encouraged an orderly discussion round the table, and even took a straw-vote at the end. But this didn't always happen.

Lenton was efficient and managerial. He was more self-effacing than most Prime Ministers. He was also a ruthless politician, and he knew a Prime Minister's power. This power had increased out of all proportion since Collingwood entered politics. The Prime Minister, they used to say piously, was the first among equals. It might be so, but in that case, the first was a good deal more equal than the others.

It wasn't a matter of *charisma*. It wasn't even a matter of personality. The awe existed, but it was practical awe. The Prime Minister had the jobs in his hand. He could sack anyone, and appoint anyone. Even a modest man like Lenton did just that. Any of us, on the secretariat of committees, who had seen any Prime Minister with his colleagues, noticed that they were frightened of him, whoever he might be.

If he didn't want a decision in Cabinet, it took a bold man to get one. In office, men tended not to be bold. Lenton, who could be so businesslike, had become a master at talking round a subject, and then leaving it in the air. It looked sloppy: little he cared: it was a useful technique for getting his own way.

Perhaps that, or something like it, had happened that day. None of us except Collingwood knew what the Prime Minister thought of Roger or his policy. My guess, for some time past, had been that he thought it was rational but that it couldn't be pressed too far. If Roger could placate, or squeeze by, the right-wing of the party, then it would be good for the Government. They might win the next election on it. But if Roger had stirred up too much opposition, if he went beyond his brief and campaigned only for the Getliffe portions of the White Paper, he needn't be rescued. Roger was expendable. In fact, it was possible that the Prime Minister would not be heartbroken if Roger had to be expended. For that pleasantly modest man had some of the disadvantages of modesty. He might not be over-fond of seeing, at the Cabinet, a colleague much more brilliant than himself, and some years younger.

I fancied that little had been said, either in Cabinet or in meetings tête-à-tête. Maybe the Prime Minister had spoken intimately to Collingwood, but I doubted even that. This kind of politics, which could be the roughest of all, went on without words.

That night, Collingwood, bolt upright on Caro's right hand, showed no sign of embarrassment, or even of the disfavour one can't totally suppress towards someone to whom one is doing a bad turn. His quartz eyes might have been blind. So far as he was capable of cordiality, he was giving it, like a moderate-sized tip, to Monty Cave. Cave was the hero of the evening, Cave looked on the short list for promotion. But Collingwood bestowed a smaller, but judicious, cordiality upon Roger. It was hard to believe that he bore him rancour. This was the behaviour, straightforward, not forthcoming, of someone who thought Roger might still survive, and who would within limits be content if he did so.

He was just as straightforward when Caro pressed him about who would speak in the debate. Roger would have the last word, said Collingwood. The First Lord would have to open. "That ought to do," said Collingwood. To Caro, to me—did Diana know already?—this was the first sharp warning of the night. The First Lord was a lightweight; it sounded as if Roger was not being given a senior Minister to help him out.

"Are you going to speak, Reggie?" said Caro, as unabashed as she had ever been in Roger's cause.

"Not much in my line," said Collingwood, as though in-adequacy in speech were a major virtue. He rarely spoke in the House, and then mumbled through a script so exe-crably that he seemed unable not only to speak, but to read. Yet he managed to communicate to the back-bench commit-tees. Perhaps that was what he meant when he looked up the table at Roger and said, with self-satisfaction, "I've done something. I've done something for you already, you know."

Roger nodded. But suddenly I noticed, so did others, that his eyes were fixed on Monty Cave. The pretence of hearti-ness, the poise, the good will, had all drained away from Roger's expression. He was gazing at Cave with intense anxiety, not with liking, not with anything as final as enmity, but with naked concern.

We followed his glance. Cave gave no sign of recognition. The rest of us had finished eating, but Cave had cut himself another slice of cheese. His lips, fat man's lips, glutton's lips, child's lips, were protruding. He looked up, eyes hard in the soft face.

Just for an instant even Caro's nerve failed. There was a silence. Then her voice rang out, full, unquailing: "Are *you* going to speak, Monty?"

"The Prime Minister hasn't asked me to," said Cave.

This meant that he couldn't speak, even if he wanted to. But there was a note in his voice, quiet, harmonious, that rasped the nerves.

Caro could not help asking him:

"Isn't there anything else you can do for Roger?"

"I can't think of anything. Can you?"

"How should we handle it then?" she cried.

Suddenly I was sure that this question had been asked before. At the morning's Cabinet? It was easy to imagine the table, Lenton droning away with deliberate amiability, not letting the issue emerge, as though there weren't an issue, as though no policy and no career depended upon it. It was easy to imagine Cave sitting silent. He knew as well as any man alive that Roger needed, not just his acquiescence, but his support. There was he, the bright hope of the Party *avant-garde,* its best debater, maybe a leader. They were waiting for him. He knew what depended on it.

"How shall we handle it, Monty?"

"I'm afraid it all depends on Roger. He's got to settle it for himself," he said in a soft, modulated, considered tone, along the table to Caro.

It was out now. For years Cave's attitude to Roger had been veiled. He had disagreed with some of Roger's policy in detail: but yet, he should have been on the same side. He knew why he was making pretexts for minor disagreements. Much more than most politicians, Cave knew himself. He hadn't forgiven Roger for holding back over Suez. Far more than that, Roger was a rival, a rival, in ten years' time, for the first place. By keeping quiet, Cave might be able to see that rival done for.

For once, though, it was possible that the career did not come first. Cave might have concealed from others, but not from himself, that he profoundly envied Roger. In the midst of all else, he was letting the envy rip. Envy, most of all, of Roger's careless masculine potence: envy, because Roger did not have women leave him: envy of what, with a certain irony, he thought of as Roger's sturdy, happy marriage. From the sadness of his diffident, frustrated sexual life, he regarded Roger. The contrast made him cruel. As he gave his answer to Caro, his voice was soft with cruelty.

She did not think it worth while pressing further. Soon afterwards the party broke up, although it was only half-past twelve. Yet, even then, as they said goodbye, Roger kept hold of himself. He might suspect, he was capable of suspecting anything by now, that Cave had in secret stimulated the attack upon him. But reproach, anger, scorn—he could afford none of them. Cave would keep his hostility quiet. In public, he would behave like a colleague. Once more, Roger congratulated him on the evening's feat. As Roger did so, Collingwood patted him on the shoulder.

Below, the cars were driving away. In the drawing-room, Margaret and I were getting up to go. Now that we were alone, Roger looked at his wife and said, with a curious harsh trustfulness:

"Well, it couldn't be much worse, could it?"

"It might be better," said Caro, bitter and honest.

The moment after, up the stairs came a rapid, stumbling tread. Sammikins marched into the room and gave a brassy hail. He was wearing a dinner-jacket, unlike anyone at the supper-party: a carnation shone in his lapel. He had been drinking, hard enough for his eyes to stare with fierce, wild, arrogant happiness. "It's too late," said Caro.

"I shan't stay long," he shouted. "I want a drink."

"You've had enough."

"You don't know what I've had." He spoke with the glee of one who had come, not only from drinking, but from bed. He laughed at her, and went on in a confident cry: "I want to talk to your husband."

"I'm here." Roger sat forward on the sofa.

"By God, so you are!" Sammikins again asked for a drink. This time Caro poured him a whiskey, and told him to sit down.

"I'm not going to. Why should I?" He gulped his drink and stared down at Roger.

He announced at the top of his voice:

"It won't do!"

"What do you mean?"

"I can't go along with you next week. It sticks in my throat."

For an instant I had thought, so had Margaret, that he was denouncing Roger for breaking up the marriage. But he couldn't have known yet about that. If he had known, his sister had protected him too much—his side of their relation was too defiant—for him to care.

Caro had stood up. She took his arm and said passionately: "No, no, you mustn't go back on him now!"

Sammikins shrugged her off. He shouted down at Roger: "I shan't abstain. That's a boring thing to do. I shall vote against you."

Roger did not look up. He snapped his fingers against his thigh.

After a pause, he said in a steady, tired, reflective tone: "I shouldn't have thought this was the best possible time to betray me."

Sammikins's face lost its fierce joy. More quietly and considerately than he had so far spoken, he replied: "I'm sorry about the timing." Then his eyes flared, and he broke out: "I don't like the word 'betray.'"

"Don't you?" asked Roger, expressionless.

"Two can play at that game. Who are you betraying?"

"Will you tell me?"

"I'll give you credit that you don't mean to. But how are you going to leave this blasted country? You've got your reasons, of course, everyone's got their reasons. We can't play with the big boys, I grant you that. But we've got to be able to blow up someone. Ourselves, if that's the only way out. Otherwise the others will blackmail us whenever they feel inclined. We shall be sunk for good."

Slowly Roger raised his head, but did not speak.

Sammikins went shouting on. "You're wrong, I tell you! You're wrong. It's simple. War's always been simple. You're too clever by half. You've just got to think of one simple thing, just to see that we're not sunk for good. It's a pity you didn't have a chap like me, I'm not too clever by half— somewhere on tap—just to say 'Oi, oi!' You're being too clever, your job is to see we're not getting sunk for good."

"I suppose you're the only patriot we've got?" Roger's

voice had turned thick and dangerous. At the end of that day, which he had endured without a lapse, he was suddenly moved, shaken, enraged. It was not that Sammikins's defection, in practical terms, counted much. He was a "wild man," he had been written off long before as irresponsible, a political playboy. If he went into the lobby against his brother-in-law, all that meant would be a paragraph in the gossip columns. It was not the defection which stabbed Roger—but the personal betrayal, for he had an affection, almost a paternal affection, for the younger man. The personal betrayal and, yes, the reason for it, the half-baked, drunken words. All through, Roger had been nagged at by the regrets, even the guilt, of someone living among choices where the simple certainties weren't enough. For Roger in particular, with his nostalgia for past grandeur, it was tempting to think of a time when you could choose, without folly, to make the country both powerful and safe. He had thought in terms as old-fashioned as that. He had often wished that he had been born in a different time, when reason did not take one into decisions which denied the nostalgic heart.

"You've only got to keep your eye on the ball and remember the simple things," Sammikins shouted.

Roger had risen to his feet, a massive bulk in the room.

"No one else tries to remember the simple things?"

"They decide what will happen to us," said Sammikins.

"Do you think no one else cares what will happen to us?"

"I hope they do."

Sammikins had not spoken in his loud, confident voice. This time it was Roger who shouted:

"Get out!"

After all his disciplined performances, the fury boiling up and over was astonishing—no, less astonishing than unnerving—to hear. The thick, driven cry filled the room. Roger began to move, hunched, on to the other man.

I was standing up too, wondering how to stop the fight.

Sammikins was athletic, but Roger was four or five stones heavier, and far stronger. With a bear-like heave, he threw Sammikins against the wall. Sammikins slid very slowly down it, like a coat collapsing from a peg, till he was on the floor. For a moment he sat there, head hanging, as if he had forgotten where he was, or who any of us were. Then, with an athlete's lightness, he sprang up—from crossed ankles—and stood erect with hardly a stagger, eyes staring. Caro got between him and Roger. She clung to her brother's hand.

"For God's sake, go," she said.

"Do you want me to?" he said, with a curious, injured dignity.

"You must *go*."

Head back, he moved to the door. From the far end of the room he said to Caro, "I expect I'll want to see you—"

"This is my house," shouted Roger, "get out of it!"

Caro did not reply to Sammikins. She went to Roger's side, and, like a united front of husband and wife, they listened to the footsteps lurching down.

CHAPTER XLI

QUARREL IN
THE CORRIDOR

Next day, when I called in Roger's office, he sat calm and stoical, like a man without passions, as though any story about an outbreak of his was one's own invention and couldn't be referred to. Yet once more his tic returned: in a distant, cold, almost inimical manner, he asked me to report what the papers were rumouring that morning. "There's not much," I said.

"Good." His face, his voice, became smooth. He was for the moment over-easily reassured, like a man jealous in love, snatching at the bit of news which comforts him.

There was a report in one paper about a meeting of a few back benchers and some scientists, which seemed to have ended in the scientists quarrelling—that was about all, I said.

Immediately, again like a jealous man, he started on the detective work of anxiety: who could they be? Where? This was the ultra-Conservative paper, they were enemies, we knew which member slipped them the gossip. Yet this man, who was venal but abnormally amiable, had already written to Roger pledging his support. Was he reneging at the last minute? I shook my head. I was positive that he was all right. Not that he minded collecting his retainer from the paper.

"One of these days," said Roger, relieved and savage, "we'll get men like him expelled from the House."

What about the scientists? I said. Who were they, anyway? He wasn't interested. Nothing could interest him except the lobbies, now. As I left him, he was working out, repetitiously, unable to shake off the obsession, who these members were, and whether he could count on their votes.

Back in my own room, I wasn't much better. The debate was to begin on Monday afternoon. They would vote the night after that. Four days and a half before it would be over. I pulled down a file from my in-tray. There was a minute written in the most beautiful handwriting, in the most lucid prose. I did not feel like reading it.

I sat there day-dreaming, not pleasantly. Once I rang up Margaret, asking if there were any news, though what I expected I hadn't an idea.

A knock sounded on my door, not the door leading to my assistants, through which visitors should come, but the corridor door, usually inviolable. Hector Rose came in, perhaps for the second time since we had been colleagues, paying me a visit unannounced.

"Forgive me, my dear Lewis, I do apologise many, many times for interrupting you like this—"

"There isn't much to interrupt," I said.

"You're so much occupied that there's always something to interrupt." He gazed at the empty desk, at the in-tray with its stack of files. He gave a faint, arctic smile. "In any case, my dear Lewis, forgive me for disturbing some of your valuable meditations."

Even now, after all those years, even in stress, I didn't know the response to his singular brand of courtesy. The bright young Treasury officials, certain by this time that he would soon be retiring, and that they would never, as they once imagined, have to answer to him, had invented a quip, the sort of quip which, like a premature obituary, gets circulated when a formidable man is passing out: "With old Hector Rose, you've got to take the smooth with the smooth."

Little they knew.

After some more apologies he sat down. He looked at me with bleached eyes and said: "I thought you ought to know that I had the curious experience of meeting your friend Dr. Brodzinski last night."

"Where?"

"Oddly enough, with some of our political acquaintances."

Suddenly, the item in the newspaper flashed back, and I guessed:

"So you were there!"

"How have you heard?"

I mentioned the paper.

Rose gave a polite smile and said: "I don't find it necessary to read that particular journal."

"But you were there?"

"I was trying to make that clear, my dear Lewis."

"How did you get invited?"

Again he smiled politely: "I made it my business to be."

He cut out the flourishes, and with sarcastic relevance told me the story. Brodzinski, in a last attempt to whip up opposition to Roger's policy, had made an appeal to some of his Tory contacts. Instead of again attacking Roger directly, he had done it through an attack on Walter Luke. He had told some of the extreme right, the pro-Suez relics, that it was Luke's advice which had led Roger into bad judgment. So Brodzinski had been asked to dine with a small splinter-group. So, by a piece of upright pig-headed good manners, had Walter Luke. So, through his own initiative, had Hector Rose.

"I wasn't prepared to have the excellent Luke thrown to the wolves," he said. "Also, I thought I might as well listen to what was going on. I have a certain influence with Lord A——" (the leader of the splinter-group, and the man

responsible for the pig-headed good manners. It sounded improbable that he should be a friend of Hector Rose's, but in
fact—in the minuteness of the English official world—they
had been at school together).

Between Brodzinski and Luke, there had been a violent
row. Lord North Street was not the only place, the night
before, where eminent persons came to physical violence.
"How these scientists love one another," said Rose. He added:
"Brodzinski could certainly be sued for defamation, if Luke
cared to go to law." With crisp detachment he gave a few
examples.

"Is anyone going to believe *that*?"

"My dear Lewis, don't you agree that if anyone is accused of
anything, literally anything, most of our friends believe it?"

He went on: "While I am about it, you might drop a word
to our potentially supreme colleague, Douglas Osbaldiston.
There appears to be no doubt that Brodzinski has been trying
to spill this particular poison into his ear."

Once before—just once, in that disciplined life where personal relations were left unstated—Rose had let fall his feelings about Douglas. He did not let himself be so direct
again, not even when I said that Douglas, whatever Rose
thought of him, was honest and fair.

"I am perfectly certain," said Rose, half-bowing as he spoke,
"that our colleague has been utterly correct. In fact, I
gathered that he had refused to grant Brodzinski an interview at the present juncture. No one could be more correct,
could he? Our colleague has every qualification for the perfect public servant. But still, I do suggest you drop a word. He
is just a shade inclined to believe in reconciliation for its
own sake. When all this is settled, he might find it was wiser
and safer to have Brodzinski in rather than out. I should
regard that as reconciliation carried to a somewhat excessive
extent. Our colleague had a slightly greater veneration than

I have for the general good sense of everybody in this part of London."

Our eyes met. For this occasion, we were allies. He said: "By the way, one fact seems to be generally known."

"Yes?"

"That he's not a hundred per cent happy about this master's policy, or shall I say his master's ultimate intentions about policy?" Rose was not given to underlining. That morning he was thinking of Tuesday's voting, not with Roger's concentration, for that was total, but with something as channelled as mine. Name by name, he gave his prognosis about last night's party. There had been twelve members present. All but one were on the extreme right, and so possible enemies of Roger's. Of these, three would vote for him, including Lord A——. (Rose was, as he might have said himself, most correct. He did not give a vestigial hint that he, a functionary, could possibly have used any persuasion.) Of the others, a maximum of nine would certainly abstain. "It's beginning to look uncomfortable," said Hector Rose. He broke off, and went on about the vote. There were bound to be more abstentions. I told him, not the full story of Sammikins, but that he would vote against.

Rose clicked his tongue. He looked at me as though he were going to give a verdict. Then he shook his head, and in a cool tone remarked:

"I take it you will let your friend Quaife know at once. That is, about the information I was able to collect. I needn't tell you, you'll have to do it discreetly, and I'm afraid you mustn't reveal your source. But he ought to know about these abstentions. You can tell him these people by name, I think."

"What good can that do him?"

"What do you mean?"

"Do you believe that, if he saw them now, he could possibly persuade them back?"

"No," said Rose.

"Well, then, all he can do is make his speech. He'll make a better speech the more hope he's got left."

"My dear Lewis, with great diffidence, I think he ought to be able to reckon up his opponents—"

"I repeat," I said with force, "what good can that do?"

"You're taking a responsibility on yourself." Rose stared at me, surprised, disapproving. "If I were he," he said, "I should want to be able to reckon up every scrap of news, however bad it was, until the end."

I stared back. "I believe you would," I said.

It wasn't necessarily the toughest and hardest-nerved who lived in public. Yet sometimes I wondered whether a man as tough and hard-nerved as Rose could imagine what the public life was like, or how much it would have tested him.

He got up. "Well, that's all the bad news for the present." He made the grim, Greek messenger joke, said this seemed as far as we could go, and began his paraphernalia of thanks and apologies.

As soon as he had gone, I looked at the clock. It was nearly twenty to twelve. This time I didn't brood or wait. I went out, through my private office, into the corridor, past the doors of my own department, round three sides of the Treasury quadrangle, on my way to Osbaldiston. I didn't notice, as I had done times enough, the bizarre architecture, the 19th Century waste of space, the gigantic unfilled hole in the centre of the building, like a Henry Moore sculpture pretending to be functional. I didn't even notice the high jaundiced walls, the dark stretch of corridor up to the next bend, the compartments where the messengers sat on stools reading the racing editions, the labels on the doors just visible in the half light, Sir W—— H——, G.B.E., Sir W—— D——, K.C.B. It was just dark, domesticated, familiar: a topological journey: the doors passing me by like the stations seen from an underground train.

Before I got into the last straight, which led to Douglas's office, I saw him coming round the corner, head forward, a docket of papers in his hand. "I was looking for you," I said.

"I've got a meeting," Douglas answered. He wasn't evading me. There was not time to return to his room. We stood there in the corridor, talking in low voices. Occasionally, in the next few minutes, doors opened, young men walked briskly past us, throwing a glance in the direction of their boss. Some would know that he and I were close friends. They might have thought that we were settling a bit of business before the meeting, or alternatively, in the way of the top stratum, at once casual and machine-like, saving time and an inter-departmental minute.

It wasn't going quite like that. As we kept our voices down, I was watching his face with a mixture of affection, pity and blind anger. It had changed since his wife's illness; we had seen it change under our eyes. Now it had the special pathos of a face which, still in essence anachronistically youthful, was nevertheless beginning to look old. Once he had been untouched as Dorian Gray, a character whom he resembled in no other particular, but now all that was gone.

Three times a week, Margaret went to sit with his wife in hospital. By this time, when she wanted to smoke, Mary had to be fed her cigarette. "How paralysed can you get?" she said, with a euphoria and courage that made it worse to watch.

Douglas had come to stay with us some nights, when he couldn't stand any more either the lonely house or the club. Once he had told us, with bitter, unguarded candour, that there were not two hours together in any day when he didn't think of her lying there, not to move again, while he was free.

All that was out of my mind. I was saying:

"How much do you know of the latest attack on Quaife?"

"What are you talking about?"

"Do you realise that they're going for anyone who has the slightest connection with him? Now it's Walter Luke—"

"You can't have a war," said Douglas, "without someone getting hurt."

"I suppose you're aware," I said angrily, "that you've been giving aid and comfort to these people?"

"What are you saying now?" All of a sudden, his face had become stony. He was as enraged as I was: the more so, because we had in private so often been open with each other.

"I'm saying, it's well known that you don't agree with Quaife."

"Nonsense."

"Can you tell me that?"

"I do tell you that, and I expect you to believe it," said Douglas.

"What do you expect me to believe?"

"Listen to me," he said. "You've felt yourself entitled to your private view. Not so private, if I may say so. So have I. I've made no secret of it. I haven't left my Minister in any doubt. I think he's wrong, and he knows that as well as I do. But no one else knows it, except you, and one or two people I can trust."

"So do others."

"Do you really think I'm responsible for that?"

"It depends what you mean by responsible."

His face had darkened up to the cheekbones.

"We'd better try to be rational," he said. "If my Minister wins, then I shall do my best for him. Of course, I shall be carrying out a policy in which I don't believe. Well, I've done that before and I can do it again. I shall try to make the thing work. Without false modesty, I shall do it as well as anyone round here."

All that he said was absolutely true.

"You think he can't win?" I said.

"And what do you think?"

His gaze was sharp, appraising. For a second we might have been in a negotiation, listening for a point at which the other would give way.

"You've done a certain amount to make it harder," I let fly again.

"I've done exactly what I've told you. No more, and no less."

"You're better at singing in unison than some of us, aren't you?"

"I don't understand."

"You realise that the line you're taking is the line that a good many powerful persons want you to take? Most of them don't really want Roger Quaife to get away with it, do they?"

With a curious detachment he replied: "That is possibly so."

"If he doesn't win, you'll be sitting pretty, won't you? You will have scored a nice new piece of credit for yourself? You'll have everything waiting for you?"

He looked at me without expression. He said, in a quite friendly voice: "One thing. You know I've had my own view all along about this business. Don't you believe it was an honest view?"

I had to say, Yes, of course I did.

I burst out, without remembering that I had once heard Cave make the same accusation to Roger: "But all you've done or not done—you must have realised that it wouldn't exactly impede your progress, mustn't you?"

In my fury, I was astonished to see him give a smile—not an intimate smile, but still genuine.

"If we worried about that sort of consideration, Lewis, we should never do anything, should we?"

After glancing at his watch he said, in a businesslike tone: "You've made me a bit late."

He went off towards his meeting, quickly but not in a rush, head thrust forward, papers in hand, along the corridor.

CHAPTER XLII

VIEW FROM THE BOX

In the middle of the afternoon, my P.A. came in with a letter marked "Urgent." It must have been delivered by hand, she said. The handwriting on the envelope looked like a woman's, but I did not recognise it. Then I found that the note was signed "Ellen." I read:

"I expect you will be at the debate Monday and Tuesday. I have got to stay away, of course. I can't even communicate with him until it's all over. Will you please—I have to ask you this—let me know how things are going? I trust you to tell me the bare truth, whatever it is. I shall be in the flat alone, on both evenings. Please ring up, whatever you have to tell me."

I thought of her that evening, as Margaret and I went out to the theatre, just as an anaesthetic against the suspense. Roger was at home working at his speech, Caro with him. Ellen was the loneliest of all. I talked of her to Margaret. There she was, hearing nothing of him. Once she had feared that, if his career was broken, she would lose him. Now the blackmail had come out, now Caro had confronted him, Ellen must have the contradictory fear. Yet I was sure that she prayed for his success. Margaret said: "She's not as good as you think she is."

I said: "She tries to be."

Margaret had met Ellen only socially, and then in the past, with her husband. It was Caro whom Margaret knew and loved, as I did not, Caro whom she had tried to comfort. Now, as we stood in the foyer of the Haymarket, avoiding the sight of acquaintances because we wanted to be together, she asked if the position was clear-cut—was Ellen facing that dilemma, either getting him, or seeing him prevail? I said, I didn't believe that either of them knew. There could be something in it? I didn't answer her.

"If there's the slightest bit in it," said Margaret, "I'm grateful I was never tested that way about you."

Monday came and dragged, like a day in my youth when I was waiting for the result of an examination. Hector Rose sent his compliments, and informed me that he expected to be in the box for the last hours of the debate the following night. Otherwise I had no messages of any kind all that morning.

I hesitated about ringing Roger up. I detested being wished good luck myself (at root I was as superstitious as my mother); and I decided that he, also, would like to be left alone. I did not want to go to a club for lunch, in case I met Douglas or anyone else involved. I was tired of pretending to write or read. Instead, while the others were at lunch, I did what I should have done as a young man, and walked blankly round St. James's Park in the sunshine, catching, and being tantalised by, the first scent of spring: then through the streets, calling in at bookshops, nibbling away at time.

In the afternoon, the office clock swept out the minutes with its second hand. There was no point in leaving until half-past four: I did not wish to sit through question time. I rang my private secretary, and went with obsessive detail into next week's work. After that, I had a session with my P.A., making sure that she knew where I would be each hour of that day and the next. At last it was four twenty-five. Not quite the starting-time, but I could permit myself to go.

Then, as I was hurrying down the corridor, I heard a voice behind me. It was my P.A., eager, comely, spectacled. My own devices had gone back on me: she knew the time too well. A lady was on the telephone, said Hilda: she said she had to speak to me immediately, it was desperately important, she couldn't wait a minute. Thwarted, anxious, not knowing what to be anxious about, I rushed back. Was Caro going to break some news? Or was it Ellen, or from home?

It was none of them. It was Mrs. Henneker.

"I should never have believed it possible." Her voice came strongly over the 'phone. What was it? I asked.

"What do you think?"

I did not feel inclined for guessing-games. It turned out that she had had a letter by the afternoon post, five minutes before, from a publisher. They had actually told her they didn't consider her biography of her husband would be of sufficient interest to the general public. "What do you think of that?"

She sounded almost triumphant in her incredulity.

Oh well, I said, there were other publishers—trying to put her off, maddened because I was not out of the room.

"That's not good enough!" Her voice rang out like a challenge.

I would talk to her some time in the nearish future.

"No." Her reply was intransigent. "I think I must ask you to come round straight away."

I said I had important business.

"What do you call this, if it isn't important?"

It was utterly and absolutely impossible, I said. I was occupied all the evening, all the next day, all the week.

"I'm afraid," she said sternly, "I consider this entirely unsatisfactory."

I said, incensed, that I was sorry.

"Entirely unsatisfactory. Can't I make you understand

what has happened? They actually say—I'd better read you the whole letter."

I said I hadn't time.

"I believe in putting first things first."

I said goodbye.

Just as I got to the end of the corridor, I heard my telephone ringing again. I was quite sure it was Mrs. Henneker. I walked on.

Down in Great George Street, the evening light bland and calm, I still felt menaced by that monomaniac voice, as though that was the cause of my worry, and not what I was going to listen to in the House. Looking up, I could see the informatory light shining above Big Ben, with a clear violet sky beyond. Though I had seen it so often, it stirred a memory, or at least a disquiet, the reason for which seemed mixed with the monomaniac voice. I was tugging at the roots of memory, but they would not be pulled out. Was it the night my wife and I went to dine at Lord North Street and, arriving too early, had walked round by St. Margaret's? The light had been shining that evening, too; yet there had been no disquiet, we had been at leisure, and content.

In the central lobby, busy with cavernous activity, members were meeting constituents, acquaintances, taking them off to tea. When I got into the officials' box, I could have counted less than a hundred members in the Chamber. There seemed as yet no special excitement in the air. The Opposition opener was speaking, like a man who is settling down to a steady lecture. He was prosy but confident, saying nothing new. It was a standard speech, gaining nothing, losing nothing. For a while I felt the needle pass away.

On the front bench, Roger was leaning back, fingers entwined, hands under his chin: Tom Wyndham sat dutifully behind him. There were three other Ministers on the front bench, Collingwood among them. A few members entered, others left. Figures were dotted here and there on the empty

benches, some not listening. It might have been a borough
council, assembled out of duty, for a discussion of something
not specially earth-shaking, such as a proposal for a subsidy
to the civic theatre.

In the box, Douglas and two other Whitehall acquaintances were already sitting. Douglas, who was writing a note on
the small desk flap, gave me a friendly smile. They were all
professionals, they had been here before. The climax was a
long way off. This was just the start, as perfunctory as the
first hour of a county cricket match, or the exposition of a
drawing-room comedy.

During the opening speech I went along to the Speaker's
Gallery. There Caro and Margaret were sitting together.
"He's not doing any harm," whispered Caro. They were going
back to Lord North Street for a sandwich some time. They
knew I shouldn't eat till the sitting was over. "Come along
then, and pick up Margaret," said Caro, in another whisper.
Now that at last we were all in it, all immersed, she could
put hostilities aside until another day. Her eyes looked at
me, bold and full, just as her brother's did when he gambled.
No one could expect her to be happy. Yet she wasn't in the
true sense anxious, and in her excitement there was a glint,
not only of recklessness, but of pleasure.

Back in my place at Douglas's side, I listened to the First
Lord making the first reply. He too was competent, more so
than I had been told. He was using much the same language
as the Opposition spokesman. In fact, I found myself thinking, as the words rolled out like the balloons from characters
in comic strips, an observer from Outer Mongolia would have
been puzzled to detect the difference between them. "Deter-
rence" was a word they both used often. The First Lord
was preoccupied with "potential scaling-down," not scaling-
down in the here and now, but "potential scaling-down if we
can have the assurance that this will influence others." He
also talked of "shield and sword," "striking-power," "capabil-

ity." It was a curious abstract language, of which the main feature was the taking of meaning out of words.

As I listened to their speeches and those which followed, I wasn't interested in speculation, or even the arguments as such. We had heard them all, for years. So I was listening, with concentrated and often obsessed attention, not to the arguments, but simply to what they meant in terms of votes next night. That was all. For all those hours, it was enough. The House grew fuller during the early evening, then thinned at dinner-time. Until nine o'clock there were no surprises. A Labour Party back-bencher expressed views close to Francis Getliffe's or mine. When it came to the vote there would, we already knew, be plenty of abstentions on the Labour side—how many we were not certain, but too many for comfort. Though these abstentions meant support for Roger's policy, it was once again the support he could not afford. A Labour Party front-bencher expressed views that a member of Lord A——'s splinter-group, or an American admiral, might have found reactionary. Lord A—— himself made a Delphic speech, in which he stated his suspicions of the Government's intentions and his determination to vote for them. Another ultra-Conservative, whom we had counted as lost, followed suit.

To the surprise of everyone round me, the first hours of the debate didn't produce much animus. It was a full-dress parliamentary occasion. Everyone had heard the passions over the issue and the personality seething for weeks. They were waiting for violence, and it hadn't come.

Then, precisely at nine, the member for a county division was called. When I saw him rise, I settled back without any apprehensions at all. His name was Trafford, and I knew him slightly. He wasn't well-off, he lived on a small family business. He wasn't on the extreme right, he wasn't smart. He didn't speak often, he asked pertinacious questions: he was never likely to be invited to Basset. I had met him because, in his constituency, there were people who had known me in my youth. I thought he was dull, determined, over-anxious to do all the listening.

He got up, heavy-shouldered, raw-skinned. Within a minute, he was ripping into an attack. It was an attack which, from the first sounding note, was virulent. He was a loyal supporter of the Government, he said: he hoped to be so in the future: but he couldn't support this particular policy and this particular Minister. The policy was the policy of an adventurer. What else was this man? What had he done? What was his record of achievement? All he did was play the field, look out for the main chance, find the soft option. This was the kind of adventurer's progress he was leading the country into. Why? What were his credentials? What reason had he given us for trusting him? Trust him? Trafford's tone got more violent. Some of us compared him with a man we could truly trust, the Honourable Member for Brighton South. We wished that the Honourable Member for Brighton South were in his place tonight, bringing us back to our principles. We believed that he had been a victim to his own high standards.

As the constituency of Brighton South was shouted out, I could not recall the member's name. I whispered a question to Douglas. "J. C. Smith," he said.

So it had got so far. The abuse went on, but the accusation became no more direct. It couldn't have been understood, except by those who knew already; yet the hate was palpable. Was this man Trafford one of Smith's disciples? It might be so. How far were they in touch with Hood, how far was he their weapon?

My own suspicion had crystallised. I did not believe that he was just a man unbalanced, on his own. Or rather, he might be unbalanced, or have become so, as he carried the persecution on. But I believed that there were cool minds behind it. There was evidence that he had a fanatical devotion to his own aircraft firm, the kind of devotion, passionate and pathetic, of one who didn't get the rewards himself, but hero-worshipped those who did. There could have been people shrewd enough to use him, shrewd enough to know that he got excitement from the sexual life of others.

I thought that there were cool minds behind him. But it seemed to me that these were business minds. They might have their links with Smith's disciples; but it didn't sound like the work of those disciples, not even the work of this man himself, snarling in the Chamber.

Adventurers were dangerous, he was saying. They might be ingratiating, they might have attractions for all those round them, they might be clever, but they were the ruin of any government and any nation. It was time this Government went back to the solid virtues, and then Trafford and his friends and the whole country would support them once more.

It wasn't a long speech. Twice he was shouted into silence, but even Roger's partisans were embarrassed and for a time hypnotised by his venom. Roger sat through it, eyes hard, face expressionless.

I hadn't heard such an outburst in the House before. What harm had it done? For a few, for Collingwood, the reference to Smith wouldn't be missed. The attack came from a quarter we should least have chosen, the respectable middle-of-the-road of the Tory members. Had it been too violent for men to take? That seemed the best hope. When two of Hector Rose's dinner companions got up to say they couldn't support the Government, they were noticeably civil and restrained, and one paid a compliment to Roger's character.

When the House rose, I couldn't trust my judgment. A policeman was shouting "Who goes home?" as I telephoned Ellen, not knowing what to say. I heard her quick, breath-catching "Yes," and told her all had gone as we expected, except—again a "Yes?"—except, I said, for one bit of malice.

I couldn't tell her what the effect would be. It had been meant to kill. It might result in nothing worse than a single un-expected abstention. "You're not holding back?" she said. I had to tell her there had been a hint about her husband: not many would have grasped it. Down the telephone came a harsh sigh: What difference would it make? Was it going to tip the balance? Her voice had risen. I said, in flat honesty, that no one could tell: I believed, for better or worse, it wouldn't count. I added, meaninglessly, Try to sleep.

Through the sparkling, frosty night, I hurried round to Lord North Street. On the stairs I heard laughter from the drawing-room. As I got inside, I saw with astonishment, with the desire to touch wood, that Caro, Margaret and Roger were all looking cheerful. A plate of sandwiches was waiting for me, since I had not eaten all day.

"What have you been doing to Trafford?" Roger asked, as though to put me at my ease.

"Do you understand it?" I cried.

"Whatever does he hope for?" Caro spoke with genuine, full-throated scorn, not pretending. She must have heard each overtone of the insinuation, but she laughed like one saying —"If that is the worst they can do!"

"Have you had any repercussions?" I asked.

"Not one." Roger spoke with studious interest, with the euphoria which sometimes breaks through in the middle of a crisis. "Do you know, I can't begin to imagine why he did it. Can you?"

I couldn't answer.

"If no one can supply any motive—why, I shall soon be forced to think that he meant what he said." His tone was unforced, free from rancour. He gave a laugh, like a man easy among his friends. He had drunk little, he was keyed up for action next day. He was hoping more simply than he had hoped for weeks.

CHAPTER XLIII

THE MEANING OF
NUMBERS

Next morning I woke early and lay listening to the papers as they thudded onto the hall floor. They didn't settle either what I feared, or what I hoped. The *Times* was playing down the whole debate: on the middle page, Trafford only got a couple of lines. The *Telegraph* gave bolder headlines and more space: if one knew the language, one knew that they were anti-Roger. But they also muffled Trafford's attack. The *Express* was angry with the chief Labour speaker. I dressed and went up Albion Gate to buy the other morning papers. I came back to breakfast, neither Margaret nor myself out of our misery, either for good or bad. In the morning light, she was ashamed of herself for having been so elated the night before.

I wondered whether Roger, too, had hated the morning. I wondered whether Caro had tried to give him comfort, as Margaret did to me. She knew, better than I did, that time and the hour ran through the roughest day.

Nothing happened—that didn't make the day smoother— until, once more at tea-time, I was within a few minutes of leaving for the House. Then a telephone call came through; this time, not from Mrs. Henneker. Instead, a friend of Sammikins had a piece of news. He had just come away from the

Lords. He wanted to tell me that old Gilbey had, ten minutes before, taken a hand.

By this time, Lord Gilbey was very ill. He hadn't been able to make a public appearance for twelve months, and his doctors were surprised that he had lived at all. Yet that afternoon, he had been impelled to make a public appearance, even if it were his last. He had arrived in the Lords. The subject for his intervention could not have seemed promising, for some peer, ennobled for scientific eminence, was moving for papers on the state of the country's technological education. This hadn't deterred Gilbey. Standing up, frail, white as bleached bread, he had supported the motion with passion. He didn't understand technology, but he wanted it, if that was the price of keeping us strong. He was for anything, whether it was technology or black magic, if competent persons like the Noble Lord proved that it was necessary to keep us strong and make us stronger. He would assert this to his dying day, which wouldn't be far off.

He had spoken for five minutes, an old soldier's attack on *adventurers,* men who were too clever for their good or ours. Adventurers in high places, careerists in high places. He begged the Noble Lords to beware of them. He wanted to make this plea, even if it were for the last time.

It was pure revenge. He might die before the summer, but hatred for Roger would live as long as he did. It didn't sound like a hero's end: and then I thought that it might be just his willingness to end like this which had made him a hero.

I was relieved to be back in the box, relieved to sit beside Hector Rose instead of Douglas. On this night it was better to have the company of an ally who wasn't a friend than the other way round. Arms folded across his chest, Rose watched with trained, cold eyes. As, at intervals of half an hour, three members whom he had designated by name got up with hostile speeches, he permitted himself to say:

"According to plan." Yet, even to him, fresh as he was, the debate was not giving any answer. The tone had become more bitter on both sides. The benches were full now, members were squatting in the aisles. There were echoes of Trafford; words like "gambler," "adventurer," "risk," "surrender," snapped into the Chamber, but all from men we had already written off. Several speakers sat down, leaving it vague how they intended to vote. When a Labour ex-Minister began a preamble on strategy, Rose said quietly: "I give him forty minutes. Time for us to eat."

I didn't want to leave.

"No, you must."

Douglas had made the same estimate about the speaker's staying-power. As we reached the Hall together, Rose gave him lavish and courteous greetings, but pointedly did not invite him to come along with us.

We hurried through the yard, across to a Whitehall pub. There Rose, who normally had delicate tastes in food, put down a large hunk of cheese and a scotch egg, and inspected me with satisfaction as I did the same. "That will keep us going," he said dutifully.

We hadn't spoken about the debate. I said the one word: "Well?"

"I don't know, my dear Lewis, I don't know."

"Any chance?"

"He'll have to pull something out of the bag himself, shouldn't you have thought?"

He meant, in the final speech.

I wanted to scratch over the evidence, to reckon the odds, but Rose wouldn't have it.

"It doesn't seem profitable," he said. Instead, he had his own recourse. He drew out a stiff, plain pocket-book, such as I had often seen him use in meetings, and began to write down numbers. Maximum possible number of members on the Government side, 315. He jotted down the figure, without an enquiry or a doubt, like a computing machine. Unavoidable absences, illness, and so on—the Whips appeared to expect eight. Available votes, 307. Rose did not hesitate: Cabinet dubious, Minister not sticking to the rules, he couldn't afford defections. 290 votes and he might be safe: 17 abstentions. (From the debate, we now knew there would be at least nine, and one vote, Sammikins's, against.)

Anything under 280, and he was in great danger.

Anything under 270, and it was all over.

Rose went on with his own kind of nepenthe. He didn't think the Opposition vote was relevant, but in his clear, beautiful script he continued to write figures. Maximum: 230. Absences: 12. Abstentions: perhaps 25.

The majority would not be significant. Roger could survive provided he received the 290 votes from his own side, plus or minus 10. That would be the figure which all informed persons would regard as decisive that night.

Rose looked up with the pleasure of one who has performed a neat operation. It struck me, even in the suspense, that the figures would be hard to explain to anyone not steeped in this kind of parliamentary process. The figures looked blank, the margins negligible. They would decide at least one career, maybe others, conceivably a good deal else.

When we returned to our places, the ex-Minister had only just finished. More speeches; the House becoming packed. The shouts of laughter were louder, so were the protests, but most of the time there was a dense silence. It was a dense, impatient silence. Men looked at Roger, sitting heavily on the front bench, chin in hand. The last perfunctory "hear-hears" after the last Opposition speech damped down. Again the silence. Voice from the Chair—"Mr. Quaife."

At last. Roger stood up, heavy, moving untidily but without strain. He was much the biggest man on either front bench. Once again, as when I first met him, in his clumsy, powerful, formidable presence, he gave me a reminder of

Pierre Bezukhov. There was loyal applause behind him. He looked relaxed, abnormally so, troublingly so, for a man in his chief trial. He began with taunts. He had been accused of so many things, he said. Some of them were contradictory, they could not all be valid. Of course, wise persons remarked that, if you wanted to hear the truth about yourself, you listened to what your enemies said. Splendid. But that principle didn't apply only to him. It applied to everyone. Even, believe it or not, to other Honourable Members, in some cases Honourable and Gallant Members, who had so reluctantly volunteered their character-sketches of himself. He listed four of the ultra-Conservatives. He did not refer, even by an intonation, to Trafford. It might be a good idea if each of us accepted just what his enemies said; it might make us better, and the world too. It would certainly rub into us that we were all miserable sinners.

It was good-natured. The House was laughing. Once or twice a barb darted out. Suddenly one heard him, not so Pierre-like, but clear, hard, piercing. Though his friends cheered, I was not easy. It might be too light a beginning. In a sense, it seemed too much above the battle. I looked at Hector Rose. Almost imperceptibly, he gave a shake of the head. In the House, in the galleries, people were saying that this was the speech of the debate. As he got down to the arguments, he was using the idiom of a late 20th Century man. He had thrown away the old style of parliamentary rhetoric altogether. Compared with the other speeches from both the front benches, this might have come from a man a generation younger. It was the speech of one used to broadcasting studios, television cameras, the exposure of the machine. He didn't declaim: he spoke about war, weapons, the meaning of a peaceful future, in his own voice. This was how, observers said later, parliamentarians would be speaking in ten years' time.

I scarcely noticed. I was thinking, was this the time that

he might choose to break loose? Once or twice he had threatened to cut the tangle of these arguments, and to try to touch something deeper. Would it help him? We were all children of our time and class, conditioned to think of these decisions (were they decisions? were we just driven?) in forms we couldn't break. Could anyone break them? Were there forces which Roger or anyone in that house, or any of the rest of us, could release?

If he had thought of trying, he had put the idea behind him. He was talking only to the House. And yet, within ten minutes, I knew that he wasn't withdrawing, that he had forgotten temptations, ambiguities and tricks. He was saying what he had often concealed, but all along believed. Now that he had to speak, he gave an account, lucid and sharp, of the kind of thinking Getliffe and his colleagues had made their own. He gave it with more force than they could have done. He gave it with the authority of one who would grip the power. But it was only right at the end that he said something which dropped, quietly, unofficially, into the late night air. "Look," he said. "The problems we're trying to handle are very difficult. So difficult that most people in this country— people who are by and large at least as intelligent as we are— can't begin to understand them. Simply because they haven't had the information, and haven't been taught to come to terms with them. I'm not sure how many of us can comprehend what our world is like, now that we're living with the bomb. Perhaps very few, or none. But I'm certain that the overwhelming majority of people who are, I repeat, at least as intelligent as we are, don't have any idea. We are trying to speak for them. We have taken a great deal upon ourselves. We never ought to forget it."

I was feeling admiration, anxiety, the exhilaration of anxiety. Now it had come to it, did I wish that he had compromised? His colleagues could get rid of him now: the bargains and balances of the White Paper didn't allow for this. The chance, the only chance, was that he might take the House with him.

"It has been said in this House, these last two nights, that I want to take risks. Let me tell you this. All choices involve risks. In our world, all the serious choices involve grave ones. But there are two kinds of risk. One is to go on mindlessly, as though our world were the old world. I believe, as completely as I believe anything, that if this country and all countries go on making these bombs, testing these bombs—just as though they were so many battleships—then before too long a time, the worst will happen. Perhaps through no one's fault —just because we're all men, liable to make mistakes, go mad, or have bad luck. If that happens, our descendants, if we have any, will curse us. And every curse will be justified.

"This country can't be a super-power any longer. I should be happier if it could. Though it is possible that being a super-power is in itself an illusion, now that science has caught up with us. Anyway, we can't be one. But I am certain that we can help—by example, by good judgment, by talking sense, and acting sense—we can help swing the balance between a good future and a bad future, or between a good future and none at all. We can't contract out. The future is finely poised. Our influence upon it is finite, but it exists.

"That is why I want to take one kind of risk. It is, in fact, a small risk, which may do good, as opposed to a great risk which would certainly do harm. That is still the choice. That is all."

Roger sat down, heavy-faced, hands in his pockets. For an instant, a long instant, there was silence. Then applause behind him. How solid was it? Was it uncomfortable? There were one or two cheers from the back benches on the other side. Ritual took over. The lobby bells rang. I noticed Sammikins stand up, head high and wild, in the middle of his friends, going out defiantly to vote against them. Half a dozen members sat obstinately on the Government benches, most of them with arms crossed, parading their determination to abstain. That told us nothing. There might be others, not so forthright, who would go out and not pass through the lobby.

The members returned. Some were talking, but the noise level was low. There was a crowd, excited, tense, at the sides of the Speaker's Chair. Before the tellers had passed the despatch box, a hush had fallen. It was a hush, but not a high-spirited one. The voice came:

"Ayes on the right,* 186." (There had been more Labour abstentions than Rose had allowed for.)

The voice came again:

"Noes on the left, 271."

Rose looked at me with cold sympathy. He said, precisely: "I consider this unfortunate."

In the Chamber, it took longer for the result to sink in. The Chairman repeated the numbers in a sonorous base, and announced that the Noes had it.

Seconds later, half a minute later, a chant opened up from the Opposition: "Resign! Resign!"

Without fuss, the Government front bench began to empty. The Prime Minister, Collingwood, Monty Cave, went out of the House together, passing close by us in the box. Cries followed them, but the shouts were focussed on Roger. He was sitting back, one arm stretched out behind him, talking, with apparent casualness, to the First Lord and Leverett-Smith.

"Resign! Resign!"

The yells broke on him. Once, he gave a wave across the gangway, like a Wimbledon player acknowledging the existence of the crowd.

Taking his time, he got up. He didn't look either at his own backbenchers or at the others. "Resign! Resign!" The shouts grew louder. His great back moved slowly down the aisle, away from us. At the Bar he turned and made his bow to the Chair. Then he walked on. When he was out of sight, the shouts still crashed behind him.

---

* I.e., those voting for the Opposition motion against Roger.

CHAPTER XLIV

"YOU HAVE NOTHING
TO DO WITH IT"

Next morning, headlines, questions in the papers: rumours in Whitehall. Beyond the windows, the February sky was clear and crystalline. In my office, the scrambled, yellow-corded telephone kept ringing. No message from Roger had reached the Prime Minister's secretary.

Collingwood was reported to have said: "This dance will no further go." (The only historical reference the old man knew, said a cultivated voice at the other end of the wire.) He was said to be bearing Roger no malice, to be speaking of him with dispassion. He had heard—this I did not know for certain until later—about Roger and his nephew's wife. He took the news with stony lack of concern. "I regard that as irrelevant," he said. He turned out to have no feeling whatsoever for his nephew. That had been one of the un-realistic fears.

That morning, there was a strong rumour, which came from several sources, that some of Roger's supporters were calling on the Prime Minister. They were trying to arrange for the Prime Minister to interview him. He hadn't resigned yet. Another rumour: he was backing down. He wouldn't resign. He would announce that he had stressed one part of the White Paper at the expense of the whole. He had been wrong, but now faithfully accepted the compromise. He would go on implementing the compromise policies: or, alternatively, he would take a dimmer job.

I heard nothing from him. I imagined that he was like the rest of us when the worst has happened, in moments still tantalised by hopes, almost by fulfilment, as though it had gone the other way: just as, when Sheila had betrayed me when I was a young man, I walked across the park deceived by gleams of happiness, as though I were going to her bed: just as, when an operation has failed, one lies in hospital and, now and then, has reveries of content, as though one were whole again.

He would be living with temptations. He wasn't different from most of those who have obtained any kind of power, petty or grand. He wanted to cling to it up to the end, beyond the end. If he went out now, untouched, unbudging, that was fine, that was in the style he would like for himself. And yet, he knew politics too well not to know that he might never come back. It would be bitter to behave as if he had been wrong, to be juggled with, put in an inconspicuous Ministry for years: but perhaps that was the way to win. Would they let him? He must be thinking of the talks that day. Others would be counting the odds, with more degrees of freedom than he had. It might be good management to make sure that he was disposed of. Some might be sorry, but that didn't count. If they gave him a second chance, it wouldn't be because of sympathy or even admiration. They owed him no support. It would be because he still had some power. They must be weighing up just how much influence he still possessed. Would he be more dangerous eliminated, or allowed to stay?

In the afternoon I attended a departmental meeting, Rose in the chair. He hadn't spoken to me that morning; he greeted me with overflowing politeness, as though I were a valuable acquaintance whom he had not seen for months. No one round the table could have guessed that we had been sitting

side by side, in anxiety, the night before. He got through
the business as accurately, as smoothly, as he would have done
when I first sat under him, nearly twenty years before. Next
year, he would be sixty, taking his last meeting in this room.
He would go on like this till the last day. This particular
afternoon, it wasn't even interesting business: it had to be
done.

As soon as I returned to my room, my P.A. came in.

"There's a lady waiting for you," she said. She looked in-
quisitive and apologetic. "I'm afraid she seems rather upset."

I asked who it was.

"She says her name is Mrs. Smith."

When I had told Ellen the result over the telephone, late
the previous night, she had gasped. I had heard a gulp of
tears before the receiver crashed down.

That afternoon, as she sat down in the chair beside my
desk, her eyes were open, bloodshot, piteous and haughty.
They reminded me of someone else's so hauntingly that I
couldn't at first listen to what she was saying. Then, down
the years, I had it. They were like my mother's, after an
intolerable wound to her pride, as on the day my father went
bankrupt.

She asked: "What is he going to do?"

I shook my head. "He's told me nothing."

"I haven't been able to see him."

She was crying out for sympathy, and yet she would reject it.

I said, as astringently as I could make myself:

"Yes, it's bad. It's part of the situation."

"I mustn't see him till he's decided, one way or the other.
You understand, don't you?"

"I think so."

"I mustn't influence him. I mustn't even try."

Then she gave a crisp, ironic, almost cheerful laugh, and
added:

"Do you believe I could?"

I had seen her so often under strain. This day was the worst. But—just in that moment—I could feel how she behaved with Roger. Given a chance, she was, more than most of us, high-spirited and gay.

"Tell me something," she said, her eyes searching mine. "Which is better for him?"

"What do you mean?"

"You know well enough." Impatiently she explained herself. She might have been reading my own speculations earlier that day. Until she met Roger, she was politically innocent. Now she could follow, by instinct, love and knowledge, the moves, the temptations, the choices. Her insight had told her much what mine did: except that she was certain that, if Roger wanted to climb down, they would welcome him.

"Which is better for him?"

"If I knew, which I don't, ought I to tell you?" I said.

"You're supposed to be a friend of his, aren't you?" she flared out.

"Fortunately," this time I could let the temperature drop, and smile sarcastically back, "I just don't know which is better."

"But you think you do—"

I said: "If we forget your side of it, then I think he'd probably, not certainly but probably, be wiser to stay if he can."

"Why?"

"If he's out of politics, won't he feel he's wasting his life?"

"It means humiliating himself and crawling to them." She flushed. She was hating "them" with all the force of her nature.

"Yes, it means that."

"Do you know that underneath he's a very proud man?"

I looked at her and said, "Hasn't he learned to live with it?"

"Has anyone? Don't you believe that I'm proud too?"

She was speaking without constraint, self-effacingness

stripped off, codes of behaviour fallen away. Her face had gone naked and wild.

"Yes," I said, "I believe that."

"If he does throw it up and comes to me, will he ever forgive me?"

It was a new fear, different from, yet grown from, that which she had once confided in her own flat yet grown from the same root. Then she had been afraid that, once he had failed, he would blame her and be unable to endure her. Now that fear had gone. She believed that, whatever happened, he would need her. Yet the doubt, the cruelty, the heritage, remained.

"You have nothing to do with it," I said. "If he had never fallen in love with any woman at all, he would have been in precisely the same position as he is today."

"Are you dead sure?"

I said immediately, "I am dead sure."

I was saying what I almost believed. If she had not been sitting beside me, wounded and suspicious, waiting for the slightest qualification, I might have been less positive. Roger had stood much less of a chance of getting his policy through —I became convinced later, looking back—than we imagined when we were living in the middle of it. It was hard to believe that a personal chance, such as their love-affair, had had any effect. And yet, and yet—their love-affair had had an effect on him: without it, would he have acted precisely as he had?

"I am dead sure," I repeated.

"Will he ever believe it?"

For an instant, I did not answer.

"Will he ever believe it?"

She was thinking of Roger coming to her, marrying her: the plain life, after Caro's home, the high hopes gone: the inquest on the past, the blame. She sat there for a moment or so, not speaking. Ellen, so self-effacing in public as to be inconspicuous, was filled with the beauty of violence, and perhaps with the beauty given her by the passion for sheer action, even if it were action destructive to herself, to all her hopes.

"I'm telling myself," she said, "that I ought to get out of it, now. Today."

I said: "Could you?" She stared at me, her eyes once more piteous and haughty. She asked: "What is he going to do?"

CHAPTER XLV

A GOOD LETTER

Some time after I had seen Ellen into a taxi, I was clearing up work in my office. The sky outside the window was already dark, the secretaries had gone home, all was quiet. The private telephone buzzed. Would I call in on Roger before I left?

Through the corridors, deserted now, I trod out the long, maze-like walk. One or two doors were open, lights of offices shone out: always the offices of the top echelon, staying late. Douglas was working, but I did not look in to say good-night. I went straight into Roger's room. From the reading-lamp shone out a cone of light which glared off the paper, was sopped up by the blotting-pad. Roger stood up, looming against the window. For the first time since we had been introduced, years before, he gripped my hand.

"Well?" he said.

I was taken aback by his vigorous, active manner. This was like a conversation which one had rehearsed in one's head and which was going wrong. I muttered something lame, about its being a pity.

"Never mind about that," he said. He gazed at me with sharp, unrelenting eyes.

"Well?" he said again. He snapped his fingers.

For an instant I thought he wanted me to take the initiative. It might have been the beginning of a business deal. But I was mishearing him. He went on:

"It's time I thought it out again from the beginning, isn't it?" He gave out a special kind of exhilaration. The exhilaration of failure: the freedom of being bare to the world.

He was certain where he was, because there was nothing else to be certain of. I thought I knew him. Ellen knew him better. But the way we had seen him that day was not the way he saw himself. The hedges, the duplicities of his nature —either they did not exist for him that day, or he saw through them. This was nothing like the night when David Rubin had begged him to back down, and Roger had played with him.

Across the pool of light, he began to talk. To begin with, as though it were obvious and had to be put out of the way, he said that he would have to go. There was no argument. He was out: so was what he had tried to do.

Then he broke out: "But not for good. Not for long. Someone's going to do it. Maybe I still can."

It was the last thing I expected. He was talking with a curious impersonality about the future. He did not mention his wife or Ellen, as though ruling out his self-bound concerns, the concern of his own guilt. He did say, as an objective fact, as part of the situation, that he would be on his own: without influence, without powerful friends. Even without money. He would have to start again. "It will be harder," he said. "It'll be harder than if I'd never done anything at all."

He looked at me with a caustic, open smile.

"You don't think I stand a chance, do you?"

Kindnesses, personal relations, had dropped away. I answered: "Not much."

"Someone's going to do it. All we want is time, and luck, and something in the air. Someone's going to do it."

Just as when he had been at the peak of his power, when

it seemed that the Prime Minister and Collingwood were
befriending him, he talked about the political process with
relaxation, with detachment. Could anyone else have done
better than he had done? Could he have avoided the mistakes that he had made? What about mine? If we had handled
Brodzinski better? How far did personalities count? Nothing
like as much as one liked to think. Only in those circumstances when the hinge is oiled, but the door may swing or
not. If that isn't the situation, then no personality is going
to make more than an ineffectual noise.

He wasn't asking for comfort. He wasn't even asking for
my view. He was speaking as though to himself, in the quiet
room. He said, If one goes too far, one's ruined. If one doesn't
go at all, one might as well not be there.

He said, Trying may have value. Even when it has failed.
The situation will never be quite the same again. He said
(I remembered when he had first said it): The first thing
is to get the power. The next thing is to do something with
it. He said: Someone is going to do what I tried to do. I
don't know whether it'll be me.

He spoke with simplicity, almost with purity. It was hard
for anyone outside to find within him that pure and simple
feeling. He cared, less than many men, what his own feelings
were. He had felt most temptations and passions, but not
that kind of self-regard. And yet, he wanted something for
himself. When he said he wanted to get power and "do
something with it," he meant that he wanted a justification,
a belief that he was doing something valuable with his life.
He also wanted a justification, in an older and deeper sense.
He wanted something like a faith, a faith in action. He
had lurched about until he found just that. Despite his com-
promises and callousnesses—or to an extent because of them
—he had believed in what he was doing. Those round him
might suspect him, but there, and there alone, he did not
suspect himself.

The irony was that, if our suspicions had been true, he would have been a more successful politician. He might even, within the limits of those years, have done more good.

It was getting on for eight o'clock. All of a sudden, Roger's manner changed. He pushed one foot against the desk and said, as though we were at work once more: "I want you to read this."

All this time, a letter had been waiting in front of him. It began, "Dear Prime Minister," in his own bold holograph, and continued in typescript. It was a good letter. There was not a sign of reproach or rancour, either overt or hinted at. It said that Roger had been honoured to be the Prime Minister's colleague. He was sorry that his policy had evoked so much dissension, and that he had emphasized parts of it to an extent which his colleagues could not share, so that both it and he had now become liabilities to the Government. He continued to believe in his policy. He could not persuade himself that it had been wrong. Since he could not honestly change his mind, there was only one course open to him, which he was sure the Prime Minister would sympathise with and understand. He hoped to be of some use to the Prime Minister and the Government as a private member.

There the typing ended. In Roger's hand, halfway down the third page, was written, black and firm: "Yours ever, Roger Quaife."

As soon as I lifted my eyes he said: "Will that do?"

"It's good," I said.

"It will be accepted, you know." (He meant the resignation.)

"Yes, it'll be accepted," I said.

"With slightly excessive haste." We gazed at each other across the desk.

"Well," he said, "you'd better see it go."

One of the red despatch boxes was standing beside the telephones. From his hip-pocket he brought out a bunch of keys and unlocked it. He did it with the ceremonial air of a man who is enjoying a privilege. Not many men had ever revelled more in having the liberty of the despatch boxes, of being in possession of such a key. He was enjoying the privilege, the physiognomic charm of office, even then.

Punctiliously he placed the letter in the box, and re-locked it. He pressed a button, and his principal private secretary—who this last week could have had no time to call his own—opened the door.

"Will you see this goes to the Prime Minister?" said Roger. He spoke in a matter-of-fact tone.

The young man, thirtyish, a high class civil servant on the climb, acknowledged it with similar matter-of-fact politeness. It might have been any one of the messages he had transmitted for Roger these last years, or would go on transmitting for years to come, although he must have been wondering now whether this was the end, and who his new master would be.

The door closed. Roger smiled.

"I might have changed my mind," he said. "That would have been unfortunate."

His voice, his whole expression, had gone tired. He had to force himself to speak again, to produce a spurt of vigour.

"I'm sorry," he said, "to have got some of our friends into trouble." He was trying to speak with warmth, with intimacy: but he couldn't do it any more. He tried again when he said: "I'm sorry to have done you harm."

"That's nothing."

"I'm sorry."

After that, he did not want to make another effort. He sat back, waiting to sit in that room alone. As I was leaving he said: "I shan't be available for some time. I'm going away."

CHAPTER XLVI

ANOTHER CHOICE

My own choice was clear. Margaret and I dismissed it in half an hour and then, friction-free, stood ourselves a drink. It seemed to both of us that we might be on the eve of a holiday, cases packed and labelled, the car ordered for nine in the morning, the ship awaiting us, rest in the sun.

I waited three days. In that time, Roger's resignation was announced and the name of his successor. It was all assimilated in the papers, Whitehall, the clubs, as though it had happened months before. I waited three days, then asked for an appointment with Hector Rose.

It was a quarter-past ten in the morning. In the Park below the mist was clearing. On Rose's desk a bowl of hyacinths breathed out the scent of other interviews, of headaching lunches long ago.

I said, the moment I sat down: "It's time for me to go now."

The elegant posturing was washed away; his concentration was complete.

"You mean—?"

"I mean, I've outlived my usefulness here."

"I should have thought," said Rose, "that that was overstating the case."

"You know as well as I do that I'm identified with this débâcle."

394

"To an extent," Rose replied, arms folded, "that is unfortunately true."

"It is entirely true."

"I don't think, however, that you need take it too tragically."

"I'm not taking it tragically," I said. "I'm just commenting, I have to do business for you with people we both know. In their view, I've backed the wrong horse. Fairly openly. It wouldn't have mattered so much doing it openly, if it hadn't been the wrong horse."

Rose gave an arctic smile.

"It's simple," I said. "I should be no good with these people any more. It's time to go."

There was a long silence. Rose considered, his pale eyes still on me, unblinking, expressionless. At last he began to speak, fluently but with deliberation.

"You have always had a tendency, if I may say so with respect, to permit yourself a certain degree of over-simplification. I can see that you have occasionally acted in a fashion which would have been, shall I say, unusual, if you had been a career civil servant. That has applied particularly in the matter of the unfortunate Quaife. But I might remind you that there have been other examples, during the course of your valuable activities. I think you should acknowledge that the Service is not so finicky as our critics are fond of telling us. The Service has been prepared to put up with what might be, by some standards, a certain trifling amount of embarrassment. It has been considered that we have gained through your having taken some rather curious liberties. In fact, we have formed the firm opinion that your presence was very much more advantageous than your absence. I dislike stressing the point, but we have expressed our appreciation in the only way open to us."

He was referring to the Honours Lists.

I said, "You've treated me generously. I know that."

He bowed his head. He considered, just as precisely: "I

can see further that after these recent events, it wouldn't be in your interests or ours for you to undertake certain commissions for us, including perhaps some which you have carried through with your usual distinction. I suggest, though, that this is really not serious *sub specie aeternitatis*. It ought not to be beyond the wit of man to make a slight redistribution of your functions. We shall still retain the benefit of your services, at places where we continue to need them. And where, you will understand, though this isn't an occasion for flattery, we can't comfortably afford to dispense with them yet awhile."

He was speaking with fairness, and perhaps with justice. He was also speaking as he might have done at any time during our twenty years' connection. Within a few months he would himself be retiring from the Service—the Service which had not given him his full reward, certainly not his desire. If I left a vacant niche, it would soon be no concern of his. Nevertheless, he was still saying "we," taking care of Service needs years ahead. He hadn't, by so much as a flick, recognised that for a short time, for a few days and hours, we had been, not colleagues, but allies. That was wiped out. He was speaking with absolute fairness, but between us there had come down once more, like a curtain, the utter difference in our natures, the uneasiness, perhaps the dislike.

I thanked him, paused, and said: "No. But that doesn't alter the position. I want to go."

"You really want to go?"

I nodded.

"Why?"

"There are some things I want to help get done. I thought we might do them this way, on the quiet. Now I don't think we can. Or at least, there's nothing more I can do on the quiet. I shall have to be a private citizen again."

"Will it be so very private, my dear Lewis?" Rose was watching me carefully.

He asked: "I take it, there is no financial problem?"

I said no. He knew it in advance. He wasn't above a dash of envy because I had been lucky. Himself, though he had been expensively educated, he had no money. When he retired, he would have to live on his pension.

"You intend to go?"

"Yes."

He gazed at me. When it came to men's actions, he was a good judge. He shrugged his shoulders.

"Right," he said. "Well, it remains to us to make it as painless as possible."

There was another silence, not a long one.

He said, without emphasis: "I should like to put one consideration before you. If you resign now, it won't pass unnoticed. You are fairly conspicuous. There will be those who will be malicious enough to draw certain conclusions. They might even hint that your departure is not unconnected with recent differences of opinion. And it wouldn't be altogether easy to prove them wrong."

He went on: "That would be somewhat embarrassing for us. No doubt you will make your own view heard in your own good time. But I suggest you have some obligation to give us a decent interval. You've been working with us for a long time. It wouldn't seem proper if you made matters awkward for us by a dramatic resignation."

I did not reply. Rose went on:

"I also suggest it wouldn't be good for you. I expect it affects you very little. You have other things to occupy you. I understand that. But still, you've done your service to the State. It would be a pity to spoil it now. Whoever one is, I think it's wrong to leave a job with hard feelings. It's bad for the soul to leave under a cloud."

I could not tell whether he was being considerate. His manner, which had become more than ever frigid, made the words sound scornful or artificial. Yet he was insistent.

I said:

"How long should I stay?"

"The end of the year? Is that asking too much?"

I said I would do it. Rose accepted the bargain, business-like, without thanks. It was only when I went towards the door that he began to thank me profusely, not for meeting his wishes or accepting his advice, but for the somewhat more commonplace feat of walking along the corridor to see him.

CHAPTER XLVII

NIGHT SKY
OVER LONDON

It was a warm summer night, a year and a half after Roger's resignation, when Margaret and I arrived at South Street for a party at Diana's. Not that either of us was thinking of the past. This was just an engagement, it wasn't more significant than others, it was part of the to-ing and fro-ing. The children were at school, we were free, it was pleasant to drive round the Park through the soft indigo evening.

In the drawing-room upstairs, the guests clattered and drank, keeping eyes alert for the latest entrant. There was a simmer of pleasure as they moved around, the pleasure of being inside the circle, like being in a party on shipboard, with the sea pattering below. It was all still going on, I thought. Going on as, for most of them, it had always been: and as, in their expectations, it always would.

I was curious, as at any of Diana's parties, about who was in favour now. Collingwood stood by the fireplace, sempiternal, satisfied, unvocal. For a while Monty Cave, who had been promoted that spring, was at his side. Cave had now outdistanced his competitors: all Diana's influence was behind him: he was being talked of as the next Chancellor. People were continuing to speculate whether Diana would marry him, but, in spite of her resolve to break away from loneliness, she, who wasn't used to dithering, went on doing so. She was hard-baked enough about the power game, but she couldn't make herself hard-baked about a second marriage. She was still capable of dreams of love. Her will deserted her. She had had a happy marriage and longed for another. She was not ready for one which was not real.

Lenton came in, did not stay long, but found time to talk, modestly, unobtrusively, to his hostess. As Prime Minister he might be busy, but he was teaching some lessons to men who thought him commonplace. One was, never make enemies if you can help it and, above all, never make enemies by neglect. Before he went, he had beamed, porcine and attentive, at each of his supporters. I noticed him whispering to Douglas Osbaldiston, whom I had not seen at Diana's before, and who, years before, when his wife was well and we were better friends, used to tease Margaret and me for our excursions into the high life.

Diana kept up with the times, I thought. She used not to pay attention to top civil servants, but here was not only Douglas, but one of his co-equals at the Treasury. Douglas had duly returned there, and had one of the top jobs created for him. All that Hector Rose, now retired, had wished for from the Service, Douglas had obtained. Margaret continued to visit his wife in hospital, and, in the months since I left Whitehall, he had frequently dined with us. Yet, between him and me, the breach wasn't healed. He had tried; the coldness was one-sided, the fault was mine.

From the ruck of the party, Sammikins halloo'ed at me. He was looking for someone to take to Pratt's, to finish off the evening. He wasn't having any luck: he had just been turned down for the sixth time, he announced at the top of his voice, his laugh ringing out like a spirited but inappropriate imitation of Roland's horn at Roncesvalles. Caro went by at that moment, magnificently pretty, looking as though she were carefree. She tapped her brother on the shoulder, threw a cordial word to Margaret, then spun round at the greeting of somebody else and addressed herself to him with vivacity. She did not come near me, or Margaret, again that night.

I felt my arm gripped. It was Lord Lufkin. He said in a meaningful and grinding tone: "That man Hood." The tone was meaningful, but for an instant I was lost. Quite lost. The party lapped and hooted round me. All this was still going on. I had forgotten. But Lufkin did not forget.

"I've got him," he said.

Lufkin was obsessive enough to go in for revenge. No one else in his position would have done the same. It seemed fantastic that a great tycoon should have spent his energy—not just for a day, but for weeks and months—working out plans for getting a middle-rank employee of another firm dismissed from his job. Yet that was precisely what he had done. He did not regard it as revenge, but as natural justice. When he spoke of it, he did not exhibit triumph or even relish. It was something he had to do, and was able to do. It was part of the rightness of things.

In the roundabout of the party, among the groomed and prosperous faces, for the first time that night I thought of Roger. He was not there. He would not have been invited. If he had been invited, it was not likely that he would have come. Margaret had asked him and Ellen often to our house, but they had accepted only once. Face to face, he was as warm and easy-natured as he had ever been: and yet he shied, like one with an active phobia, from the places and people he had known best in his period of power.

He was still in the House. But, now the divorces had gone through and he had married Ellen, his constituency party would not run him at the next election. He had not lost his hope. He and Ellen were living modestly, in an ambience quite unlike the glitter of Lord North Street. His income, such as it was, came from two or three directorships which Lufkin had stiffly but judiciously put in his way. As for the marriage, we had not seen them at close enough quarters to be anything like certain, but Margaret, prejudiced against it, had nevertheless come to believe that it was firm and good.

Ellen she had not quite brought herself to like. This was partly out of feeling for Caro and partly, I thought to myself with a degree of inner amusement, because in some of the qualities of their natures, she and Ellen were not altogether dissimilar. Both were active, both were capable of violent feeling, both were natural partisans, though Ellen had nothing of the easy flow inbred in Margaret. "She is a one-man dog, you know," Margaret had once said to me with a rueful grin, "she hasn't anything left over for the rest of us. And that I find a little hard to take. Still, it's not hard for him to take, and I suppose that's the important thing."

Parting from Lufkin, I went through the heat and dazzle, out to the balcony in search of her. There she was, in a group with Francis Getliffe and others, and I took her aside. Lufkin's news filled my mind, absented me from the party. I felt as though I had suddenly recaptured a long dead grief or joy, and I had to tell her.

She listened, looking at me and then into the brilliant room. She knew, more quickly than I did, that I was not really telling her about Lufkin or Hood, but about Roger's failure and our own. I was really speaking of what we had tried, and failed, to do.

"Yes," said Margaret, "we need a victory."

Her spirit was strong. She was looking back into the room. Just as I had done earlier, she was thinking how it all went on. "We need a victory," she said. She was not giving up, nor letting me.

Francis Getliffe joined us. For an instant Margaret and I stopped talking, awkwardly. We might have been caught gossiping about him, using his name in malice. Francis wasn't with us any more. He had given up. Not that he had changed his opinions: but he could not endure another struggle. He had retired to his house in Cambridge and to his research. Already, that evening, he had talked about a new idea with as much excitement as when he was young.

Defeat can cut into friendships, I was thinking, as much as being on different sides. Francis and I had been intimate for thirty years. Yet now part of the spontaneity had had to go, almost as much as it had gone with Douglas. It was a tiny price to pay for having gone through the struggle: but still, it was a price.

We talked a little, the three of us, of the college and Cambridge. We went to the end of the balcony. Over the garden, over the rooftops, shone the rusty, vivid night sky of London, the diffused recognition of all those lives. We talked, more eagerly now, of our children, with the special tenderness of old friends, who have seen each other's families growing up. The memory of the struggle, even the reason for it, dimmed down. We talked of the children, and were happy. The only puzzle remaining to us that night was Penelope. She and Arthur Plimpton were both in the United States and they had both got married, but not to each other. Francis gave a grim, quixotic smile and thought it was a joke against himself.

Under the town's resplendent sky we talked of the children and their future. We talked as though the future were easy and secure, and as though their lives would bring us joy.